Cobble City

Cobble City

Todd Monger

Library of Congress Control Number: 2018909598

ISBN:	Hardcover	978-1-9845-4606-7
	Softcover	978-1-9845-4605-0
	eBook	978-1-9845-4604-3

Print information available on the last page.

Rev. date: 09/04/2018

To order additional copies of this book, contact:
Xlibris
1-888-795-4274
www.Xlibris.com
Orders@Xlibris.com
779976

CONTENTS

CHAPTER 1

It Begins

IT CANNOT BE said when this story began, but it was a time when barbarians ran wild among the lands, ravaging and destroying every civilization in their path. They had no mercy, raping and enslaving the women while brutally murdering any male not willing to follow.

In a small village is a group of very special young men who will grow to be great leaders in the fight against the barbarians. Mount is the leader of the men; he is becoming a very strong, powerful warrior. When he was born, he was so big that his mother said it was like pushing out a mountain, and that's how he got his name.

Always right next to him since he was old enough to walk is his younger brother, Marc; he got his name when their father said, "Another boy, that marks the spot." So that became his name. Marc trains with Mount every day when they have time from their chores. Always with them is Jax; he is a smaller man than the brothers, but no one dares mention it. He is the inventor of the village, always thinking of ways to make things easier, including making tools and weapons out of items from the earth.

Last of the men is a special tall, thin young man with special powers. His name is Hem. He lives with his father; his mother passed away some time ago. Hem gets visions and dreams of stuff to happen; he has energy in him that he can bring out from his hands, and with his father's help, he learns more and more each day. Together, the four help Dorn, the leader of the village, with seeing over the men of the village's progress and seeing over the protection of all in the village.

Dorn, the father of the boys, is a very tough, smart large man; he is the one who began it all with a few of his people who decided to leave their home. Now Dorn lets any good-hearted people live in the village;

all anyone has to do is accept a job to do each day. Every person in the village has one, from building houses to growing food to cooking the food and hunting. The village has come a long way since the days Dorn was fighting scavengers, raiders, and headhunters every night with the men who followed him. But now, most nights are peaceful; and everyone works together to keep everyone clothed, fed, and out of the weather with a place to sleep.

In the past few months, though, Hem has been having visions and dreams of a large vicious group of scary-looking big men going into other civilizations, taking over, and making the people their slaves. They destroy the cities, then move to the next and do it all over again. Hem is scared that it won't be long before these men will be at their village, raiding their homes. Mount has sworn to all that this will not happen to them; with Jax's help, they have been working on a wall surrounding their village. The available men work on the wall every day, for Hem has never had a vision not come true, and they hope they get it done before any kind of attack.

One early morning, as Mount and Marc are with the men building the wall, they see Jax running toward them. He had been out of the village all night exploring, looking for items of the earth that could be used for tools and weapons while marking the areas of land and drawing maps.

"Good morning," he says as he walks up to them. "I was way out past the valley and found an area where the ground was opened. It went deep into the earth. When I looked down into the hole, I found these unusually strong rocks, so I took them back to my shop. And when I put them over heat, the rocks melted to liquid."

"Well, that's great, a rock that melts. How is that any help?" Marc asks.

"Well, I'm hoping that when it cools, it will turn hard, and I can shape it to any form," says Jax.

Mount is very impressed with Jax's findings. "You going back to your shop to work more?" he asks Jax.

"Yes, I should be there the rest of the day. So unless you need me, I'll see you later at dinner," Jax assures Mount. Jax goes in the direction of his shop, and Mount and Marc go back to working on the wall.

Mount hears someone yell his name; when he turns, he sees Kurt running in his direction. Kurt is Hem's helper; he lets Hem try different spells on him and does anything for him. Marc sees Kurt and tackles him to the ground; he always picks on Kurt every time he sees him. After Marc is done, Mount helps Kurt up and dusts him off. "What's Hem making you do today?" Mount asks Kurt, laughing.

"It's something you will have to see yourself. Hem wants to show both of you," Kurt tells them. They tell Jeremy they have to see Hem, so Jeremy takes charge of the men as Mount and Marc follow Kurt to Hem's house.

When they get to Hem, they find him walking in circles while talking to himself. Kurt gets his attention and lets him know the brothers are here.

Hem thanks Kurt, then tells him to light the logs in the firepit. He then tells the brothers that he is learning to channel his powers where he can bring out his visions from the flames of the fire. Kurt gets the fire going, and soon, a large flame is burning. Hem walks up to the flames and tells the three men to stand back. He closes his eyes and holds his hands into the air, then yells out, "Show me what evil comes to destroy us!" He raises his hands higher as the flames shoot up into the air, and a giant fireball forms from the flames.

The fireball opens, and an image of the huge powerful barbarian army appears; they are going through a large community of villages, beating down all the people, even the children. Then the image moves through the army, showing just how large it is; then it gets to the end, and standing there is the most gorgeous woman they had ever seen. The image goes right up on her; she is stunning, with beautiful long dark hair, lovely soft lips, and deep blue eyes. Then suddenly, her blue eyes turn to a blood red, and then the gorgeous woman transforms into a scary huge demon. The demon looks at the men and screams, "You will die!"

Then the demon's huge arm swings at the men, and the fire explodes everywhere and goes out as it knocks all the men to the ground. The men stand up.

"That was the best thing I ever saw!" Marc yells.

"What was that?" Mount asks.

"I'm not sure," Hem answers. "But I'm sure we will soon find out in the days to come. Whatever it is, it seems she or it is in control over those men. I need to go let my father know what happened and see what he thinks. I will see you two at dinner," Hem tells the brothers. Kurt follows him back to his house, and then Mount and Marc go to tell Dorn what they have just seen.

A yell fills the room when Serina wakes out of her trance. "Get Boar in here right away!" she screams at her personal slaves.

Lisa, her main girl, goes to her. "I sent one of the girls to find Boar. He should be here soon," she tells Serina, trying to calm her down.

In a few minutes, Boar comes in and kneels to Serina. "What can I do for you, my queen?" he asks. Boar grew up with the barbarians, learning to fight as young as ten; he is now the leader of the army. He has killed more men than can be counted and has taken many cities all for Serina.

Serina will not be happy till she finds a great city worthy of her greatness to call her kingdom. So far, no place has been worthy. For her army to grow, she lets her army of barbarian men do as they please, destroying everything and having their way with the women. Serina tells Boar to stand; then she tells Boar of her vision of a great beautiful huge city, one like she has never seen before. "All their people were beautiful, and we had control of them all. Then from out of nowhere, a man appears, and he has powers just as powerful as mine. Then strong, powerful men surround him, and he looks at me and says, 'We will stop you.'"

Boar laughs. "Really, that's what worries you? Please, we have destroyed everything in our path. Our army is the most powerful army on this earth, and you're worried about a few warriors and a man with powers? My men will destroy anyone who gets in our way." He then grabs a male slave who was cleaning, then hits him in the nose, and blood splatters on him. Boar then goes to beat him down.

That's when Serina screams, "That's enough! We need all the men for the army. You must trust my vision."

Boar kneels. "I'm sorry, my queen. I'll get back to training the men and see if there is news on the explorers. I hope they have found the city in your vision. I'm more than ready to go take a new city for you. We have been here too long."

Serina smiles at hearing her army's commander ready to fight a war for her. "Rise, my warrior. Go keep training the men. Have them ready. I can feel it will be soon."

Boar stands. "Yes, my queen. And don't worry, if we run into the ones in your vision, I will kill each one of them for you."

Serina's smile becomes serious. "I'm sure you will, Boar. Now go and don't let anyone disturb me till the men have returned."

Serina watches Boar leave the room; she hates the male species, which all started with her father. They said that he was a good upstanding man who was an important person at one time. He had a very good job with a powerful man whose family invented a drink from a fruit called grapes. He had a very good life; he was even able to get the most beautiful girl in the village to be his life mate. Then she became pregnant with his child; he was the happiest man on the earth.

Then the day arrived when it was time for the baby to come. During the delivery, there were problems; the mother lost a lot of blood and died, and they could save only the baby. He was devastated, wanting nothing to do with his new daughter. Luckily, the wife of the man's boss took over taking care of her; but before she turned eight, the woman died. The man named Mr. Wine didn't want to care for a child who wasn't his own, so he gave Serina back to her father. By now, her father was a worthless drunk who sat around and drank what was called wine all day.

She soon became her father's caretaker through the years, even going to work for other people to get by. But she had to hide anything of value, or her father would trade it for more wine. The years go by, with Serina taking her father's abuse. She was now a woman, and like her mother, she was the most beautiful woman in the village. All the men loved her, and all the other young women hated her. It did not matter; her father would never give his slave away to a man to be his mate because then he would have no one to take care of him.

One day, Serina took a job from one of the richest families in the village; she was cleaning their house for them when she overheard Lisa, the daughter, talking with others in one of the rooms. She was to become the mate of Kris, the eldest son of the Wine family. Lisa saw Serina listening in on her conversation. Lisa wanted so badly to be more beautiful than Serina; she was a pretty girl, but not nearly as beautiful as Serina. But she was from a wealthy family, and she was sure to let Serina know every time they ran into each other.

Lisa went to Serina and asked her to join her and her friends. Serina didn't want to, but Lisa wouldn't take no for an answer. Lisa seemed nice as she offered Serina something to eat and a glass of wine; then she let her know that the best-looking and richest man in the village chose her to be his life mate. Then it started. Lisa told Serina she would probably die an old maid, that by the time her father was done with her, no man would want her. Then she started on how poor they were and how she wore rags out of the garbage. As Lisa was getting to what a drunk her father was, Serina ran out of the room, crying; then she left the house without finishing her job.

She came back home and started running for her room to cry; but before she got to her room, her father yelled for her to come to the room he was in. She did her best to wipe her face as she went to see what he wanted. Serina walked in the room to find her father sitting in a chair, looking angry. He looked at her. "I know you've been working. I'm out of wine. I need you to go to the tavern and get me a jug."

Serina started to cry, knowing what was about to happen. "I didn't get to finish the job, so I didn't get paid," she told her father in a low voice, looking at the floor.

"What do you mean you didn't get paid?" he screamed at her. She started to cry and tried to explain what happened, but her father wouldn't listen; he just started telling her how she ruined his life—how he had a perfect life; then she came and ruined it. Then for the thousandth time, he let her know she killed his wife and that he would never forgive her. He stood and hit her in the face. She fell to the floor, crying. Her father screamed, "If you can't get me my drink—the only thing that makes me happy—what good are you to me?"

He pulled her off the floor by her hair. "I guess there is only one other good reason to keep you around," he told her; then he pulled her close and forced her to kiss him. Serina started screaming and pulling away, but her father pulled back on her hair and smacked her across the face. She fell back down to the floor; then her father got on top of her and ripped the top of her dress open. As he rubbed her breast with his hands, Serina screamed and did her best to get away.

Because her father hadn't had a drink, her screams and having to hold her still were giving him a headache. He finally stopped and got off her. "You best go finish your job and get that money, or else, you can leave here and live in the wild." He then left, and Serina lay on the floor, crying.

Her father needed a drink bad, so he went to the tavern where he used to work. He approached the new guy in charge, begging him to let him get a drink. Over in the main corner table was the owner, his old boss, Mr. Wine. He was there with his sons, celebrating the elder son having chosen his life mate. They were interrupted by his begging, and Mr. Wine went to him and told him he was making a scene and then asked how he could help his old friend. He begged Mr. Wine for some wine, telling him he hadn't had a drink all day.

Mr. Wine and his three boys all laughed at the poor man as he groveled at their feet. Mr. Wine pulled a chair over. "Join us for a drink. We are celebrating my son picking a life mate." He sat down; and Chad, the middle son, poured him some wine. He quickly drank it down and ask for more. They all laughed, and Chad poured his glass full. The talk became of women as they downed more and more wine. Soon, the talk became of how long he planned to hold on to Serina and how she would make a nice life mate.

He got almost protective of Serina, making it clear that Mr. Wine's other sons had no chance of Serina being their life mate. That's when Mr. Wine smiled. "How do you plan to keep drinking? I have a way where you can come here and drink all day long," he told him as he poured him more wine.

He picked up the glass, took a big drink, then said, "What do I have to do?"

Mr. Wine smiled. "Let my son enjoy your daughter before he commits to one woman."

Serina's father said, "Fine." Then he went back to drinking. "You will find her at home. That's where I left her," he told them as he filled his glass back up to the top.

"Go find her and have fun. She's all for you, son," his father said, laughing.

Chris stood up to leave, then turned to his brothers. "Come on, I don't want to go alone. She won't want to be with me. She's made that clear more than once." Chad and Cyle got up from their seats and followed their brother out of the tavern. They went to Serina's house. Chris went to the door, pounding on it.

Serina, not sure what they wanted, went to the door.

When she opened it, Chris shoved the door open, and the three brothers walked in. Chad shut the door behind them. Serina quickly asked, "What do you boys think you're doing?"

"Well, our father made a deal with your father, and now you are Chris's present for the day," Cyle told Serina, laughing.

Serina got upset. "You boys are crazy. Get out of my house right now!" she screamed. Serina went to open the door, but Chad grabbed her by the hair and pulled her away from the door.

Serina got mad and slapped Chad across the face; it made him very angry, so he hit her in the face, and she fell to the floor. Serina got up and fought; she started hitting Chad with everything she had. Chad yelled for his brothers to pull her off him. They tried but were having trouble pulling her away; she started hitting them as they tried to grab her. Then the door opened, and their dad came in; he screamed, "What the hell are you boys doing?" He then grabbed Serina by her hair and started smacking her across the face. "Does Daddy have to show you boys how to do everything?"

He pulled Serina's face close to his. "I paid good money for you, girl. Now one way or another, you will work it off."

Serina screamed, "Please don't do this!"

That's when he grabbed her dress, ripped it off her, and threw it on the floor. She fought the best she could, but the man hit her hard in the face; then he demanded his sons to hold her down. The boys grabbed her arms as their father hit Serina in the face till she couldn't take any more and went still. He then pulled his pants down and told his sons, "Guess we all get a present today." Then he went down on Serina and raped her with hard thrusts, trying to hurt her; as he did, he looked down to see no blood. "This little slut isn't no virgin! Guess we know why Daddy wouldn't sell you to me." He laughed and then gave a moan as he finished up. He then told Cyle, "Today's the day you become a man. Drop your pants. It's your turn, boy."

"I get a turn?" He swiftly removed his clothes with excitement.

Serina tried to stop him from getting on top of her, and his dad yelled, "You going to let a little girl get the best of you? If you don't get on her, I'll have your brothers beat the shit out of you!" Cyle got upset and scared of getting beat up, so he started punching Serina as hard as he could; she finally gave in and let Cyle have his way with her. Being excited and it being his first time, he was done fast. His brothers cheered for him as he finished up.

Chad then yelled, "My turn!" Then he ripped his clothes off. Chad was wilder than his brothers; he grabbed Serina by her hair and forced her to kiss him. When he pulled away, she spat in his face; he became enraged and started beating her in the back of her head. As she screamed, he laughed and hit her harder. "Lie down and spread your legs and beg me to put my cock inside you," he told her as he jerked her by the hair to the floor.

"No!" Serina screamed, then hit him back with everything she had. Blood dribbled down Chad's lip as everything became quiet.

Chad smiled as he wiped the blood from his lip. Serina crawled to a corner and balled up. "Leave me alone! Please don't do this!"

Chad went over to her and started kicking her with all he had. "Lie down and tell me you want it because you're a dumb slut!" he screamed as he kept kicking her.

Serina finally couldn't take any more; she begged him to stop, then lay on the floor and let Chad on top of her. He didn't let up as he wrapped his hands around her throat and choked her while he raped her as hard as he could; as he finished, he hit her right in her jaw.

The punishment was too much for Serina to take; all she could do was lie there. "Come on, it's time for big brother to get his last piece before it's the same piece every night," Chad urged him on.

"You didn't have to beat the hell out of her. She was a pretty girl. Now I don't know if I want to," Chris told his brother.

"Don't be a little wuss," his father said as he took her dress from the floor and wiped her face with it. "See? All better, she looks beautiful."

Chris bent down and rubbed his finger down Serina's face. "She is a beautiful woman. It's a shame she turned me down when I asked her to be my life mate, told me I was too much like a brother." Then Serina got his finger in her mouth and bit as hard as she could. Chris screamed and started hitting her in the head as his brothers and dad laughed at him. Serina let go, and Chris jumped around and shook his hand, trying to make the pain stop. "It's not funny, assholes!" Then he reached down and grabbed Serina by her hair to pull her up, then dragged her over to a table.

"If you thought that was funny, you will love this." He picked her up and put her on the table; he forced her legs apart as she was begging him not to. Chris dropped his pants and moaned as he started to rape her.

As best she could, Serina laughed and said, "The oldest brother seems to be the smallest."

Again, his brothers and dad started laughing at him; he got infuriated and started punching her hard in her chest. "Think I'm small, do you?" Chris grabbed her and turned her over on her stomach. "Let's see how small I feel in your ass!" he screamed at her, then started forcing his hard penis in her asshole.

Serina gave a small grunt, then told Chad, "I've shit bigger than that."

Chad, Cyle, and their dad again started laughing hard at him. He then started thrusting in her as hard as he could, then grabbed her hair; and each time he pushed forward, he would slam her face into the table. Before he was done, a puddle of blood was dripping off the table.

He let go of her hair and pulled up his pants. Serina's body fell limp on the table, and she didn't move. "I think you broke her, brother," Cyle told Chris as he went over and gave her a nudge.

"Damn, son, you didn't have to kill her! Now I'll have to let that drunk drink at the tavern for a long time!" Mr. Wine screamed at his son.

Things were quiet as they stood looking at Serina's motionless body; then Chad spoke up. "No need for that, Father. Just go tell him we told her that he sold her to us. Then she got very angry, got all her stuff, and left, saying she was running away, never to be seen again."

Mr. Wine smiled. "That story could work," he told his son. "This is what we'll do. I'll go back to the tavern and tell him your story that she ran away." He laughed. "Hell, I'll tell him the deal's off and he owes me for all of my wine he drank."

"That's not right, Father! You are evil," Cyle told his father, shaking his head.

"While I'm doing that, you boys wrap her body in something, then gather her stuff. Then take her to the caves and throw all her stuff and her body in one of the caves."

"All the way to the caves? That's a far walk! Plus we have to carry her and all her stuff there—it will take all day!" Chris yelled at his dad.

"Shut up, you little crybaby!" his father yelled back. "You stay here so your soon-to-be mate doesn't start asking me where you are and getting on my nerves."

Chris smiled and looked away from his brothers. "If you insist, Father. Thank you."

"Are you kidding me? I have to do this with just Cyle? It will take us two days!" Chad yelled at his father.

"Well, you best get going. And if someone sees what you two are doing, I'll say I know nothing. So you'd better not get caught!" screamed his dad.

Chad stopped talking, and he and Cyle started finding something to wrap the body up in. Mr. Wine yelled, "Again, don't get caught!" Then he and Chris left the house and went back to the tavern.

The boys snuck the body through the village and started the long walk toward the caves where people used to live in a long time ago. Serina's body started getting heavy as they made their way there; they stopped more than once to rest. It seemed like forever, but they finally made it to the caves.

It was still daylight, so they were still able to see a good way inside the caves. "Let's take her over to the caves on this side. I think the wolves use them when it rains. It shouldn't take too long for them to sniff her out and eat her remains," Chad told his brother. So they took her body inside the cave till it was so dark they couldn't see. "This is good," Chad told Cyle. Then they dropped her body on the ground.

When she hit the ground, she made a noise. "Is she still alive?"

Chad went up to her body and kicked; again, Serina gave out a low moan. "She is!" they both screamed and ran as fast as they could out of the cave.

Serina had somewhat come to, but she had been beat so bad that she can't move. From all the crying and screaming, she was left without a voice, so she couldn't scream. But she knew where she'd been brought and knew no one was around to hear her even if she could scream. She did her best to get up, but she was very weak and in extreme pain. She started to cry as she began to think she was going to die there.

Her sobs echoed throughout the cave, but as she lay there in the dark, she swore she heard someone call her name. She stopped her crying, and the cave went quiet. As she listened, she could hear water dripping from the cave's ceiling; and just as she started to think she was hearing things, she just barely heard her name almost whispered in her ear. She lifted her head up just enough to give out a soft "Hello?" Again, there was nothing but silence as she listened; she thought she must have heard her mom calling to her from the other side.

She went back to crying, and then she heard "Don't cry!"

Then a bright light filled the cave; from the light, it looked like a woman, but the light was too bright to be sure. Serina found it in her to sit up. "Who are you?" Serina asked her.

"I know what those men have done to you. I'm here to help you, plus help you get your revenge on them," she heard the voice from the light say. "Come over to me. Feel my light, and you will see for yourself how I can help."

Serina told her, "I can't. I'm hurt and can't get up. You come over to me please." Then she tried to stand but couldn't.

"I'm sorry, child. If you want my help, you must come to me. I must know you truly want my help." Serina tried to get up but again fell back to the ground. The voice started to encourage her to try again. Then with everything she had, Serina pushed herself up, then stood to her feet. With everything she had, she slowly walked to the light. "That's it, child. Come closer," the voice told Serina. She went into the light and was lifted off the ground, and her whole body glowed from the light.

When Serina was lowered to the ground and came out of the light, she was completely healed. She couldn't believe it. As she looked over her body, the bruises were gone. This time, she asked, "What are you?"

"I told you, dear, I'm here to help you. Would you like to have the power to get revenge on those men that hurt you?" the voice asked.

"How would I ever get revenge on them?" Serina asked.

"I can give you the power to not only defeat those men, but also have every man bow to you and make you a queen."

"What would I have to do to get these powers?" she asked.

The light became brighter, and the voice said, "Just hold out your hand to me."

Serina slowly walked back to the light and nervously held out her hand. Then the voice said, "Now just say, 'I give you my body and my soul.'"

Serina softly spoke the words. Then the voice loudly said, "LOUDER!"

Then as loud as she could, Serina yelled again, "I give you my body my soul!"

Then the voice changed to a scary low voice, saying, "Good!"

Then from the light came a scary huge arm with long sharp claws; it took hold of Serina's arm and pulled her in close enough to see that behind the light was a scary huge creature that she had never before seen in her life. "Look into my eyes," he told her.

Then as the demon possessed Serina, she gave out the loudest scream ever heard. Chad and Cyle heard her scream from where they were, and the boys started running as fast as they could back to the village.

At the village, Mr. Wine and Chris were back at the tavern; he did just as Chad said and told Serina's dad that she ran away before his boy had a chance to be with her. Then he felt bad as he watched the man cry, so he told her dad he could drink the remainder of the day; he even joined him again and had Chris join as well. Chris agreed to one drink before they had to go meet Lisa at the holy place. They drank quietly, not wanting to say anything about what really happened to Serina.

Before they finished their drinks, Chad and Cyle came walking into the tavern; they sat at the table, and both poured a drink for themselves. The two boys both drank down their glasses fast. Their dad looked at them. "Did you boys get your chores done before coming here?"

Chad answered, "Yes, sir." Then he filled his glass and again drank the whole glass in one gulp.

Serina's dad laughed and said, "That's how you drink!" Then he took his glass and drank it all. They all cheered as he drank it down; then Chad filled his glass back up.

The men sat chatting and drinking for some time; then Lisa's mother came in to tell Chris she was ready to say her vows if he was ready to come to the holy building. Chris stood and told her to tell Lisa he would be there soon; she said that it was fine and went out the door to go tell Lisa.

Chad looked at his brothers and father. "Well, it's that time. You guys ready to go?"

Mr. Wine stood up. "I'm proud of you, son. You picked a fine girl for a life mate." He hugged his son, then said, "Let's go make you a man." Then he told the other two boys, "Let's go." Then they all went to leave.

Then as they approached the door, the building started to shake; everyone screamed as things began falling to the floor. "What's going on?" Chris screamed as he grabbed a post to keep from falling.

"We need to get out of here!" Cyle screamed as he tried to crawl to the door.

That's when the door swung open; the place stopped shaking as someone walked into the building. When the person came in, they could see that it was a woman. Chris walked closer. "Lisa, is that you?" Then when he got closer, he screamed, "No, you're dead!"

The woman grabbed Chris by his throat and picked him up off the ground; she walked over to where everyone could see that it was Serina. Mr. Wine and his other two sons ran to hide as Serina squeezed Chris' neck till blood started pouring out of his mouth; as Serina turned to the others, laughing, she slung Chris' dead body at them. "Who's next?" she said. "Isn't that what you asked your sons earlier after you beat me down to the ground and let your sons take turns with me?"

Her father stood up. "What is going on here? You need to stop this!" Then he tried to hit Serina, but she caught his arm and broke it.

He screamed as Serina laughed. "You will never touch me again!" Then she grabbed him by the head and twisted his head completely off his body. As she laughed, she looked at her father's head and said, "What, no kiss?" Then she threw her father's head across the room at Mr. Wine and the two brothers hiding behind a table.

Serina used her new powers and sent the table flying across the room. Mr. Wine pushed his sons toward Serina, then tried running toward the door. Serina held up her hand, and it froze Mr. Wine in his tracks. "Where do you think you're running off to?" Serina asked.

Mr. Wine began crying as pee started running down his pants. "Please don't kill me. I'll give you anything you want," he begged.

Serina walked closer to him. "You and your boys tried to kill me, then took me off and left me for dead. You tried to take my life, so now I'm taking yours!"

Mr. Wine started to scream as Serina closed her hand into a fist; as her hand closed, Mr. Wine's bones could be heard breaking. Once her hand shut, it silenced his screams as his head dropped, and blood poured from his mouth and nose; he was dead. Chad and Cyle were both on their knees, begging for their lives. She looked at them, then raised both her arms; when she did, both boys went flying into the air and through the roof of the tavern.

Serina turned to the other men in the tavern. "Run. Go tell everyone in the village that there is a new ruler and to come bow before me."

As the men looked at her, that's when Chad and Cyle came falling from the sky; and both slammed on to the floor, which caused blood to splatter all over the men. It made them run out of the tavern, screaming for their lives. "Tell everyone to come here to bow to me, or I will kill them!" She then went to the door and out to the center of the village.

Serina looked around as people were running in fear; then in the distance came one of the men from the tavern with a large group of the men who were guards of the village. They approached her, and the man screamed, "Lie down on your stomach and hold out your arms, witch!" They all had torches and spears pointed at her.

"This is your last chance to bow to me as your queen before you all die," Serina told the group of men.

Then the leader of the guards ordered his men, "ATTACK HER!"

The men started to charge at Serina; she laughed as she held up her arms at the men, and fire came from her hands. The men screamed as they were burned to ash; the men who didn't charge all started bowing down to Serina. "If you don't serve me as your new ruler, you will die!" Serina yelled to the scared, screaming people running to hide. Then another group of men came from the back end of the village to see what all the commotion was about. Serina told them, "Kneel before me before you die."

The biggest man of the group laughed and went to attack Serina; the man was three times her size, but she picked him up off his feet by his neck and squeezed till the life went out of him. She then threw his body at the men, and they bowed down to her as well. "If you cannot bow to me and serve me, then you will die!" Serina again yelled to the people as most were on their knees. Then she saw a girl slowly crawling on her knees toward her.

The girl approached Serina's feet and looked up at her; that's when Serina saw that the girl was the bitch Lisa. Lisa started to beg Serina, "Please don't kill me or my family. We will serve you as our queen. I will personally be your servant. You can tell me to do anything."

Serina looked down at the girl as she begged for her life. "Kiss my feet," Serina demanded of Lisa. Lisa didn't hesitate; she kissed both of Serina's feet. Then Serina told Lisa to rise. Lisa stood with her head lowered down to Serina.

Serina didn't know where the feeling came from; she lifted Lisa's head up with her hand and kissed her with a deep, long kiss. "I think I will let you and your family live. Your home is mine now, so go there and wait for me," Serina told Lisa.

"Yes, my queen," Lisa told Serina, then went running off to her family's house.

Serina then put her attention back to the people; she went over to one of the men who was kneeling down on the ground, waiting for orders. "Rise, young warrior. You will lead my army," she said.

"Yes, my queen," the young man said, then rose to Serina.

"You will command the men to go through the village, find every person, and have them agree to follow me or die," Serina commanded her new leader. "The main house on the hill is where you will find me. Come get me when you have gathered all the people here." Then Serina went to her new home to find her servant Lisa as the young man gathered the men to do Serina's bidding. Serina smiled as she looked at the fear in the people's faces.

When she got to her new home, Lisa was true to her word; she was waiting at the door with her family, each waiting to see what they could do for Serina as they gave her food to eat and wine to drink. Lisa had her best dresses out. "All my best dresses are yours now," Lisa told Serina. "Come with me. I have a warm bath ready for you. I will wash and dress you, my queen." Serina followed Lisa to a back room where there was a large tub of water surrounded by lit candles.

Lisa walked over to Serina; she pulled Serina's dress down her body to the floor. Serina and Lisa were both amazed at the perfect form of Serina's body. Lisa started to rub Serina's shoulders as Serina looked in a mirror; she was so much more beautiful than before. Her teeth were straight and white, her skin was silky smooth, her hair was long and shiny, and there was something different now that she could feel the hate and evilness in her. Plus she was very much enjoying Lisa rubbing her body; she was getting turned on.

Serina tried to fight it; she had never thought about women her whole life, but she could feel the demons in her, and they wouldn't let her—their being in her was making her lust for Lisa as she kept rubbing her back. Now Serina was the prettiest girl in the village before, but Lisa was the second prettiest; she had long light brown hair and a very lovely body. Serina finally stopped fighting it; she turned around toward Lisa and started kissing her. It was a deep, long kiss. Then Lisa pulled back and dropped her clothes; then she and Serina got in the tub.

Lisa washed Serina's body, but it didn't take long before Serina pulled Lisa toward her, and they started to kiss. "Let me wash you. Then we can go to the bedroom," Lisa told Serina.

Serina lay back and let Lisa wash her; as she did, she looked over Lisa's body. "You are a very beautiful woman yourself. I now have the power to not only make you more beautiful, but to keep you that way forever," Serina told Lisa.

Lisa kissed Serina. "What would I have to do?" she asked Serina.

Serina had Lisa help her out of the tub, then dried her off and then dried herself off. She had Lisa go down to her knees. "Take my hand," she told her. Lisa gave Serina her hand. "This will hurt more than any pain you have ever felt," Serina said; then her eyes lit up, and Lisa screamed as she felt her body transforming. It seemed to take forever as Lisa kept screaming from the pain; then the pain stopped, and she heard Serina tell her, "RISE UP." Lisa stood and looked in the mirror.

She was more beautiful than ever; her figure was a perfect hourglass. She was so happy she couldn't believe her eyes. "You like?" Serina asked Lisa as she came behind her and rubbed her hands across her body.

Lisa turned and kissed Serina with a deep, long passionate, kiss. "Come with me to my room and make love to me please," Lisa almost begged Serina. Serina loved her creation. Lisa was now close to her beauty, and something inside her wanted to ravish Lisa's perfect body.

Serina followed Lisa to her bedroom. "This is your room now, my queen," Lisa told Serina, then dropped the cloth that covered her. Serina dropped her cloth and took Lisa to the bed; then something inside her took over as she lustfully ravaged Lisa's body. Lisa lay back, enjoying Serina's lips kissing her body all over.

After she heard a growl, Lisa then opened her eyes to a scary evil-looking large demon; it was ugly in the face but had a perfect muscular body with the largest penis she had ever seen between its legs.

As she screamed in fear, the demon spread her legs and put the large penis in her. Lisa's screams soon turned to moans, which drowned the screams from the people outside as the demons thrust in and out of Lisa.

Serina's new army of men went through the whole village, dragged each person out of their homes, and made them give allegiance to their new empress or be beaten to death.

Lisa woke up early to find Serina back to her beautiful self; she went to get her some food and a new dress before she woke her. She couldn't help but enjoy what happened last night; it was the best feeling she had ever felt.

Serina woke up to Lisa, who was already up. "My queen, the leader of the men is asking for you outside." Serina rose and saw Lisa had fixed herself up nice; behind her was Lisa's sister with food and her mother with a pile of dresses for Serina to choose from. Lisa started to feed Serina as her mother showed her all the dresses. She picked one of the nicest dresses and told everyone but Lisa to leave. Once alone, Serina had Lisa help her get dressed so she could go out front.

Serina followed Lisa through the house and out to the front. When she walked out, the people all kneeled; it was the first time she witnessed the real power she had possessed as she saw all the people in fear. "Know that you will serve me from now on. As long as you do as I say, I will let you live. If you ignore my orders or try to run, I will make sure you suffer."

One man who hadn't seen what Serina was able to do now stood. "Why should we listen to you?" he asked.

The people who had seen her powers all started to lie on the ground in fear. Serina looked at all the people—some cowering in fear and some standing, waiting for her to answer the man. "Let this be a lesson to every person here," she said loud enough for all the people to hear. Then she turned to the man who asked the question, and her eyes turned blood red. "If you don't listen, you die," she said in a very evil voice. Serina then held up her hand in a fist; when she opened her hand, the man's body exploded in pieces. Everyone screamed.

"Anyone else want to question me?" Serina asked. No one else dared say anything as everyone was on the ground in fear. "Good! Now I want everyone to get ready for a journey. I now hate this place. It's not good enough for your queen to live here. We will leave here, and you will find me a new home fit for me, even if we must take it. Everyone, get to work. Pack everything worth taking. Get all food. We will never return here again."

"My queen, I'm back," Serina hears, and it wakes her from the daydream she is having. Lisa is kneeling in front of her. The years have gone by; her army is the most powerful army on the earth. She and her army have destroyed civilization after civilization as she has searched for the place she will finally call home. Till she does, she allows her people to destroy the structures of the cities they take over so she can demand to move on to the next.

Serina can feel that the next place her explorers find will be the one this time; she is tired of always moving. She must find the place she will remain. Serina's attention then goes to Lisa; she is still as young and beautiful as she was that first night they were together. "Rise up and join me," Serina tells Lisa.

Lisa stands, but instead of sitting, she goes to the back of Serina's chair and starts rubbing her shoulders. "You seem tense, my love. Are you still having visions of the men?"

"I'm still not sure what to think of it," Serina tells Lisa as she starts enjoying Lisa rubbing her shoulders.

"How would you like the slave girls to get your bath ready?" Lisa asks.

"That sounds nice, but not now," Serina tells Lisa as she pulls her hand down and starts to kiss it. Then she stands, grabs Lisa's hand, and leads her to the back room where the bed is.

"Oh, I know what you want," Lisa says as she drops her dress to the floor. The demon has taken over more of Serina through the years. Serina can't control the lust that it has of women. She calls for two of her personal slave girls to join them.

Serina and the two girls lay Lisa down and ravish her body. Serina can go all day making love to her favorite girls. It's the only thing that keeps her mind off where her explorers are and when they will get back as well as who the men in her vision are. Serina pulls Lisa up into her arms, then commands the slave girls to be with each other while she and Lisa watched. "Nothing else to do today. We should lie back and enjoy the show," Serina tells Lisa, and they both lie back and relax for the day.

Back at Mount's village, it is time for the evening meal, Marc's favorite time of the day. They go to their normal table to eat. Hem is at the table waiting with his father, Ebert. The brothers say hello as they sit down. The young server girl comes to the table with water for them both; when she sets it down, she looks at them and says hello in a soft, sweet voice. They both say hello; then the girl goes running off to a group of other young women servers, and they all start giggling.

Some of the elder women walking by the table stop. "When are you boys going to pick life mates? There are plenty of fine single young women to choose from. Most boys your age have life mates," one of the women tells the boys.

The men all start shaking their heads. "No, we are way too busy for life mates right now," Mount says.

"Who wants a life mate?" Jax asks as he comes walking up to the table.

"No one!" Mount screams.

"All I want to do is eat," Marc tells them all as the server girl comes with food for them.

"I'll never fall in love with anything but my work," Jax says, sitting down.

They all start laughing as the woman walks away, saying, "It will happen, trust me."

As they start eating, Mount tells them, "Let's change the subject please."

"What was that we saw in the fire?" Marc asks Hem.

"That just may be the end of the world as we know it!" Ebert screams out at them all.

Hem laughs at his dad. "Don't scare everybody, Dad. He's not wrong, though. Whoever the woman is, there is one thing for sure—she is pure evil."

"She is as powerful as she is beautiful. No telling how powerful—most likely more powerful than I will ever be. She knows we know about her. She is trying to block my visions, but I felt her powers. She can kill a person without touching them. She doesn't even need the huge barbarian army she has following her," Hem explains. "We train every day. Our people are strong people too. We must find a way to defeat her and her army."

"Maybe I have the way. Follow me back to my workshop," Jax says, smiling.

All the men look curious as they get up from the table and start following Jax—well, everyone but Marc, who quickly starts shoving food in his mouth, then takes what he can carry as he runs to catch up with the others.

Jax leads them through the village to the back where his house and workshop are; they go around back of his workshop. There is a large stick with a sharp point at the end of it and a bunch of melons that look split in half. "How did you get such a sharp point on that stick?" Mount asks.

Jax smiles again. "I was able to use the strange material for something great. Heating the material with fire turned the material into a liquid like water, but when it cools, it turns back solid and strong."

"How will that help us with fighting?" Marc asks.

"Watch," Jax tells him; he goes over to a pile of melons, picks one up, and shoves it on the point of the stick. He goes over to a table and starts unrolling a large cloth; inside the cloth is a strange shiny metal-looking spear.

"That's the neatest thing I've ever seen!" Marc yells out.

"You haven't seen nothing yet," Jax tells Marc, then walks over to the melon and swings the strange object at it; it slices the melon in half as the top part goes flying in the air and splatters all over the ground.

"Now that was the neatest thing I've ever seen!" Marc screams, then starts begging Jax to let him have a turn; but before he can get to it, Jax hands it over to Mount.

"I like this," Mount says as he starts swinging it around, then twirls it in circles. Jax sets up another melon; and Mount then runs at the melon, jumps with a full twist, and slices the melon in half. Hem is very impressed with Jax's invention; he goes to his knees and thanks man's creator for giving Jax the knowledge to make such a weapon.

Marc finally gets his turn; he slices the melon in two and then turns to Jax. "Will you make me one?"

Jax looks at Marc, then at Hem and Mount. "I might have enough to make one more if we're lucky."

"I can go back and find more. It's a long journey, at least five sunrises, to get to the mountain area where I found the material in the ground. At the time, I wasn't sure what I had, so I didn't grab it all. There is lots more where I found this."

Mount looks at Marc and Hem; then he tells Jax. "We're going with you. That way, we can all carry back what we can."

"We have never been past the woods. Father will never allow us to go," Marc tells Mount.

"Let's go show Jax's new discovery to him. When he sees what this new weapon can do, I know he will agree to let us go," Mount answers Marc.

The four men leave Jax's workshop and walk toward the brothers' parents' house. Dorn had his house built on top of the highest hill of the large valley, so it gives Jax time to tell them of the great adventure it will be going out in the wild. "There are dangers everywhere you turn, from poisonous plants growing to wild animals that could rip you to pieces and wild savage headhunters that eat human flesh," he tells them.

"I can't wait. It will be fun!" Marc excitedly says.

"We need a good challenge. If we can't do this, how will we ever defend our home?" Mount asks.

"This will be easy compared to Mount's training sessions," Marc jokes as everyone laughs.

"We'll train every day while we are gone—harder, if I have anything to say about it," Mount says with a stern voice.

Marc doesn't have time to comment back because from a distance, they hear their names being yelled. Running down the hill is the boys' younger teenage sister, Missy. She runs to Marc and jumps in his arms, then goes over to Mount and jumps on his back.

Mount carries Missy on her back as they walk the rest of the way up the hill. Missy then jumps off his back and runs ahead of them into the house. Soon after, the door opens again, and Dorn comes walking out of the house. "Hello, boys. What brought you all to the top of the hill?" he asks.

"Hey, Dad!" both boys say to their father.

"Hello, Dorn," both Jax and Hem say to Dorn.

"We came to show you the invention Jax has made. We think it will help our people in case we are ever attacked," Mount says.

Mount pulls the weapon out from the cloth he had it wrapped in. Dorn's eyes light up when he sees the shiny object. "Can I see that?" Dorn asks. Mount hands the weapon to his father. Dorn takes the weapon and gets a feel of it; he then rubs his thumb down the blade. It cuts his thumb, and blood pours down his arm.

"Careful, Dad!" Mount yells.

"How did you make such a thing?" Dorn asks Jax.

Jax is setting up a melon on a stick as he explains, "I found the material in the ground on one of my scavenger hunts. It's a strong silver rock. Then when I put it to fire, I was able to shape it into what you see here. I call it steel. Now take the steel and swing it at this melon," Jax tells Dorn.

Dorn takes the steel weapon and swings it at the melon; it splits in half, and Dorn is amazed by what it can do. "I want to go back to the mountains where I found this rock and bring back more to make things with," Jax tells Dorn.

Mount walks over to his dad. "We want to go as well, if you are okay with it, sir."

"You and your brother want to go with Jax to get more of that rock?" Dorn asks.

"Yes, sir," they both say at once.

"Hem is going too," Mount tells his father.

"That is fine! How long do you boys plan to be gone?" Dorn asks them.

"We shouldn't be gone any more than six to seven sunrises. We are going all the way to the mountains. Plus I have a table on wheels I call a wagon that we will push to be able to carry more rock back," Jax says.

Dorn has them follow him into the house and sit in the entertainment room. From another door comes out the boys' mother, Doris. "There's my babies!" she yells as she goes to each boy for a hug. Doris then yells, "Missy!"

Missy comes running into the room. "Yes, Mother?" she says.

"Get your brothers and their friends some water."

Mount stops her. "Mom, we are fine. We have to go pack."

"Pack for what?" Doris says, getting worried.

"Dad will tell you everything," Marc tells their mom as they leave the house.

Back at Serina's village of barbarians, it's starting to turn dark; and Boar has been walking through the streets, looking at his men. He can't help but wonder if his men can handle a real fight; they have been at this village for some years now. Most of his good warriors have aged; hell, he has aged himself. Plus in the past, none of the other places they attacked knew they were coming. How would his men do if they attacked a place where the men were ready to fight?

As he makes his way to the center of the village, his male servant Hex comes running up to him. "What can I do for you, sir?"

"Hex, gather all the men to the center of the village. I need to talk with them," Boar commands.

Hex does as Boar says, and he goes running through the village, yelling to all to come to the center. Soon, all his men are surrounding him; then Hex comes through the crowd next to Boar. "Quiet them down!" he growls at Hex.

Hex screams, "QUIET!"

Boar stays silent as he walks up to his men, looking seriously at them all. Then he talks as loud as he can so all the men hear his words. "My warriors, we have attacked and destroyed many civilizations for our queen, Serina." The men all cheer for Boar. "I have talked with our queen, and she has told me of a man that we will soon face. He has powers as she does and a powerful army as well. Are you men ready for a fight?" Boar screams.

The men all scream, "YEAH!" as they cheer.

"Well, it's time to find out. In the morning, we will have a pit fight. I want to know who my real warriors are and who I can depend on to help me lead us into battle to win a war. All men will line up, and all men will fight till I have a champion, and that man will be my second-in-command." The men go crazy as they try to show Boar they are ready. "I suggest you stay away from the wine and the women and go get some rest. You'll need it. Now go as you are. Have a good night. I'll see you all in the morning."

Boar looks to Hex. "Tomorrow should be good. I didn't mention it, but I've been bored and plan to put myself in the tournament. I need a workout." Both men laugh as they walk toward Boar's shelter.

Then from behind them, they hear, "Sir, we are back." They turn to see that the explorers Viper and Cobra are back from their mission of finding a new civilization to take from the people.

"Did I hear 'tournament'?" Cobra asks.

"You heard right," Hex says to the men.

"It's good to see you men back," Boar tells them.

"How was your journey? Did you find anything?" Boar asks the two.

"You won't believe the city we found. It's the biggest city we've ever seen, with huge structures like we've never seen before," Viper reports to Boar.

"The people are light-haired with the most beautiful women ever seen—next to Serina, of course," Cobra adds.

"So you went in and talked with the people?" Boar asks.

"Yeah, they are very nice—let us come in, fed us, gave us a place to sleep. They should be easy to take over," Viper assures Boar.

"So you didn't meet a man there who seemed to have powers like Serina's, or did any of the men seem like they would put up a good fight?" Boar questions them both.

Cobra and Viper shake their heads. "No, not at all," they both say.

"Why?" Cobra asks.

"I'll explain on the way to Serina's shelter. She will be excited to see you two are back," Boar tells them. They follow Boar to Serina's place. "Wait here while I announce our arrival," Boar tells them, opens the door, and goes inside.

Lisa is waiting for him. "Serina is waiting for you. Bring the men in and follow me," she tells him.

Boar goes out and gets Cobra and Viper; they come in and follow Lisa to the back where Serina is waiting. The men enter the room and kneel to Serina; she goes over to the men. "So you have returned with good news, I hope?"

"Yes, my queen, we found a huge city—one like we've never seen before, with huge structures made from stone built to the sky," Viper informs Serina.

"Come over here and hold out your hand," Serina orders Viper.

He walks over to Serina, kneels in front of her, and holds out his hand. Serina takes the warrior's hand; when she does, her eyes light up, and everything Viper has done and seen shows up in an image in a large mirror. It shows the men's trip there; then it shows a beautiful large city, and just how the men said, there are large stone buildings far in the sky. There are many of them that surround the largest one of all—it was huge.

The vision moves into the city, where all the people are moving through the city; they all seem like each other, with all seeming to have light golden blond hair. Serina also sees there are no men who look like any kind of guard or warrior or any who seem to have powers like the man in her vision. She lets go of Viper's hand. "That is the city I've been seeing in my dreams. It was meant for your men to find it. That will be my new kingdom. We will make our way there in just a few days."

"Lisa, you get the women ready to leave. And, Boar, you will get the men ready," Serina tells them. "We will leave here in two days. Now go!"

"What about the men from your vision? Aren't you worried they may try to stop us?" Boar asks.

Serina becomes fuming mad. "Don't worry about the men in my vision. You just worry about getting my men ready to march and attack those people and getting me my kingdom. Besides, they are nowhere to be seen."

She adds, "I will go meditate and see if I can find them in my visions. I feel the one with the powers is trying to block my visions, but I know they have nothing to do with my city. Take our two men. Let them pick a slave girl to be with. Make sure they are fed and get a good night's sleep for their efforts."

"Yes, my queen," Boar says; then the men leave. Lisa then helps Serina to her bed to rest for the night, then leaves to go gather the women to start getting everything packed up.

CHAPTER 2

The Journey

IT IS NOW early morning into the next day; the sun is starting to peak over the horizon. Already, the news of Jax's new invention has spread through the village; and all the men have gathered at the front of Dorn's house, watching Mount give an unbelievable demonstration of what the new metal can do. All the men praise Jax's abilities as they see the new weapon cut through everything; then one of the elders yells out, "What do we need such a thing for? All that thing will do is get people hurt or, worse, dead."

Mount steps up to the man. "This is what we need to make sure we stay alive to keep our people safe."

"Safe? From what? We have never seen any attack for ages. What you are referring to is nonsense from a strange-acting boy who has been lucky a few times with stuff that's happened, so that makes him have special powers?" the man yells back at Mount. Then he looks over to Dorn. "You best get control of your boy before he destroys all we built."

Hem can't take any more; his father tells him he has a gift from their creator—he is special but can't use his powers for jokes. *But once won't hurt*, he thinks to himself. Hem waves his hand, and the old man's robe flies up over his head, showing his naked body. Everyone laughs; then while he stumbles around to pull it down, he slips in the mud. The man finally stands and gets his robe down; everyone is still laughing. "That was the wind! You have no powers!" the old man yells, walking away.

"So you boys ready for your big journey?" Dorn asks them.

"We are ready!" Marc screams excitedly.

"I have a surprise for you, Marc," Jax says, then pulls out another sword.

Marc can't believe his eyes as he takes the weapon. "My very own sword!" he cries out.

"Plus at my workshop, I put a table on wheels and call it a wagon. We can push it along with us and bring back ten men's worth of the silver stone," Jax tells them all.

"Let's get it and get going," Mount says to them all. "You ready?" he asks Hem, who was with Ebert.

"Ready," Hem tells Mount, then hugs his father goodbye.

At the barbarian village, Boar is slowly waking up from a long night of celebrating with Viper and Cobra. His favorite slave girl, Jonna, is lying next to him asleep. He wakes up excited, having her lying right up next to him, so he doesn't even bother waking her up as he slides inside of her; she quickly wakes up, moaning. "You know how to wake a girl up," she cries out as she starts moving with Boar's motion. It doesn't take long before Boar lets out a moan and collapses on top of her.

"Doesn't someone have a tournament to win?" Jonna asks Boar.

"Yes, I do," he says as he gets up and gets dressed.

Jonna sits up on the bed and puts her arms around Boar's neck. "I'll be cheering for you," she says and kisses him.

He grabs her ass. "You'd better be ready. I get really horny after winning in anything." He laughs as he goes out the door.

"Good morning, sir," Hex says to Boar; he was waiting for him with food. "You need to eat. It will give you the strength you need to win in battle."

"Are the men up and ready?" Boar asks Hex.

"Yes, sir, and the pits ready," Hex tells Boar.

"Good, now go get all the prisoners as well. I want to know who is a warrior and who is cleanup crew." Boar laughs.

Hex goes to do Boar's orders as Boar goes to the pit where the men are waiting. Boar makes his way to the center of the pit; the men cheer for him as he gets there. Then with a few men, Hex comes leading in all the prisoners.

Boar eyes a certain one they captured alone in the nowhere lands of the sands. He is different from him and his people; he has darker skin, talks different, and has a crazy fighting style. His men barely caught him; it took over ten of them to bring him down, and that was after he put down over ten. Boar wants to take him on one-on-one; he knows he can take him. That's why he chose to put the prisoners in the tournament.

Hex lines all the prisoners up at the front, and Boar gets everyone's attention to explain the rules of the fight.

Back at Dorn's village, Mount, Marc, Hem, and Jax have gotten back to Jax's workshop, where Kurt has gotten the wagon packed and ready to go. The wagon is perfect; it has handles on each side to make it easier to push. The men all push the wagon toward the front of the village, where all the people have gathered to see them off. Jax, on his past journeys, has drawn maps; and he marked the land. So after they all say their goodbyes, Jax leads them out of the village into the wide open fields.

Not far into their trip, Marc starts complaining. "How long do we have to push this thing before we rest?"

"Stop whining! We just started this trip," Mount snaps at him.

Marc stays silent for some time as they push the wagon through the tall weeds in the field; then he yells out, "Look at those huge animals in the distance eating the grass! Wonder if we could eat them, or too bad, they can't pull this wagon for us."

Hem laughs. "That's not a bad idea. Let me go ask them."

"If we can eat them?" Marc asks.

As the three others stay in the wagon, Hem slowly walks over toward the group of animals. With his father's help, he has learned he can read the thoughts of animals. He can send his thoughts to the animals, and they understand him. He gets close, then stops. "Hello, my friends. I'm called Hem. Don't be scared. I am a friend."

The large animals stand looking at one another; then the largest one of them comes walking toward Hem. "Why would we be scared? We could crush you small strange animals," the large animal tells Hem.

Hem laughs. "Yes, I'm sure with your size, we would be in trouble. What do you call yourselves?"

The animal stands tall. "We call ourselves horses," he tells Hem.

"We are human. It's so nice to be able to communicate with you. I was hoping to ask for you and your companions' help."

"How could we horses help you humans?" the horse asks.

Hem points toward the wagon and men. "Those are my friends. We are trying to push that wagon to a far destination. We were hoping you all could help us by pulling it for us."

One of the other horses comes over. "Why would we do that?" the horse asks Hem.

"We are on a mission to save our people and to save the lands around us from a large vicious army of barbarians. They come through and destroy the lands and kill anything living that crosses their path. We have a plan to stop them, but we need to gather some special rocks far away near the mountains. With all of your help, we could not only get there faster, but as strong as you are, we could carry back much more," Hem says.

The horses gather around in a circle away from Hem; they are shaking their heads and making grunt noises. Then after a short time, the leader comes back over to Hem. "We have talked it over, and if our lands are in trouble, we are here to help you in any way we can."

Hem smiles. "Thank you so much. You don't know just how much this means to us. Come meet my friends," Hem tells them, then leads them over to where the others were waiting. Hem tells them, "These are the horses. They have agreed to help us with our mission."

Marc runs over to them, petting each one. "They are so beautiful," he says.

Mount, Jax, and Kurt go over and join Marc in petting them. "You really understand what these animals are thinking?" Mount asks Hem.

"Yes, it's amazing. I talk with them just as I talk with you," Hem tells Mount.

"Can I ride one?" Marc screams out.

"I don't think they want us to ride them," Hem tells Marc.

Then the younger-looking one of the horses steps over to Hem. "He can ride me if he wants. It should be fun."

Hem tells Marc, "This one says you can ride him."

Marc runs to the horse and hugs it. "Thank you," he says, then stops. "Do we call them all 'horse,' or can I give him a name?" Marc asks Hem. Hem then explains to the horses that humans have names to be different if they would like names, and they agree to having names. Marc looks at his horse. "I'm going to call you Colt," he tells the horse.

"He likes it," Hem tells Marc.

Then Colt lowers down to let Marc climb on his back, and Marc slowly climbs on.

"This is crazy!" Marc yells.

"Hold on to his mane!" Hem yells to Marc.

Then Colt takes off running across the field; they could hear Marc screaming with excitement. As Mount watches his brother go across the field on his newfound friend, he feels a nudge on his shoulder. He turns to see the leader of the horses behind him.

"He seems to like you," Hem tells Mount.

Mount starts petting the large solid black horse. Then the horse bends down to let Mount climb on him. He grips the horse's mane, and the animal takes off running across the field. Mount gives out a yell as he hangs on to the horse; he never has felt such a rush. They catch up to Marc and Colt.

"This is the most amazing thing ever!" Marc yells over to Mount.

"We will get to the mountains in no time with their help," Mount tells Marc.

"What did you name your horse?" Marc asks Mount.

Mount pets the horse as he looks off into the sky for a moment; then he says, "Stallion."

"That's a good name," Marc says.

"Let's race," Mount says to his brother; and then without saying a word, Marc takes off on Colt, leaving Mount and Stallion behind.

Mount tells Stallion, "Let's see what you can do." Then Stallion takes off, running like the wind. Mount hangs on for his life. In no time, they were catching up with Colt and Marc; and with ease, Stallion shows why he is the leader of the pack of horses. Stallion and Mount ride back up to where the humans and horses are still waiting.

"Hem, you are the greatest person on the earth!" Marc yells as he rides back up on Colt; then he yells at Jax, "What are you waiting for, Jax? Get on one. It's the best thing ever!"

"I'll pick one when I'm ready!" Jax screams back.

Then the white female with golden spots walks up to Jax, and he starts petting her. "You are the most beautiful creature I have ever seen," Jax says to the horse and kisses her on her head. She lowers down to let Jax climb on her, and he says, "I'll call you Mustang."

Mount jumps off Stallion and walks over to Hem, and they watch Jax go across the field on Mustang with Colt and Marc right behind them. Mount laughs. "Looks like the female is faster than most of the males," he says about Mustang. "Your gift was special before. Now you can communicate with animals. Wonder what else you can do."

Marc and Jax come riding back up to them. "Which one will you ride?" Marc asks Hem.

Hem walks over to the solid brown horse with white spots. "This will be my horse. He is the eldest of them all and very wise like myself. I'll call him Pinto." Hem then pets the horse.

"That leaves you, Kurt. Jump on a horse," Marc tells Kurt.

"No, thank you. I'll just ride on the back with Jax or on the wagon," Kurt says to Marc.

Then Jax tells Kurt, "No worries. With the setup I plan to use to tie the horses to the wagon, I'll need you to guide them."

"That sounds good to me, sir. Let's get started," Kurt says to Jax.

Jax gathers the supplies he brought with him; he gets all the rope he made and then a long piece of wood, and he is able to tie the horses to the wagon with what he had.

Marc laughs. "Look, now it's like you have two horses."

Mount smiles. "It's like everything is coming together. Let's get moving!" he yells to everybody.

Kurt gets on the wagon, and the horses start to pull it across the field, with the other horses riding right with the horses pulling the wagon. Hem rides with Pinto ahead of everyone, and they lead the way across the land, heading toward the mountains. "This will get us there in half the sunrises. Good idea, Marc," Mount says to his brother.

At the barbarian village, all the men have now gathered to the pit area. Hex is in the middle of the crowd, yelling for everyone to be quiet. Once he gets everyone to shut up, he lets them know Boar is about to speak. Boar then walks to where Hex is in the center of all the men. "My warriors, I've been told by the queen we will leave here tomorrow to go conquer a new city for her." The men all cheer, hearing they get to go kill a bunch of people and take what's theirs.

"I have seen the vision of our queen. This new city is as far as you can see. Many people live there, so I need to know who my best warriors are, who I can trust to lead a group of men and claim victory. Today the winner of the fight will stand next to me and give out my orders to the men as we take the city." The crowd of wild, fired-up men cheer for Boar as he holds his arms in the air, enjoying the love of his men for him. "Let's get started!" Boar screams.

Boar looks over his men. "Who will survive the tournament and help me lead the army?"

All the men start yelling at Boar, "Me!"

Then the largest one of the strongest of the barbarian men comes pushing his way to the front of the crowd. "Everyone knows I'm winning this thing," the large man tells Boar.

"Ace, there you are. I have a surprise for you," Mount tells him. Back when they captured the strange prisoner, Bree, Ace was one of the men badly hurt by Bree.

Boar turns to the guards over the prisoners. "Bring the prisoner Bree to the center of the pit," he commands.

"Thank you," Ace tells Boar with a smile on his face. "It's revenge time," he says as he makes his way to the pit.

The guards drag Bree to the center of the pit; then one of the guards hits Bree hard with the wooden side of his spear before they untie his hands, and Bree falls to the ground as the guards run away. Ace takes advantage as he runs over to Bree and hits him in the back as hard as he can.

Ace then picks Bree up over his head; he spins him around as the crowd goes crazy from the excitement. He throws Bree into the front of the crowd, and the other men start hitting and kicking Bree back into the circled pit. As Bree lies on the ground, Ace is walking around the circle of men, flexing his muscles and calling out to them, "Who's the best?" While Ace is busy showing off, it gives Bree time to gather himself. As Bree gets up, Ace has his back turned.

"Look out!" Boar screams.

Ace turns to see Bree back on his feet; he runs at Bree and goes to hit him with his forearm to put Bree back to the ground, but Bree is very fast. He moves out of the way from Ace's charge. As Ace goes by, Bree hits Boar on the side of his leg at the knee. Boar goes down screaming and holding his knee in pain. Bree walks over to Ace and kicks him so hard in the head that he drops to the ground out cold. The cheers go silent for a moment; then they get louder than ever, never seeing anything like that before.

Boar is screaming mad; he orders five of the men in front to take the prisoner down. The men slowly go in and surround Bree as one of the men goes over to Ace to help him up; in a daze, he slowly sits up. The man helps Ace to his feet; then Boar comes over to them and starts handing out clubs to all his men. Bree has dropped to his knees and has his eyes closed in a meditation. Ace looks at Bree, then looks over to two of the men. "You two go over and beat the prisoner to the ground. Kill him if you can," he says.

The two men run at Bree, and one swings his club. Bree catches the club and blocks the other man's swing with it. As he does, he twists the man's arm till it snaps; and the man screams as Bree comes back with the club, knocking the man out with a blow to the head. The second warrior tries to hit Bree again with his club, but Bree ducks the swing and comes up with an uppercut to the man's chin, then hits him with a combo of punches till the man falls to the ground.

Bree then turns to Ace and the three other men, and with his hand, he motions them to come to him. As Ace points the men in the directions to go, they all surround Bree.

Inside Serina's chambers, Serina has called for Lisa. She comes in and kneels in front of Serina. "What is all the commotion outside?" Serina asks Lisa.

Lisa stands up. "My queen, Boar has called for one of his pit fights and made the first fight Ace against the dark-skinned prisoner. The prisoner has beat Ace and four other men when I came to you."

Serina shuts her eyes; and in a vision, she sees the prisoner killing half her army, along with Boar, as he escapes.

Back outside, Boar has seen enough; he goes to the center of the circle, where Ace stands with the other men. "Are you all a bunch of wimps? You can't take down one man!" he screams at them. "Give me a club. I'll beat him down!" Boar tells them as he takes a club from Ace, then walks toward Bree.

"Time for you to die, dark one!" Boar screams at Bree, charging him with his club.

Bree quickly takes the weapon from Boar and sweeps his legs; then when he goes to hit Boar with the club, he suddenly goes to his knees, screaming in pain.

"This ends now!" Serina screams as the crowd of men quickly clear the way for her as she makes her way to where Boar and Bree lie on the ground. She kicks Boar in the stomach as she walks up to him. "GET UP!" she screams.

Boar slowly gets up as Serina turns back to Bree and starts hitting him hard with her powers; he screams as she makes it worse. "Why do you keep causing me so many problems?" she yells as she punishes him. She lets up just as Bree is close to death.

Boar is back on his feet. "My queen, why did you not kill him?"

"I want you to end this nonsense now. We need all our men in good shape. How will we take my new kingdom with a bunch of hurt men? You will never call one of these fights again unless I say so, understand?" Serina says very sternly. "Now get the prisoners back in their cages! We need them to be ready to march in the morning!" Serina screams.

"Yes, my queen," Boar says as he kneels to her.

Serina turns to all the men. "I think you have more important things to do besides playing games. Everyone will get to work to be ready to leave here in the morning. I will curse this land. If you try to stay, you will die," Serina warns all the warrior men.

"When we take control over my new kingdom, I need you to be smarter about things. There are better ways to do things than to have your men kill each other. Now go show me you're worth being my leader by getting this place packed up and the people ready to leave," Serina tells Boar. "I'm going back to my chambers. Lisa is in control. You will answer to her till morning." She then leaves the area and goes back to her chambers.

Boar stands and watches Serina walk away; he hates when he must answer to Lisa, but he won't dare say anything about it. Lisa puts just as much fear in the people as Serina. If Lisa goes to Serina about you, most times, you will die.

Boar yells for Ace. "Gather up the men and give the orders for an evacuation! I want this place packed up by dark!" he screams at Ace. Ace gets the men to work as Boar walks around, making sure everything gets done.

It's now the middle of the day. Mount, Marc, Jax, and Hem are now comfortable with the horses and have been covering triple the ground that would have been covered walking. Jax rides up to Mount. "It would have taken us two days to get to this point walking."

Mount laughs. "All thanks to Marc for being lazy."

Marc isn't even paying attention. "I'm hungry. When are we going to stop and eat?" he asks.

Everyone laughs as Hem says, "It's probably a good idea. The horses could use the rest."

"There is a stream over this way," Jax tells the men, and they lead the horses to the stream; next to it is a large field of grass for the horses as well.

Then as Kurt sets up a camp and gets a fire started, the other four men go to hunt some food. Jax, always being gone in the wilderness, is the best hunter of them; he has them quietly follow him as he follows the river. It isn't far down the river before Jax has them stop. "Be quiet," he tells them. Then on his knees, he crawls over to a tree and hides behind it.

Jax slowly bends around and looks ahead, then quickly pulls back around and hides; he then looks back and motions Mount to come to him. Mount tells Marc and Hem, "Stay here till I say so." Then he does as Jax and crawls slowly to him at the tree.

"Look around the tree and be quiet," Jax tells Mount.

Mount slowly looks around the tree; he sees a small group of large animals that look like horses, but not as tall and real wide. He pulls back around to Jax. "What are they?" he asks.

"Not sure, but one will feed us the whole trip," Jax says, then motions for Marc and Hem. "Behind the tree a way down the stream are some animals drinking. We only need one to feed us for the whole trip. We must be quiet. If they get spooked, they will run. They aren't too fast of an animal, but faster than us." Jax looks at each man. "Ready to do this?" he asks.

Hem stops them. "Something is not right. We'd better not do this," he tells them.

"What's wrong?" Mount asks.

Hem shuts his eyes, shaking his head. "I'm not sure. I just feel we are in danger," he says with concern in his voice.

Jax looks at Hem, not sure if he really has powers; he shakes his head. "This could be our only chance to have food. I say we do this, or we'll die from hunger. You ready to do this?" Jax asks Marc.

Marc shakes his head up and down. "I'm ready," he tells Jax.

"Good, you sneak around past them. Then I will charge them, making them run in your direction," Jax tells Marc.

"Then when one comes by, I'll kill it with my sword," Marc finishes Jax's sentence.

"You got it. Go on," Jax tells Marc, who slowly goes around the animals and gets behind a tree a few feet from them.

"Trust me, Jax, something bad is going to happen. I feel it," Hem tells Jax one more time.

"Everything will be fine. Don't worry," Jax tells Hem; then he starts walking toward the large animals. Mount and Hem watch from the tree as Jax starts running toward the animals, screaming.

Just as Jax said, the animals get startled and run away from the river right in Marc's direction; and when one of the largest ones comes running by Marc, he jumps out from behind the tree and stabs the large animal with his sword. The animal lets out a loud scream and starts jerking around, then takes off running. Marc takes off running after it. "Come back with my sword!" he yells at the animal because the sword is still in its chest.

When Mount, Hem, and Jax catch up with Marc, he is standing over the dying animal; it's jerking, and Marc is trying to get to his sword. Mount comes up and finishes the animal off. "Don't let that poor animal suffer like that," he tells Marc, then pulls out the sword and hands it to him.

"I was about to when you walked up!" Marc snaps at Mount.

"You looked scared to me," Jax says to him; then everyone laughs. "Let's eat!" Jax yells out. "See, Hem? We got our food, and nothing went wrong," Jax assures Hem.

Then from behind them, they hear a vicious growl; then it seems to be all around them as the growls get louder. The men circle around the dead animal as they watch a pack of huge wild wolves surround them. "Okay, this is bad," Jax says as all the men start to pull out their weapons.

"No sudden moves, or we will be dead," Mount tells them all.

"Shouldn't we just kill them before they kill us?" Marc asks.

"We may have no choice," Mount tells his brother.

"Wait," Hem tells them. "Let me try talking with them." Hem starts walking closer toward the wolves; he holds his hands up. "Hello, my friends. We mean you no harm."

The largest of the wolves steps forward. "Whatever you creatures are, you need to leave here. These are our lands, which makes that our food."

Hem smiles. "We apologize. We are just passing through. We will leave here without the animal," he assures the wolves. "We should slowly leave here without the animal," Hem tells the men.

"We can't leave our food with them. We'll starve," Jax says.

"I say we make clothes out of them," Marc tells Jax as he holds up his sword.

The wolves start growling and coming closer to the men; they have forgotten about the dead animal. They want fresh meat. Mount joins Marc and Jax and holds up his sword, getting ready for the wolves to attack. Hem jumps in front of them and holds out his hand. "Become man's best friend!" he yells out; then a large flash comes from his hand.

The wolves go from almost viciously attacking the men to rolling around on the ground, begging for the men's attention. Hem walks over to the wolves as the others yell, "Hem, no!"

The wolves all attack Hem; the others look away, thinking he will be ripped to shreds; then they hear him laughing as he pets all the wolves, and they all lick him. Hem looks over to the others. "It's fine, fellows. They are loyal to us now. Come over and pet them. They love it."

Marc comes running over, then calls one of the wolves to him; the wolf charges Marc and knocks him on the ground, licking him all over the face. He rolls around on the ground, playing with the wolf. Mount and Jax still stand at the dead animal, guarding it. Mount puts his sword away. Jax tries to stop him, but Mount goes over to the wolves. Mount starts petting and playing with them; then Jax finally walks over to where Hem is and starts petting one of the wolves slowly.

Once he gets comfortable with the wolf, he looks over at Hem. "If I didn't see it myself, I would have never believed it. You have a very special gift. I will never doubt anything you do again," Jax tells Hem.

The leader of their pack comes up to Hem. "I'm not sure what you did to us, but we can calmly focus now, and we all thank you. We have talked and have decided to be your protectors and stay with you, humans. Have each of your human friends choose a wolf to be their guardian."

Hem calls the others over to him and gathers them in a circle. "My spell worked too well. They want to be our personal protectors and stay with us as our pets. We can each pick one to stay with us," he tells them.

"Oh yes, we get our own wolf as a pet. That is awesome!" Marc yells out excitedly.

"This is a very good thing. We can all sleep at nights, knowing we have wolves watching over us," Mount says to Hem.

"I thought the horses giving us rides was incredible. Now we have wolves watching over us. Like I said before, you are amazing, Hem! I'll never doubt you again," Jax says, grabbing Hem's hand.

"Do we get to name them?" Marc asks while he pets each wolf, trying to decide which one to make his pet.

Hem asks the elder wolf if they mind getting names. "The wolves enjoy the idea of getting names," Hem tells the men. "Why don't you pick first?" Hem tells Mount.

"I'll take the leader for mine," Mount says as he goes to the wolf and pets him. "I'll call you Maverick," Mount tells the wolf. "I promise to take as good of care of you as you will me." Maverick licks Mount up his face.

Marc then goes to the wolf that has been jumping around and playing the whole time. "You are my wolf," he says to the wolf, and it jumps on him, licking his face. "I'm calling you Rowdy," he tells the wolf, then calls him. "Follow me, Rowdy." Then Marc takes off running, and the wolf goes right behind him.

Hem then looks at Jax. "Your turn," he tells him.

Jax walks over to one of the females. "You look smart," he says to the wolf. "I'll take her," he tells Hem.

"What's her name?" Marc yells.

Jax looks her over. "I'll call you Charm," Jax tells the wolf as he pets her.

"Good name!" Marc yells to Jax as he is still rolling around with Rowdy. "What about the other two?" Marc asks Hem.

"I thought we could give the other two to each of our dads," Mount suggests to Hem.

Hem explains to the wolves, and they are more than happy with that. Hem tells the male, "You will be called Woe." And he tells the female, "Your name will be Desire."

"Then of course, I want the elder wolf, and I shall call you Savvy," Hem tells the wolf. "We'd better get back to camp. Kurt must be wondering where we are," he tells everyone.

"Knowing Kurt, he is somewhere hiding by now." Marc laughs.

The men get the dead animal and drag it back to the camp as the wolves stayed right with them just as they promised. When they get back, Kurt has a nice camp set up with a large fire burning; and the horses are over in the field, feeding.

When Kurt sees the guys walking up with wolves around them, he screams and jumps on the wagon. The guys all start laughing at Kurt. "Get him!" Marc says to Rowdy. and the wolf runs over to the wagon, then jumps up next to Kurt, who is frozen in fear.

"He won't hurt you!" Jax yells to Kurt, but Kurt won't budge.

Marc jumps into the wagon and starts petting and wrestling with Rowdy. "Look, he won't hurt you. None of them will, thanks to Hem." Kurt slowly reaches out and pets Rowdy. "See? He loves being petted," Marc says to Kurt as he slowly starts petting Rowdy a little more and rises up from balling up in fear.

"How did you do this?" he asks Hem as he jumps off the wagon and goes to pet all the other wolves.

"Mount and Jax, take the dead animal. Cut it up and put pieces of meat on the fire to cook. Then give the wolves all a piece of the meat for their meal."

Half the day has gone by. Serina, in her chambers, asks for her slave girl to go find Lisa. A few minutes later, Lisa comes running into the room and goes to her knees in front of Serina. "How is the progress going with packing up for us to leave in the morning?" Serina demands to know.

"Everything is packed, and the people are ready to go. They are having their meal, and I will shut things down after they all eat," Lisa assures Serina.

"Good, very good, Lisa. Now go have Boar get Ace and come back with them."

Lisa goes and finds Boar at his home, still upset over how his tournament turned out. When Boar sees Lisa, he snaps, asking, "What do you want?"

Lisa is not happy with his tone. "If I'm here, it's for our queen, Serina. Shall I let her know you are not happy to see me?" Lisa quickly lets Boar know.

Boar drops to his knees. "No, I'm sorry. What are my queen's orders?" he asks.

"Serina requests your presence in her chambers. She said to bring the warrior Ace with you," Lisa tells Boar.

"As you wish," Boar tells Lisa and stands. "I'll find Ace and be right there."

"Don't keep the queen waiting too long. I'd hate to see something happen to you," Lisa says and laughs going out the door.

After Lisa is gone, Boar slams his table with his fist, and it falls to pieces to the floor. He hates being ordered by a woman but won't dare cross Serina after seeing some of the things she has done through the years. Boar goes through the town looking for Ace, who is supposed to be watching over the men.

After looking around and asking a few of the men, he finds Ace getting his wounds looked at; but by now, he is having sex with the slave he had look at his wounds. Boar comes in. "Is this how you look after the men?" he screams. Ace jumps from being startled by Boar and tries his best to get his pants on. Boar looks at the slave girl. "Get out of here!" he demands.

"I'm sorry," Ace says with his head down, waiting to be hit.

Boar looks at him, shaking his head. "Stand up! Serina has asked for both of us in her chambers."

"Me too? Is she mad?" Ace asks in fear.

"No, but if we don't get there, she will be," Boar warns Ace. So they both run through town, ignoring the others trying to talk with them to quickly get to Serina's house.

Very nervously, they make their way to Serina's back chambers. Lisa is there waiting with Serina, who is sitting in her throne; they both go to their knees in front of Serina and lie at her feet. "Are the men ready to march to our new homeland, Boar?" she asks.

"Yes, my queen. The men have everything ready to be brought on the journey," Boar answers.

"That's excellent. Everything is going as I have seen. The dark slave, he has a gift. Don't worry about what happened this morning. The slave can't be beaten one-on-one, but I will one day need his gift. So we will keep him alive, understood?" Serina warns the men.

"Yes, my queen," they both say loudly.

"In my vision, I've seen you both. You both fight a good battle for me, and we take the large city with ease. Both of you go rest, for I will see you at sunup," Serina tells them.

Mount, Marc, Hem, and Kurt all sit around the fire, each full from eating the meat of the animal. "That was the best thing I have ever eaten in my life," Mount tells Jax, who is still cooking up meat over the fire.

"I ate so much I can't move," Marc tells them.

Hem laughs at Marc. "I'm the fullest I've ever been," he says.

Kurt lies back on the ground. "I could go to sleep," he says, shutting his eyes.

Mount looks at the men. Jax still has a lot of meat to cook, the other three look like they can fall asleep, and the wolves are all full of meat and lying around the fire.

Even the horses seem to be enjoying standing around the river. Mount stands up. "With the help of the horses, we have traveled in one day what would have taken three. And now we have the friendship of the wolves, who swore to protect us. I say we call it a day. Get a good night's sleep and get an early start in the morning," he tells all of them.

Everyone quickly agrees with Mount, and Jax tells Kurt, "Gather enough wood to last for the night while I finish here." With Marc's help, they go get wood while Mount and Hem set up a place to sleep, then call it a day.

CHAPTER 3

The Great City

IT IS EARLY morning, and Boar is seeing over the last few things before they leave. On all trips, Serina and Lisa are carried in a large carriage that takes ten of the strongest men to carry, and it needs to be brought up to the front of her house. Boar has Hex make sure that the carriage is ready; then knowing it will be a long trip, he finds his favorite slave girl, Jonna, and sneaks off to his house with her to make love one more time before the long journey.

The sun starts peaking over the horizon. Jonna runs out of Boar's house, scared Lisa will have her beaten if she isn't with the other slaves ready to leave. Boar jumps up as well and makes his way to Serina's house, where he finds Hex and Ace waiting for his orders. No sooner than he gets to them Lisa comes out. "Is everything ready for us to leave?" she asks Boar.

"Yes, my lady. Our queen's carriage is ready for her, and then we can start our journey," Boar lets Lisa know.

Lisa turns and goes back into the house. Soon, the door opens again; and with all of Serina's personal slave girls covering Serina from the sun, she comes out and quickly gets in the carriage. The demon inside her hates the sunlight. Lisa walks up to Boar, who is ordering the men to gather around the carriage, and loudly says for all the men to hear, "You may want to warn the men what happened to the last group of men who dropped the carriage."

Lisa then enters the carriage with Serina, and Boar looks at the men. "You heard her, men. If you dare drop the carriage, you will die a painful death."

Then Boar leaves Ace in charge of watching over the carriage as he goes to the front of the large group of people, where the trackers Viper and Cobra were waiting to lead the way to the great city. Boar stands in front and gives the order for the people to start marching. Then he stays and makes sure no one stays behind before he leaves, but in fear of Serina, all the people leave their old homes on their way to a great new life they have been told.

After a long good night's sleep, Mount is awake right when the sun starts peaking up. He looks over and sees Maverick lying next to him next to the fire; he still can't believe that Hem has powers like he does. Marc is asleep, using Rowdy as a place to put his head on. The wolf is asleep, but Mount can see the happiness on the wolf's face with Marc lying on him. He sits up and pets Maverick on his head, and he scoots closer to Mount, enjoying being petted.

"Hungry boy," Mount says as he gets up, then kicks Marc. "Wake up!"

"Oh, come on! I was having a great dream about Susie from home!" Marc cries out, so loud that it wakes everyone else up.

"Damn, Marc, shut up!" Jax screams.

As Mount leaves Marc and Jax arguing with each other, he goes over to Hem, who is sitting under a tree with his eyes shut. "I still have trouble understanding my visions. I don't see any danger ahead of us, but let's just be careful," Hem says as he opens his eyes.

Before Mount has any time to answer Hem, Marc comes behind him and puts a choke hold on him. Mount flips Marc over him to the ground. "Good try, little bro." He laughs. Marc stands up. "Now stop playing and help Jax and me pack up while Kurt is cooking. Then we will take a break real fast and eat before we leave," Mount tells his brother. "Why don't you stay here and see what you can do? We'll have Kurt tell you when it's time to eat," Mount tells Hem, and he and Marc go help Jax.

Marc looks over to Mount. "We have to break fast to eat—that's funny. So for now on, I think I'm calling the morning meal 'breakfast.'" Mount shakes his head at his brother, laughing. "You wait, one day, everybody will call the morning meal 'breakfast.' You wait and see!" Marc tells Mount.

“Whatever. Let’s just get done packing so we can eat and go,” Mount tells Marc.

“Eat breakfast,” Marc says as they hand Jax the last load to put in the wagon.

The sun is now up, and they are on the horses and heading toward the mountains; as the horses run across the fields, the wolves all keep up with ease. They even run ahead from time to time, checking to see if it’s safe for their new human companions. They have been riding the horses as fast as they can run for some time now; then Jax slows Mustang down.

“I hope we are stopping for a pee break!” Marc yells out to Jax.

“I could go myself, and the horses could use the rest,” Hem tells Jax.

They stop, and all of them jump off their horses and go over to some bushes to relieve themselves. When Mount finishes, he looks over at Hem and sees that he looks worried. “Something wrong?” he asks Hem.

“I’m not sure. I feel like we are being watched,” he tells Mount.

Then the wolves come up, barking. “What’s wrong, boy? Where are Marc and Rowdy?” Mount asks Maverick.

Then Marc comes pulling up his pants with Rowdy behind him. “Why are the wolves barking? It scared me so bad I almost fell in my shit!” he screams.

Everyone laughs at Marc as he is still trying to fix his pants. “Quiet down,” Hem tells them, then calls everyone closer to him. “We are not alone here. The wolves can smell a different scent,” he says quietly.

Marc laughs. “Please let someone attack us. I’m ready for a good fight.”

Then from a distance, in the direction of a patch of trees, loud screams are heard by the men. “I know those screams,” Jax says. “They are Neandertals, a vicious large group of men with no morals. They will eat human meat to survive.”

“There’s too many for the wolves to scare off and way too many for us five men to fight. We should get on the horses and leave while we can,” Jax suggests to the others.

Mount agrees, but before they can get to the horses, a large group of men surround them; they are savages who live under only one rule survive. The men circle around; then the biggest of the men speaks up. "You are on our land with no permission, so today you will die!" the leader screams at them.

Marc starts to yell something, but Mount stops him. "We are just trying to get to the mountains. We were not touching anything on your land," Mount says to the man.

The leader looks to his men. "Kill them!"

The wolves all come next to their humans and viciously growl and show their teeth to the Neandertals, and they hesitate to attack. Mount and Marc hold up their swords, not sure what will happen when they stab someone with it.

The leader gets very angry at his men for hesitating; he hits the nearest man and again screams, "ATTACK!" The men then run toward the men with the wolves. The wolves don't hesitate; they all run at the charging men and jump at their throats, taking them out fast. Mount and the others watch in amazement as the wolves devour through the men. Maverick is ripping through the men, but a group of the men surround him, and one of the men hits him with a club.

Mount gets very upset and runs over to where Maverick is and puts his sword through the man's chest; blood spurts all over the other men as the man falls to the ground dead. Then Marc comes behind him, swinging his sword at the Neandertals' heads while Jax and Kurt come at them with the daggers Jax had. They easily were defeating the savage men, but no one notices two of the men about to attack Hem, who has no weapon.

Savvy senses Hem is in trouble and runs to him; the wolf jumps on one of the men, ripping at his throat, but the other man has a large club raised over his head and is about to hit Hem with it. Hem cowers down with his hands over his head, and when the man goes to hit Hem with the club, a light surrounds Hem and blocks the club's blows. Not believing what he is seeing, he keeps swinging at the light; then Savvy comes behind him and rips his throat out, and the man falls to the ground dead.

As Mount, Marc, Jax, and Kurt look around, the Neandertal men were either running away or dead. Mount goes over to check on Hem;

he is stunned at what he was able to do. "Did you see what happened?" Hem asks Mount.

Marc comes over and puts his arm around Mount. "I saw you. It looked like you were glowing," Marc says.

"I was, and I could feel the power coming out of me. The men could not break through," Hem says excitedly.

"Did you see me cut the one's head clean off?" Marc says, still pumped from the fight.

Jax comes over, laughing and wiping blood from his face. "I saw Rowdy save your ass more than once," he says to Marc.

"Yeah, he did," Marc says as he goes over and starts petting Rowdy as Rowdy jumps all over, licking Marc.

As Marc lets Rowdy lick the blood off his face, Mount laughs. "We need to go wash this blood off," he tells them all.

"There is a small stream of water not far I was heading toward," Jax tells Mount. They get on the horses, and just as Jax said, not very far is a small stream of clear water.

Marc is the first to jump in the water and starts washing off; everyone else joins him, washing off the dried blood from the Neandertals. Soon, the men are splashing around, having fun; then out of nowhere, a tree falls, almost hitting them all. When they get out of the water, they all find Hem trying to form his energy shield and instead shot out a power ball that took out the tree. "I'm not sure what I really did," Hem tells them, holding up his hands away from them. "Dad said I have abilities I don't know about."

"That's for sure! Look at that poor tree." Marc laughs.

Mount looks serious. "We did good just now. I hate having to kill, but we needed that. We now know we can handle ourselves in a fight, and we know Hem can take care of himself," Mount says. "Just look at that poor tree," he says, laughing.

"We should get back on the trail. We can still be close by dark," Jax tells them, and they get on the horses and go back on the move with Marc bragging about how good he is on the way.

The day goes by, and they travel the rest of the day with no problems; then right when it seems the sun is starting to go down far in the distance, they see the tips of the mountains. Mount rides up to Jax. "So what's the plan when we get there?" he asks Jax.

"I want to go back where I found the material as there was still plenty there to get. Then we will search the area around it for more till we get all we can carry," Jax tells Mount.

"It's almost dark. We'll never make it. Let's stop and set camp for the night," Mount says.

Serina has the large group of people stop; she tells Lisa, "Get out of the carriage and have the people set up for the night."

Lisa opens the door to step out; all the people fall to their knees, thinking Serina is about to get out, but Lisa shuts the door and announces, "We will stop for the day. The men will set up Serina's tent first, then the rest of the camp. I want the women to start cooking the meal for after the men are done." Then Lisa remains out with the people to make sure things get done.

Serina stays in her carriage, waiting for Lisa to return; she lies back to rest and goes into another vision of the great city.

Back at the other camp, everyone has eaten, and Hem goes off early to rest; while he tries to sleep, he starts to see a beautiful huge city with large stone buildings reaching to the sky. He can see the people going through the town; they all seem so happy while the children play in the streets. Then out of nowhere, just like in his past visions, a large group of vicious men come in, destroying everything.

They start killing the people, even the children. Hem falls to his knees, watching the people die. Then just like his other visions, the beautiful woman comes in leading the large army; but this time, she looks over at Hem like she could see him and shoots a large fireball at him. Hem opens his eyes, jumping around, scared over his vision being so real.

Lisa opens the door of the carriage, and it wakes Serina. "Something wrong, my lady?" she asks.

"He was in my vision. The wizard was back in my vision, but I burned him to a crisp." Serina smiles.

Hem jumps up and runs to find Mount; he finds all of them still practicing their fighting moves. Hem motions to Mount to follow him and walks away from the others. "What's wrong?" Mount asks Hem.

Hem tells Mount, "I had a vision of a large beautiful city, one like I've never seen before. But in my vision, the same army from my other visions with the beautiful woman comes in and destroys the city and kills all the people."

"You think it has already happened?" Mount asks Hem.

"I don't think it has," Hem says.

"Do you think the city is nearby?" Mount asks Hem.

"In my vision, I seen mountains, so it could be," Hem answers. "We'll ask my animal friends in the morning. Right now, we should rest." Mount agrees and calls it a night for everyone.

The next morning, they eat and get back to riding toward the mountains; once they get close, Hem uses his power to call a gorgeous hawk from the air. It comes and sits right on his arm. Marc rides over to pet it. "That's the craziest thing I ever saw."

Hem talks with the hawk. "Good morning. I'm so happy you chose to come down to see me," he says to the large bird.

The bird looks at Hem. "I had to make sure you really were calling for me," the bird tells Hem as he flaps his wings.

"Don't be scared. No one here will hurt you," Hem says, and the bird calms down and sits still on his arm. "I called you to me to ask if you have seen any large man-made objects with people living around them," Hem says to the bird.

"Yes, a lot of people live across the other side of the mountains—nice people that leave me food, never have tried to attack me in any way," the bird tells Hem.

"Would you be willing to show us the way there?" Hem asks the bird.

"I will stay on this side of the mountain till you are ready to go. Just call me with your thoughts, and I will come to you." Then the bird flies away high in the air.

"Bye, bird!" Marc yells.

Hem tells Mount, "I was right, there being a city of people on the other side of this mountain."

Mount looks at Hem. It's quiet for a moment; then he looks over to Hem. "We need to go there and warn those people what is about to happen to them."

Hem looks skeptical. "Most of our people don't believe I have powers. You think we can make strangers believe?"

"We must try. We can't just let them die," Mount tells his friend.

That's when Jax yells to them, "We are here! There should be plenty of the metal in the ground here."

Later, after they set camp near the river coming out of the mountains, they are eating. Mount and Hem tell the others of Hem's vision of the nearby city being attacked. "I want to go warn them," Mount tells them. Everyone agrees that will be the right thing to do.

Jax says, "Kurt and I will stay and start looking for the metal. With the tools I made, we shouldn't have any problem."

So it was agreed that Mount, Marc, and Hem will go in the morning and warn the city of Hem's vision.

Morning comes. Hem tells the wolves Desire and Woe to stay with Charm at the camp with Jax and Kurt. Kurt has their food ready to eat and another meal for the travel. The three get on their horses and wave goodbye as Maverick, Rowdy, and Savvy run ahead to make sure everything is safe for their humans. Not far down the trail, Hem calls for the hawk; and soon, they hear the loud screech of the large bird. Then it starts circling around them. "He will lead us to the city," Hem tells the brothers.

They follow a rough rocky path right through the middle of the extremely large rocky mountains; it is very hot. The horses and wolves both are very thirsty. Mount tells Marc to quiet down from complaining; then as they listen, they can hear moving water. They lead the horses toward the sound of the water; it gets louder as they get closer.

They move around one side of the mountain and find a large water stream moving from down the mountain and running right through the middle of all the mountains.

The men lead the horses to the stream; then Marc jumps in, and the wolves follow him. Mount and Hem sit on the bank to drink and watch Marc jumping around, playing with the wolves. Mount looks over to Hem. "Think we will make it to the city by dark?" he asks.

Hem looks to Mount. "I do believe we will make it."

Then over the sound of the water, they hear a loud vicious growl, and then Marc screams like a girl. When they look, a huge cat has Marc pinned with his large paw on a rock, about to smack him with the other.

Right when the large animal swipes his bulky paw at Marc, all three wolves jump on the cat's back and knock it off Marc and into the water. The cat gets up and jumps at Savvy. Maverick and Rowdy pull the cat off, and the cat starts swiping at them both. Hem can hear the thoughts of the animals. "What are you dirty dogs doing at my water? Take your nasty humans and leave," the cat tells the wolves.

Maverick growls a laugh. "We don't take orders from a smelly cat. We hate cats. You leave!"

Then the wolves jump the mountain cat; they start trying to rip the large cat to pieces. Finally, the cat cowers down to the wolves. "Okay, you win. Drink all the water you want. Just let me live. I have cubs back at my den."

"Get up and slowly leave and don't try nothing, stupid cat." The cat says nothing; it jumps from the water and runs off in the direction he came.

Mount, Marc, and Hem look at one another, amazed. Marc runs to the wolves, petting and praising each one.

After making sure that every animal got water and they collected some for later, they get back on the trail as the hawk starts to lead them again. The trail gets easier for the horses to travel, and they start to make good time getting through the mountains. Then Marc says, "Look, what is that way in the distance?"

Mount and Hem both start looking; then Hem smiles. "It looks like we are looking at man-built structures. I think we found the city." As Hem says that, they can see the way out of the mountains.

As they come out of the mountains, not far in the distance is the huge city; it is the most beautiful thing the men have ever seen. The hawk flies over the city and circles around, then flies off into the distance as they get closer to the city. When they get close enough to see the entrance to the city, they can see around five men at the front; soon, they are close enough for the men to see they are on large animals with scary-looking animals walking with them.

The men quickly run into the city, shutting the large doors to keep them out. "Where are they going?" Marc asks.

"I feel they fear the wolves," Hem tells Marc, then jumps off his horse and calls the wolves over to him. "The people here seem scared of you, so I want you all to go back inside the mountains and find a place to rest till we return," Hem explains to the wolves.

Savvy lets Hem know, "We will be close. Just call our names, and we will come running." Then they run into the woods.

Hem looks at the brothers. "We should walk from here."

"Oh man! We have to walk?" Marc cries out, getting off Colt.

Mount hears him and snaps. "Are you kidding me? Just a few days ago, all we did was walk. Don't get lazy on me."

The men walk next to the horses, slowly getting to the door; they can hear the noise of people behind the walls and door. Marc starts to worry. "If they attack us, are we going to fight them?"

"NO!" Hem snaps at Marc. "I sense no danger from these people."

They get to the door. "Let me and your brother do the talking. We don't want to fight. We are here to help these people," Hem says to Marc.

"Whatever," Marc says as he kicks the dirt.

"Hello in there! We mean you no harm. We are here to help you," Mount yells to the people inside.

Nobody says anything back to Mount; he looks at Hem, then goes to try again. But right before he yells, the door starts to slowly open. Out walks a well-built older man with white hair and a long white beard.

He seems very wealthy with nice clothes on; he has four middle-aged men come out behind him but stay behind him as they walk out toward Mount, Marc, and Hem; none of the men are near the size of Mount or Marc as they get close. The elder man speaks. "Hello, friends. My name is Gamble. These are my sons behind me. This is our home, Cobble City. What can we do for you fine men?"

Mount steps up and shakes Gamble's hand. "Hello, sir. My name is Mount." He points to Marc and says, "This is my brother, Marc."

Then Mount points to Hem. "And this is my best friend and advisor, Hem. We have traveled a long, far ways from here with another friend who is collecting a special rock out of the mountains. Now my friend Hem has visions that have been known to come true, and he saw a large army of vicious men coming here to take your city."

Gamble is looking at Mount like he isn't all there. "We have never seen an attack inside the city. No one can get through our giant stone walls or bust through our doors."

Hem steps up to them. "These men will get through. They have a leader with powers of her own. She will not quit till she has your city, your home."

Gamble is still shaking his head. "I don't know you men, and the two of you are two of my men. How do I know you three aren't here to rob me and my people?"

"Give me your hand," Hem tells Gamble. Hem has been practicing with his father to make the other person see his visions. Gamble slowly gives Hem his hand. "Close your eyes," Hem tells Gamble.

When he does, Gamble starts seeing the army bursting through the city wall, coming in and beating down all his family. Gamble then pulls away from Hem's grip. "What kind of trickery is this?" he screams as he pulls away.

Hem is a little upset that Gamble pulled away. "This is no trick," Hem says, then shuts his eyes, and he starts to glow all over and then slowly rises into the air. Gamble and his sons all start backing away as they watch Hem float in the air.

"What are you?" Gamble nervously asks Hem.

Hem comes back to the ground. "I'm human like you. I just have a gift I really don't understand yet," Hem tells the old man.

"Does this woman have powers like yours?" Gamble asks Hem.

"Yes! Stronger than mine—plus she is pure evil!" Hem warns them.

Gamble gathers his sons around him. Mount can hear one of the sons telling Gamble, "We can't trust these strangers. So he floats in the air? They probably want to rob us themselves."

They can see Gamble shaking his head side to side, looking like he is disagreeing with his son. Finally, Gamble turns back to Hem, Mount, and Marc. "It would honor us if you all would join us for dinner," he says with a smile.

Then one of the sons yells out, "Open the gate!"

The gate opens to a crowd of people waiting to see what the strangers look like. As they walk through the town, they look at all the beautiful buildings, but not Marc—he is saying hello to every female he walks by.

There is a strange similarity with all the people; they all seem to have light golden hair like the sun. Mount and Marc are a lot bigger than all the people; the children keep coming up to them, then screaming and running away. "These are all your children?" Mount asks Gamble.

Gamble smiles at Mount. "I am a very old man, and since I was a young man, I've had five women for mates that have all given me children over time. And the children grew and had children and so on and so on."

"Then some are my brother's children, but he is no longer with us. Together, my brother and I were the ones who built this city."

"You have a beautiful family," Marc says, still eyeing all the women they passed.

Then Gamble says, "Here we are."

The guys look up to the most beautiful and largest of all the structures. "This is my castle. Come inside." Then he opens the door to a group of beautiful women waiting on them. Then Mount and Marc both drop their jaws as they look at the most beautiful girls.

There are two out of the girls that look just alike. Marc smiles at the girls and spits out, "Hello."

Gamble laughs as he sees the girls shy away and their faces turn red. "These are my twin daughters, Amanda and Amy," he tells Mount and Marc.

Marc hits Mount with his shoulder. "Say hello," he tells him.

Then Mount says, "Hello, ladies," as he lowers his head.

Gamble then claps his hands to get attention. "These gentlemen are here from a far land and are joining us for a meal. I want you all to go with the twins."

Then he takes the girls to the side. "Go let Angel know to make room for our guest, then help her get everything ready."

The twins go to leave with the other girls; they look at Mount and Marc and, with a giggle, say, "Goodbye." Then they run ahead and out of the room.

Gamble then tells the men, "You must be tired after such a long trip. Let my son Adam show you to a room where you all can rest till dinner."

Hem was more than happy to go rest after a few days of sleeping on the ground.

Gamble yells, "Adam!" Soon, a young near-teen blond boy comes in the room.

"Yes, Father?" he says.

"These are our new friends." Then as he points to each one, Gamble tells Adam, "This is Mount, Marc, and Hem."

Adam says, "Hello." Then he looks at Mount. "You're huge," he says to him.

Everyone laughs, and Gamble tells Adam, "Take the men up to the empty rooms on the top floor with the beds, then come back to see me."

Adam goes to the stairs. "Follow me, gentlemen," he says and starts up the stairs.

The men catch up to Adam, who is almost at the top; he then starts to lead them down a long hallway that had paintings and statues everywhere. "This place is beautiful," Hem says to Adam.

Not as impressed, Adam says, "I guess. It's been here since I can remember." They finally stop at some doors, and Adam goes to one and opens it, and they follow him into the room. It has soft-looking places to lie down and a balcony that looks over the city. "You can rest here," Adam tells them, then goes out and shuts the door.

"Pleasant little fellow." Marc chuckles; then Mount and Hem both join in laughing. "Do you think these people will believe us?" Marc asks Hem.

Hem looks at Mount, then Marc. "Let's take advantage of these nice beds. We'll worry about that when the time comes," he tells Marc, then lies down.

Marc looks at his brother. "We've never been outside our home. And now we are in the most beautiful city, the only other city we have ever been in, with the most beautiful women we have ever seen. There's no way I can sleep!"

Mount sits on his bed, looking at his brother, then says, "You're right, I can't sleep either."

"I'm right?" Marc says, amazed.

Mount takes the pillow from the bed and throws it at Marc. "Let's get out of here before you wake up Hem," Mount tells his brother.

"I hope we see those two twins. They are the most beautiful girls I have ever seen," Marc says, standing.

Mount looks at him. "Are you kidding me? Look at how rough you look! They will never look at us," he says.

Marc smiles. "US?" he says to Mount, but then a knock comes to the door, and Marc goes over and opens it. It's another boy smaller than Adam; he walks into the room.

"Hello, fine sirs. My name is Alix," the boy says.

Marc laughs. "Son of Gamble?" he says to the boy.

"Yes, sir," the boy says.

Mount pushes his brother to the side. "What can we do for you, Alix?" Mount asks.

"Not what you can do for me—it's what I can do for you," Alix says. "My sisters sent me here. I think you met them. They look just alike," he tells them.

Marc comes back and shoves Mount to the side. "Yes, yes, we did meet them!" Marc tells Alix.

"They want me to take you to the bathing room and have you fitted for some clean clothes," Alix tells them both. "Wake your friend. He should come as well."

Then Marc jumps on Hem. "WAKE UP!" he screams.

Hem, with everything he has, cannot push Marc off him. "Get your brother, Mount!" Hem yells.

Mount pulls Marc off Hem. "Come on, we are going to go clean up." Mount laughs.

Alix leads them down to the bottom of the castle, where in a room is a large stone tub filled with hot steaming water; none of them have ever seen anything like it. Marc rips his clothes off and jumps in the water. "It feels great. Come on, you two!" he says to Mount and Hem.

They both undress and enter the tub; then Alix hands them a funny scrubber. "This will help clean you," he tells them.

As they are washing, Mount grabs the hair on his face. "I wish I could get rid of my beard," he says.

Marc jumps out and gets his sword. "Watch this. I did it by accident when we were riding the other day," he takes the sword and rubs it down his face, and it takes the hair from his face.

"That's incredible!" Mount says and gets his sword, and both he and Marc shave their faces clean, but not Hem.

"I like my beard. I'm going to let it grow to my feet," he tells them.

They get out and dress in the robes given to them by Alix. "I like these clothes," Marc tells his brother. Mount isn't sure of them as they are tight.

"Come on. I'll take you back to your room," Alix tells them, and they follow him out of the bathing room.

When they get back to the room, they find Adam waiting on them; he can't believe the change in Mount and Marc. "I almost didn't recognize you two," he tells them.

"Thank you," Marc says, holding out his chest.

"Everyone is in the dining area, waiting for the guest of honor," Adam tells them.

"Is that us?" Marc asks Adam.

"Yes, so please follow me, gentleman," he tells the three men, and they follow him out.

They follow Adam back down to the main room of the castle, then down another long hallway. Soon, they start hearing noises of people talking; the noise gets louder as they finally get to a set of doors. Adam opens the doors, and the noise becomes silence as they walk into the room. Then sitting at the center table with his sons from out front is Gamble; sitting next to him is his only living spouse. Gamble stands up. "Come, my new friends, join us," he tells them.

Mount, Marc, and Hem go to the empty seats; and with Gamble and his family, the eldest looking son looks at them. "So which one of you has dreams that come true?" he asks.

Hem clears his throat. "I'm the one who has visions," he tells the son.

Jed, the youngest looking of the sons, asks, "Why should we leave our home over whatever it is you saw?"

Gamble hits the table with his fist. "Enough! The men just sat down. Let them eat."

"Yes, Father," his sons say.

"Sorry, please eat," Jed tells them.

As they were eating, the men start small talk about where they are from. Marc's attention goes over to the table across from them with all the women, who are laughing and talking about how different and handsome they look now. Then Marc sees the twins sitting at the table at the end; he pokes Mount. "Look, it's the twins. I dare you to go say hi," he tells him.

Mount glances over and locks eyes with Amanda, then turns his head quickly and snaps at Marc. "We're not here to find mates. Stop now."

Mount then looks over to Gamble and his sons. "I have to speak. I've known this man as long as I can remember. All our lives, I watched him do incredible things—bring energy from his hands, talk with animals like they were human. And lots of times, he has said something would happen before it happens." Gamble and his sons look at one another and whisper.

That's when Mount stands up, looking at Gamble, and yells loud enough for the whole room to hear, "Know right now that a large group of bloodthirsty barbarian men will come destroy your city and kill every one of you or make you their slaves!" Mount sits down.

Everyone in the room is silent for a moment; then the whole room starts laughing, and some chant, "Make them leave!"

Hem stands and walks over to a torch hanging on the wall; he reaches into the fire and pulls the fire over with his hand. He takes his other hand and forms the fire into a large ball.

Everyone, including Mount and Marc, stares in amazement as Hem holds the giant fireball in his hand; then some of the women start to get scared. A scream is heard, then another.

"Enough!" Jed yells to Hem; he laughs, then makes the fireball small and puts it back on the torch.

The eldest son stands. "These men are the evil ones I don't trust." Then he yells, "Tell them to leave, Father!" Then most of the people start cheering with agreement for them to leave.

Hem holds up his hands. "We will leave in peace. We didn't mean to bother you, good people."

Mount and Marc stand. "Good luck to you all," Mount tells them as they go to walk out of the room. They go out of the room and start down the hallway; they don't get far before they hear a loud "STOP!"

The men turn around to see Gamble running out of the dining hall. "Please accept my apology for my children. They know no better," he pleads. "I believe you, sir. It would be an honor if you and your friends would take me, my wife Jill, and all my younger children to a safe place."

Hem smiles. "It would be our honor to lead you and your family to safety."

Gamble falls to his knees. "Thank you, Great Wizard. Please stay for the night so I can get my family ready for travel."

Hem gathers with Mount and Marc, then turns back to Gamble. "Have your family at the front of the city at sunrise and have them ready for a long journey."

"Yes, we will be ready, and you gentlemen can go back to the room and rest while I get my family ready," Gamble tells the three.

They bid Gamble good night, then go back through the castle and find their way back to their room. They go in, and all three lie back in the beds to get some sleep before the journey back to where Jax is waiting for them.

Mount sits up and looks at Hem. "Well, it's turned out better than we thought. At least Gamble believes us."

Hem rolls over and looks at Mount. "We've done all we can do. Let's just hope Gamble can talk his close family to come with us."

Mount agrees. "You're right. There's nothing else we can do," he says, then lies down.

Then Marc yells out, "There is one more thing we could do!"

Mount laughs. "Okay, I'll bite. What can we do?" he asks.

Marc jumps out of his bed and jumps on top of Mount. "We need to find out if the twins are coming with us," he says, holding Mount down.

Mount pushes Marc off him, and Marc hits the floor. "Well, we do need to check the horses before we go to sleep. If we run into them on the way, it won't hurt to ask," Mount tells his brother.

Marc jumps to his feet. "What are we waiting for?" he says, excited.

Hem laughs. "Do check the horses, but have fun while you're gone. I'll stay here to pray for the ones who stay here." Mount and Marc tell Hem goodbye and go out the door, and Hem goes to his knees to pray for the people.

Mount and Marc find their way out of the castle to the streets; the people try their best to avoid the large men as they make their way out to the front of the city. The horses are still where Hem had them wait. Marc goes to Colt and pets his head. "Where should we take the horses to feed?" Marc asks Mount.

"We'll take them to the grassy fields near the mountain entrance. We need to check on the wolves while we are out," Mount tells Marc.

"Wonder where the twins are," Marc says.

But before Mount has a chance to answer, they hear a woman's voice behind them. "They sure are beautiful." They turn around to find both twins standing there.

"Thank you," the guys say at the same time.

"Would you like to pet them?" Marc asks them.

The girls both go over and slowly start walking close to the horses. "They won't hurt you," Mount says as Amanda starts petting Stallion; then Stallion bucks his head, and Amanda jumps back into Mount. Amanda then jumps away as her face turns red, and they both smile at each other.

Amy is petting Colt; she laughs at her sister, then asks Marc, "Where do you all come from?"

Marc tells her, "We came here from a far distance on the other side of the mountain."

Then Mount takes over. "We came here looking for a certain rock our friend Jax uses to make different things like this sword," he says, pulling it from its case.

"What are you two doing out here?" Amanda asks.

Mount tells her, "We are about to ride the horses and take them to the field to graze on the grass."

Amanda gets excited. "Can we ride with you?" she asks Mount.

Marc quickly says, "Yes, you girls can ride with us."

"But to be safe, you girls better ride with us," Mount tells them.

Excited, the girls agree to ride with the boys, and the boys help the girls up on the horses. Mount and Marc both get on with each girl on their horse. Mount calls for Pinto to follow, and they start to ride.

Both girls yell with excitement as the horses start to move. Mount laughs. "We felt the same our first time on them."

"Let's race!" Marc yells to Mount.

They both tell each girl, "Hang on!"

Stallion, Colt, and Pinto take off running away from the city toward the fields; the boys both smile as each of the twins is hanging on with everything she has.

Back at the room, Hem has been praying and goes into another vision; he sees he is at the barbarians' camp.

For as far as he can see, there are tents set up for the large army of men. His vision takes him to a huge fire rising to the sky; around it is the same scary-looking large man from his other visions. He is surrounded by other men, some just as large as him; they are all talking among one another. Hem gets close enough to hear them. "We are very close. We should be there by this time tomorrow," Hem hears him tell the leader.

"Good, very good job," he tells the man, then has a smaller man get the men's attention.

The man starts hyping his men up to be ready tomorrow to take their new home from the people who live there. Hem starts getting a bad feeling as he sees the evil in each man's eyes. He then starts to focus on where the real leader—the beautiful woman with the powers like his own—is. His vision takes him over to a large carriage that was closed in. Hem's vision takes him into the carriage, where he finds the beautiful woman lying on the floor of the carriage.

She is nude, and three other beautiful women are also nude and kissing her all over her body. Hem can't believe what he is seeing, but he can't stop watching as the women moan with pleasure. Then the woman rises, then looks straight at Hem. "Enjoying yourself?" she asks him.

Hem wakes from his vision, shaking and sweating all over; he goes to a bowl with water and splashes his face. "How did she see me?" he asks himself as he wipes his face. "I must stop her somehow," he says and starts to pray.

Lisa sits up and starts rubbing Serina's shoulders. "Something wrong, my love?" she whispers into her ear.

"I could feel the wizard watching us right now. When I sat up to let him know I had seen him, he disappeared," Serina tells Lisa.

"He was watching us?" Lisa gasps.

Serina shuts her eyes. "Yes, but I don't feel his presence now, and I still don't see him during our attack," she assures Lisa. Serina looks at Lisa. "Don't worry, dear. After we settle into our new home, I will send Boar to hunt these men down and kill them."

Lisa smiles. "I never worry with you." The women start to kiss and lie down with the other girls.

Mount and Marc have led the horses to the fields to feed on the grass; they help the girls off the horses, and they are now talking among each other. Mount starts to explain to the girls. "Hem, he does more than see visions. As you can see, he also talks with animals."

"That's how the horses let you ride on them?" Amy quickly asks.

Mount laughs. "Yes, that's how we are friends with the horses. Plus we have more animal friends," he says.

"Where are they?" Amanda asks.

Mount faces toward the mountains, whistles real loud, then yells, "Come here, Maverick! Here, boy!"

Soon, they hear an animal howl; then all three wolves come running from out of the mountains. When the girls see the wolves charging at them, they both jump into each brother's arms. Marc stands brave and says, "Don't worry, I'll protect you." That's when Rowdy tackles Marc to the ground as both girls scream till they see Marc is laughing as the wolf is licking him all over his face.

Mount laughs. "Don't worry. Hem did something, so now they protect us. They are man's best friend now," he says as he pets Maverick and Savvy. Maverick jumps up and licks Mount on his face. "Good boy," Mount tells him.

Marc tells Amy, "Come over and pet him. He won't hurt you." Amy goes over to Rowdy and pets the wolf as he rubs his head with every stroke. "See, he likes you," Marc says.

Amanda goes over and starts petting Maverick with Mount; they touch hands and lock eyes, smiling.

Marc is now wrestling with Rowdy, trying his best to show off. Rowdy takes off running, and Marc grabs Amy by the hand. "Come on," he tells her, and they both run after Rowdy.

Meanwhile, Mount and Amanda are still staring each other in the eyes as though nothing else exists. Mount looks away to see which direction they ran, but Amanda gets it back quickly. "So do you have a female life mate waiting for you back at your home?" she asks him.

Mount turns a shade of red as he answers, "No," looking down at the ground.

Out in the middle of the field, Marc is having trouble keeping up with Rowdy and Amy; she is a very fast girl. Right when Marc is about to give up, he sees them stop; he slows down to a jog and catches up and comes behind Amy. "Got you," he says as he grabs a hold of her. He then looks over at Rowdy, and he is standing in attack stance, growling.

Amy grabs a hold of Marc and whispers, "Down the hill is a group of wild boars. They will tear a human to pieces with their sharp pointy tusks."

Marc starts pulling Amy back. "They must be hunting for food. I need to get Mount." That's when Rowdy lets out a loud howl to call for his brother wolfs.

It gets Mount's and Amanda's attention as well. "Let's go," Mount tells Amanda and helps her on to Stallion.

Then she takes off. "I got this!" she yells. Mount jumps on Colt and takes off after them. Amanda seems to have no problem controlling Stallion; as Mount rides up, they can see the wolves in front of Marc and Amy.

In the distance, vicious large boars are coming right for them. "Ride in. Get your sister and get back to the city!" he tells Amanda, then reaches over to pull out his sword from its case hanging off Stallion. "Marc and I will take care of those beasts," he says.

Then Amanda reaches over and kisses Mount. "Good luck!" she tells him.

In his mind, he is doing a backflip off Colt, but he manages to spit out, "You be careful."

They both go riding in as Amanda gets Amy on to Stallion to ride off. Mount jumps off Colt.

Mount gets Marc's sword from it' case hanging on Colt and throws it to him, then helps Amy on to Stallion and smacks Stallion on his behind. "Ride, Stallion!" he yells to the horse. Stallion runs away toward the city.

"Shouldn't we ride with them?" Marc asks.

"If we ride off, they will tear the wolves to pieces. Plus I've heard Jax talk how he killed a boar on one of his trips, and it's the best meat he ever ate," Mount tells his brother.

"That's all you had to say," Marc says.

As the boars and wolves are at a standoff, Marc and Mount attack the boars, stabbing them with their swords as the wolves then easily take down one a piece. That leaves three remaining; they charge Mount and Marc. "Stab them in the head!" Mount tells Marc. Marc stabs his sword straight through the head of one; it falls to the ground, but Marc's sword gets stuck. One of the other boars charges at Marc.

Mount sees the boar running at his brother, so he jumps on the boar. He grabs the boar by its tusk, pulling the boar back, as Marc struggles to get his sword out of the dead boar's head. Marc frees his sword and cuts the boar's head off; blood covers Mount as he is left holding the boar's head. They then look around to see the wolves, all three ripping the third boar to pieces. Mount and Marc go to the wolves, petting and praising them for doing such a good job. Then over the hill, Amanda and Amy, who are still on Stallion, come riding back to them with Colt and Pinto with them.

The girls jump off to see the boys are okay; then Amanda hugs Mount, and Amy hugs Marc for being their heroes. Both men get lost in the moment; it is their first to be hugged by a woman, unless you count their mother or sister. After a short time goes by, Maverick rubs up on Mount to get his attention. Mount smiles. "It's late. We should get you girls back to the city."

"I'm not even tired," Amy says, looking at Marc.

"I could stay up all night," Marc says, looking back at Amy.

"Still, we need to find a place to put these dead boars to take them with us tomorrow, and we don't need any other animals getting the scent," Mount tells Marc. "We will need the meat with the extra people with us," Mount finishes.

Then Marc turns to Amy. "Will you and your sister be leaving with us and your father in the morning?" he shyly asks Amy.

Amy turns red as she says, "Yes, we will be with Father and our other younger brothers and sisters."

Marc picks Amy up in the air. "That's the best news I've heard all day!" he yells out as she lets out a scream when he twirls her around.

Mount yells to Marc, "Use those muscles to put the boars on Pinto to carry back to the city!" They both get the animals and tie them on Pinto's back. They then help the girls on the horses and get on behind them. "We need to go slow so Pinto doesn't drop the boars," Mount tells Marc and winks, letting him know it's to spend more time with the girls.

Marc smiles at his brother. "Yeah, we'd better go really slow so we don't lose or food."

After a slow quiet ride back to the city, with each couple enjoying the closeness, Amanda points out an empty building where they can put the animals in. Mount and Marc put the meat in the building; then with the girls still on the horses, they walk all three to the front of the city to tie them up for the night. They then walk the girls to the castle and to their rooms.

The four stand in the hallway, each couple looking in the other's eyes. One says, "Good night," but no one moves. Finally, Mount leans in and kisses Amanda; and when Marc sees his brother, he does the same and kisses Amy.

Amanda then grabs Amy and pulls her in the door with her. "Good night," both girls say; and as the door closes, both Mount and Marc stand there silent. Once the door shuts, Marc jumps on his brother's back and gives a quiet yell. Mount carries him off so the girls won't hear.

They race down the hallway back to the room; when they walk in, they find Hem awake and not looking as happy as they are. "What's wrong?" Mount asks Hem.

Hem looks over to both the brothers. "I had another vision while you two have been gone. She is very close, and her army of barbarians are as far as the eye could see."

"How long till they get here?" Marc asks.

"Tomorrow most likely," Hem says.

"We have to get the ones willing to leave out of here in the morning. We'll die if we stay," Mount tells them.

Marc smiles. "I have the one I want to leave with. How about you, brother?"

Hem looks at Mount. "What does he mean by that?" Hem asks.

"It's nothing. We saw the twins, Amanda and Amy. They are coming with their father in the morning," Mount tells Hem.

"Don't let this get in the way of our mission, boys," Hem says in a stern voice. Mount goes to assure Hem that won't happen, but before he can, Marc goes over to Hem and starts rubbing his shoulders.

"Don't worry, buddy, that won't happen. What we need to do is find you a girl."

Hem pulls away. "I'm way too busy to worry about girls, thank you."

Mount steps in. "Maybe we should get some rest. It will soon be daylight," he tells them. They both agree, and all three lie down in a bed.

Then Marc rises back up. "Just wait, Hem, it will happen to you when you least expect it." Then he lies back down, and the room goes quiet as Hem says nothing back but starts thinking of what he saw in his vision of the woman.

Mount wakes as soon as light breaks through the window; he wakes Hem, then kicks Marc till he is whining like he does every morning. As they get going to meet Gamble and his family to lead them away, not far from where they are at, Boar is up and getting the barbarians ready for one last march to their new home.

When Mount, Marc, and Hem get to the front where the horses are waiting for them, they find Gamble and his family waiting as well. "Good morning, men," Gamble says to them, smiling.

Mount and Marc go find a work carriage, and thanks to helping Jax through the years, they find materials to turn it into a wagon for the horses to pull Gamble and his family. The twins are helping their older sister Angel with the smaller children; they get the kids settled in the wagon before Gamble and their mother, Jill, get in the wagon. They tie the horses to the wagon, and each man still rides his horse. As Mount and Hem talk over the journey ahead, Marc is at the back of the wagon, talking with Amy.

She introduces her sister Angel and the other children to him; he starts playing with the kids as Mount explains to Gamble, "Our friend is waiting on us. We will go meet him before our next decision." Mount goes to the back of the wagon, "You ready, or you going to play all morning?" he asks his brother.

Marc jumps out of the wagon. "You're going to say good morning to Amanda," he says, pushing him.

Mount stands on the wagon. "Good morning," he says as he grabs her hand and kisses it.

The younger kids all laugh at Mount. Amanda smiles. "Good morning, Mount. You seem to lead very well. We should be good in your hands," she tells him.

Mount gets Marc and gets him on Colt, and they start to leave out of the city. As they go to leave the gate, Jed comes with all the other brothers and most of the family in the city. Jed stands in front of the horses and has them stop; with his hand in the air, he yells, "Father, get out of that strange carriage! Nobody is going with these strangers!"

Marc goes to jump off Colt, but before he does, Mount tells him, "Don't, Marc. This is between them."

Gamble stands. "Please come with us. Don't stay here to die," he pleads.

Jed laughs along with others. "That's crazy talk from some kid! No one is coming to take our city. Now get out of that carriage," he says, getting angry.

"No! I believe the wise man no matter how young! I'm taking my small children to safety!" Gamble yells at his son, then yells to all, "My children, you are all my family. Please go with us for the night!"

All of Gamble's people start talking among themselves, but Jed quickly quiets them down as he asks his father, "Why should we listen to these men? They came out of nowhere, and one says he sees the future. For all we know, they have men waiting to come here and steal everything once we are gone. Get my brothers and sisters out of that carriage, and you and Jill take them back to the castle!" Jed demands.

Gamble sits silent for a moment, then says, "No! We will leave with the wizard. For your sake, I hope he's wrong, my son." Gamble then tells Hem, "Sir Hem, you can lead us out of here."

Hem has the horses start to move as Jed and Gamble's other children start to clear a path for the horses. As they start leaving the city, Jed yells out, "Fine, Father, go! But the castle is mine!"

Then another yells out, "No, I'm moving in there!"

As they leave the city, all Gamble can hear is the sound of his children fighting over who is going to take over his home.

They get inside the mountains, and the wolves come from the trees and join them. Hem nods his head, and the wolves go ahead of them to make sure the way is safe for the humans. The day goes by. As the horses pull them through the mountain trails, the kids start to get restless, so Angel suggests, "We should stop and feed the children." Mount agrees, and they stop near the river. Mount and Marc set up a fire and cut out some meat from the boars, and the girls cook up the meat.

Once the children are eating, the twins join the men; and as they are all enjoying the meat from the beast animals, Amanda tells her father, "Mount and Marc saved our lives from these beasts we feast on."

Gamble looks at the boys. "Is this true? Did you save my daughters from these animals?"

Mount smiles. "They were never in any danger. We had everything under control."

Marc then speaks up, elbowing his brother. "They probably wouldn't have survived without us."

"Most likely not," both girls say.

Gamble looks very seriously at Mount and Marc. "My family has a long tradition. It's believed if you save a life, that life belongs to you," he tells the boys.

Mount sits looking at Gamble in silence; then Marc asks Gamble, "You want your daughters to be our mates?"

Gamble laughs. "That's up to you, but it's law that they will serve you their remaining life," he demands.

Mount finally stands. "Sir, we took them where the boars came out. So really, this is our fault. There is no need for them to become our servants," he pleads.

Gamble then stands up to Mount. "I'm sorry, this isn't your choice. The girls know the laws we live by. They will remain with you," he tells Mount, who is getting upset.

Mount goes quiet again; he thinks to himself, *I can't deny the man of his laws. Actually, it will be nice having Amanda around from now on.*

Mount looks at the old man. "Fine, but let's be clear about this—I saved Amanda while my brother, Marc, is the one who saved Amy," he says.

Gamble smiles. "Fine, Amanda serves you, and Amy serves your brother, Marc."

Each girl goes over to the man she now takes care of. Mount and Marc each assure them they will never be treated like a servant. While all of this has been going on, Hem has gotten the horses ready to travel again. He suggests, "We should get moving again to get to the other side of the mountains by dark."

Hem, Mount, and Marc get everyone back on the wagon; and they lead the horses through the trails. In the back, they can hear Angel arguing with her father. "I'm older. I'm supposed to be set up with a man first."

With the wolves leading the way, the trip comes with no complications; it is starting to get dark, and they are coming out of the mountains. They soon get to where Jax and Kurt have camp set up and find them there just about to eat. Jax and Kurt jump to help when they see their friends back from their journey. Marc gives Kurt the boar meat to cook up as Jax helps with the new guests. Mount introduces Jax and Kurt to Gamble and his family. "Hello," they both say; then Jax sees Angel.

Gamble introduces Jax to his daughter. Jax goes down to one knee and takes her hand. "You, my dear, are the most beautiful creature I ever laid eyes on," he tells her, then kisses her hand.

Flattered, Angel gives a giggle and says, "Thank you." Then she asks Jax, "Would you like to help me unpack the wagon?"

Jax jumps at the opportunity as he goes off to help Angel. Marc goes with the twins to get their brothers and sisters ready to sleep for the night as Mount, Hem, and Gamble discuss what is going to happen to Cobble City.

It is now dark. Cobra calls for Boar to the front. "What do you need?" Boar asks when he gets to the front.

Viper points out to the distance where the brightness of the lights from the city can be seen. "We are here," he says as he points. They march toward the lights till they could see the strange tall buildings.

Boar goes to Serina's carriage and has the men set it down. Boar yells to Serina inside the carriage, "Mama, we are here!" The door to the carriage opens. Lisa steps out, then helps Serina out.

The women stand and stare at the city. "It's even more beautiful than in my visions," Serina tells Lisa.

"Yes, my queen, I couldn't have dreamed a place more beautiful!" Lisa says in amazement.

"Get it for me, my great warrior Boar. I want it to be mine by sunrise," Serina demands to Boar.

Boar smiles. "My queen, taking over cities just happens to be my specialty." He then goes off and starts telling the men, "Line up in attack position and get ready to march in." The men cheer as they line up.

As the men get ready to attack, they start lighting torches. So many are lit that the dark sky is brightened. The gleam of the light gets the attention of the gate watchers at the city. The men walk closer to the light till they are close enough to see it's a huge group of blood-crazed men, just as the wizard had warned them. The men go running into the city, screaming, "The wizard was right! The army is outside, getting ready to attack!"

Jed comes from the castle after hearing all the screaming. He goes to one of the guards and grabs the man by his arm. "What are you all screaming about? You are waking the whole city! he screams."

The man looks Jed in the eyes; he is shaking because he is so scared. "They are here, cousin, just as the wizard said. WE ARE GOING TO DIE!" he screams.

Jed pushes the man down to the ground. "Stop scaring everyone. There is no one outside," he tells the man, then starts walking toward the front of the city to see for himself. Each one of his brothers starts gathering behind him.

Jed and his brothers get to the front of the city with the rest of the city slowly gathering behind them. They can see the light of the torches; the people start getting scared. You can hear them saying, "Why didn't we go with Gamble? Why didn't we listen to the wizard?"

Jed isn't going to look like a fool; he speaks to his people. "We don't know if they want trouble. Maybe they are just passing through. Who will go with me to see what they want?" he asks his people.

Out of the crowd, a few of his brothers and cousins raise their hands to say they will go with him. With his brothers next to him, they walk toward the charging army. Boar sees the small group of men coming toward them; he's not sure what to do. This has never happened. Boar stops the men from marching and lets the men come closer to see what they are up to.

Jed stops at a short distance from Boar and his gigantic army. "Please, we are peaceful people. We don't want any trouble," he tells Boar.

Boar has Ace, Viper, and Cobra follow him as he walks closer to the group of men. When Boar gets to Jed, he asks, "Are you the leader of these people?"

Jed looks back at his family, then looks back to Boar. "Yes, I'm the leader of this city, and I'm here to ask if you and your men can nicely walk around our city. We can't occupy such a large group of people."

Boar looks at Ace and gives a short laugh. "They can't occupy a group as large as ours! What should we do?" he says, shaking his head.

Boar quickly turns back to Jed, grabs him by his throat, and lifts him off the ground. "Guess if the city isn't large enough for this many people, one group needs to leave." Then he drops Jed to the ground.

Jed comes up to all fours as he desperately tries to catch his breath; he slowly stands and looks Boar in the eyes. "This is our city. We kindly ask you to leave!" He is being stern with his message.

Boar is bored with Jed, and that's how he got his name—because everyone becomes a bore so fast to him. He picks Jed up by the neck. This time, he says nothing; he just starts squeezing his throat as Jed starts shaking from not breathing. Then soon, his body goes limp, and Boar throws his body to the ground.

Boar then turns to the rest of the group of men. "So who is in charge now?" he asks them. The other brothers start pointing at one another; then they all fall to their knees and start begging for their lives. Boar and Ace laugh as they watch all the people at the city fall to their knees as well.

"Serina said it would be easy," Ace tells Boar.

"Yes, she did! Watch these people while I go tell Serina the good news," Boar orders Ace. Boar leaves, and soon, the men clear a path as Serina makes her way to the men with Lisa and Boar leading the way. Ace and the other men go down to a knee as Serina approaches.

"Rise," she tells them as she walks up. Serina looks at the group of men standing in front of her. "Who leads your people?" she asks. None of them say anything to her; she starts to get angry and points to one. "You come here," she tells him.

He looks at his brothers as they look away; then he walks over to Serina. She smiles. "Don't worry, I won't hurt you," she tells him as she grabs a hold of his hand. She sees in a vision his life at the city and how each person is a relative in some way. Then she sees his father, Gamble, and his brother and how they are responsible for building this beautiful city. Serina lets go of the young man's hand; she starts to look around at the people. She then goes back to him. "Where's your father? I don't see him," she asks.

Gamble's son Jim stands, trembling in fear. "He left this morning with three strangers that showed up here last night," he tells Serina. When she hears of three strangers, she gets very upset and grabs Jim's hand again. She sees his memories again; they show her how Hem, Mount, and Marc came to warn all the people of their attack and how they didn't believe them; she then sees how Hem used his powers and how the father left with them, but she can't read where they were going.

Serina lets go of his hand and looks to Lisa and Boar. "They were here," she tells them both. "The men from my vision came here and warned them of our attack. I saw the one using his powers for the people. He is as powerful as I am," she lets them know. "We must find them and destroy them. They will not ruin my dream!" Serina yells to them.

Lisa goes to Serina. "Mama, we just took the city you have been dreaming of. Forget the men for now. Let's go enjoy your new city," she softly says to Serina.

Serina looks at the city in the distance, then hugs Lisa. "You're right. Let's go to our new home," she whispers into Lisa's ear. Serina turns to Boar. "Have our men gather up the people and have them agree to serve me or die," she tells him. Boar orders his men to go through the city and line all the people up in the front.

Serina has Lisa and her personal servants follow her into the city. As she passes the people being forced to line up, an elderly man yells out to her, "This is our city! You have no right!"

Serina stops and looks to the man. "You people have built a beautiful city, but you have only one choice—serve me or die," she firmly tells the man.

"I would rather die than serve you!" the man screams at her.

Serina walks closer to the man, making sure all his people are watching. "Then you shall die," she tells the man as she holds up her hand, and the man rises off the ground. He starts choking for air before Serina turns her wrist, and the man's neck snaps; the people scream as he falls to the ground.

Serina looks at all the other people. "Anyone else not want to serve me?" she screams to them. All the people go silent as she walks closer to them.

Jim has all his people go down to a knee, and he tells Serina, "Please, we will serve you any way we can. No one else needs to die."

Serina smiles as her vision is coming true. She tells Boar, "Take a couple of men to check the castle and make sure it's clear." Then with Lisa and her servants, they follow Boar to the castle.

Hem has awakened from a dream where he was at the city and watched as the people cowered down and handed the city over to Serina; he also saw Jim tell her of their being there. He gets up to go find Mount, who is asleep next to Amanda; he is able to wake him up and calls him over to the fire. "I have seen the takeover. They cowered down and gave the evil witch the city. Worse, they told her of us being there, and now she wants us dead," he tells Mount.

Mount stands still, looking into the fire, then turns to Hem. "We have to go back."

Just as he says that to Hem, Marc comes walking up behind them. "Go back? No, I want to go home!" Marc almost whines to his brother.

"Sorry, little bro. I must know what we are up against. I have to see this army of barbarians with my own eyes," Mount tells Marc with the look on his face that he has when there is no changing his mind.

Hem looks at Mount with concern. "You sure about this? If we are caught, we will most likely die."

"Who is going to die now?" Jax asks as he comes up to the fire.

Hem tells Jax, "I saw Gamble's people get taken over by the barbarian army. Now Mount thinks we should return to see with our own eyes what we are up against."

Jax agrees with Mount. "It's best we see if they are as large as you see in your vision so we know if we have a chance to win in a fight," Jax says.

"I've also seen his people tell the evil queen of theirs that we were there and took Gamble with us. Now she wants us dead," Hem lets Jax know.

Mount steps in. "I just want to sneak in and look things over and quickly leave. They will never know we were there."

Jax again agrees. "That sounds good, Mount. We need to know how big this army of men really is."

"Can we make it really quick? I want to go home," Marc says as he kicks a log in the fire.

Mount pushes Marc. "Don't be a baby. We will go home soon enough. But when we do, don't you want to feel safe at nights? This way, we will," Mount tells his brother.

Mount looks at Jax. "I know you want to come with us this time, but I was hoping you and Kurt could take Gamble and his family back to the village, and then you could get a start on making more weapons," he asks of his friend.

"No, that's fine. I can do this for you, Mount," Jax tells him.

"It's settled then. In the morning, when you head home, we will go back and see this great army with our own eyes," Mount says to them all.

Amanda and Amy come up to the fire. Amanda goes up to Mount. "Will we go with you?" she asks him.

Mount takes Amanda by the hand and leads her over to where Amy is standing with Marc. "It would be best if you both go with your family and Jax to our home and wait for us there. It will be safer," Mount tells them both, and Marc agrees with his brother.

Amanda becomes upset. "And what will happen to the two of you? What if we never see the two of you again?"

Mount grabs Amanda by her hands. "Nothing will happen. We just want to see how large this group of barbarians really is. We will sneak in and sneak out."

Amy then says, "Do you both promise?"

Mount and Marc say, "We promise," at the same time.

Jax comes up to Mount. "I'll need a horse for each wagon."

Mount tells Jax, "That's fine. Marc can ride with me on Stallion. You can use Colt."

"I'll hook up each horse at sunrise," Jax tells Mount.

"Sounds good. We should all get some rest. It will be sunrise soon," Mount tells Jax; then Mount and Marc go off with the twins to lie down.

Jax stands at the fire, watching them leave, as Angel walks up; and they lock eyes.

Sunrise comes. Mount tries to get up without waking Amanda, but she also rises. "Good morning," she says to Mount.

"Good morning," he says to her, helping her up from the cot they made to lie in. Mount yells at Marc, "Wake up!"

Marc slowly starts to move with Amy's help, and the girls go help with the small children as Mount and Marc go help Jax with the horses. Jax tells the brothers, "You two seem happy this morning. Did you two . . ."

Before he says any more, both brothers say, "No," and smile.

"What did you do all night?" Marc asks Jax.

Jax smiles the biggest smile he's ever smiled. "We talked all night. It was wonderful," he tells them.

Marc laughs at Jax. "You only talked? I at least got a kiss. How about you, brother?" he asks Mount. Mount rolls his eyes at his brother. "He kissed her," Marc says.

"Who did Mount kiss?" Hem asks, walking up to them.

"Forget about it. We have work to do," Mount tells them all.

They finish getting the wagons ready, and they tell Gamble and his family it is time to travel.

The family all climb into the wagon, and the three sisters will guide the horse. As Amanda and Amy get into the wagon, they each go to their man and give them the deepest, longest kiss either man has ever experienced. Then as the wagons move up the trail, the brothers stand and watch until they disappear.

"We have to hurry and get back home," Marc says to his brother.

"We won't take too long. I just want to look at what we are up against. Then we'll go home, I promise," Mount says.

"I can't believe we have to share a horse. This will be a long trip," Marc tells Mount.

Mount pushes his brother. "Don't start crying already! Tell him, Hem."

Marc jumps on Mount's back, and they roll on the ground. The wolves jump in, and they all start wrestling in the grass. Hem laughs, then finally says, "We should get going if we want to be there before dark."

Mount sits up and pets Maverick. "Ready for another adventure, boy?" he asks him as he stands up.

CHAPTER 4

Going Back

MARC COMPLAINS AS he gets on the back of Stallion. "I can't believe I have to ride on the back. Why couldn't you give them Stallion and let me keep Colt?"

"Stop complaining. It's going to be long enough of a trip with you on the back. Plus Stallion hides in the dark better than Colt."

Hem has the wolves run ahead to make sure they have a clear path as Marc and Mount keep arguing back and forth; finally, Marc stops as Mount has Stallion run to catch up with the wolves.

The day is going by, but they are quickly making their way through the mountains; just as they are getting close to the opening, Hem stops them. "Quiet down. The wolves are telling me they sense something," Hem quietly tells the brothers, and they get off the horses and walk to the wolves. The wolves are bent down in attack mode, growling, when they get to them. Then they quickly duck down when they see a group of men, most likely barbarians.

Marc looks at Mount. "Are we going to fight them?" he asks.

Mount sits quietly, then finally says, "No, we will wait here till they leave."

Marc becomes upset. "Come on, brother, we can take them." He stands and pulls out his sword.

Mount grabs him and pulls him back down. "Are you crazy? Do you want to die?" Mount says to Marc.

Then they hear one of the men yell out, "Runaways!"

That's when they look down and realize they are dressed as Cobble City people.

The five men come charging at them, and one of them yells out, "Lie down on the ground or die!"

Mount tells Marc and Hem, "We have to kill them. No one can know we are here."

Marc smiles. "Now you're talking."

The barbarians are now right behind them, holding wooden spears at them, and the one man again says, "Lie on the ground or prepare to die."

Hem turns; and from his hands, he releases a power ball that knocks all the men down to the ground, not able to move.

Mount and Marc go to the men on the ground. Marc kicks one, and the man doesn't move. "You knocked them all out cold. They won't wake up for some time," Mount says to Hem. He then looks around and says, "I have an idea. Let's take their clothes, then tie them up to a tree."

Marc gives his brother a weird look. "Take their clothes? Why?" Marc asks Mount.

"We will dress in their clothes and take Hem in as a prisoner. Once we get a good look at things, we are going home," he tells his brother.

Hem agrees with Mount. "That should get us by the guards at the front of the city, but we should wait till it's completely dark before we try to go in. Some of Gamble's people might recognize us and give us away," Hem explains to Mount.

"Agreed. Then Marc and I will get the clothes off the men and find a good place to tie them up. Why don't you get the horses and wolves to the river and have them stay there while we are inside the city? By then, it should be dark enough to enter the city," Mount tells Hem.

Mount and Marc drag off the men, get their clothes, and tie them to a tree in some thick brush. They take the clothes and go to the river, where Hem went to take the horses and wolves. They find Hem in the river washing off, so the brothers decide to join him in the water, and they all wash off; then when they get out and dry off, Mount and Marc put on the barbarians' clothes. Hem couldn't help but laugh at the two in their new outfits. "Real funny!" Marc snaps at Hem.

Mount looks down at himself, giving a small laugh; he then looks over to Marc and Hem. "We'd better get going. By the time we get out of the mountains, it should be good and dark."

Hem tells the horses, "Stay near the river." He tells the wolves, "Maverick, you and the others watch over the horses while they are gone."

Rowdy doesn't want to stay. Marc goes to him and pets him. "Stay here, boy. We will be right back, I promise," he tells his wolf.

They start their hike down the mountain trail; as they are walking, Mount reminds them, "By now, the men we tied up will most likely be missed. Let's be careful." They get out of the mountains just as it is fully getting dark; from the distance, they see the lights of the city and follow them till they can see the front of the city. As they look around, they see no one guarding the entrance to the city; it looks quiet from where they are. They slowly and carefully walk in the entrance and see no one.

Mount looks around, and just as he is about to ask Hem what is going on, they start to hear voices and screaming. Once they get inside the main part of the city near the castle, they find all the people of the barbarians in the streets of the city drinking, eating, and having a good time as women everywhere are running around with little or no clothes. Mount, Marc, and Hem stand watching, not ever seeing anything like it before. Marc laughs as he watches the people. "These people are wild," he tells Mount and Hem.

Then a large man the size of Mount and Marc comes up to them. "Why is this slave out of the building? We locked them in," he asks Mount. Mount looks over to Marc, then looks at the barbarian. "We had him doing work for us. We will take him back once he is done," Mount tells the man.

He looks at Mount, and Marc is slowly going for his sword, but then the man says, "Fine, just make sure he gets locked back up. Plus we just took the city. Work can wait," he says, fully thinking Mount and Marc are barbarians.

Marc lets go of his sword as the man walks away and goes back to having a good time. "Well, we now know that Gamble's people are still alive. Can you see where they put them in the city?" Mount asks Hem.

Hem closes his eyes to concentrate, then opens them. "They are locked up in a building at the back of the city," Hem tells Mount.

"Lead the way," Mount tells him. They make their way to the back of the city, and again, no one is guarding the large building.

They get to the door and find it locked. Marc uses his sword to break the lock; when they open the door, the people fall to the ground, thinking Mount and Marc are barbarians. Hem walks ahead of the brothers. "Don't be scared. We are here to help you," Hem says loud enough for all of them to hear.

The people look up, and most of the people recognize Hem. Jim crawls to Hem, "Great Wizard, you returned after we laughed at you. Thank you, Great Wizard!"

"Don't thank me yet," Hem says as he touches Jim. "Relax," Hem tells the man as he shuts his eyes; he then sees the vision of how they gave up with no fight to the barbarians. In the short time they have had control, the barbarians had forced them to work for them. The largest barbarians were taking the women as they pleased, and the few that did say anything died. The ones they didn't need got locked in this building with no food or water. Hem lets go of Jim.

"We need to get these poor people out of here," Hem tells Mount as he explains what the barbarians have been doing to them.

Mount looks over the room. "I don't know if we can sneak all the people out now that they have them working already. Plus we just came here to look, not to free them. They had their chance," Mount reminds Hem. Mount then shakes his head. "Look, I'll take Marc, and we will look around to find a way to get who we can out. You stay here and talk with them, see if they can help us in some way," Mount tells Hem.

"Yes, I'm sure they can help us in some way. You two be careful out there," Hem tells the brothers.

Mount and Marc both say, "Promise." Then they go out the door and make it look locked again. The brothers start walking back to the castle; going through a group of buildings, they hear women screaming and crying. Marc can't help but follow the noise; he hates hearing women cry. They go into a building and find three barbarian men forcing three Cobble City girls to have sex with them. Mount tries to grab Marc, but Marc goes into the room, demanding them to leave the girls alone.

The men turn and see Marc; he is wearing their clothing, so they think he is one of them. The men laugh; then one says, "Wait your turn. You can be next." Then he turns back around.

"The woman is crying! She doesn't want you doing that!" Marc yells.

The men stop and turn to Marc. "Do you have a problem, boy?" one says as they all grab their clubs. Marc says nothing; he takes a step back and pulls out his sword.

The men laugh, never seeing anything like it. The men start coming at Marc; he looks back to see Mount isn't with him. One of the men swings his club at Marc; he ducks and sticks the man with his sword. Blood pours out of the man as the other two scream and go to run. That's when Mount comes in with his sword, putting it in one's chest; and he falls to the ground, bleeding. Scared, the other man backs to a corner, screaming, "Who are you two men? You are both dead!" He tries to attack Marc.

Marc pulls out his sword from the dead man and swings it at the charging man; it takes his head off, and the body falls to the floor. Marc looks at Mount. "Where were you?" he screams.

Mount smiles. "I was keeping a lookout for more men. I thought you could handle it," he tells Marc.

"I could have handled it!" Marc snaps back.

Then they start making their way to the castle again. "I know you could have," Mount says as he puts his arm around his brother as they get to the castle.

Then as they walk in front of the castle, Serina is standing up high on the balcony, and she is looking over the city. Mount sees her; he stops, letting Marc walk ahead as he can't stop looking at Serina and her beauty. His thoughts become of climbing to the balcony and kissing Serina as he has never had this lustful feeling for a woman that he had just seen.

As Serina stands with Lisa looking over the people, Lisa notices Mount staring up at Serina; she points him out to Serina.

Serina is intrigued by Mount's well build; she can't remember seeing him before. Then she uses her powers to see the thoughts of Mount, who is now thinking of laying her down in bed. She smiles as she enjoys the thoughts of the young man; then she loses the vision.

Down on the street, Marc has come back for Mount. "You with me, bro?" he asks when he puts his arm around him.

Mount, not sure what just happened, answers, "Yeah, I'm with you." Then he starts walking with Marc.

Serina watches Mount walk away; then she walks back into the castle. "I need to rest," she tells Lisa.

Mount lets Marc drag him through the city. "Where are we going?" Mount asks his brother.

"Can't you smell that?" Marc asks as he drags Mount closer to the smell till they get to a building where the smell of food was strong. They go into the building to a large cooking area, where Gamble's people are cooking for and serving the barbarians.

Marc runs over to the food and starts shoving some in his mouth. Mount comes over, gets some food, and has Marc go sit down with him to eat. As they sit and eat, Mount tells Marc, "Back at the castle, I saw her, the one from Hem's fire vision. She was beautiful."

Marc becomes upset. "Why didn't you tell me? I wanted to see her too!" he yells at Mount.

"I'm not sure. It was like I was in a trance till you came back and put your arm around me. I couldn't stop staring at her—she is so beautiful," Mount tells Marc.

"Whatever! I can't believe you didn't point her out to me," Marc says, still upset.

Mount looks at Marc and bends in closer to him. "I think she saw me," he says.

Then a slave girl comes to them with a jug. "Would you men like a drink?" she asks them.

"Yes," they say at the same time.

She gets two mugs and pours from the jug. It comes out a dark-colored liquid; she fills each mug and hands each brother one. Marc puts his nose over the drink and gives a large sniff. "It smells good," he says, then takes a drink.

Mount takes a drink of his; they both really like the new discovery as they can't stop drinking it. They both quickly finish their mugs, and they look at each other as they start feeling the effects of the wine. "I feel good," Marc says to Mount before he starts laughing. He stands up and waves the girl to come back over to them. "What is this drink?" he asks her as she fills their mugs back up.

She looks at him strangely. "Wine—it's only been served at night forever," she says to Marc.

Mount steps in. "He's playing with you. Do you mind leaving the jug with us?" he says to her.

The girl laughs at them. "You're crazy," she says to Marc, then sets the jug down and leaves.

Marc gets the jug and fills both mugs and smiles. "I love this drink," he says to Mount, then starts drinking; he sets his drink down and looks around at the half-dressed women everywhere. "We'd better get out of here. I might start liking it here," he tells his brother, then takes a drink and has a passing girl hug him.

Mount takes a drink. "I don't know how we can sneak out Gamble's people without being seen. So don't get comfortable, but I need more time to think."

All the time Mount and Marc have been sitting at the table, not far from them, Boar and Ace are at a table with other warriors. Marc has caught Boar's attention as all the girls keep going over to hug him, with a couple doing more than just hugging. Ace notices Boar staring. "What's wrong, sir?" he asks Boar.

Boar points at Marc, "Who is that warrior?" he asks Ace.

Ace looks over at Marc, then looks at Mount. "They look young. They must be fighters. Our army is so big that I can't name them all," Ace answers.

Boar smiles at Ace's answer as he keeps staring at Marc. "Go tell them to join us at this table for a drink," Boars orders Ace.

Ace walks over to the table Mount and Marc are sitting at. "Hello, warriors. Our leader has told me to have you join us at our table," he says as he points to Boar.

Mount stands. "Thanks, but we're tired. We need to go lie down somewhere," he tells Ace, trying to get Marc to stand up.

Ace stops them. "Boar doesn't take no for an answer. I suggest you boys go over and sit down," he quietly warns them.

Mount pulls Marc up. "Let me do the talking," he whispers to him, walking over.

They walk up to the table; before Marc sits, he looks at Boar. "Hello, leader!" he screams out. They all laugh as the two men sit down.

"How are you warriors tonight? I see one of you is feeling good," Boar says as he watches Marc fill his mug up with more wine.

Mount smiles. "Yes, sir, just celebrating an easy win," he says, and they all hold their mugs up and slam them together; then Mount and Marc join in late, and they all drink.

Boar asks, "How long have you two been warriors? I don't remember seeing you two before."

Mount shakes his head. "Not long at all," he answers.

"So did I make you warriors before we marched here?" Ace asks them. Both brothers shake their heads yes. "I remember you boys were slaves," Ace says.

"Then we had a growth spurt," Marc says as he showed his muscles.

Mount steps in. "Yes, you made us soldiers. But then we never fought, so we have been in the crowd of the other soldiers," he tells Boar.

Boar shakes his head. "Congratulations on becoming soldiers! Sorry you boys got no action. These people were the weakest of all the cities we've took over." He laughs, then holds up his mug, and they all join him and take drinks.

"What're your names?" Boar asks them.

Marc is about to say his name when Mount blurts out, "Maverick is what they call me, and this is my brother, Rowdy."

"Good names, fellows. Stay, drink with us, Maverick and Rowdy," Boar says as he fills all the mugs on the table. They sit down with the barbarians and drink mug after mug as Boar brags of all the kills he has. Marc is feeling good; he now has one of the slave girls rubbing his shoulders. Mount can't stop thinking of the woman as he's acting like he is listening to Boar.

Serina is back on the balcony, looking over the city. Lisa comes out and stands next to her. "Are you okay?" she asks. Lisa has been with Serina since the day she got her powers; she tells Lisa everything.

"Earlier right here, we saw a young man. Then without trying, I saw his thoughts of being with me, and it made me feel strange," she tells her friend.

Lisa isn't sure what to say. Serina has hated men for so long. "Who was this man?" Lisa asks curiously.

"I've never seen him. He looked like one of our warriors," Serina says with a lustful look on her face, thinking of him. She then goes to Lisa. "Hold me," she tells her. "This can't happen to me. I can't have feelings for a man." She then pulls away from Lisa. "I have to go kill this man. This feeling has to go away," Serina tells Lisa.

"Why would you do that? He could be the one that finally makes you love," Lisa says.

Serina screams, "NO!" Her eyes start to glow, but then she calms down.

Serina walks back over to Lisa and hugs her again. "You are the only one I want. I will always love you, you know that." She kisses Lisa. "No, that was a warning. That is why I read his thoughts without trying. I must kill this warrior. He will be trouble, I feel it," Serina says as she leads Lisa back inside to her chambers.

"Now go find me a robe from one of the slaves. I must sneak out without being seen so I can track this young warrior down and rid of him before the sun comes up," she tells Lisa, who then goes out.

At the table, all the men are good and drunk. Jonna has joined them and is sitting on Boar's lap. The server girl is still rubbing Marc's shoulders as they all are still enjoying the drinks. Boar looks over to Marc. "She seems to like you. Why don't you take her for the night?" he tells Marc. Marc looks up at the girl, but all it does is make him start thinking about Amy.

He goes to tell Boar he can't, but Mount stops him. "Let's go relieve ourselves, brother," he tells Marc as he drags him out of the building.

"Were you going to tell him no?" Mount asks.

Marc shrugs his shoulders. "I can't be with that girl. I want to be with Amy," he says to Mount.

"Look, we have to act like barbarians. If you tell him no, they will know something is going on. We can't get caught. Being with that girl is better than dying and never seeing Amy again, so go back in there and act like a barbarian. I really got to pee. Go back in there," Mount tells his brother.

Marc goes back into the building as Mount finds a dark corner to relieve himself. Mount goes to the back and starts to pee; he doesn't see Serina coming, and she follows him to the back and watches as the handsome young man relieves himself on the side of the building. She finally raises her hand, thinking of crushing his windpipe. She stops as Mount turns and sees her and quickly goes to cover himself up. Mount can't believe the beautiful woman from the balcony is watching him pee; he turns to her and starts walking toward her, and Serina lowers her hand.

When Mount gets to her, he says nothing; he goes to a knee and grabs her hand. "You are the most beautiful creature on this planet," he tells Serina, and the buzz from the wine gives him the courage to kiss her hand. Mount slowly stands; getting a good look at just how perfect she is, he shies away. "I thought you were an angel from the heavens," he softly says to her.

Serina smiles as she sees this well-built, handsome man still shying away from a woman's attention. "No, I'm just a servant girl of the queen's. What are you? A warrior of the army?" she asks.

"I am," Mount quickly answers. "I was just having drinks with our leader, Boar," he brags to her.

Serina laughs at him. "You must be important to him," she says. "What's your name, great warrior?" she asks him.

Mount is about to say his name, then stops. "My name is Maverick, he tells her still thinking she was the queen" he tells her.

Serina smiles. "I'm called Lisa," she tells him.

Mount again kneels to her, takes her hand, and kisses it. "It's a pleasure to meet you," he says.

She is impressed with Mount. "For a barbarian warrior, you sure are respectful," she tells him.

"My mother taught me to treat all women with respect, my lady," Mount says as he turns red. He stands, and things go quiet; then he asks her, "Do you have somewhere to be?"

Serina sees he is flirting with her; she likes it. "I don't know. Why do you want to know?" she asks him.

"If you are not busy, I thought we could walk together and talk," Mount tells her.

Serina wants to see what type of man he is. "I'm a slave. You could just force me to come with you," she tells him.

Mount looks seriously at her. "I would never force a lady to do anything," he tells her as she looks him in the eyes.

She thinks of leaning toward him but stops. "I would really enjoy walking with you, Maverick," she tells him.

He grabs her hand, and Serina not only lets him but also grips his hand as they walk through the city. Mount walks her to the creek that runs outside the city.

The night is clear; the light of the stars and moon light the way. They get to the creek that runs out of the mountains, and the wind blows a small breeze. As they walk alongside the bank of the creek, Mount stares at Serina's beauty being lit up by the moon. Serina looks over and notices Mount looking at her; she flashes back to many years before, thinking of the first boy who was nice to her. Then she snaps out of it and starts to remember that she needs to rid herself of this man.

Then when she starts thinking of killing him, he puts his animal fur over her shoulders. "You look cold," he says as he does it.

Serina isn't sure what to do as she pulls the fur over her. "Thank you," she says to him, turning and looking up at the well-built man. She can't stop the lustful feelings as she rubs her hand down his chest. "You must be cold," she says.

He smiles at her, looking in her eyes. "I'm not cold with you around," he tells her, then kicks himself as she laughs and walks away.

They quietly walk beside the creek; then still feeling the wine, Mount takes a chance and grabs Serina's hand with his. Not sure what to do, she decides to let it happen and enjoy the moment. They get to a wide part of the creek, and Mount picks up a small stone and says, "Watch this." He throws the stone sidearm, and it skips a few times across the water and sinks.

Serina smiles. "Pretty good," she says, then picks up a stone; and with a little power boost, she skips her stone. It goes all the way across the water on to the bank of the other side.

"Impressive!" Mount tells her.

"I've been good at that since I was a little girl," Serina tells him.

"Bet you can't do it again," Mount tells her with a smile on his face.

"What would we bet?" she asks, interested.

"If you do it, I'll carry you back to the city," Mount tells her.

Serina agrees and picks up a stone, getting ready to throw. Then Mount says, "If you don't make it, though, I get a kiss."

She laughs. "It's a bet," Serina says, then gets ready to throw.

Mount comes next to her. "Line up. Get a good throw," he tells her.

Serina steps back and goes to throw; right when she does, Mount pokes her in the side with his finger. It messes her throw all up; the stone sinks to the bottom as it hits the water. Serina starts laughing like she never has before as she smacks him over and over. "I can't believe you did that!" she yells at him.

"I'll take my kiss now," Mount says to her with a large smile on his face. Serina gives him a look that could kill as she knows she must kiss him.

Their eyes stay locked as each one takes a step closer to the other. Serina moves closer in, then pulls away, teasing Mount. She moves back closer, then quickly gives Mount a kiss on his cheek; and when she tries to pull back, Mount puts his arms around her and kisses her on the lips. Serina is shocked and pulls away; and when Mount tries to apologize, he is stopped by Serina coming back and giving him a long, slow wet kiss. Both are getting into the kiss as each one is feeling feelings neither has felt.

The kiss doesn't stop as neither wants it to end. After a few more minutes, they finally pull away; and each one looks in the other's eyes, not saying a word. Mount can't believe he has met such a beautiful, charming woman; he grabs her in his arms as he thinks of taking her with him. Serina melts in Mount's arms, never wanting the night to end as she forgets about the real world for the moment. Mount leans into her ear. "I wish we could stay right here forever," he softly says to her.

Serina moans, "Yes," as she melts into his arms. But then she opens her eyes and pulls her head away from Mount's shoulder. "I must get back before they notice I'm gone," she tells Mount. Scared of her feelings, she pulls away from Mount and turns to walk back to the city.

Mount watches her walk away, then goes running after her and stops her. "I can't let you go back. You are too beautiful of a woman to be a slave! I want you to run away with me," Mount tells her.

Shocked, Serina gives a laugh. "You must be crazy!" she tells him, then starts walking back to the city again. Mount catches up with her, grabs her, and kisses her. Serina kisses him back, then pulls away, smiling. "You're crazy," she tells him again.

She goes to walk away, and Mount grabs her arm. "You belong with me. I'll love you forever," he tells her.

Serina, still not fond of the word *love*, says, "The queen is all-powerful. She would hunt us down and kill us both," talking about herself.

"Worth it," he says.

Serina looks at Mount, shocked. "You would die for me?" she asks him.

"Come with me! I'll make sure we escape without dying. Then I will love you till we die as old people with beautiful kids surrounding us," he tells Serina.

She isn't sure what to do anymore; she runs to Mount, and they hold each other in their arms as they go into a deep, long kiss. Serina takes Mount by the hand. "Follow me," she tells him and then leads Mount through the city till they find an empty building.

They go into the building, and it is filled with wheat from the harvest. Serina has Mount lie down on a large pile, and she straddles him as they keep heavily kissing. She stands up in front of Mount and drops her robe. He can't believe how perfect her body is as he stares at her. She then rips Mount's animal skins off him and lies back down with him as they start making love. Serina slowly starts moving up and down on Mount as they both moan with pleasure.

Outside, Boar has left the eating room and is walking back to his new house, where Jonna is waiting for him. When he goes by the building where Mount and Serina are in, he hears the noises; and curious of what the noise is, he goes to the door and opens it, then slowly peeks into the room. He sees two people having sex in the wheat stack, but it is so dark that he can't see who they are. So he leans in for a closer look. Then he can't believe his eyes.

Boar quickly gets out of the room and stands outside the door. "No way," he tells himself. He slowly moves back in for another look and can see it is the queen, and she is so into making love that she doesn't even notice Boar behind them. "I got to see who she is with." But she is blocking his face; after riding him hard, she finally goes down to kiss the man, and Boar sees it's the young warrior Maverick.

Boar slips out of the room; he is mad. *I should stop them!* he thinks but doesn't. *She will kill me if she sees me*, he thinks.

Boar leaves the building and starts going back to his place. *There's no way in hell that little punk warrior will make his way up by sleeping with Serina. I have to think of a way to rid myself of him and his brother. I can't put them in a pit. I have to think of a way to kill them both*, Boar thinks to himself. He gets to his place and walks into the room to find Jonna standing in the middle of the room covered in only a small towel, which she drops to the floor.

Boar grabs his woman; being excited from watching Serina and the young warrior, he starts kissing and licking her all over as he picks her up and carries her into the bedroom. He throws her on the bed and rips his clothes off; he then gets on top of her and pins her down. He starts thrusting inside her as he takes his anger out on her. Jonna gives out a sexual scream as she enjoys when Boar gets rough with her; he turns her over and shoves his manhood inside her as he pulls her hair.

Back at the wheat storage building, Serina is still riding Mount as they both are moaning with pleasure. Mount is loving being inside

Serina; he is thinking to himself that he can keep doing this forever. He flips Serina over, where he is on top of her, and he takes control. Then suddenly, he gets a strange feeling, and he yells out as he releases all inside of Serina; it is the greatest feeling he's ever felt as his whole body goes into the most relaxed state he has ever been in.

Serina lies in Mount's arms; she is so happy now as her whole body is numb from the pleasure. Everything is quiet; then Mount speaks up. "I hope this means you will run away with me. I never want to be without you again," he tells her.

Serina lies quiet as she thinks of what she is going to tell him. "I so want to go with you, my love. I dream of a life with you," she tells Mount.

"So you will go with me?" he asks her.

"Yes, lets' get some rest till morning. Then I will run away with you," Serina tells him.

Mount hugs Serina. "I will die making you happy," he tells her.

Serina smiles as she feels a safe happiness, a feeling she hasn't felt in so long. Mount leans in and starts to kiss Serina; while they kiss, Serina opens her eyes, and they were glowing. Mount falls into the wheat pile, knocked out. "Sleep, my love," she says as she runs her fingers through his hair. A tear rolls down her cheek. "If only things were different, my love." She runs her fingers through his hair again, but this time, her eyes light up. "It's best you don't remember."

Serina leans down and kisses him once more, then lays him down to sleep in the pile of wheat. She stands, covers herself with the slave robes, and leaves out of the building to sneak back through the city to her chambers. She enters the room to find Lisa waiting for her to return. "I was getting worried. Did you find the young warrior?" Lisa asks. Serina says nothing; she goes to her clothes and changes out of the slave robe. Serina comes back over to Lisa. "What happened? Where have you been?" she asks.

Serina tells Lisa everything, but never anything like what she is about to tell her. "This stays between us," she tells Lisa, and that really gets Lisa's attention.

"Yes, Mama," Lisa says.

Serina lights up like a little girl. "I found the young warrior," she tells Lisa. "I went up to him, about to crush his windpipe," she says, then stops.

"What happened?" Lisa asks her.

Serina looks at Lisa and shakes her head. "He was so nice to me I couldn't do it. Something came over me," she says, confused.

Lisa gives a scream of excitement. "You got feelings for a man!" she screams, laughing.

Serina says nothing; she just smiles. Lisa stops laughing. "It was more than that." She gasps.

"You kissed this man!" Lisa says, almost asking.

Serina looks at Lisa, then blurts out, "We had sex."

Lisa screams. "You slept with that handsome young warrior?" she says.

Serina grabs Lisa by the hands. "It was wonderful, the greatest moment in my life! And when it happened, he put his seed inside me," she says to Lisa.

Serina smiles as she rubs her stomach. "I'm with child. I can feel it already growing inside me," she tells Lisa as she looks down at her stomach.

Lisa is stunned. First, Serina comes back telling her of being with a man, and now she is saying it produced a child. "Will you have the child?" Lisa asks her.

"Yes, of course," Serina says as she walks over to Lisa and puts her arms around her. "We will raise this child together," she tells Lisa. Lisa puts her arm on Serina's, liking the sound of having a baby around.

Then she turns and looks at Serina. "What about the father?" she asks.

"I left him asleep after I wiped his memory of us meeting. He will think he just drank too much wine when he wakes, not remembering anything," Serina tells her.

Lisa likes hearing that, and then she leads Serina to her bed, where they lie together. Lisa holds her as she falls asleep. As Lisa lies there thinking of the joy of having a child to raise, the sun starts peeking through the balcony window as she too falls asleep.

At Boar's place, he sits up in his bed, thinking of what he saw and what he must do to rid himself of this young warrior. Jonna sits up next to him, rubbing his back. "Come lie down with me. The sun is starting to rise," she tells him.

Boar pushes Jonna off him, gets out of bed, and gets dressed. "Hex!" he yells across the house, and soon, Hex comes in still half-asleep.

"Yes, sir?" he says, yawning.

"Wake up. We have a long day ahead of us. I want those two young warrior brothers dead before the sun sets," he demands to Hex.

"I'm hungry. Let's get some food," he tells Hex.

Boar leaves Jonna in bed, and the men go to the building where they eat. As they sit down and wait to be served, Hex is giving Boar ideas on how to kill the brothers. As Boar is eating while listening to Hex, he starts watching a group of boys; they have one of the boys' towels rolled in a ball and are throwing it back to one another as they keep it away from the other boy. Boar starts to laugh as the boy runs around, trying to get his towel, and begins to cry.

As the other kids start to laugh at the boy for crying, he goes running at the boy who has his towel; and when he tries to throw it, the one boy hits the other right in his nose. The boy drops the towel and grabs his nose as he goes down to the ground, screaming. The other boy stands on top of his towel, looking around for one of the other boys to come at him; but the boys all run, leaving their friend there hurt. Boar watches the boy pick up his towel and leave as the other finally runs off crying, leaving a trail of blood.

Boar laughs at what he just saw, how the bigger kids were playing keep-away from the smaller kid, who took out the biggest of them all. He sits thinking of him and his leaders playing keep-away from the young warrior brothers. They have Serina's crown and throwing it around. "Whoever puts the crown on Serina's head is the ruler of the army," Boar says. Then as he and his men keep throwing around the crown, each of the men are punching the brothers as they try to grab the crown.

Soon, both brothers have been beaten down; they are both on the ground, bleeding. Boar takes the crown and walks over to Serina, who has been watching the whole time. He walks behind her and places it on her head. She stands smiling and holds Boar's arm up in the air, calling him the winner. Then when the brothers try to stand up, Serina blasts an energy ball from her hand, and it blows the warriors' body parts everywhere.

Then Boar hears, "Sir, you done?" It is Hex.

"I got the perfect game," Boar says, smiling.

In the wheat storage building, Mount is slowly waking up as the sun hits him in the face. He sits up; his head is pounding. He looks around the room, wondering where he is. He then looks down and realizes he isn't wearing any clothes; then he sees his clothes lying on the ground. He picks them up, and they are ripped up. He can barely get them to cover him. He goes over to the door and slowly opens it, not sure where he is at. Then it hits him. *Where is Marc?* he thinks to himself.

Mount starts to walk the streets, doing his best to avoid the people walking by him; as he looks around, he can't understand why he can't remember what he did last night. He reaches an area where he can smell food, and he follows the smell to the building where they prepare food. He slowly walks in and looks around; he sees the food, gets some, and sits down to eat. On the other side is Boar, sitting alone; he sees Mount and walks over to him. "Where did you end up going? Your brother have a good time?" he asks.

Mount starts thinking, not really sure who Boar is; he seems familiar as he looks at him with a blank face. "I'm not sure what happened," Mount says, confused.

Boar shakes his head, knowing Serina has done something to him. "You and your brother need to learn to handle your drinking if you want to hang around the big dogs," he says, slapping him on the back. Still confused, he catches the remark against Marc.

"Where is my brother?" he asks Boar.

Boar becomes upset. "Do I look like your brother's keeper? Find him yourself! And when you do, both of you better get ready. I have a challenge for all warriors to compete in, so I suggest you find him!" Boar yells at Mount, then storms out of the building, looking for Hex.

Mount starts to eat again as he tries to think of what happened to him; then in comes Marc, stumbling to the table. He sits down and reaches over to grab some of Mount's food; he smells terrible. Mount backs away. "You stink!" he says.

"What happened to you?" Marc asks Mount.

Mount shakes his head. "I'm not sure. I can't remember much of last night. I just woke up in an empty building with no clothes on," he tells Marc.

Marc becomes upset. "It probably was Boar and Ace. I know it was! I got drunk and passed out too. I woke up in the garbage," he explains to his brother.

Mount starts thinking that maybe last night was just a prank on the new guys. "Well, now that we are known, how we sneak out of here will be hard. Hem won't like this," Mount says.

"Have you talked with Hem?" Marc asks.

"No, I'm sure he is fine. Right now, we have a problem. The leader, Boar, came to me and said all warriors have to compete in a competition," Mount tells Marc.

Marc gets excited. "Really? I hope I get to hurt someone. After what they did to us, it's payback time," he tells his brother.

Mount laughs, then smells Marc. "Right now, let's get you to the river so you can wash off that smell," he tells Marc, who then grabs more food. Then they leave for the river.

When they get to the river, Marc runs and jumps into the water; he washes off, then joins Mount, who is sitting on the bank of the river. "So we are in a warrior tournament?" Marc asks Mount as he picks up a small stone and skips it across the water.

Mount sees the stone go across the water, and it's like he's seen that before; he looks at Marc. "Did we come here last night?" he asks his brother.

Marc shakes his head. "You left me last night. If you were here, it wasn't with me," he tells Mount. "Are you okay?" Marc asks his brother.

Mount pushes Marc back into the water. "I'm fine. Now let's go win a warrior tournament!" he yells at Marc. Marc climbs back out of the water, and the brothers go back to the city.

When they get to the front gate, they find a crowd of people gathered on the outside of the city. They get closer to see Boar and Hex ordering a group of slaves around as they clean the brush and rocks up out of the field. Hex is lining up large wooden barrels on opposite sides of the field.

Mount and Marc get close to Boar, and he sees them coming. "The smelly brothers are here!" he yells.

As he and the other warriors laugh, Mount grabs a hold of Marc to keep him from starting a fight. Marc pulls away. "So what you got planned up?" he asks Boar.

Boar gives an evil grin. "See the two barrels? They are both fifty steps away from the rock in the middle of the field. The rock will be replaced with this ball I made. Two men will line up at each barrel. When Hex says 'go,' the men will race to the ball."

Boar continues, "Once you have the ball, you put it in the other's barrel to score. The only rule is no weapons. All else is fair. You can beat the other team down till they can't get up. First team to score five times wins!"

"Sounds fun," Marc tells Boar. "When do we start playing?" he asks.

"The field's almost ready. You'd better worry about getting ready to find out what it feels like to be a warrior," Boar warns him.

Marc walks away with Mount looking at the field. "We've been training for this our whole lives," Marc says, laughing.

Mount stops and puts his hand on Marc's shoulder, pointing over to the far side of the field. Marc looks to see Hem working with the slaves. They both walk over to Hem. Mount grabs Hem and pulls him close, "What are you doing?" he asks Hem.

Hem realizes it's Mount and Marc and goes from scared to mad. "What happened to you two? You were supposed to find a way to sneak these people out and be back!" he snaps at them both.

Both tell Hem, "Sorry."

Then Mount pulls Hem close. "We were noticed. See the large man standing at the side? He is Boar, the leader, and he demands all warriors to play in this tournament."

Hem looks worried. "I've been talking with slaves that came here with the barbarians, and they all say Boar's games are deadly," he tells the brothers.

Marc laughs. "I'm not worried. How about you, Mount? We will destroy them no matter what he chooses us to play," Marc says, flexing his muscles.

Mount looks at Hem. "It's your call. We can leave now if you want," he tells him.

"No, we can't leave these people here. Plus I have to see this evil queen for myself. They say she is all-powerful," Hem answers Mount.

"Yes, we are going to play. It's payback time!" Marc says.

"Yes, maybe she will show up at this tournament. I must know if we can get these people out without her catching on."

Then from the center of the field, Hex yells, "All warriors gather round!"

Hem tells Mount, "Slaves are allowed to watch. I'll be close."

Hem then goes back to work with the slaves as Mount and Marc follow the other warriors to where Hex is standing with Boar. Once all the warriors are gathered around, Hex yells, "Shut up! Our leader wants to speak!"

Then Boar stands in front of the warriors. "Find a partner! This is a two-man game!" he yells, then has Hex explain the rules.

"If you lose, you're out. If you win, you play again till there are only two teams that play for the championship. The champion team will be free from training for a week."

All the warriors team up, and the games begin as the first two pairs of warriors line up on each side to play. Hex sets the ball in the middle of the field; he backs away, then yells, "GO!" Then both teams charge at the ball as the crowd screams. The fastest of the men gets to the ball, but when he goes to pick it up, one of the men from the other team comes and kicks the guy to the ground. The other teammate comes in and helps his teammate kick the other to the ground.

They both jump the other man, and both start beating him down. While they aren't looking, the man on the ground gets up, gets the ball, and runs to the barrel before the other two notice; and he puts the ball in to score a point.

As the day goes on, each game gets more brutal and bloody; some of the games ended early over the men getting too hurt to play. It was now Mount and Marc's turn; they go line up at their line, getting ready for Hex to drop the ball.

Marc looks over at Mount, laughing. "Look how small them two are! This should be fun!" he tells Mount.

"Get your head in the game!" Mount snaps at Marc as Hex drops the ball.

Marc becomes upset at his brother snapping at him; he takes off running, and by himself, he runs past their competitors, picks up the ball, takes it, and slams it into the barrel. He goes running back and lines back up next to Mount. "Good job," Mount tells Marc.

"Yeah! Let's get them!" Marc yells out to his brother.

"My turn," Mount tells Marc.

When Hex drops the ball, Mount goes charging at the ball and picks it up; and just as Marc did, he runs over one of the men and drags the other with him to the basket as he puts the ball in to score. The crowd is cheering loudly for Mount and Marc, which gets the attention of Boar, and he yells to the brothers, "It won't be that easy when you play us!" as he puts his arm around Ace.

The rest of the game is just as easy as Mount and Marc score three more times with no difficulty.

"It will be a while before we play again. Can we go get some food?" Marc asks Mount.

"Sorry, brother. We need to go talk with Hem," Mount tells Marc as he starts walking toward the group of Cobble City people, looking for Hem.

They find Hem with the people; he sees them coming and walks toward them. "Good job out there, boys! I've got good news and bad news," he tells the brothers.

"What's the bad news?" Mount asks Hem.

Hem gives Mount a disappointed look as he kicks the dirt. "I've not seen the queen nowhere. I just knew she would come out for this. I'll never get to see what we are up against," he tells Mount, upset.

"Calm down. What's the good news?" Marc says to him as he slaps Hem's back, almost knocking him to the ground.

Hem shakes away from Marc. "I've been talking with Gamble's people. They have told me a couple of places where to sneak out of the city unnoticed," he tells Mount.

Mount grabs a hold of Hem and brings him close to act like he was in trouble. "That's perfect. Gather his people now. Sneak away while everyone's attention is on the game."

Hem thinks about it but knows this is the best time to get them out alive. "I'll take them into the mountains where the wolves and horses wait for us," Hem tells Mount.

Then Hex from a distance yells, "Maverick, Rowdy, you boys are next!"

Hem laughs when he hears the names they used. "Be careful, we will be right behind you!" Mount tells Hem, and the brothers head back to the field.

Hem then gets Jim and tells him the plan; then they both go to gather all the people and sneak out of the hidden exit built in the back. The day goes by as Hem and Jim slowly sneak everyone away to get out of the city.

At the games, it almost gets easier each time as Mount and Marc keep destroying each pair of barbarian warriors they play against in the games. Boar is getting crazy mad that none of his men have been able to take out the brothers.

It is getting dark. The slaves set torches down both sides of the field; they give off enough light to keep the games going. It is now down to four teams, so two more games, and they will have the championship teams set to play the last match for the win. The first game is Mount and Marc against two vicious barbarians, Cobra and Viper. The men line up as Hex walks to the center of the field; he places the ball down, and the four men run to the ball.

Marc gets to the ball first. Cobra comes up and tackles him to the ground, but Marc is able to throw the ball to Mount. Mount goes running toward Viper, who gets ready to tackle him to the ground. Mount comes up to Viper, does a spin, and goes past him. As he does, Viper grabs a hold of Mount by his leg, but Marc comes running up and kicks his arm off Mount. Then Mount runs to their basket and puts the ball in. Marc runs and hugs Mount, and they go back to their side of the field.

Cobra and Viper do the best they can against the brothers; they are even able to score two points, but Mount and Marc are just too much for them as they win, easily scoring five. They didn't get to celebrate long, though, as Boar and Ace more than easily beat Tyke and Cage five to nothing. It is so easily seen that the two let Boar and Ace win as they never tackled them one time. Mount and Marc go to Boar and Ace as they were celebrating their win.

Boar goes over to Mount as he is getting the people excited for the next game. "You and your brother have done good today, but if you two know what's best, you won't play so hard. It would suck to be on night guard duty, wouldn't it?" he says to Mount as he waved at the people. Boar goes back over to Ace, and they both start laughing as they go to their line.

Marc walks with Mount; as Mount tells his brother what Boar said, Marc laughs. "Fuck both of them. Let's kick their asses!" he tells Mount.

Mount laughs. "I want to, but we can't," he tells his brother.

Marc looks shocked. "Why not?" he asks Mount.

"We don't need the attention if we are going to sneak out of here later," he explains to Marc.

Marc lets out a moan. "Fine, this sucks." He grumbles as they line up on their side.

Hex goes to the middle of the field, places the ball down, steps away, and yells, "GO!"

All four men go running to the ball. Marc gets to it first; and as he goes to pick the ball up, Ace comes from behind, knocking him down.

Marc pulls Ace to the ground, and they start wrestling around on the ground; as they fight, Boar runs up on them, grabs the ball from

Marc, and takes off running. Mount runs after Boar. As he catches up to him, Boar bends down and grabs a handful of dirt; and when Mount gets close to Boar, he throws the dirt into Mount's eyes. Mount bends over, rubbing his eyes; then Boar kicks Mount to the ground and easily goes to their barrel and throws the ball in.

Marc has broken away from Ace and comes running at Boar, but Mount grabs him. "Remember why we are doing this," he whispers to his brother.

Marc pulls away. "Let's get this over with," he says, and they start walking back to their line as Boar and Ace scream, "Losers!"

As Hex starts to place the ball down, Mount is still wiping his eyes. "You okay?" Marc asks.

"I'm good. Let's stay back and let them get the ball," Mount tells Marc.

Hex drops the ball, and before he yells, Boar and Ace go running and get to the ball first. Ace picks up the ball, and he and Boar both start charging at the brothers. Boar goes right at Mount and jumps on top of him, taking him to the ground. Marc goes to help Mount, and Ace goes to their barrel and puts the ball in for another score. Boar gets up, and he and Ace start celebrating as the people start going crazy. Marc helps Mount up. "How much more can we take of this?" he asks.

"Let's score one," Mount says.

They high-five as they step up to their line; they watch Hex as he drops the ball. This time, when Boar and Ace start to run, Mount and Marc do the same. Marc gets to the ball first, and this time, he turns and gets ready for Ace to attack. Ace comes charging at Marc and tries to stiff-arm him, but Marc ducks Ace's swing, then turns and throws the ball to Mount. Ace turns to throw another punch when Marc uppercuts Ace right in his chin, and he falls to the ground, knocked out.

Mount goes running toward Boar, who is guarding his barrel. Mount stops close to Boar, shows him the ball, then throws it straight up into the air. Boar follows the ball with his eyes, looking up. When he does, Mount hits Boar the hardest he has ever hit anyone. Boar falls to the ground, knocked out; the ball comes back down, and Mount catches it, then walks over to the barrel and forcefully throws the ball in for the score. The crowd goes quiet as they look at Boar and Ace both lying on the ground, not moving.

In Serina's chambers, she is still resting as she thinks of what happened the night before and feels her child grow inside of her. Then she is disturbed by the cheers of the crowd outside. She gets up, goes to the balcony, and sees enough to notice that all the people of the city are gathered watching something. "Lisa!" she yells.

Soon, Lisa comes running in. "Something wrong, Mama?" she asks.

Serina comes in from the balcony. "Where is all the noise coming from?" she asks Lisa.

"Boar has the warriors playing a game in the field out front of the city," Lisa tells Serina.

"I must see this. Get my carriage," she tells Lisa.

By the time they get there, she sees Boar and Ace in a massive battle with two other warriors. As she keeps watching, she notices that one of the other warriors is her lover. She keeps watching as Mount is not only holding his own but also getting the better of Boar. She starts thinking of him being next to her as her mate and leader of her army.

Now there are still a few of Gamble's people that want nothing to do with Hem or Jim as they are sneaking away. Now the rumor that Mount and Marc are not warriors, but the wizard's protectors has gotten around, and some of the other warriors have come to Serina to tell her what has been said. Serina looks over at her lover, who is still on top of Boar, hitting him. Then she tells the warrior to bring to her one of the slaves. She then takes the hand of the slave. She goes into a vision of the night before they attacked; the wizard was there to warn them of their city being taken over. She sees with him the two warriors on the field with Boar and Ace. Then her vision goes to the next morning, and she sees them taking to safety the leader of the city and the ones that would go with them. Serina opens her eyes and lets go of the slave's hand; she is very angry as she stares down at the brothers.

Serina walks out on the field to where the men are fighting; she holds out her hand and makes a fist. When she does, Mount and Marc both fall over, gasping for air. "Where is your wizard companion?" she screams at them both.

"We serve you. I don't know no wizard," Mount chokes out.

Serina goes to Mount, picks him up by his throat, and holds the big man off the ground. "Don't lie to me," she says, then starts reading Mount's thoughts. She sees that the wizard was here and that he snuck out more slaves. Then she loses him as they left the city. She opens her eyes and throws Mount back to the ground.

"Leave him alone, you bitch!" Marc screams as he tries to attack Serina, but she sees him coming and shoots a power ball at him that sends him flying and then hitting the ground. Serina then starts choking both brothers; they slowly start going out, almost near death.

Then Lisa yells, "Madam, stop! Don't kill them! You may need them to get the wizard back here."

Serina drops her hand, and both brothers start gasping for air. She looks at Lisa. "Yes, maybe it's best to keep them alive for now. Have Boar see them to the tower rooms above my chambers," she tells Lisa.

Lisa has Boar come over; he has been hiding in shame. "Take the two men to the tower rooms above Serina's chambers."

Boar is more than happy to do it. He and Ace get a few more men, and they beat the brothers all the way to the tower rooms, then lock them in separate rooms.

Hem has now gotten the Cobble City people out of the city and inside the mountain trail where the wolves and horses are waiting. They have been waiting on the brothers to join them for some time now; then sitting alone, Hem goes into a vision. He sees Mount and Marc getting beaten, dragged off, and locked away high in the castle. Hem comes out of the vision and goes to Jim. "I've seen my friends were caught. I must go back for them," he tells him.

Jim agrees to help Hem get his friends out, and the wolves are not staying behind this time. Hem knows he will need the wolves to get Mount and Marc out. The people tell Hem all about the castle and its secret passages to the top, where Mount and Marc are being held. "We will go back early morning when most of the people will still be asleep, but with the sun up. I sense the queen is less powerful in the sun. So get some rest. I'll wake you soon," Hem says, then goes to rest.

Back at the city, Serina is with Lisa inside her chambers; and she is furious that the wizard came in and out without her sensing his presence, then snuck slaves out with him. Now she can't locate where he went. Lisa tries to calm Serina down. "Madam, you know those two prisoners are important to the wizard. Like you said, he'll come back for them," Lisa tells her.

Serina smiles. "Yes, I will set a trap for him. He will be caught, and I will see him die," she says with an evil tone in her voice.

"We have men searching the area. Most likely, they will find him if he is still nearby," Lisa tells Serina.

"Yes, maybe. I must rest now. Come get me if he is captured," Serina orders Lisa. She lies down, trying to concentrate on the wizard's whereabouts and his next move; but as she lies there, her mind keeps wandering off to the night with the prisoner above her. She tries to stop thinking of him; but she still can feel the touch of his skin, the wetness of his soft lips, and the extreme feeling that came over her in his arms.

Serina can't take it anymore; she needs that feeling again—she must see him. Serina takes the back stairway that leads to the locked rooms; she stands outside the door of the room with Mount inside. He is lying on the cot, asleep. *He is so handsome*, she thinks to herself as she stares at him sleeping. She opens the door, walks into the room, and goes over to where Mount is sleeping. She bends over. "Wake up, my love," she softly says, and Mount wakes up under Serina's powers.

"Follow me," she tells him as she takes his hand, then leads him down the stairway and to her chambers. Serina is so focused on Mount that she doesn't see Lisa come into the room. Lisa quickly hides, wanting to see what happens.

Under Serina's spell, Mount wastes no time as he starts passionately kissing her. Serina cannot control her urges as she kisses him back. She loves the feel of his strong arms wrapping around her; then he forcefully rips her clothes off.

Hem's vision of Mount wakes him from his sleep. "Mount's in danger," he says to himself as he sits up. He goes and wakes Jim. "I had a vision. My friends are in trouble. We must go now," he tells Jim.

They get the horses, and the wolves are waiting as they get on the horses to leave. Hem tells the wolves, "Go ahead and check for barbarians. They must be looking for me by now." Then they run up the trail toward the city. Hem prays he makes it in time to save his friends as they go through the mountains.

Mount now has Serina on her bed, making love to her as Serina moans with pleasure. Lisa is hiding, watching the two having sex; she is angry, thinking back to how Serina killed her fiancé the day she was to become mates with him and then made her a servant. So she has never been with a real man—only what comes out of Serina, which is not human. As she keeps watching the two, she can't help but get turned on by the sexy man thrusting himself in and out of Serina.

Serina is now at a soft scream as Mount makes her feel like she has never felt in her long life; she rolls her eyes in the back of her head as she has another orgasm. Serina digs her nails into Mount's back as her body quivers; under Serina's powers, it just stirs him up as he keeps thrusting inside her. She then takes charge as she rolls Mount over and gets on top of him; she starts riding him slowly as she feels another orgasm. Mount then gives out a moan, and Serina feels the warmth of his seed all inside her.

Serina makes sure her lover falls right to sleep, then lies next to him, enjoying the moment. Lisa slowly sneaks out without Serina noticing as she lies there in thought of killing her lover for his betrayal. She stands over Mount, looking him over as she holds up her hand to crush the wind out of him. Something stops her—she can't do it. She drops her hand and walks away, leaving Mount lying there. Serina must think before she kills the father of her unborn child; he one day could join her.

Hem and Jim come out of the mountains, finding the wolves waiting for them; at the front of the city are some guards, so Jim shows Hem a secret way in. They leave the horses at the back of the city as Jim

.m a secret tunnel that leads to the castle. Hem tells the wolves, .ere till I call for you." Then Jim leads Hem inside a small empty .ng with a door. Jim opens the door to a large dark tunnel; there corches to light at the front.

The men get the torches lit, and there are other torches on the walls as they walk down the tunnel; they light the other torches, and soon, the tunnel is lit up. They seem to walk forever; then finally, they get to a small wooden door. It is stuck from never being opened, but after a few pushes, it finally opens. It goes into a small dark room with a stairway going up, so the men slowly start up the stairs. They get to the top to find a door in the flooring; when they push it up, they find themselves in a supply closet.

They open the door to the closet and see they are in the main hallway of the castle, close to where Gamble's room is. "What now?" Jim asks Hem.

Hem closes his eyes. "My friends are close. I need you to go upstairs and free Marc as I go get Mount out of Gamble's room. Follow me and take the stairs inside the room." They go to the door, and it's locked; but with Hem's powers, he unlocks and quietly opens the door. Hem sends Jim up the stairs and then starts looking for Mount.

He goes to a door and peeks around the corner; he sees Mount lying on a bed nude, with Serina standing over him. Hem thinks to himself, *What should I do?*

But before he has time to think, Serina turns around. "Come in, wizard. I've been waiting for you."

Hem stands straight up as he walks into the room. "Back away from my friend," he says in a deep voice.

Serina looks Hem over, then starts to laugh. "You are just a young boy," she says to Hem. "I don't listen to no man, especially one that is no man!" she screams.

Serina then forms an energy ball from her hand and throws it at Hem. He quickly forms a force field around his body; it blocks the ball and sends it across the room. Serina is impressed by Hem. "You do have some power," she says to him.

"Let my friend go," Hem tells Serina again.

"You don't understand. He is under my spell. He belongs to me now, and soon, you will too," she says, then throws another energy ball at him. Hem ducks behind a table, then comes back up and throws one back.

That makes Serina extremely mad as she blocks his power ball away; she starts throwing everything she has at Hem. He forms his shield, but Serina's powers are just too strong as he can't keep his shield formed. Then finally, her power ball hits him and knocks him to the ground. Serina stands over Hem. "Did you really think you could stop me?" she says as she uses her powers to raise Hem in the air. She has been using all her power on Hem, and Mount is able to snap out of her trance.

Serina tells Hem, "You will die now." But before she does anything, Mount comes up behind her and hits her over the head with a chair; she falls to the floor as Hem does as well.

Hem stands up and goes to check on her. "She is breathing," he tells Mount. "Thank you. She was just about to kill me. Her powers are so much stronger than mine," Hem says to Mount.

"How did I get here, and why am I naked?" Mount asks while he picks up his clothes.

"I'm not sure. You were captured. She said she had you in her control," Hem tells Mount.

Mount rubs his head. "We need to get out of here before she wakes up," he tells Hem.

"First, we need to go check on Jim. He went to find your brother up the stairs in the other room," Hem says.

Mount follows Hem into the other room. When they start to go up the stairs, they hear someone coming down, so they quickly hide. It's Marc with Jim behind him. "Mount, you're okay! I saw her come get you last night. I thought you'd be dead!" he says to Mount.

Mount laughs. "Good to see you're okay too," he says.

"What did she do to you?" Marc asks Mount.

Mount looks puzzled as he thinks. "I don't remember. All I know is I woke up, and she was trying to kill Hem. So I broke a chair over her head. She is in the other room, knocked out," he tells Marc.

Hem then says, "Yes, and we need to get out of here before she wakes up, or we will all be dead."

So they follow Jim back to the closet. "We're hiding in here?" Marc asks.

Jim laughs. "Follow me," he says, then opens the door to the tunnel.

"Oh man, this is great!" Marc says as they enter the tunnel.

They quickly run through the lit-up tunnel. As they do, Hem uses his powers to have the horses be at the building where the tunnel comes out of.

Back in Serina's room, Lisa comes in and finds her on the floor; she shakes her, and it wakes Serina up. She is the maddest Lisa has seen her since the day she became her servant. "Find Boar! Tell him the prisoners have escaped. Find them immediately!" she screams.

Lisa goes to find Boar and tells him about the brothers escaping. Boar is almost happy to hear the news; this is his chance to kill those two. Boar calls Hex into the room. "Go tell all warriors to meet me at the front of the castle," he tells him. Hex runs out the door.

Meanwhile, Lisa leads Boar to Serina's chambers. When they get there, they find Serina out on the balcony; they both back away when they see she is doing a chant as she uses her powers.

As Serina is doing her chant, the sky starts to turn dark; then out of nowhere, a giant storm forms with strong gusting winds, large drops of rain and hail, and frightening thunder and lighting. She turns to see Lisa and Boar. "Find them!" she screams at Boar.

Boar goes out to the front of the castle, where all his men stand in the storm, waiting for orders. "The young warriors are trying to escape the city. I want them dead!" he screams to the men, and they all scatter, searching the city for the brothers.

Mount, Marc, Hem, and Jim have made it to the end of the tunnel and find the wolves waiting for them inside the building. They can hear the storm outside the building. Marc goes to open the door, but Hem quickly stops him. "That is no regular storm. It's the work of Serina. She is awake and has all her men looking for us. We must be very careful," Hem tells them all.

Marc laughs and opens the door again. "I'm not scared of a little storm," he says. Then lighting strikes right at him; he shuts the door.

Everyone laughs as Marc stumbles away from the door. "That's crazy! How are we going to get through that?" Marc asks.

"The wolves can get us to the horses. Then we can get to the mountains and should be safe," Hem informs them.

They get ready, and Marc opens the door for them to go out into the storm; the wolves lead the way, trying to avoid the warriors hunting for them. It is so hard to see in the rain; it is easy to sneak by, and Mount and Marc quickly take down the few they ran into.

They get to the front of the city, where the horses are waiting; some men are waiting as well. "There are a lot of them. We need our swords on the horses," Marc says to Mount.

Then lighting strikes near the men. "Now is our chance!" Mount screams to Marc, and they run to the horses for their swords. The men run to attack the brothers, and the wolves run up from behind the brothers, and the men stop. Mount and Marc attack, but before they kill them all, one gets away.

Before they can get on the horses, Boar is there with twenty men or more surrounding them. Mount looks at Boar. "Just let us leave in peace. We don't want to fight," he says to him.

Boar laughs. "Attack!" he yells to his men.

Mount and Marc start cutting through the men with their swords; the warrior men scream in terror, never seeing such weapons as blood flows in all directions. Some of the men go to attack Hem and Jim. Hem forms a shield around them; then the wolves attack, ripping the men up.

Boar stands in shock as he sees the beasts helping them and the brothers cutting through his men with strange weapons he has never seen. As most of Boar's men have fallen, Mount gets Hem, and Marc gets Jim; and as the rest of the barbarian army arrive, they escape on the horses. As Boar screams for the men to go after them, Marc is yelling out as they ride toward the mountain trail. The men go running after them, but the horses quickly disappear in the pouring rain.

Boar screams, “Get back in the city!” He knows they won’t be able to catch them riding those large animals. He goes back through the city; then when he gets to the castle, the rain stops, and the sky clears up. Seeing this, he knows Serina must know the brothers escaped with the wizard.

Boar walks into Serina’s room; she is standing, waiting for him. He drops to his knees. “I’m sorry, my queen. My men have seen a lot, but never the weapons they have, and the fierce dogs seemed to listen to the wizard,” Boar pleads.

He then stands. “I will gather my best men. We will track them down and destroy them all,” he tells Serina.

“NO!” she screams. “I want him alive. I will kill the wizard myself! Bring me the prisoner Bree. He has the skill to defeat them without killing them,” Serina demands of Boar. “Send the trackers with him along with two guards to watch him. Now go get the prisoner and bring him here.”

Boar does as he is told; he finds Ace and tells him, “Bring the slave to the castle.” Ace does as he is told.

Boar and Ace come into Serina’s chambers with Cobra, Viper, Tyke, and Cage surrounding Bree with his hands tied together behind him. The men push him into the room, and Ace hits Bree in the back of his legs, and Bree falls to the ground. Serina becomes angry seeing him hit Bree, and Ace goes flying across the room. “I don’t want him hurt!” she screams at Ace, then turns to Tyke. “Help him up!” she screams at him. With Cage’s help, they get Bree to his feet.

“Bree, my favorite slave, today is your lucky day,” Serina tells him. Bree looks over to Serina as she walks toward him and looks him in the eyes. “You do as I say and go with my men as they track down a certain man traveling with two other men and most likely a group of slaves. You can kill his protectors but bring him back here alive, and I shall let you go free,” Serina explains to Bree.

Bree doesn’t have much of a choice. “I agree,” he tells Serina.

"Cobra, you and Viper get ready to leave. Tyke and Cage, you will go with them to watch the slave. It's your job to make sure he doesn't run, so go with Cobra to ready yourselves for the trip."

They all agree and leave her chambers.

"Boar, you and Ace take the slave for a meal before they leave. Then have your men ready just in case they get stupid and come back." They also agree to Serina's orders and shove Bree out of the room.

Mount and Marc have gotten the horses into the mountains; they are all glad the rain stopped, and it has cleared. Hem tells Mount, "The Cobble City people we got out are waiting on us at the mountain river where we left the wolves." Then they lead the horses toward the river.

"Think they will try to come after us?" Marc asks.

"Most likely will," Hem answers, and Mount hits Hem.

"We have a good head start. Thanks to the horses, we will get far away before they come near us," Mount tells Marc.

Then Mount speaks up. "We will get to the others and keep moving. The horses will help with the children and elders by carrying them. We won't stop till nightfall," he explains to them all, and they agree and then speed up the horses.

Before long, they are at the river, where the people waited. They do as Mount says, and the horses carry the kids and elders, and they get a far distance away from Cobble City before the sun starts going down.

At Cobble City, the men have Bree tied up, and they are ready to start tracking the wizard and his men. Serina is angry. "They probably have gotten a far distance away, riding those animals. So I am giving you all the energy where you will never get tired till your mission is complete. When they stop and rest, it will give you the time you need to catch up." Serina waves her hand, and a dark smoke comes from her fingers. "Breathe in the smoke," she tells them, and all five men breathe in the smoke.

The men all start jumping around, ready to go. "This is great," Cobra says to Serina.

"Don't fail me," she tells the men as they start their way out of the city.

Cobra quickly finds the animal prints that left a trail going into the woods. They light torches as they make their way into the mountains, and they all can feel the effects of the smoke as none are tired and all can easily keep going all night. Cobra and Viper watch for the animal tracks as Tyke and Cage keep an eye on Bree.

It's dark now, and Mount decides to stop till daylight; they have been following the river and set up camp next to it. While they set up camp, the wolves track a lamb and bring it back to be eaten. Marc has been watching Kurt, and he does his best to clean the meat, and the Cobble City women cook up a good meal for everyone. Soon after they eat, everyone lies around the fire to go to sleep as the wolves keep watch.

Mount and Marc lie next to each other, looking up at the stars. Marc looks over to Mount. "I can't wait to get home. I miss the twins," he tells his brother.

Mount gives a laugh. "Me too, little brother. It will be nice to see them, but we must figure a way to defeat the barbarians and get them their home back." He gets serious with Marc.

Hem sits up. "We need to talk with our fathers. They will know how to help us," he tells the brothers.

The men slowly fall asleep, talking about their home.

The barbarians quickly cover ground, tracking the animal prints in the ground; thanks to Serina's spell, they have not stopped all night, and Viper is sure they will catch up to them before the sun rises. Sure enough, right when the light is starting to show, Cobra stops them and points to a light in the distance. "Look, there's a fire in the distance. It most likely will be them. Be quiet and follow me," he tells them all. Cobra slowly guides the men toward the light; soon, they see the fire in the distance.

Around the fire is the wizard, his protectors, and the missing slaves; and right with them all are the fierce-looking animals. "Those beasts seem to protect them. If we charge down there, they will tear us to pieces," Cage, the biggest of them, says with fear in his voice.

"I'm not going down there," Tyke tells them. "None of us are going. That's why we brought the slave. He will go first and take the wizard's protectors out. Then once they are down, he can make the animals go away," Cobra tells them, and they go to Bree.

Cobra looks at Bree. "If I untie you, will you go do what the queen asks of you?" he asks Bree.

"Yes, I'll do as I was asked," Bree tells Cobra, who unties the ropes from Bree's hands. The men back away from Bree as he stretches his arms.

Bree walks over to where he can see the people around the fire; he looks around and notices the wolves lying with them. He turns and looks at the barbarians, who are keeping a distance from him. "Which of the men do you want to take back to your queen?" he asks.

Viper points to the one they think is the wizard. "That's him. You can kill the rest if you have to," he tells Bree.

"Why do the animals sleep around them? I've never seen anything like it," Bree says.

"They protect them. I saw the beast tear into some of our men when they were escaping," Cage tells Bree.

Bree keeps looking down at them. "It would be best if we let them wake and get moving. Then hopefully, the wolves will leave them at some point. Then that's when I can attack," he tells the barbarians.

They gather around in a circle. "You all think we can trust him?" Tyke asks them all. The others shake their heads, none of them saying a word.

"We have no choice. We must trust him," Viper finally tells them, and they all agree to let Bree do his plan.

So Cobra goes to Bree. "We will do things your way," he tells them.

"Fine, then we wait here in the distance and let them get up and start moving. We need to stay back, though, because the wolves will smell our scent," Bree tells them, and Cage quickly moves back.

At the camp, Mount is now waking up; seeing the light starting to form in the distance, he gets up, stretches, and walks off to relieve himself. He gets back and sees Hem up; he is standing at the fire. Mount starts walking toward Hem but stops where Marc is lying asleep. Mount bends down at Marc's ear. "Wake up!" he screams. Marc jumps up, startled.

"Mount, come over here," Hem tells him, and Mount walks over to Hem.

"What's wrong?" Mount asks.

"I sense we are being watched. It must be the barbarians. There's five of them, and I get a strange feeling about one of them. The others seem scared of him," Hem tells Mount.

Mount looks around in the distance, seeing if he sees something. "Should we send the wolves to kill them?" Mount asks Hem.

"They are keeping their distance over their fear of the wolves, but we can't take the chance that one could get hurt," Hem lets Mount know.

"Then we'll have the wolves leave so they will attack," Mount says.

"You want them to attack?" Hem asks.

"Want who to attack?" Marc asks and walks up to them, still trying to wake up.

Mount looks at Marc. "Up the hill are some barbarians who have tracked us down."

Marc gets excited. "Really? Let me get my sword. Let's get them," he tells them.

Mount stops him. "No, we want them to attack us so they think we don't know they are here. Hem has the wolves going off to hide. We can sit here and wait," he tells Marc.

Hem talks with the wolves as Jim, Mount, and Marc have the Cobble City people hide. The wolves argue with Hem but finally agree to leave, but not out of hearing distance, just in case things go wrong.

In the distance, the barbarians are watching with Bree, and they see the people scattering around; then as they watch, they soon realize the wolves are no longer around. "Slowly and very quietly, follow me," Bree tells the barbarians; then he leads them toward the camp.

Hem joins Mount, Marc, and Jim at the fire. "They are coming, and they want to kill us," Hem tells them.

Marc grips his sword. "Let them come. I'm ready," he says to Hem.

Then they hear noises coming from the distance; then from behind the trees out walk five men.

Cobra looks at Mount. "Did you think you were just going to walk away?" he asks him.

Marc speaks up. "We were hoping to!" he tells Cobra.

Cobra gets very angry from Marc's comment. "Well, Rowdy, you hoped wrong!" he screams, and Marc starts laughing. Cobra looks at Bree. "Kill him!" he screams.

Bree hesitates, not wanting to kill. Cobra gets in his face. "You gave our queen your word. If you want to be a free man, you will do it!" he says to Bree.

Bree lowers his head but then looks up at Marc and goes toward him. Marc starts backing away as he holds up his sword. "Don't do it. I don't want to hurt you," Marc says.

"I'm sorry," Bree tells him.

Then Marc swings his sword at Bree, and Bree moves away from the sword while quickly hitting Marc, taking the sword from him, and putting him to the ground. Bree then swings the sword at Marc, but before it touches him, Mount blocks the swing with his sword. Bree then swings at Mount, and he blocks that swing as well, and they start trading swings back and forth as they move around the area.

Hem goes over and helps Marc up. "What should we do?" he asks Hem as they watch Mount dueling with Bree. Hem looks at the barbarian men; they were all into watching Mount and Bree fight that they have forgotten all about Hem and Marc.

"Mount can take care of himself. We need to contain the others while they are distracted," Hem tell Marc.

Just as Hem says the words, Bree disarms Mount and pins him up to a tree with the point of the sword at his throat. "Kill him!" Cobra yells to Bree, but he just stands there, holding the sword and looking Mount in his eyes. Again, Cobra screams, "Kill him, slave!"

Bree drops the sword. "No, I won't kill an innocent person!" he yells back at Cobra.

It's enough to break his attention, for Mount to kick Bree away from him; then he dives to the ground, gets his sword, and jumps back on his feet. Cobra has the others attack Bree while he isn't looking; they are able to knock the sword away as they all punch and kick Bree to the ground. "You were told you would die if you didn't do what you were told!" Cobra screams at Bree. Viper goes over and picks up a large rock, then goes over and raises it over his head to hit Bree.

Mount has had enough; he goes over and swings his sword. It cuts Viper's hand clean off his arm. Viper grabs his arm, screaming as blood pours out. Cobra tries to hit Mount with a club, but Mount holds up the sword, and the club falls to the ground as it hits the sword; then Marc comes from behind and punches Cobra so hard that he falls to the ground, knocked out. Marc goes over, picks up his sword, and joins Mount, holding their swords at Tyke and Cage. "Don't kill us!" Cage begs the brothers.

Mount puts his sword at Cage's throat. "Get your friends and slowly go in that direction," he says as he removes the sword and points to the direction they came from.

Viper screams to Tyke, "Get my hand!" Tyke helps him off the ground, and then they pick Cobra up and drag him with them.

"Tell your queen we will be back to throw her out of these good people's city!" Marc yells as they watch them leave. He smiles as he looks at Mount and Hem, who are not happy he told them they are planning to come back.

Marc quickly changes the subject. "So what are we going to do with this guy?" he asks, pointing to Bree.

"Well, he's the best fighter I've ever went up against," Mount tells Marc, then goes over to Bree and helps him up.

"Please don't hurt me. I've been a prisoner of theirs for a few years know. They forced me to attack you," Bree says to Mount.

"Yes, I realized that when they went to kill you." Mount laughs, then looks over to Marc and Hem. "I say we let him go his way. He is no threat to us," he tells them.

They agree, and Mount tells Bree, "Today's your lucky day. You are free to go home."

Bree goes to his knees in front of Mount. "I can't do that, sir. You saved my life, so now my life belongs to you forever or till I return the favor," he says to Mount.

Mount smiles and tries to get Bree to stand up. "No, that's not necessary. You are a free man. Go home to your family," he tells Bree.

"I can't do that. I would be a disgrace to my god and my people. I must stay and serve you, or it will shame me," Bree demands.

Mount doesn't know what else to say. "Fine. I will allow you to serve your life debt, but I will not allow you to be my servant. Truthfully, I have a female servant waiting on me at home who is my servant for the same reason," he tells Bree, and they all have a laugh.

"You are a born hero. I can see it in your eyes," Bree says to Mount.

Marc goes over to Bree. "Welcome to the family," he says putting his arm around him; then he looks at Mount and Hem. "Can we go home now?" he asks them.

CHAPTER 5

Returning Home

WITH THE COBBLE City people, the trip takes a lot longer than expected; but after six sunrises, they are finally close to being home. Marc gets excited knowing they will be there by the middle of the day if there are no problems. Thanks to the wolves keeping any dangerous animals away from the people, they are making good time; another hour and they will be in the wheat fields where they first befriended the horses. Marc does his best to hurry the people.

The hour passes quickly, and they see the fields. Marc gives out a yell; he is so happy to see the fields. "We should be there just in time to eat," he tells the others. They walk their way through the tall fields of wheat grass, and it doesn't take long before they can see the wall that surrounds the village.

Soon, they are close enough to where Marc yells out, "We're home!" His yell is so loud that it gets the attention of the guards on top of the wall.

They turn to the village and yell, "They're back!"

Mount looks at Bree as they get closer. "You should like it here. All the people here are good people. We will get you a house built. And later, if you have any, we can go get your family and bring them back here," Mount tells him.

Bree smiles. "It looks great. Thank you for your kindness, but no, I have no family to go get," he tells Mount.

Finally, they get to the gates of the city; they hear someone yell, "Open the gates!" As they open from the other side, all the people are at the gates cheering for the three men.

The gates open; and all the people gather around Mount, Marc, and Hem, welcoming them home. Jax comes through the crowd. "What took you all so long?" he asks them.

They all say hi to Jax. Mount tells Jax, "We saw her. She captured us. We barely made it out alive."

Marc cuts in, saying, "We kicked their asses and got Gamble's people out!"

"Where are Gamble and his people?" Mount asks.

Before Jax says anything, Amanda comes up behind him and puts her arms around him. "Finally, you're home!" she says.

Mount turns around and hugs Amanda; he almost forgot how beautiful she is. He turns his head to see Marc hugging Amy. "I missed you," he tells Amanda as he squeezes her tighter. He looks back around and sees both their fathers standing not too far in the distance, watching them as they smile. He lets go of Amanda, takes her hand, and leads her with him over to their fathers.

"It's good to see you home, son, both of you," Dorn says to Marc as he comes up to them.

"Jax and our new friend Gamble have told me how Hem's visions are all true and the sorceress and her barbarian army took their home from them," Dorn says to Mount.

"It's all true," Mount says, then motions to Bree to come join them. "This is Bree. He has been a prisoner of theirs for some time. She sent him to kill us for his freedom, and he ended up helping us escape," Mount tells his father.

"Because your son saved my life, I'm now his to command till I repay the favor," Bree lets Dorn know. "I was caged for a long period. They would barely feed me, and they beat me regularly. The barbarians have no rules. They take what they want. And if anybody tries to stop them, their leader, Serina, has strange powers. She can kill you with a wave of her hand," Bree explains to Dorn and Gamble.

Dorn puts his arm around Bree. "I promise you will always be safe here, my new friend. Come, let's celebrate your freedom and my boys and Hem being home with more of Gamble's people safe."

They all walk with Dorn to the center of the town, where Doris and Missy come up to Mount and Marc, welcoming them home. The women have quickly gotten a feast together when it was heard they were home. They hug their mom and sister, who go back to getting the food ready.

The twins come get them and take them both over to the side. "We have been staying at your house. We hope you don't mind, but we want you to come look if you like the changes," Amanda tells both the brothers.

They follow the girls to their home; once there, the girls stop them at the door. "We hope you like it," they say together. Mount and Marc walk into a whole new house; it is clean and has flowers and places to sit down on. Then they follow Amanda and Amy to the sleep rooms; their clothes are clean and folded. They smell nice and now have a place to lie down for two. The girls lead them to the last room, which now has a wooden tub with water being heated for a bath.

Hem makes his way through the people and arrives home, where his father is waiting. Ebert is in the prayer room. "Welcome home, son. Come join me," he tells Hem, who sits next to his father. "Jax came back with Gamble and his family, saying you found the evil sorceress and her army of barbarians," Ebert says.

"Yes, Father," Hem tells him and explains what they did when they went back to the city. "How will we protect ourselves from such a large army?" Hem asks.

"Pray, my son," Ebert says.

Back at Mount and Marc's house, they have undressed and gotten into the warm water. They are lying back, relaxing for the first time since the bathhouse at Cobble City. The twins come in with clean clothes, and each shaves and washes her man. The men sit back in the tub. "Can you believe we have those two beautiful girls as our personal servants?" Marc asks.

Mount sits back. "I can really get used to this," he tells his brother with a smile on his face.

The brothers finally get out, get dressed, and find the twins waiting for them to go to the celebration. They get to the celebration and find Jax with Angel, and they have a place for them to sit next to them. Mount and Marc notice they seem close with each other. They each pat Jax on his back. "Good job," Marc tells him. Just as it is time to be served, Hem comes and joins them all as his dad goes to sit with Dorn and Gamble and their wives.

Now that everyone is at the dinner celebration, Dorn stands and gets everyone's attention. "We are here tonight to celebrate the return home of Ebert's son and that of my sons. While they were gone, they—thanks to Ebert's extraordinary son—found and met our new friends, Gamble and his family. Unfortunately, it was under a bad situation. The barbarians from Hem's visions attacked and took their home from them, and it is up to us to help them get it back and keep the barbarians from coming here and taking or home."

The people stand and cheer for Dorn as he walks over to where Jax, Hem, and his sons are sitting. "I have full trust these four men have the courage and wisdom to defeat this powerful army." The people cheer louder as Dorn has them all stand up.

Mount walks to his father. "I promise to you, Father, and all of you people that have always been family to us that we will figure out how to defeat the barbarians and their evil sorceress they call their queen!" Mount yells to the people.

Mount pats each one on the back as the people start chanting his name. Dorn quiets the people down. "Everyone has been working on a feast for our sons' return home so everyone can enjoy the meal and celebrate their return," Dorn tells everyone.

The men sit and enjoy their meal as they enter in small talk about their adventures. Mount asks Jax, "Were you able to make more weapons with the steel rocks you collected?"

"Follow me," Jax tells them all, then leads them to his workshop.

When they get there, Bree is outside, waiting for them. Jax agrees to let Bree stay in his father's empty house. "You settled into your home?" Jax asks Bree.

Bree kneels to them. "Yes, thank you, sir," he says.

Mount walks over to Bree. "Bree, you are a friend, not my servant. There is no need to kneel to any of us," Mount explains to him.

Bree smiles. "I'll try to get used to it, sir," he tells Mount.

"Follow me," Jax tells them and leads them into his workshop, where swords hang on the walls around the room.

Bree is amazed by all the strange shiny objects. "Go ahead and pick one out," Jax tells Bree.

"I can have one?" Bree asks, shocked.

"Any one you want," Jax answers as he points over to the swords.

Bree walks over and looks at all the swords; he picks one up and looks it over. He then starts spinning, twirling, and swinging the sword like no one has ever seen; he then starts to work some punches and kicks, showing off all his moves. "I'm glad you decided to be on our side," Jax says, very impressed.

Mount smiles. "With all the bad that happened, it was a really good thing that we found you, Bree."

"Well, he found us," Marc says, laughing. Then Bree laughs with him, and everyone starts laughing.

"It's been the four of us together since we were kids. I would die for any one of these men, and I hope you will feel the same way one day," Mount tells Bree. "Remember one thing—I respect your life debt with me, but you will never be considered a servant, but only a friend with us," he finishes, and everyone agrees.

"I am the lucky one to have found you wonderful people," Bree says to them all.

"When are we going to go eat? I'm starving!" Marc yells out.

"Sounds good! Everything should be ready by now. Let's go eat," Mount says, and they leave the workshop and go back to the eating area.

The sisters have all their plates ready; even Bree has a plate at the table. The girls join the men, and as they sit and eat, over at the kids' table, some of the kids are trying to get Marc's attention.

Finally, Amy tells Marc, "I think those kids are trying to get your attention."

Mount laughs. "Marc usually sits with the kids when we eat," he tells the girls.

But instead of them laughing, they say, "How sweet! They must have missed you since you've been gone," Amanda tells him.

"You should go over there and talk with them," Amy tells him.

Marc jumps up, runs over to the kids, and starts slapping hands with them.

"He will make a good father one day," Angel tells the twins, and they giggle.

To change the subject, Mount asks the sisters, "How do you like it here since you all have been here?"

"It's been good. Everyone is so nice," Amy says.

"I've really enjoyed being here," Angel says, looking at Jax.

"It's better now that you are back," Amanda tells Mount as she puts her hand over his.

"It's good to be home," Mount says as they stare in each other's eyes.

Then just as each lean in to kiss, Marc comes up and slaps Mount on the back. "I was telling the kids about the game we played. They want to play."

"That's so sweet," Amanda says.

Mount is about to get upset with Marc for ruining his moment with Amanda but says, "Go find a couple of wooden barrels and have Kurt stop helping the women and find something to use for a ball."

As Marc runs off to get Kurt and find the things they need, Mount has the kids follow him out to the empty field outside the gate. He marks the center of the field, then counts off each side and marks where to put the barrels.

Soon, Marc and Kurt come with the barrels and a ball made from some cloth. The kids gather around Mount and Marc as they explain how to play the game. Soon, they divide the kids into two teams, and each brother coaches a team as Kurt takes the ball to the middle. The kids line up and run to the ball; one of the bigger kids gets the ball and drags a couple of smaller kids before they drag him down. He throws the ball to his teammate, and the other boy runs to the barrel and scores.

Mount and Marc have the children play to five; then they call it quits and go join the twins, who have been watching the whole time. They walk back into the village to go sit down, but before they do, Kurt comes to them. "Jax wants everyone to the center of the village to show what he was able to do with the silver rock," he tells them.

So they follow Kurt to the area where Jax and Bree are standing at a large table with different objects covering it and the whole village standing around.

When they get to the front of the crowd, the twins go running to Doris and Missy. "You girls glad my boys are home?" Doris asks the twins as she hugs each one.

Mount and Marc hug their mother, then Missy. "I think you have grown since we've been gone," Marc says to his sister.

"I see you have gotten close to the twins while we've been gone," Mount says to his mother.

"Yes, they told me how you boys saved them, and now they must serve you. I wasn't happy when I was first told," Doris tells her boys.

Mount assures his mother, "I denied Gamble's request, but he would take no for an answer. He made us agree to the arrangement, just the same with our newfound friend, Bree. I saved him as well, and now he won't stop looking after me till he returns the favor."

Doris smiles at her son. "You were just meant to save lives," she tells her son. "But I hope you boys do the right thing and make mates out of those lovely young women. That's why I suggested they stay at your house," she says with a smile.

Jax then gets everyone's attention. "It's time to show all of you what I was able to make from the silver rocks I call steel," he tells the people. Then as Bree picks up different weapons and starts doing demonstrations, Jax tells the people what he calls the weapon and explains the different ways to use it. The people cheer as they go through each one.

Mount goes over to Jax and Bree. "It's a miracle what Jax is able to do with the materials the earth provides," he says to everyone. "This will ensure our victory if anyone comes and tries to take what we've worked so hard to have. Now, everyone, go and enjoy the evening. And again, it is so wonderful to be home!"

Everyone cheers Mount as the crowd of people start celebrating around the village. The four friends stand around the fire when Dorn and Gamble come up to them, calling it a night. They say good night, and the twins go with them to make sure they all get to their homes safe.

They get Gamble to his house, then follow Dorn and Doris to their home. Doris has the girls come in and has Missy get some drinks. They all sit down, and Doris wastes no time. "So my boys seem to really care for you girls," she says to them, and they both quickly confess their love for her sons.

"We wish to make them our mates," Amanda tells Doris.

Doris is happy to hear that. "You beautiful girls have no business being servants to my boys. I will talk to them. They will make you their mates," Doris lets them know.

At Jax's workshop, the men are standing around, talking. "You and Angel seem to have gotten close while we've been gone," Marc says.

Jax smiles. "I'm very fortunate to have met such a goddess. I'm the luckiest man on the earth," he tells Marc.

Angel comes behind Jax. "And I'm the luckiest woman on the earth," she says as she kisses him on the cheek. She then looks at Mount and Marc. "So now that you boys are home, do you plan to be with my sisters or keep them as servants?" she asks them.

"I plan to ask Amy to be my life mate tonight," Marc assures Amy.

Mount looks at Marc but stays silent. "Do you not feel the same about Amanda?" Angel asks Mount.

"I think he's scared," Marc jokes.

Then Mount becomes upset. "I'm not scared," he informs Marc. "Amanda is a wonderful, beautiful woman. I would be a lucky man if she agreed to be my mate," Mount tells them all.

Angel grabs a hold of Jax. "You ready to call it a night?" she says in his ear, then kisses his neck.

Jax looks at his friends. "Well, I think it's late. We're going to bed," he tells them with a smile on his face.

Marc smiles. "I'm tired too. Let's go home, where we both have a beautiful woman waiting for us." He then laughs. "Did I really just say we have women waiting on us at home?"

Mount then laughs. "Let's go home," he tells his brother.

They all tell Jax and Angel good night, then go outside. Bree goes to his new home; and Mount, Marc, and Hem walk to their houses. Hem's house is next to the brothers' house.

Hem says good night and walks into his house; then the brothers start walking toward their house. "I don't know about you, but I really like Amy. I want to be with her. Do you want to be with Amanda?" Marc asks Mount.

Mount is confused; he really does like Amanda. She is perfect. But every night he goes to sleep since they left Cobble City, he can't help but dream of the sorceress Serina; and in the dream, he is making love to her—and worse, he enjoys the dreams.

"The twins are very beautiful. We are very lucky for how we found them and even luckier that Gamble made them our servants. I think he did it so we would end up with them. But it's one good thing that has happened on our quest to save our village."

"You didn't answer my question, bro," Marc tells Mount.

"I do care for Amanda very much. I do want to make her my life mate," Mount tells Marc as they come up to the door of their house.

Marc stops Mount from going in. "Let's make a promise right now that we make them our mates tonight," Marc says as he holds out his hand to his brother.

"Let's do it," Mount says as he shakes his brother's hand; then he opens the door to the house.

When they walk in, they find their house all lit up with candles. They hear Amanda yell out, "Go sit down! Relax, there are drinks waiting for you!"

They go sit down; when they pick up the drinks, they see it's the barbarian drink called wine.

"I swore I'd never drink this stuff again," Mount says to Marc.

Marc smells it. "I don't want to wake up in garbage again." he says.

Then the twins walk in the room; they are both in sexy see-through clothing and fixed up very beautifully. Both brothers, at the same time, take big drinks of the wine as they look at the twins. Amy goes to Marc, and Amanda goes to Mount, and they both start rubbing the men's shoulders as they relax and drink the wine. "This is awesome," Marc moans out.

Just as they both get relaxed, Amanda picks up a jug and fills their mugs back up with wine. Then each girl grabs her man by the hand, and both lead them to their rooms.

Amanda has Mount get out of his clothes and lie down on the bed while she puts out the torch lighting up the room; the only light is a candle she brought with her. Mount is so relaxed being back in his bed after the long journey; then he is taken to heaven when Amanda drops her robe and joins him in bed.

"I have dreamed of this every night we have been apart," Mount tells Amanda as he puts his arms around her. They go into a long passionate kiss. Then in the quiet house, they can hear moans coming from the other room; they both laugh.

"Little brother didn't waste no time," Amanda whispers to Mount. Hearing them gets both very excited. Mount starts kissing Amanda, then starts working down her perfect body, not missing an inch.

Being Mount's first time, for some strange reason, he knows exactly what to do as he stops and slowly kisses her breasts and makes her moan. He then works his way down between her legs; when he kisses her there, she screams out with pleasure, and Mount gets so excited hearing her enjoyment. He soon can't take any more as he moves back up to her and slowly puts his manhood inside her. Amanda digs her nails into Mount's back as he starts moving in and out.

Way into the morning hours, both pairs seem to see who can make more noise as each couple is making love. Finally, the house goes silent as both couples fall asleep from exhaustion.

It's not long, though, that the sun is coming through the window; then not long after that, someone starts knocking at the door. The twins almost run into each other as they both jump up to go see who is at the door. Both go and quickly open the door, trying not to let the noise wake the men; it's Kurt out front.

Kurt smiles and looks down when he sees the girls. "Good morning. I've been sent here by Dorn to have his sons come to his house," Kurt says in a shy voice.

The twins laugh at his shyness. "Thank you, Kurt. We will tell Mount and Marc and have them come there," Amanda tells him, and he gives a nod and goes off running back up the hill to Dorn's house.

Amanda shuts the door. "Should we go wake them and tell them their father has asked for their presence?" Amy asks Amanda.

In Mount's room, he starts to wake up; he stretches as he thinks to himself, *That was the best sleep I've had in forever. Making love to Amanda seemed to stop my dreams of Serina.* Then he thinks of the night before making love to Amanda.

Suddenly, the door opens, and Amanda walks in and sees Mount's bulge under the cover. She smiles as he pretends to be asleep; she walks over to the bed and starts kissing him on his neck. Mount opens his eyes and pulls Amanda up to his lips; they start passionately kissing.

Just as Mount starts trying to remove Amanda's clothes, she grabs his hand. "Kurt was here. He said your father wants to see you at his house," she tells him.

"No!" he cries as he stops pulling on her clothes. "How can I go like this?" He points between his legs.

"If I take care of it, you won't make it to your father's house," Amanda says with a smile on her face.

Mount gets up and gets dressed; they go out of the room and find Marc and Amy in the sitting room, kissing like teenagers. "Good morning!" Mount yells.

"How was your all's night?" Mount asks.

"Well, from the sound of things, just as good as yours was, I guess I could say," Marc says.

Amanda goes to Mount and puts her arms around him. "Well, maybe not that good," Amanda says, smiling.

"Better," Amy says, then goes back to kissing Marc.

"You girls want to accompany us to our dad's house?" Mount asks the twins.

"Yes," they both say.

"Let us get ready real fast," Amanda tells Mount.

"That's fine. Marc and I can take the wolves out and check on the horses."

Amanda smiles. "That sounds fun. We will get ready and meet you in the fields before we go to your father's house," she tells him, then kisses him long and hard on the lips.

Marc runs over to Amy. "I want one," he tells her; then they start kissing as well.

After a minute, Amanda is the one who stops with Mount; then she pulls Amy out of the room. "We'll meet you in the fields," she says as they disappear.

Mount goes to the door. "Let's go, boys!" he yells, and Maverick with Rowdy go running out the door behind him.

The brothers go by Hem's house, and Marc screams, "You in there, Hem?" Both men stop looking at Hem's house.

Then the door opens, and out walks Hem. "Good morning. You both on your way to your father's house?" Hem asks as he walks up.

"We are going to the fields to check on the horses while the wolves play," Marc answers him.

"You both know your dad will be furious if we don't get there soon," Hem warns them.

"Come on, Hem. I want Bree to be there. He knows more about Serina and her barbarians than anyone here," Mount tells Hem.

"Well, let's hurry. Get Bree, check on the horses, and get up the hill to your dad's house. My father and Gamble are waiting as well," Hem says as he starts walking faster toward Bree's house.

Before they reach the house, they find Bree out front helping Jax with something he was working on. Bree turns. "Good morning, my friends. Can I do anything for you this morning?" he asks as he lowers his head.

"No, Bree, and stop doing that. It's not necessary," Mount tells him.

Jax laughs. "Here, you are just one of the guys," he tells Bree.

"There is one thing. Come with us to our leaders' meeting. We really could use your wisdom on the barbarians," Mount tells Bree.

"First, we are going to see the horses in the field," Marc says to make it clear to everyone.

"Last one to the field cleans up horse crap," Mount tells Marc, then takes off running. Then all the men take off running after Mount and leave Marc standing there.

Everyone gets to the field, and soon, Marc comes running up last as the others laugh at him for being last. "The girls even beat you here," Mount tells Marc as he shows they are behind him.

Amy goes to him. "When you clean up the horses' poop, go take a bath," she says, then kisses him.

"The horses are doing great. They are all happy here in the fields. The wolves are in the shade. We'd better get to your dad's house," Hem tells the brothers.

Marc grabs him by the head. "Don't worry," he says.

Mount laughs as Marc rubs Hem's hair. "Kurt went to tell Father we would be there soon. It will be okay," Mount tells Hem.

"Let's go, boys. No need to keep your father waiting just to bug Hem," Amanda tells them both.

"Yes, Mama," Marc says. As they start walking back into the village, he whispers to Mount, "They know us so well. We may be in trouble."

Jax hears Marc and laughs. "If they are like their sister, you are in trouble," he says; then he feels a smack across his head.

"I heard that!" Angel says as she comes up.

Jax turns. "Good morning, my love," he says as he kisses her on the lips. "I only meant that in the best way," he tells Angel.

"Follow us. We are going to my parents' house on the hill," Mount tells Angel.

They all make their way up the steep hill to the large house. Dorn had his house built on top so he could always look over the village. They get to the top, and Mount slowly opens the door. Marc steps in his way.

"Ladies first," he says to Mount as he opens the door and lets the sisters walk in first.

"Thank you," they each say as they go in.

"There you boys are! Your father's waiting for you in his meeting room," Doris says as they all come in.

The men go into the room and find Dorn, Ebert, and Gamble with a few other elders of the village sitting at the large table in the room.

Dorn stops talking and looks over to his sons. "Glad you boys could find the time to come here," he says very sternly to both.

"Sorry, Father," they both say to him.

"I wanted Bree to be here for anything said. He knows what we are up against," Mount tells his father.

Melton, the elder over growth of all the fruits and vegetables, tells Dorn, "Give the boys a break. They have been gone a long time, and if they agree, they will be gone longer."

"Agree to what?" Mount asks them.

Dorn looks at all the boys. "Sit down, all of you. It's time for each one of you to know where you come from," he tells them all.

They all sit down at the table as Dorn stands and walks to the front. "It is such a good thing to see that you all have become so close to each other growing up. I'm sure you have realized that each of you seems different from each other," he tells them and starts walking around the table till he gets to Bree. "I'm not sure you realized it, but we have been talking with Bree for most the morning. He has told us all about the sorceress and about just how large her army of barbarians is," he says, patting Bree on his back.

Then Dorn looks back at the others. "Ebert and I have discussed what to do, and we have come up with a way to stop the barbarians," he tells them, and they all look with attention. "I came from a far-off land from a group of people that call themselves Gargantuans. I had a fallout with my people and left my home with your mother and a few others. On our journey to find a new home, I met your father, Jax. He was also kicked out of his village, and he and your mother came with us," he tells everyone.

"Then I met them coming from our home, Hem. We are called Timberlands, and our people live in the Timberland Forest. We live way above in the giant trees," Ebert tells Hem.

"Well, that sounds neat. I would like to go meet them. But how is knowing all this going to help us defeat the barbarians?" Mount asks his father.

"You four will go to each of your homelands. You will talk with each one and get them to help with our fight against this large army."

"Another trip away from home? We just got here!" Marc cries out.

Mount shuts him up. "This could work with three groups of people, Jax's inventions, and Hem's special abilities. We could have a good chance of defeating them and driving them out of Gamble's home!" Mount agrees with his father. "So do we all agree to go find our people and ask them for help?" Mount asks them.

"I agree," Jax says.

"I agree," Hem says.

Marc looks at Amy, then Mount. "Can the twins go?" he asks.

"It would be best, my sons. It never hurts to have a woman's influence when you're trying to win people over," Dorn tells them.

"Yes!" Marc screams and goes out of the room to go tell Amy.

Ebert laughs. "When I met your mother, I would do anything for her," he tells Hem.

"I still do," Dorn says, laughing, and everyone laughs with him. "So it's settled. Ebert and I will draw out maps for you to each place, and I have a map that Jax's father drew long ago. That will be the hard one. He said it's hidden in the canyons," Dorn says.

Doris comes in the room. "It will be time to eat soon, men," she tells them.

"Good timing. We will go eat. Then while you boys get ready for your journey, we will get those maps ready so you can leave in the morning," Dorn tells Mount.

"I will have us ready to leave, and I will come home with an army of our own, I promise," he tells his father, then turns to Gamble. "And I promise we will get your city back for you," he says to him.

Gamble stands, then hugs Mount. "Thank you," he says.

They all then go out of the room to the sitting room, where Marc is with the twins and Angel. "Are we really going with you on your journey?" Amanda asks Mount.

"Yes, we would like if all three of you will go with us to find each of our people so we can talk them into helping us defeat the barbarians and get your home back," Mount answers.

Amanda hugs him. "This will be so wonderful! We will take care of all the cooking and packing," she tells Mount.

"You girls are the best thing that has ever happened to us! But right now, let's go eat lunch," Mount says.

"Yes, let's go! I'm starving," Marc says, and they all leave the house and make their way down the hill to the eating area.

The women get the food as the men go sit down; then as they are eating, Gamble stands. "I want to say I feel it was meant to be for those barbarians to take our city so we could meet you wonderful people. I just want to thank you all for wanting to help us get our home back," he says.

The people all around clap for Gamble; then everyone enjoys a good meal as they talk among one another. Once they are done eating, Jax stands. "I want to show you what I was working on with Bree early this morning," he tells them all.

They all say their goodbyes and go to Jax's workshop; they go inside and find the cart they took on the trip, but now instead of being tied up with rope, it has been put together with steel spikes and has seats built on it with a long wood pole to attach the horses to.

"Nice work," Mount tells Jax as he walks around, looking at the wagon. "This will work perfectly," he says as he looks it over.

"I built it so four horses can pull it easily," Jax says, smiling at his work. "We should take all the weapons we can carry. I haven't been very far in the direction we will travel. A lot of scavengers are in the area. I never took the chance on them following me back here," he informs them all.

Marc laughs. "I hope we do run into some scavengers. I will take them by myself," he says, flexing.

The door opens, and the three sisters walk in. "There's my man," Amy says as she goes to Marc, feeling his muscles.

Amanda goes to Mount. "Your mother wouldn't let us help with cleanup because we are leaving, so we went and packed up our clothes for the trip," she tells him.

"And I have our clothes ready as well," Angel tells Jax as she leans in for a kiss.

Jax has Angel climb into the wagon and sit in the seat to see if it was comfortable. Amanda starts helping the men load up weapons. She picks up a sword, walks behind Mount, and pokes him in the butt; he jumps, and everyone laughs. Mount picks up a sword. "You want some of this?" he says, holding up the sword. Amanda swings her sword and knocks his sword out of his hand. Everyone cheers for Amanda as Mount, a little embarrassed, picks up his sword. She again tries to knock it out of his hand, but this time, Mount is ready and blocks her swing. He then strikes at Amanda, and like a pro, she blocks his attack.

As Amanda swings back, Mount is very impressed. "Seems I won't have to worry about you on our trip," he says to her as he blocks her swings. Mount has never felt feelings like he was feeling just then. *She is the one*, he thinks.

While he is thinking, it is enough for Amanda to knock his sword out of his hand and point the sword at his chest. Mount is almost in shock as everyone in the room is cheering Amanda on; but Mount quickly takes her sword, swipes her feet, and pins her down, kissing her.

Amanda pulls away. "Now that you got me, what are you going to do with me?" she says as she runs her hand down to his crotch. Mount smiles, then goes to kiss her again; she squeezes his crotch as hard as she could squeeze. He rolls away in pain as Amanda gets her sword and points it at Mount. "Now what should I do with you?" she asks.

"Take me home to bed," Mount answers, and Amanda smiles.

"That will be the perfect punishment," she says and starts leading him out the door. "See you all in the morning."

Marc laughs. "She has made Mount a totally different man," he tells everyone.

Jax and Hem agree. "In a good way," Hem says.

Amy punches Marc. "Have I changed you?" she says.

"I know I'm ready to catch up with them and do what they are doing," Marc tells her as he kisses her.

"Sounds good to me," Angel says to Jax.

Hem and Bree laugh as the two couples leave. "I'm happy for my friends, but I hope they can keep their focus on the mission," Hem tells Bree.

"Mount is a good man, very smart. But love is a very powerful thing," Bree assures Hem.

Hem agrees that Mount is a good leader, then changes the subject. "Would you like to go with me to tell the horses and wolves about the journey we are going on?" Hem asks Bree.

"Yes, I would be glad to," Bree answers.

"Excellent! You need to get used to the horses. While we are there, you can pick one to ride on for the journey and name him if you would like," Hem lets Bree know as they go toward the fields.

Hem and Bree go to the fields; as they investigate the distance, they can see all the horses in the fields and at the stream while the wolves are running through the grass, chasing and playing with one another. Hem closes his eyes; he can feel the happiness in all the animals as they enjoy their new home. He then uses his powers to call all the animals to where he stands with Bree; from every direction, the animals come running to where they stand.

Bree steps back behind Hem, still nervous around the wolves. Hem laughs. "It's okay. They won't hurt you. They love to be petted," he tells Bree, who slowly walks over to Rowdy and puts his hand out. Rowdy sniffs his hand and then pushes Bree's hand with his head; then Bree starts rubbing his head, seeing the enjoyment on Rowdy's face. Then all the wolves come over, begging for his attention. Bree pets each wolf as Hem tells the story of how the wolves became part of their lives.

"Rowdy is Marc's protector, Maverick is Mount's, Charm is Jax's, Woe is my dad's, Desire is Dorn's." Then he walks over to Savvy. "And this is my protector, Savvy," he tells Bree. Bree is very impressed with Hem and his special gift. "Come now. Other horses have joined ours. You can pick one to ride and give the animal a name. They seem to like that," Hem tells Bree. As he did with the wolves, he again tells the story of how he befriended the horses and how each of them has a horse to ride.

Bree goes to the horses and starts to pet them. All the horses that have no human seem to come to him, hoping he will pick them to ride. Hem laughs as he hears the horses fighting over Bree's attention. Then from the center of the pack walks out a beautiful smoky gray horse with a white mane; then it bumps Bree with his snout. Bree turns around, laughing. "Hello there," he says, and the horse licks him on his face. Bree pets his face.

"I think he likes you," Hem says.

Bree jumps on its back. "What now?" he asks.

"Give it a small kick in the side and hang on!" Hem screams at Bree as he almost falls off when the horse takes off running. The horse takes Bree across the field; it doesn't take Bree any time to get used to being on the horse as he gets it to turn around and run back to where Hem is.

"That was the greatest feeling ever!" Bree yells to Hem as he goes back to where Hem is standing.

"I had a feeling you would enjoy riding him. He wants to know his name," Hem says.

"I will call him Bronco," Bree says as he pets the horse's head.

Hem goes to the horse. "He wants to call you Bronco," he tells the horse. It nods his head, letting them both know he likes his name. "Bree and Bronco, they go well together!" Hem laughs.

Bree jumps off Bronco as Hem calls all the animals to the center of the field. He tells them of the long journey they will accompany the humans on; he tells the horses that will stay to help with the farming and tells the wolves they will all go.

"The journey is in the direction no one has ever been, so no one knows what they will come across," Hem tells the wolves.

Maverick steps up. "It will be our pleasure to go with you all on your journey, and we will protect all of you humans," he lets Hem know.

"Thank you," Hem tells Maverick.

Then from a distance, they can hear the children running through the village, yelling, "Time to eat!" Hem and Bree leave the animals to rest up for the journey in the morning.

Bree and Hem slowly make their way to the eating area; as they look around, they see most people are eating. Just a few are in line; but nowhere to be seen are Jax, the brothers, and the three sisters. So Hem and Bree get their food and go sit with the elders. They all make small talk about where Mount and Marc are and what they are doing. Everyone finishes; and Dorn, Ebert, and Gamble leave to go finish the maps for the boy's journey in the morning. Hem and Bree go back to the fields as Bree tells Hem of his life.

"My people live where it is necessary to be able to defend yourself. At one time, my people were getting killed by other tribes. My grandfather believed the creator would show him the way. As he prayed to him, the fighting style came to him quickly. He showed it to the other males of our tribe, and they were soon able to drive off the attacks and take back their lands. Now my tribe, when I last was there, is the most powerful tribe in the lands." Bree then starts doing kicks and punches for Hem.

From inside the village, kids come running out to the fields to watch Bree do his moves. Soon, the kids are cheering and trying to copy what he is doing. Both Bree and Hem start playing with the kids. "Show them something," Bree tells Hem.

"I'm not sure what to do," Hem says. Then he smiles and holds out his arms at his sides; he closes his eyes, then starts to glow as he rises into the air. Bree is very impressed as he watches Hem float in the air; the kids all cheer for Hem.

Hem descends back to the ground. "Go ahead, try to attack me," Hem tells Bree.

"I couldn't hit you," Bree says to him.

"Kick me then. You won't hurt me, I promise," Hem says, confident of himself.

Bree backs up, then runs at Hem. When he jumps to kick him, Hem forms his force field; and Bree hits it and falls to the ground as Hem stands, not hurt. "That's handy," Bree says, getting up off the ground. The kids are now surrounding Hem, wanting to see more; he then calls the horses over for them to pet.

Bree looks at Hem. "You are a very impressive man," he tells him as he helps a smaller kid pet one of the horses.

Then from the village, Kurt comes running out and approaches Hem. "Dorn and your father have the maps ready. They have asked for you to come to his house with the others," he tells Hem.

"Thank you, Kurt. Now go tell Jax, and Bree and I will go get Mount and Marc. Then we will meet you at Dorn's house," Hem tells Kurt.

Kurt nods his head and goes off out of the fields, back to the village toward Jax's house.

Hem and Bree leave the fields, go through the village, and make their way to Mount and Marc's house. Hem goes to the door. But before he knocks, the door opens, and Mount is there. "Do our fathers have the maps ready?" he asks.

"That's why I'm here. Kurt told me they want us back at your father's house. They must be done," Hem answers Mount.

From inside the house, Amanda's voice is heard. "Let's go, you two! Mount is waiting." Then from behind Mount come the twins with Marc behind them.

Mount shuts the door, and as they start walking toward the hill, they hear, "Wait up, y'all!" They turn around to see Jax, Angel, and Kurt walking toward them from the distance. They wait for them to catch up, then make their way up the hill again to Dorn's house.

Mount opens the door, and they all go in; this time, Mount tells the girls to join them in the other room. They all go in to the room to find Dorn, Ebert, and Gamble sitting at the table, talking.

"There you all are," Dorn says.

Everyone sits down, and Dorn shows them the maps. "Between us, we have drawn out the way to all three of these villages."

"You will get to the Timberlands first. It's deep in the woods, and their homes are up high in the trees," Ebert tells them. "Then you will follow the woods till the end. Then you will come across a huge set of canyons. The Dales' village is hidden in the canyons. That's all we can tell you. Then you will go out of the canyons and travel till the land turns to water. This is where the Gargantuans live."

"We can only wish you luck. None of us left our people under good terms, so it will be a very difficult task for you to convince them to come help us fight," Dorn tells them.

Mount stands. "I give my word to you, Father, we will convince them to help us no matter what it takes."

Then he holds out his hand for each man to take; they all stand and join their hands with Mount's. "We give our word," they all say together.

Then Ebert gives a prayer to the creator to guide and help their boys on their journey.

Mount then stands. "We all need to go get rest so we can leave at the break of dawn," he tells the elders. They all say their goodbyes and leave the house. "We will meet at the workshop at sunup," Mount tells them.

"So much for getting used to being home," Marc tells them, and they all laugh.

"We must do what it takes to defeat the barbarians and their evil leader," Mount tells Marc.

"I just hope we can convince all three groups of people to come help us," Hem says.

"We will," Mount tells him, putting his arm around him.

CHAPTER 6

The Start of Their Quests

FINALLY, AFTER A long trip back home, the barbarians come out of the mountains and can see Cobble City. Slowly, they make their way to the city. Now in fear, they go through the city to the castle, where Serina's chambers are. When they get to the front of the castle, they find Boar and Ace waiting for them. All four men go to their knees. "I'm sorry, sir, we failed you." Boar looks at the bruised and beat me up; then he sees Viper holding his arm with his hand missing.

"What the hell happened to you men?" Boar screams.

"We are so sorry. They were ready for us, like they knew we were going to attack!" Cobra cries out.

"It was that wizard. He saw you coming," Boar tells them.

"We had the slave attack, but then he turned on us and helped them. And then the one called Maverick pulled out a shiny weapon none of us have ever seen and cut Viper's hand off like it was nothing," Cage tells Boar.

"The vicious animals that seemed to listen to the wizard didn't help matters," Tyke says.

Boar screams and punches the wall. "I should have gone with you men! I blame myself," he says to them. "I will lead an army to hunt those bastards down and kill them one by one as they watch each other die!" Boar yells to the men. "Now the queen already knows you men failed. She is waiting for you. I will do what I can to keep you men alive. Now follow me," he says, then starts walking into the castle. Scared and tired, the men follow Boar and Ace to Serina's chambers.

As they walk in, Ace turns to them. "Keep your heads down and don't look her in the eyes," he warns them.

They stand and wait with Ace as Boar goes into her private room. It doesn't take long for him to return with Serina; she doesn't say a word. Instead, she walks over to the men and holds her hand up; with her powers, she picks up all four men into the air. Then when she moves her arm forward, the men fly across the room and slam into the wall. "How could you fail me?" she screams as the men fall to the ground.

"I should execute each one of you slowly," Serina tells them as she starts to use her powers.

Boar stops her. "My queen, let's not kill them just yet. We may need them later. You haven't even read one of their minds to see what did happen," he tells Serina.

Serina walks over to Viper and places her hand on his shoulder; as she closes her eyes, she goes into a vision, seeing Bree attack Maverick, then how he turns and helps them defeat her barbarians. Then she sees the strange weapon that cuts off Viper's hand.

Serina opens her eyes, then pushes Viper to the floor with disgust. "I should have sent more men. I had no idea how useless you men are!" she screams as she goes to kill Viper.

Boar stops her again. "My queen, we need these men. They can help with hunting down the wizard and his men with a larger group of men, and then we will destroy them and that traitor slave, if he is still with them."

Serina stops and starts to think, then looks at Boar. "Yes, we need to find them and kill them," she says. "For some reason, I can't seem to locate them. I think the wizard is blocking my powers," she finishes telling him.

Then Serina turns to the four men. "Fine, I haven't killed anyone lately. But I'll let you live so you can go back where you lost the fight, and you track down where the wizard and his men went and where they live," she tells them.

"Thank you, my queen," they all say to her as Boar and Ace get them up and start pushing them out the door.

"Don't come back without knowing where they ended up!" she warns them.

They all get out to the main hall of the castle. "I thought you were going to help!" Cage screams at Boar.

Boar grabs him by his throat. "You're alive, aren't you? You easily could have been dead!" he tells him. Boar lets him go and starts walking out of the castle to the streets with the men behind him.

Cage catches his breath. "We might as well be dead! We just got home, and now we have to leave!" he cries out.

Boar starts getting upset with Cage. "Stop your whining, or I will kill you!" he screams at him. "Besides. Cobra is the best tracker ever." He turns to Cobra. "Can you find the wizard and his men?" he asks Cobra.

Cobra looks at them with a cocky expression on his face. "I'll find them no matter where they went. Don't worry, boys," he says with confidence.

The men get to the building where the food is served. "If I were you men, I would enjoy a good meal and find a female slave to be with for the night." Ace laughs at them.

They get their food and sit at a table; a slave girl comes around and fills their mugs with wine. Boar holds up his mug. "Safe journey on your quest. Come home alive!" Boar yells out to them, and they all raise their mugs, then drink. They spend the evening eating and drinking wine. Soon, they have women surrounding them, and they just had a party for their return home and now one for their new journey and safe passage home.

Mount awakes to an empty bed, wondering what happened to Amanda. He gets up and goes through the house to find no one; he goes to Marc's room. "Wake up, Marc. Is Amy with you?" he asks.

In a grumpy voice, Marc yells out, "No!"

"Well, get dressed and let's go find them!" Mount yells back at him.

Marc gets up, and the brothers go outside. Maverick and Rowdy come running, happy to see their humans; both Mount and Marc pet their wolves. "Can you find the women?" Marc asks the wolves.

Rowdy starts sniffing in the air, then howls and takes off running. "Let's go!" Marc yells to Mount.

The wolves take them to the eating area, where the men can see lights inside the building. They get to the building, go inside, and find the twins with Angel and their mother. "There are my lazy boys," Doris says as they walk in.

"Good morning, Mom," both the boys say to her.

Then both go to their girls and kiss them. "I wondered what happened to you," Mount says to Amanda.

"What are you all doing?" Marc asks as he grabs a piece of meat.

Doris smacks his hand. "This is for your journey. You can eat before you leave," she scolds Marc.

Angel changes the subject, saying, "Jax is in his workshop. He has been working with Bree all night," she tells Mount and Marc.

"We should go see if they need any help," Mount tells Marc, then turns to Amanda and kisses her again.

"We will finish here, then bring the food there to pack up for our trip," Amanda tells him.

Both men leave the women and go to Jax's workshop, where Jax and Bree are working on the straps to tie the horses up with. Hem is watching them work, sitting in the driver's seat of the wagon. "Finally, I thought you two changed your minds!" Jax yells out as he sees them come in.

"Funny!" Marc barks at Jax.

"You boys ready for an adventure?" Hem asks them as he pretends to lead the horses. Mount laughs, looking at Hem.

"I'm ready!" Marc yells out.

"How's everything look, Bree?" Jax asks him.

"I think we are ready," Bree tells him.

"Good, let's push it out front and hook up the horses," Jax says.

Except for Hem, everyone gets behind the wagon to push; as they do, Hem yells out, "Push!" When they get out front, Hem calls the horses from the field. In a few seconds, the horses come running into the village. Jax and Hem start tying the horses to the front of the wagon while Mount and Marc load supplies.

To help the women out, they take the wagon to the food building and help the girls load up the food into the wagon. "That's everything,"

Mount says as they load the last of the food into the wagon. "Let's take the wagon to the front of the village. Then we will eat before we leave," he tells them all.

When they get back to the eating area, all the people are there to wish them well on their journey. They quickly eat and say their goodbyes; then the women get in the wagon as the men ride separately on their horses.

Everyone follows them out of the village, and they start in the direction toward the Timberland Forest. Once they get away from the village, Hem calls for the wolves. "Go ahead and clear the way of any dangerous animals," he tells the pack. They run ahead, sniffing in the wind, looking for any trouble. They start quickly traveling some distance. Mount thinks that at the pace they are going, they could be there in a day or two.

At Cobble City, the sun is rising. Cobra wakes up, pushing the slave girl off him as he looks around for the others; he gets up, finding his clothes. Once dressed, he sees Cage lying in the floor. He kicks him hard in the back. Cage screams. "Get up, you lazy ass! If we are not out of the city when it's fully light, she will kill us!" Cobra screams at Cage.

Cobra goes into the next room to find Viper up and getting dressed. "I heard you," he says.

Tyke comes in the door. "I have food ready to take with us. Let's get out of here," he says.

As they are about to leave, Hex comes up to them. "Boar wants me to make sure you men are out of the city and tells you all good journey," he tells them as they go running through the city.

The four men get the food Tyke packed and grab extra weapons as they leave the city and start walking toward the mountains. "Well, we're alive. So what do we do now?" Cage asks.

"We go back to where we last left them. Most likely, we can find prints off the animals and go from there," Tyke tells Cage.

The day has gone by fast; it has been a beautiful day. The sun has been shining all day, so they have been able to travel a greater distance than Mount ever thought they would cover. He rides up to the wagon, where Amanda was sitting. "Want a ride?" he asks her.

Amanda says nothing; she stands up, and without hesitation, she jumps right into Mount's arms on to Stallion. She turns and sits in front of Mount. "Hold on," she says before getting Stallion to take off running.

The wolves run with Stallion as they cross the field. Bree comes riding up on Bronco; then Marc on Colt comes running up. Soon, they are racing across the field. They get to the top of a hill, and they all stop as they look at the largest set of woods that seem to go as far as they could see. Soon, Hem comes to the top of the hill, with Angel behind him guiding the horses up the hill. Once Hem gets to the top, he stares off into the distance, looking at the deep, dark forest.

After a few minutes go by, Mount rides up next to him. "Are you okay, Hem?" he asks.

Hem looks over at Mount. "I'm not alone," he says to Mount. "I can feel their powers. They know we are coming," he tells them all.

They start slowly riding toward the forest. "I always wondered if there were others like me. I'm finally going to learn why I am how I am," Hem tells Mount as they get closer to the giant trees, which seem to get larger and larger as they get closer.

"When we enter the forest, everyone be on guard. I can feel someone there watching us right now," Hem warns them all. "Stay with us. Don't run ahead," he tells the wolves. "I can feel they are not used to having strangers come into the woods. They may try to attack. We must not kill anyone. We need to try to let them know we come in peace and don't want any trouble," Hem tells them.

"I won't hurt nobody. But if they come at me, I might have to hurt them a little," Marc says, laughing.

"I can't believe this is where I'm from. I wonder if I'll meet anyone that remembers my mother. Dad would never talk about her much. It always seemed to upset him, so I never would push him to talk about her," Hem tells Mount.

Mount starts to think about how soon they will be at his people's home; he will be just as excited, but they've never met these people. "I know this must be exciting for you, but let's be careful. They may be your people, but they are strangers," Mount warns Hem as they get there.

CHAPTER 7

The Timberlands

DEEP INSIDE OF a large dark forest and up at the top of the biggest, tallest trees is a magical, beautiful city. The spirits of the forest made the city for the people so they would be safe from any attacks from outsiders and from the dangerous wild animals that live in the forest. The spirits watch over the people of the Timberlands, and certain people can pull and use the powers of the spirits. Most of the people can't use the powers of the spirits; they use a weapon made from wood that shoots sharpened arrows, which is called a bow.

The best warrior and best shot with a bow is a man called Fierce; he is the leader of the Timberlands warriors. He has been summoned by Coral; she is very strong in using the spirits' energy and is second-in-command. "You called for me?" he says as he enters the room of the leaders.

Coral is there sitting with the others who make the decisions. "Yes, thank you for quickly getting here, Fierce. I have seen strangers at the entrance of the forest. One seems to be able to pull energy from the spirits," she says.

"He is trying to block my visions. His powers are strong for an outsider. I must know who he is," she tells Fierce. "Take your men. You will find them at the start of the woods. They seem to be looking for us, so make sure they find us. Go now," she commands Fierce.

"I will be back soon with all of them captured," he tells Coral, then leaves to gather his men. Coral goes back to check if she can see more in her visions.

Back at the start of the woods, Mount has found an opening large enough to get the wagon through.

Hem closes his eyes as he feels Coral trying to read his thoughts; he tries to reverse it on her so he could read her thoughts. But Coral's power has intensified, and she easily blocks Hem from seeing anything. Hem opens his eyes and rides over to Mount. "Someone is trying to get inside my head. Whoever it is, their powers are way stronger than mine. We need to be very careful."

They have the horses slowly walk as they get deeper into the forest; the wolves suddenly stop and start growling. Hem stops the horses and motions everyone to be quiet. "We are not alone," he quietly tells them. Then as soon as he said the words, an arrow flies just past his head and hits the tree next to him.

"Stay right there, or the next one won't miss," says a voice that seems to be coming from high above them.

The wolves look up into the trees and start growling and barking. Hem quiets them down. "Hello! We are friends! We mean you no harm! We just need to talk with your leader!" Mount yells up into the trees.

Then from one of the trees comes a man flying down, holding on to a vine; he lands down on the ground in front of all the strangers. Then from the trees all around them come men holding bows with arrows pointed at all of them. Fierce pulls his bow and points an arrow straight at Mount's head. "What brings you people inside our forest?" he asks Mount.

Mount holds his hands up. "We are here to ask for your people's help. We want no trouble. You can lower your weapon," he tells Fierce.

Fierce laughs, and all his men in the tree join him laughing. "Why would we help you? It would be best if you turn around and leave our forest," Fierce warns them.

Mount jumps off Stallion; when he does Fierce shoots his arrow, just missing Mount's head. "The next one is between your eyes," he says, pulling out another arrow.

Mount becomes upset. "We are here to warn you people of a great danger!" he yells to them all, and again, they all start laughing.

"We fear no danger. We are protected by the spirits of the forest. No one can hurt us inside these woods," he tells Mount.

Hem jumps off Pinto and walks toward them. Fierce points his arrow at Hem. "Stop right there!" he tells Hem, and when Hem doesn't stop, he shoots his arrow. Hem holds up his hand and forms his energy shield, which seems stronger; the arrow hits the shield and falls to the ground. Fierce can't believe his eyes. "How did you do that?" he asks Hem.

Hem holds up his hands in the air. "My name is Hem! My father's name is Ebert. He once lived here. I believe I am part of your people!" Hem yells to Fierce.

Fierce gets extremely upset. "You are no Timberland!" he screams, then shoots his arrow straight at Hem.

Hem isn't ready; he can't form his shield. Then right before the arrow hits him, it stops. Bree flipped off Bronco, landed in front of Hem, and caught the arrow with his hand; he looks at Fierce as he breaks the arrow over his knee.

"That's enough!" he yells at Fierce, but that only angers Fierce even more; he pulls an arrow and shoots it at Bree, who flips in the air. The arrow flies by under him; he then does a flying jump kick at Fierce, which sends him to the ground. The other warriors come out of the trees with their bows aimed at Bree, but before they can shoot, Bree quickly puts the men to the ground.

Marc yells out, "Yeah, Bree! You are the greatest!" He pulls out his sword to help Bree.

Fierce slowly gets up. "You got lucky, stranger. Bring it on!" he screams at Bree.

Then comes a loud scream. "Stop!" From the trees come four women floating down; they are the councilors of the people. Coral is the head councilor; she is the one who yelled. They land on the ground, surrounding Mount, Marc, Hem, and Bree. The wolves come growling at them. Coral holds up her hand, and the wolves cower down, whining.

Hem becomes upset. "Stop that! They mean you no harm." Then he blocks her powers.

Shocked, Coral fires an energy ball at Hem, and he blocks it with his energy shield. Then she lowers her hand. "Who are you?" she asks. Then she thinks of the leader of the Timberlands, Shaman; he has turned evil and has done something to the spirits of the forest. The prophecy says a stranger will come and bring peace back to the forest. *He cannot find out about this*, Coral thinks to herself. The other consolers sense her thoughts as she looks at Hem.

Hem is mesmerized by Coral; he can't believe there are others like him and one so beautiful. He walks closer to Coral. "You have such control of your powers. I have trouble controlling mine at times," he says to her.

The young women behind Coral laugh as she is not sure what to say to him. "Our people draw the energy from the spirits of the woods. Not all can, and more women than men can pull the energy in," she explains to Hem.

"That's how I got powers," he says to her.

"You must have Timberland blood if you can pull the spirits' energy," Coral tells him, confused. "Where did you all come from?" she asks them again.

Hem looks at her. "Take my hand," he tells her as he holds it out. Knowing she will see his memories, Coral grabs a hold of Hem's hand and closes her eyes. She sees them in their small village, then how they went to find metal and find Cobble City and save the people, then how they went back to find the barbarians and the evil queen with powerful powers, and then how they fought their way out.

Coral slowly opens her eyes to Hem looking right at her; they lock eyes as neither lets go from holding hands. Then Marc shoves Hem. "You two okay, buddies?" he screams.

They both let go of their hand holding and look away from each other, both a little embarrassed. "We are fine!" Hem snaps at Marc as all the girls around giggle.

Coral gets serious again. "Those people look dangerous. I would love to say we will help, but I'm just councilor. It's not my decision," she says.

"Whose decision is it?" Hem asks her.

Coral looks to her other councilors; she doesn't want Shaman to find out about Hem. He will kill him for sure. "You don't want to meet our leader, Shaman. He will not help you," she tells Hem.

Mount steps in. "We have traveled a long way. We must talk to your leader. We won't go till we talk to him. Please show us where to find him," he tells Coral.

"You become the leader of our people by being the most powerful in using our powers. He won't like you here," she says.

Hem goes closer to Coral. "My father, Ebert, told me he once lived here with my mother. She died shortly after I was born. He says her name was Sara," he tells her. When he says his mother's name, all the councilors gasp and start talking with one another. "Did you all know my mother?" Hem asks them.

Coral quiets the girls. "Yes, I was a small girl, but I do remember your mother and your father," she tells Hem; then she tells the warriors to lower their weapons.

"Your mother was not only head councilor, but the only woman leader our people ever had. It was the most peaceful of times as well," she tells Hem.

"My mother was most powerful? That's nice to know," Hem says, smiling.

Then Blair grabs Coral by the arm. "Should we tell him who we think he is and why he is here?" she quietly asks Coral, then turns, giggling with the other girls.

Hem looks at Coral, curious. "Who do you think I am?" he asks her.

"Our people are in fear of Shaman. He has made our people his slaves, and there is a prophecy that says a stranger that is a great yielder of the powers will come bring peace back to our people," Coral tells him.

Behind them, Marc starts laughing. "You saying Hem is your savior?" he says to Coral.

Suddenly, the wind starts blowing strongly; then from nowhere, a strange black smoke starts to form. All the Timberland people drop to their knees in fear.

When the smoke clears, there stands Shaman; he looks around at the warriors, then at Fierce and then turns to Coral and the other councilors. "So there are strangers in my forest, and I'm not told?" He then turns to the strangers. "Why have you entered my forest?" he asks them.

Hem walks closer to Shaman while Mount, Marc, and Bree join in behind him. "Hello, my name is Hem. I'm the son of Ebert and Sara. We have come to ask for your help," he tells Shaman.

"Ridiculous! The son of Sara died long ago with his mother and father when they betrayed the council," Shaman says with an evil laugh.

"That's a lie!" Hem screams at Shaman, which angers Shaman. He holds out his hand and fires a powerful ball of energy. It hits Hem, Mount, Marc, and Bree; they all fly back into a tree and fall to the ground. Shaman then looks around to Coral and the other girls.

"I know what you're thinking," he says, then turns and walks over to Hem, who is lying on the ground.

"I've heard the whispers. I know of the prophecy Titan told of before the spirits disappeared." Shaman then bends down and pulls Hem up by his hair. "Do any of you really think this kid is your savior?" he asks. "Do you really think this kid can overpower me?" he screams. "Get up and leave my forest or die!" he screams at all of them.

They all stand up, and Hem tries again. "We are not here to fight you. We came to warn you of danger," he tells Shaman.

"The only one in danger is you!" Shaman screams. He then fires another energy ball at Hem, and this time, Hem forms his shield and blocks the ball.

Shaman goes to Fierce. "Kill every one of them, even the women!" he screams at Fierce. Fierce holds up his hand, giving the signal for his men to aim their arrows at the strangers.

"Please don't do this!" Bree pleads with Fierce.

"I have no choice. I'm sorry," he tells Bree.

Coral goes to Shaman. "Stop this now! You cannot kill them!" she yells at him.

"If he is your savior, he will save himself from dying," Shaman tells her.

Coral then claps her hands, and a bright flash blinds Shaman; she then goes to Hem. "You and your friends need to come with me if you want to live," she tells him.

"We are not scared of him. I can take Shaman," Hem tells her.

"Son of Sara, you have the power to defeat Shaman, but you don't know how to use the power. I can take you where you will learn to use it," she assures him.

"We need to go with her," Mount says. Hem agrees.

The girls leave the wagon, and they follow Coral through the woods.

Shaman rubs his eyes, slowly getting his sight back. "Get them!" he screams at the warriors. He stops Fierce. "You stay here. Let them go," he tells him. He then turns to the other councilors and looks at Chantel, who is Coral's younger sister. "I know you two have a connection," he says to her. "Fierce, take her to my chamber cell and lock her in it," he tells him.

Blair and Tia stand in front of Chantel. "There is no need to lock her away. We will go to the councilors' room and stay there till Coral is found," Blair pleads.

Shaman doesn't say a word; he fires an energy ball at them, and they all fall to the ground, stunned. He then turns to Fierce. "Take them all to my chamber cell and lock them in it." He then turns to the woods in the direction they ran; using his powers, he is able to talk with Coral. "I know you hear me, my dear."

She does hear him; she stops everyone and looks at Hem, who hears Shaman too.

"I have the councilors. I locked them away in my chamber cell. They will stay there with no food or water," he tells her.

Coral becomes upset hearing what Shaman has done. "Leave them out of this!" she tells him, but she just hears his evil laugh go through her head.

"Bring me the strangers. You have till sunup tomorrow. If you are not at the top of the trees with the strangers, I will kill all three girls," he tells her.

Coral screams, "NO!"

Hem grabs her in his arms. "I promise that will not happen," he tells her; then he tells all the others what Shaman has done to Coral's sister and other councilors.

Marc looks at his brother. "Let's just go back. We can take them," he says.

Coral stops him. "You must give me till morning to help Hem bring out his powers," she says.

"Can you teach him in one night?" Jax asks her.

"It's up to him and if he can harness the powers of the spirits. We don't know what Shaman did to the spirits, but we can still pull their energy, and it's strongest in the deepest part of the forest," Coral answers him. "We best get moving. Shaman most likely will send men after us," she says.

They move through the heavily wooded area; it seems to get thicker as they move closer toward the center, and the wolves seem to run off more dangerous animals. Then suddenly, it seems to get dark; the trees are so thick. Then all they can hear is a small breeze moving through the trees. Coral then stops them. "We can stop here. We will be safe," she tells them. To be safe, Hem has the wolves patrol the area. Mount, Marc, Bree, and Jax start clearing the area and building a fire.

The sisters start making some food with what they were able to carry as Hem starts questioning Coral. She takes him to the fire and has everyone gather around. "Long ago, when the Timberland people were happy, we were led by a powerful wizard named Volans. He was a very peaceful leader, and at the time, he named your mother head councilor. Then Volans became very old and was dying. Shaman was the next in line to be leader, but Volans saw the evil in Shaman, so he planned to choose your mom," she explains.

"The news was surfacing through the people that Volans planned to choose a woman to lead the people. There were mixed feelings among them, but everyone knew that Shaman was not nice. And Ebert, your father, was not powerful enough to defeat Shaman in the standoff for leadership."

Hem stops Coral. "Why would my father be part of this? He has no powers," he says to her.

Coral shakes her head. "He must hide them from you because it is law that to be with someone who can pull the spirits' powers, you must be one too," she tells Hem.

Hem laughs, thinking back. "That's how he seemed to always know how to teach me things even though he said he doesn't know why I was special," he tells them all.

Coral goes back to her story. "Before Volans could name your mother leader, he died, and Shaman went to the people to name himself leader. But when he did, the people demanded the new leader be Sara. So Shaman challenged your mother to a power standoff, and for the first time, a woman was to compete for leadership of the people," she tells them.

"The challenge was set to take place the next morning, but when the councilors went to get your mother, they found her dead, with your father kneeling over her and covered in her blood. Shaman quickly blamed your father for your mother's death, and they found a club covered in her blood in the same room."

Hem stops Coral. "No, that can't be true!" he yells, then gets up and walks away from them all. Coral runs after him and stops him by grabbing him and holding him in her arms.

Hem lets out a good cry on Coral's shoulder, then pulls his head up. "What happened after that?" he asks her.

"Shaman demanded for your father to be arrested for killing your mother. But before the warriors could get to him, he ran with you. Shaman sent the warriors after you both, and when they returned, they said they had killed the both of you. Thank the spirits that was not true!" she tells Hem.

Mount comes up behind them. "So who did kill Hem's mother, Sara?" he asks her.

"It was left as Ebert being the one who did it, but none of the people ever believed he did it," Coral tells Mount.

Hem pulls away from her. "Shaman must have killed her. I must learn my powers and go confront him. He will tell me the truth," he tells them with a serious look on his face.

"You must go to the thickest part of the woods. Somehow, Shaman has trapped the spirits there, but if you can get there, the spirits should come to you," Coral tells him, pointing the way toward the center.

Hem looks at the thick brush surrounding the tall trees and then looks over at Coral; he then looks back at all his friends. He starts walking toward the brush when Mount stops him. "I can't let you go alone," he tells Hem as he grabs his shoulder.

"He must go alone. He will be fine. The spirits are our protectors. They are the reason we have our power. They would never hurt a human," Coral informs Mount.

"It's okay, Mount. I have to do this. I feel them calling for me," Hem tells him.

Amanda comes behind Mount and pulls his hand off Hem as everyone comes over. "Scream loud, and I will come running!" Marc says.

"We all will come running," Bree follows up.

"Thank you, my friends. I know you will, but I will be fine. I can feel it," Hem tells them, then turns and walks into the thick brush. He hears Coral yelling, "Good luck!" as he enters the brush and disappears.

Hem slowly walks among the trees, getting deeper into the forest till he comes out into a large area clear of trees and brush. He looks around, and it is the most beautiful place he has ever seen—a clear blue spring of water flowing through like it came from nowhere, exotic flowers he never seen before, and small trees with the best-tasting fruits he has ever tried. Hem fills himself up with fruit till he can't eat any more; then he looks around a little bit more, then yells out, "Hello!" He hears some birds flying off; then the sound of the water returns as he looks around.

Hem again yells, "Hello!" He starts thinking to himself, *What am I waiting for? I've never seen any kind of spirit in my lifetime.* He takes another second to look around, then shakes his head and turns to leave.

But before he turns, a bright light forms out of nowhere; it is so bright that Hem must close his eyes, lower his head, and block the light with his arm. He then hears a deep voice saying, "Son of Ebert and Sara, you survived and made your way home."

Hem goes to his knees. "Are you the spirit of the woods?" he yells out into the distance, looking for something to appear out of the light.

"Yes, I am one of the spirits. We felt your presence as soon as you entered the woods, and I can help you as well." Then the light gets brighter and moves toward Hem. He goes into a trance as he stares into the light. "Prepare yourself," he hears the voice say. Inside Hem's mind, he sees everything; it starts with his past as he sees his mother and father with him as a baby.

It goes to them standing in the councilors' room in the trees. Sara challenges Shaman to the wizards' duel for leadership. His parents leave the room, and Hem sees Shaman tell his personal guards to kill Sara and set up Ebert for the crime.

Then he hears, "Great Hem, we have been waiting for you to come home. I feel your energy pull. It is very strong. You are very special." Then he starts seeing all the ways he can use the powers he gets from the spirits.

After seeing all the ways to use his powers, he comes out of the trance; the light is gone, but in front of him are two males and a female. The female smiles. "Hello, Hem. It's nice to finally meet you," she says to him. "He looks just like his mother," she turns and tells the males.

Hem stands up, not sure what to say. "Who are you all?" he asks them.

The eldest and very wise-looking one smiles. "I am Titan." Then he points to the other male. "This is Legend," he says.

The female stops Titan. "I'm Energy, and we sure have been waiting for you a long time," she tells him. "Now you can go defeat Shaman and lift his evil spell he tricked us into," Energy explains.

"What did he do?" Hem asks the spirits.

Legend looks at Titan for approval, then looks at Hem. "Long ago, when Shaman killed your mother and blamed your father and we found out, we arrested Shaman. He told us he had your father and you trapped in here. When we came to look for you, Shaman used our powers against us and trapped us in here. We can't go past the trees. An energy field stops us," he tells Hem.

"Long ago, Shaman was our best pupil. He could use the pull of our powers to the full extent. He was a good person when he was young, but the older he got, the more he was able to use our powers. He got obsessed and stopped listening to us. Then he found a way to trap us here and still be able to pull from our powers. The only good thing is so can the others. That's why we ask you to stop Shaman and free us from this prison, my son," Titan tells Hem.

Hem drops to his knees. "I promise I will stop him," he tells the spirits.

Hem raises his head, but the spirits are gone. He stands up. "Hello?" he yells out but hears nothing. "I will defeat him! I will free you all!" he yells out. Hem then quickly turns around as he hears something in the thick brush; he stands up straight, waiting for what comes out, and then he hears his name being yelled.

"Hem!" It's Mount.

"I'm over here!" Hem yells.

Then out from the brush comes Mount with Bree behind him. They see Hem and stop. "Is that you, Hem?" Mount asks.

"Yes, it's me," Hem says, then curiously looks into the stream to see that his appearance has changed; he looks older and wiser. He now has a long beard with long hair; he likes his new look.

"Are you okay?" Bree asks him.

Hem smiles with a small laugh. "I'm great! I have never been better!" he says to them and then tells how he met the spirits and how with their powers he learned about his powers and his past. "I must go face Shaman so the spirits will be free from his spell," he tells them.

"Well, you won't face him without us," Mount tells Hem as Bree agrees.

"Thank you, both. I won't be able to do this without you," Hem tells them.

"Let's get back to camp and tell Marc and Jax what is going on," Mount tells them.

"Marc will be happy he may get to hit someone," Hem says, and Mount agrees as they all laugh.

They make their way out of the brush and back to the camp. "So how do you like Coral? She sure seems to like you," Mount teases Hem.

They then come out of the woods and can see the camp; before Hem has a chance to say anything, Coral comes running to them. "It's you!" she screams, then goes and hugs him. "I knew you would come back more a man, but you look so different—more handsome!" she tells Hem. They walk over to the camp, holding hands.

"Hem's got a girlfriend," Marc sings out loud, and Amy hits him, stopping him from teasing Hem.

"What happened to you?" Jax asks Hem.

Hem sits with them and tells them of how he met the spirits and how they are trapped; he lets them know he has mastered his powers and must stop Shaman.

As Hem explains his story, Shaman has zoned in with his powers and has been listening to Hem tell what he is planning. He knows they plan to attack, and Hem is going to try to defeat him. Shaman is furious; he goes into his chambers, where the other councilors are locked in a cell. "Coral turned against me. Who will be my new head councilor?" he asks.

The girls are all sitting in the floor, tired and hungry. Blair stands up, walks close to Shaman at the bars, and spits in his face. This makes him very angry. "You bitch!" he screams, then fires his powers at them; all three girls fall to the floor, stunned. "So you girls are with the enemy, are you?" he says as he opens the cell door. He walks in, kicking each girl. "You will all die then, starting with her," he says as he grabs Chantel by her hair, dragging her out of the cell.

Blair and Tia both try to stop him, but he slams the door on them, locking them in the cell. They scream, "Please don't kill her!"

Shaman laughs as he holds her, rubbing her body. "Why would I kill such a lovely young woman?" he tells them, then forces Chantel to kiss him. "I need a good woman to produce my seed," he says as he rips her clothes off and throws her on his bed. He turns and laughs at Blair and Tia, who are screaming, "Stop!" He proceeds to rape Chantel; when he is done, he throws her back in the cell.

Back out in the forest, Coral is leading Hem and the others through the trees; she suddenly stops and lets out a scream as she sees the vision of what Shaman has done to her baby sister. Hem grabs a hold of Coral after seeing the vision himself; she lays her head on his shoulder, crying for a minute, then looks up and tells everyone what she has seen. Mount goes to Coral. "We are all very sorry for what happened. This might not have happened if we never came here," he tells her.

"Please don't blame yourself. Shaman was looking for a reason to hurt me for some time. I refused to be his partner," Coral tells them.

"I promise you, we will go there, and we will defeat him. He will not get away with what he did. I have full faith in Hem, and he knows we are right behind him," Mount tells her.

Coral breaks the hug she was in with Hem and straightens herself up. "It is time for Shaman to go down. I have full faith that you all will make it happen," she tells them, then looks Hem in the eyes and smiles. The sisters can see love in the air as Coral slowly turns away from Hem and starts leading them through the trees.

Shaman is now standing on the large balcony built to look over the forest; he has seen in his vision that Hem has somehow found the spirits and is coming to challenge him. He has gathered the warriors and given Fierce the order to kill them all, even the women. Shaman announces to the people, "The strangers have kidnapped Coral and are trying to trade her for valuables!"

Coral stops them. "We are near. I have seen that Shaman has told the people of the city that you all have kidnapped me and for them to kill you all. But I ask of you, try not to hurt them. They know no better listening to Shaman."

Marc looks at Mount. "What should we do if we can't fight?" he asks him.

Mount looks at Marc, then looks at Coral. "The people trust you. We just need to get the people's attention so you can tell them we are not the enemy. We are here to help," he says to her.

"I know what we can do," Jax says, then pulls out a large round piece of steel with a handle from the large bag he's been carrying. "We can use this to block the arrows as we hide behind it," he tells everyone.

"It is only large enough for two people. One of us will have to take Coral and get her close enough to talk with her people," Mount plans out.

"I'll do it," Marc says. Mount looks at him. "I can do it," Marc assures his brother.

"This sounds dangerous. I can go with her. Together, we can form an energy shield to protect us from the arrows," Hem says.

"It sounds like a good plan, but we need you to find your way up to the tree houses where Shaman is at. You need all your power when you face him," Mount tells him. He agrees his focus must be on taking Shaman down, and Coral tells them of a hidden stairway in the middle of the tree house at the largest tree.

Mount suggests that he and Jax go with Hem to find the hidden passageway and get Hem to the top, where Shaman is waiting with his personal guards. Amanda goes over to Mount. "What can we do?" she asks him.

Mount kisses her. "I was hoping you and your sisters would stay here where it is safe," he says to her.

Amanda becomes upset. "We can do more than stay out of the way!" she snaps at him.

"This is going to be dangerous. These people want to kill us. Please stay here till it's safe," Mount pleads.

The sisters all agree with him, and they each hug their man before they leave. Marc goes over to Mount. "You ready to do this?" he asks his brother.

"I'm ready, and you be careful. I won't be there to save you this time," Mount says, smiling.

"Back at you, bro," Marc tells him. Then they quickly hug, but not fast enough.

"You boys want to be alone?" Jax yells out.

"Funny!" Marc and Mount both yell at him.

"Everyone, come here! Join hands before we do this," Mount tells everyone.

Everyone forms a circle, and Hem says a prayer to the creator to keep them safe; then the sisters stay back and watch their men go toward the trees whose tops had houses built on them. They don't go far before Coral points to something. "There in the distance is the stairway to the houses in the trees. Over to the left, you can see the tallest and largest tree. Inside of it is a secret stairway in the tree," she tells Mount and Hem.

They move in closer, but before they get to the stairs, they hear, "Fire!" Arrows fly at them.

Marc grabs Coral and hides her behind the shield as the others hide behind the trees. The shield works as the arrows bounce off and hit the ground. Then from behind the tree at the stairway, Fierce comes out with ten warriors behind him, all holding large wooden clubs. Bree goes running over to Coral and helps Marc back her away from danger. Then as the men start to charge at them, they suddenly stop and back away from Rowdy and the other wolves coming out of nowhere.

Coral then pulls away from Marc and comes out from the shield. "Fierce, stop! This these people are here to help us. This is the son of Sara. He has been with the spirits of the woods. They have showed him how to use his powers to defeat Shaman!" she tells him.

"He is supposed to be the one from the prophecy. This kid is going to beat Shaman in a powers duel," Fierce says to Coral, pointing at Hem.

"Let him go face Shaman. What do we have to lose? We are slaves to Shaman!" Coral yells at Fierce.

Fierce drops his weapon and kneels to Hem. "Go, and may the spirits be with you," he says to Hem.

With Mount leading the way, they take off toward the tree with the secret stairway in it.

"Traitor!" the Timberland warrior Drake yells at Fierce, then hits him hard with his club. It knocks Fierce to the ground. Drake raises his club to hit him again, but Bree quickly jump kicks, hitting the club out of his hand. He then sweeps Drake's feet and puts him to the ground as the wolves circle around him.

Drake screams, "get them!" He backs away from the frightening beasts, growling and showing teeth, but the other warriors lower their weapons; this infuriates Drake as he finally gets back on his feet. "Come on, I'll kill you!" he screams at Bree, motioning him to attack. Bree has had enough. He hits Drew fast and hard; it knocks Drew out, and he falls to the ground.

Coral goes to Fierce. "Are you okay?" she asks him.

"I'm good," he tells her. "How are you?" Fierce asks her.

Coral gathers the other warriors and tells them what the plan was to take Shaman down. As she is explaining the plan with Bree and Marc, telling them how they can help, no one notices Amanda, Amy, and Angel sneaking by, going toward the tree with the secret entrance. The girls have been watching from a distance the whole time, and they do their best to go in the direction of Mount, Hem, and Jax. They get past everyone and are in the middle of all the largest trees.

"Coral said the secret door was at the largest of the trees," Amanda tells them as they look over every tree.

"Maybe we should go back. We promised we would stay back, out of the way," Amy suggests to her sister.

"We can't go back and just do nothing!" Amanda snaps at her sister as she keeps looking over each tree she comes up to.

"I agree with Amy. We should go back before we get lost," Angel says to Amanda.

Amanda stops and looks at both of her sisters; then as she is about to say something, she stops. "Quiet! I think I heard something," she tells them. The two sisters gather next to Amanda, and she pulls them near a tree to hide as they can hear someone or something coming. When the noise gets close, Amanda peeks around the tree to see what it is. "Maverick!" she yells.

"It's one of the wolves," Amy says, scared without the men around.

Amanda goes walking toward the wolf. "He is here to watch over us, I know it," she says as she starts petting him. "Can you find Mount?" Amanda asks Maverick.

Maverick lets out a bark, then starts sniffing up in the air, then goes down and starts sniffing the ground; he moves around, sniffing all over. Then he looks at Amanda and barks. "He wants us to follow him," she tells her sisters, then drags them both off behind Maverick, going through the woods. Maverick takes them a short distance, then starts sniffing around again; he gets to the largest tree, stops, and starts to bark. "I think he's trying to tell us something," Amanda tells her sisters.

She goes over to Maverick. "What is it, boy? Did you find something?" she asks the wolf. Maverick goes to the thickest part of the tree, jumps on his hind legs, and starts scratching the tree with his front paws. Amanda starts looking closer at the tree. "Angel, look. I think it's a door," she tells her.

Angel goes over to the tree. "I think it is," she says; then both she and Amanda start trying to open it. They both try everything to open it.

As they do, Amy walks over to a branch. "It's no use. We won't get it open," she says as she grabs the branch, pulling down on it to hold her up; when she does, the branch bends down. She thinks she broke it. The branch doesn't break when it is lowered, but the door to the tree opens. They look inside the tree to see a secret stairway going up to the top. "Should we go up them?" Amanda asks her sisters. "We came this far. We can't go back now," she tells them, then goes into the tree.

Mount, Jax, and Hem have made their way to the top of the stairway; it leads to a door. Jax picks the lock of the door and slowly opens it. It leads to a large room with chairs all around a large table. Mount goes into the room to make sure it is clear. "It's clear!" he yells to Jax and Hem, and they go inside the room.

"It's beautiful," Hem says as he looks over the room. Jax shuts the door so it doesn't look like anyone came in.

Mount walks to the head seat. "Think this is your chair," he says to Hem, joking.

Hem turns and looks at the large table, then at Mount standing at the head chair. "I want to help my people get out of Shaman's control, but where we live is my home. I can't stay here," he tells Mount with a worried look on his face.

Mount smiles. "Let's just worry about Shaman right now. We will worry about them wanting you to lead them when the time comes," he tells Hem.

"You're right. I'm worrying about being their leader when I might not be able to beat Shaman," Hem tells Mount.

Jax is at the door, about to look out. "Can you see what is waiting for us outside this door?" he asks Hem.

Hem shuts his eyes, then starts shaking his head side to side. "I can't see anything. I feel his powers blocking mine," he tells them as he opens his eyes back up.

Jax then slowly opens the door and looks out; they are high at the top of the trees. Each tree has a house built on it, and there is a large wooden bridge that connects each tree that goes farther than Jax can see. He shuts the door. "It seems to be clear," he tells Mount and Hem.

"One good thing is I can return the favor. He shouldn't be able to see where we are," Hem tells them.

"Good, then let's move slowly and quietly. We will find him," Mount says.

Jax then opens up the door back; they slip out of the room and sneak on to the bridge. They all can't help to stop and look at the beautiful view from high in the trees. Mount then starts leading them across the bridges.

In Shaman's chambers, Shaman feels his people's disloyalty; he sends his personal guards down to the bottom; and they are giving Marc, Bree, Fierce, and the Timberlands loyal to Coral a good fight. Marc looks over to Coral. "We are doing our best not to kill any of your people," he says, but then she stops him.

"Our good people are fighting with us or hiding. The men you fight are loyal to Shaman and evil as well. Do what needs to be done," she tells Marc.

He looks at Bree. "You heard her. Let's end this," he says.

Marc calls for Rowdy; he has been carrying Marc's sword on him in a leather case. He bends down to Rowdy. "Stay with me and help protect us," he tells the wolf, hoping he understands. Rowdy gives a howl, and the other wolves come stand beside him. Marc stands up next to Bree. "There are a good twenty men blocking the stairway. What should we do?" Marc asks. "Jax gave his bag. Maybe something inside can help," he says as he opens the bag.

Bree looks in and pulls out pieces of strange-looking metal with holes in them. "Put your fingers through the holes," he tells Marc.

"Jax calls them brass knuckles," Bree tells Marc as he slips them on his fingers.

"We're ready," Marc says, looking at them, but he doesn't give them a chance to answer. Marc goes charging at the guards with the wolves behind him. Realizing he just got left, Bree takes off running after them.

Fierce and a few of the others stay back and fire arrows, giving the men a diversion; with the wolves attacking first, most of the guards run, screaming in fear. The ones who stay to fight quickly get put down by the three men. Bree is in love with his new weapon as he crushes the skulls of a couple of attacking guards. Marc slices through the men blocking the stairway; they fall to the ground, screaming as blood pours out. As the men look around, they see the rest of the guards running away.

Above in the trees at the balcony, Shaman gives out a loud scream as he senses the defeat of his guards. He knows they will be coming up into the trees. He takes a minute to think of what to do; he then goes into another vision. He sees that the sisters have snuck up the secret passageway, and now they are up in the trees, snooping around. Somehow, they have made their way to his room and are about to go inside. Shaman comes out of his vision and sends his guards to capture the girls.

Outside his room are the girls; they can hear a funny noise from inside the room. Amanda tries to open the door, but it's locked. "Stand back," Angel says as she pulls a small dagger from her boot. "I've learned a few things being with Jax," she tells her sisters as she uses the dagger to pry the door open. Soon, the door comes open. Angel slowly opens the door so they could look inside.

"Let's go inside and see what that noise was," Amanda tells them.

They go inside, and the room seems to be empty. "Hello!" Amy yells.

The girls stand there and hear nothing. "I know we heard something," Angel says as they look around the room.

"We'd better leave and go find Mount," Amanda tells them. Then as they go to leave, they start hearing the faint screams they heard before; then they hear a bang on the wall. The girls start checking the walls, listening for more screams; then Amanda finds a handle. When she pulls it, a secret door opens, and they see the women locked in a cage.

"Are you girls okay?" Amy asks them.

Blair jumps up to the bars of the cell. "Thank the spirits you found us! Shaman locked us in here. He plans to kill us," she tells the sisters.

"How can we get you out of there?" Amanda asks them.

"There should be a key somewhere hanging on the wall," Tia tells them.

The sisters start looking for the key. Soon, Amy yells, "I think I found it!" as she holds it up in the air. Amanda gets the key from Amy and goes to put it into the lock, and the key opens the door.

Blair, Tia, and Chantel come running out of the cage; they each hug the sisters for setting them free. "We must go warn the people of Shaman's evil plan," Tia says to them.

"Right now, Hem and Mount are tracking down Shaman. Hem plans to challenge him in a wizards' duel. You are safe now," Amanda tells them.

"We hope your friend can handle himself. Shaman is a very powerful man. He will not be easy to beat," Chantel tells them.

Then when they go to leave, the door opens, and guards slowly fill the room.

Marc, Bree, and Fierce have fought their way up the stairway, defeating all of Shaman's men; they get to the top right into the center of the large tree city. "Hide!" Marc yells as they hear more men coming.

When they hear the men close, they jump out ready to attack, only to see it is Mount, Jax, and Hem. "I see you all made it up here," Mount says to them.

"Yeah, we did, and I think we took care of all his men on our way up," Marc brags to his brother.

Then up above them, they hear Shaman. "You don't think you have won," he says with an evil laugh; he is standing on a balcony above them. As they look up to see him, he disappears, then reappears in front of them. He forms an energy ball and fires it at them all.

Hem quickly forms an energy shield and blocks the ball.

"Get him!" Marc yells, holding up his sword.

Shaman backs away. "You do that, and your women will all be dead by the time you get to them," he says with an evil laugh.

Coral steps up and asks Shaman, "What did you do?"

"He sent his guards to kill them. They are down that way," Hem tells them as he points toward Shaman's room.

"We will go save them. Will you be okay here?" Mount asks Hem.

"I will be fine. Go save the girls," Hem tells Mount.

Mount, Marc, Bree, and Fierce go running toward the room and leave Hem with Coral to face Shaman. Shaman starts laughing. "Coral, you really think this little boy will defeat me?" he says to her.

Shaman then looks at Hem and holds up his hand. Hem rises off the floor and slams into the wall, not able to move. He walks up to Hem and puts his face inches away from Hem's. "So, boy, what are you going to do?"

Hem is doing his best not to show his fear; all he can think of is yelling for Mount. "Man up. You have powers too," he says quietly to himself. Hem starts to concentrate and slowly lifts his arm and is able to form an energy ball and hits Shaman with it.

Shaman falls to the ground as Hem lands on his feet, free of Shaman's hold. Shaman stands up mad, but with a shocked look on his face from being overpowered.

On the other end of the tree houses, Mount, Marc, Jax, and Bree find their way to Shaman's room. Marc doesn't hesitate as he runs and busts through the door with his shoulder. The others come in behind him as they find the girls have all been locked in a cell as at least ten of Shaman's guards stand ready to fight. The leader of the guards tells the others to surround the strangers, and they circle around the men. "Lie down on the ground and surrender, and Shaman may let you live," the leader tells them. Marc can't help but laugh as the guard repeats,

"Lie down on the ground." Then all four men start pulling out their weapons.

Jax sees Bree with the brass knuckles. "You like using them?" he asks Bree.

Bree slides them down his fingers. "Let me show you what they can do," he says.

Mount stops Bree. "We don't want to fight you," he says. Mount lowers his sword. "We are here to help you, not hurt you."

The leader laughs, and the others join in. "You four men hurt all of us?" he says to Mount, then looks at his men. "Well, fellows, think we should give up to four boys?" Then they all laugh. The leader then looks at them. "I've had enough. You had your chance," he tells them, then yells to his men, "Kill them!"

But just as he yells the words, they hear a scary loud growling noise. Maverick, Rowdy, and the other wolves are standing inside the doorway.

At the main balcony, Shaman is on his feet and regains his composure. Hem pulls Coral behind him and slowly backs her away. "You really don't think you are the Timberland's savior, do you?" he asks Hem angrily. "I rule these people—not your mother, not your father, and sure as hell not you!" he screams, then shoots an energy ball at Hem.

Hem blocks his power and fires his own as Shaman blocks his off; then they start going back and forth, trading blows with their powers.

The wolves have come into Shaman's room, showing teeth and growling. "I suggest you men lie on the ground before you all become our friends' lunch," Mount tells the guards.

The leader looks at his men as none of them attack. "I said attack them now!" he screams. The other guards look at one another as the wolves get closer to them; then one by one, each of them starts lying down on the ground.

Maverick and Rowdy go to the leader, who is the only one still standing. He does his best to show no fear till a growling Maverick snaps close to his crotch. A large wet spot appears on his pants; then a puddle forms on the floor around his feet. Marc starts laughing. "He peed his pants!" he screams out. The leader of the guards falls to the floor, crying.

Mount finally calls the wolves off him; he goes over to the man, trying not to step in the mess. "I'll take the key to the cell door, if you don't mind," he says. The man hands Mount the key, and he throws it to Jax, who goes to the cell and frees the girls.

Hem and Shaman are still trading shots back and forth. Shaman is just too strong for Hem, who is starting to wear down. Shaman can see it as he starts taunting him. "Boy, did you really think you would beat me after one lesson from the spirits?" He laughs. "Who do you think put them there? If they can't beat me, you never will!" he tells Hem, then hits him with a powerful blow. "Now, boy, you will die! And I get the pleasure of killing you myself, not like when my guards killed your mother!" he says evilly.

Hem is on the floor; he looks up at Shaman laughing. Then Shaman throws another energy ball at him, and for the first time, Hem holds up one hand and forms a shield stronger than with two. "You had my mother killed!" he screams as he shoots his own energy ball; it is powerful. Shaman blocks it, but it knocks him back. Hem starts walking closer to him. "You blamed my father and tried to kill him!" he screams, shooting another energy ball stronger than the last.

This one hits Shaman and puts him on the floor; hurt from the blast, Shaman stands up and grabs Coral, putting his hand around her neck, then pulling her close. "Don't move, boy, or I will break her neck," he tells Hem, backing away.

"No, stop!" Hem yells to Shaman.

Then from behind him come Mount and the others. "Shaman, we have defeated your guards! Let her go and surrender!" Mount yells at Shaman.

All it does is anger Shaman more. "NO!" he screams, then picks Coral off the ground by her neck.

"Leave my forest now, or I will kill her!" Shaman screams at them as he holds Coral by her throat, choking her.

But before any of them have time to react, out of nowhere, an energy ball hits Shaman, knocking him and Coral to the ground. Hem runs over and grabs Coral as everyone is looking to where the blast came from; then from the other side out walks Chantel. "You will never touch me again!" she screams as she forms another energy ball and throws it at him, but this time, Shaman blocks it.

He then hits Chantel hard with his powers; it knocks her down and out. "Little bitch!" he screams out. Coral sees this and gets very angry; she fires her own energy ball at Shaman. He's not looking, and it hits him, but it's not strong enough to knock him down. Shaman turns to see Coral standing there and starts laughing; then when he is about to hit Coral, Blair and Tia come join her. All three of them start hitting him with their powers. It starts to wear him down, but he can still block them all.

Hem then comes over and starts hitting Shaman with his powers, and with the four of them, they put Shaman on the ground; he is in pain, begging them to stop. Then when he looks close to death, a loud "STOP!" is heard.

Titan, Legend, and Energy appear. Hem and the female councilors all stop as they see the spirits. "You have done well. We are free of Shaman's spell. We will take care of him from here," Titan tells them. From every direction of the bridges that connected the trees come the people.

Shaman slowly rises on his knees. "Thank you, Great Spirit, for saving me," he says, groveling to Titan.

"You won't be thanking me when you are serving your punishment," Titan tells Shaman. Titan then turns to Hem. "We knew you would find a way to defeat Shaman. As soon as he went down, so did the force field around the woods." Then he has Hem come next to him. "My people, Shaman had us trapped in a force field. He tricked us and imprisoned us in the deepest, darkest part of the forest," Titan explains.

"We are back, and we are very sorry for letting Shaman rule you. We will deal with him. He will no longer hurt anyone again—that's a promise. And the one who made this all happen and, if he wants, your new leader of council, son of Sara and Ebert, Hem!"

The crowd starts cheering and clapping for Hem. Mount and Marc go up behind Hem and raise him up so the people can see him. As the people cheer Hem on, Shaman slowly rises to his feet and then lets out a loud yell.

He grabs a dagger off Jax and runs at Hem with the blade. Titan turns and freezes Shaman just as he is swinging his arm at Hem with the dagger. "That's enough of you!" Titan says to him. He then turns to Legend and Energy. "Take him to our domain and put him in the prison," he tells them.

"Yes, sir," they both say. Then Legend grabs Shaman, and with Energy, they disappear.

Titan turns to Hem and the councilors. "He will be imprisoned just as he did us. You will never have to worry about him again," he says.

"Good luck, Hem. If you need me, just say my name, and I will be here," he tells Hem, then disappears.

The girls each go to their man as they all start celebrating. Hem goes to Coral, and she hugs him. Fierce goes to Chantel, checking on her. Meanwhile, Bree is checking on Blair. Coral announces to the people, "Tonight we celebrate!" The people cheer loudly.

"Let's show our new friends how good the food and the people really are!" Chantel yells to them.

Coral looks at them. "I know you all must need some rest," she says.

"That does sound wonderful. We haven't seen a bed in many of days," Angel says to her, speaking for everyone.

With all that just happened, Mount is not ready to go lie down; there is too much to discuss now. But he looks at his crew and at Amanda and can see how tired they all are, so he stops from saying anything. The houses in the trees seem to go on forever as Coral takes them all to separate rooms to rest. Bree is showed to a room, then Jax and Angel, then Marc and Amy.

Coral leads Hem with Mount and Amanda behind him; she shows him the entire hidden palace, explaining to him how great the need is for him to stay and lead his people. Coral finally stops at a door. "This is where you two can rest till dinner," she tells Mount and Amanda as she opens the door.

"I need to speak to Mount," Hem tells Coral and Amanda.

They walk down one of the bridges. Hem is quiet for a second; then he looks at Mount. "How will I tell her I don't plan to stay here?" he asks Mount.

"You did good. I'm proud of you. I know you will do the right thing. But right now, go get some rest. We will discuss it at the dinner tonight." Hem hugs Mount.

"You are my best friend. I couldn't have done it without you," Hem says.

"Well, we still have a much more powerful sorceress to defeat with a larger army. Right now, we just need you to convince these people to help us fight," Mount tells him.

They walk back to the room where Amanda and Coral are inside, waiting for them to come back. "Go get some rest," Mount tells Hem.

Coral leads Hem out of the room, leaving Mount and Amanda. Once they have crossed over a couple of bridges, Hem stops Coral. "So where do I go rest at?" Hem asks her.

"If you choose to be our leader, your room will be the grand room. That was Shaman's room. But I was hoping to take you to my room," Coral tells him and shies away a little.

"I would love that," Hem nervously says.

It's now later in the evening. Hem is awakened by a loud knock on the door. He covers himself, then goes over and opens the door. A young boy is standing outside. "Hello, sir. I was sent here with these clothes for you," he tells Hem, holding up the most beautiful robe he's ever seen.

"Thank you," Hem says, taking the robe; then the boy goes running off. Hem drops the cover wrapped around him and puts the robe on.

The door then opens, and Coral smiles, seeing Hem in the robe. "You look wonderful." Then she goes over to him, leans in, and kisses him. "Very handsome," she says.

Hem smiles, still wondering if this is all real. He hugs Coral. "Marc said we would be together. I'll never hear the end of it from him and Amy," he says, laughing.

Coral laughs with him. "You love your friends," she says to him.

"They are more than friends. They have been my family my whole life. Mount, Marc, and Jax are brothers to me."

Coral's smile turns to a sad look. "I know you want to go back to your home with them," she says. Then she looks him in the eyes. "But think about it. This is your home too, and the people here are your family, and we need a leader," she tells Hem. Then she kisses Hem again. "Plus I know we just met, but I love you and don't want to lose you."

Hem hugs Coral. "I love you too, and you will not lose me, I promise," he swears to her. "I must talk with Mount. He will understand. I think he already knows I belong here," he tells her.

Coral kisses Mount long and hard. "Come, your friends are already eating," she says.

She takes Hem by the hand; they leave her room, and she leads him across a few bridges to a building with a large door. They enter the room, and when the Timberland people see Hem, they lower down in respect of the savior. Hem isn't sure what to do. "Thank you!" he yells out. "No need to kneel," he says to them all.

Then Marc stands up from the table that he is at with everyone else. "SPEECH!" he screams out as loud as he can.

"Thank you, Marc," Hem tells him as everyone laughs.

Hem looks at the people of Timberland; not ever giving a speech before, he isn't sure what to say. He looks over to Mount, who smiles and gives him a "You can do this" nod; then he looks back at the people. "People of Timberland Forest, I'm so happy my friends and I came here and ended Shaman's rule over the forest. You will no longer have to serve anyone again." When he finishes his sentence, the people cheer loud and start chanting his name. Then the people come up to meet and shake the hand of the one who defeated Shaman.

Coral comes and breaks it up. "Let Hem take time to eat," she tells the people and takes Hem to the table where Mount and the others are sitting. He sits down as Coral bends down and kisses him. "I need to check on how things are going with the meal," she says to him and excuses herself. Hem watches Coral walk away.

Marc quickly smiles. "Somebody became a man!" he screams out. Hem turns red as a large smile forms on his face. "I know that look!" Marc yells.

"The look you give me," Amy says, laughing.

"Welcome to the club, my friend," Jax says, putting his arm around Angel.

"Congratulations!" Amanda tells Hem. "You two seem to belong together, like it was meant for you to come here and meet her."

Hem's eyes go wide. "I thought the same thing afterward," he tells Amanda.

"It's like you belong here," Mount says to them, talking about Hem.

Things go quiet for a second. "I didn't come here to stay and lead these people. We have our own quest to think about, our own home to save . . . Why bother leading them if their future could be doomed by Serina? I have felt her evil powers. They are strong," Hem tells Mount.

"These people need someone to show them the way now. Unfortunately for our cause, that person is you. But don't worry. We can go to the Dale Canyons and Gargantuan Shores while you stay here and get order. Then we will be back," Mount says.

Hem sits quiet for a moment. "I don't see you all getting into too much trouble without me. But Coral and I talked earlier, and she would like you to take Fierce with you on your journey. He really wants to see the world outside the forest," he tells Mount.

Mount sees no problem with Fierce joining them on the journey; he liked having another great warrior with him. They tell Fierce to be ready; then the food is served, and they celebrate the rest of the evening away as each couple sneaks away—even Bree with Blair and Fierce with Chantel—before the night ends.

CHAPTER 8

The Dale Canyons

IN THE PAST days, the barbarians Cobra, Viper, Tyke, and Cage have made it back to the area where they fought the wizard and his warriors. Tyke is able to find prints from the animals and has slowly been tracking them. Along their way, they run into a group of Neandertals who thought they had an easy meal, but the four barbarian men easily slaughter the savage men and force the women to become their slaves. The barbarians take over the small camp the people called home as the women feed them.

Full, they lie at a fire. "We must be getting close. The tracks seem to be more fresh and easier to find," Tyke, the tracker, tells them.

"Do you think you can find the wizard and his men by following these tracks?" Cage asks.

"The animals seemed to be friends with the wizard. I know the tracks will lead us to them and that traitor Bree," Tyke tells him.

Cobra comes out of a tent; he has been having his way with one of the females. "I'll kill that fucker myself," he says.

"Put some clothes on!" Tyke yells out.

Cobra pays no attention. "Get these bitches to gather anything worth taking from this dump!" he yells at Tyke and Cage. He turns to go back in the tent; as the woman is coming out, he grabs her. "Where are you going? I'm not done with you yet," he says, disappearing into the tent with the woman screaming. He pokes his head out. "Get going! In the morning, we are leaving," he tells them. They get up and do as he says, ordering the women to pack up what is worth taking.

Morning comes quickly. Cobra soon comes out of the tent dressed and has the woman join the other women packing up; he turns to Tyke. "Where is Viper?" he asks him.

Tyke points to the only other tent still up. "He's in there with one of the women," he says.

"Still?" Cobra screams. He goes to the tent. "You've had plenty of time to get off. Now get dressed and let's go!" Cobra screams.

Viper quickly comes out of the tent, still pulling on his clothes. "What's the hurry?" he yells at Cobra.

"I want to go home one day, and we can't do that till we find them!" Cobra screams, throwing a club at Viper. Nothing else is said as they start traveling.

The sun quickly shines brightly high up in the trees; everyone is up, and Hem leads them all down the long stairway back to the ground. He calls for the horses, and they soon bring the wagon to them; as the women load up supplies in the wagon, the men feed the horses. "This all happened fast," Hem tells them. "Maybe I should go with you all," he says.

"We'll be fine. You are needed here. Plus we will be back before you know we are gone," Mount tells Hem, then hugs his old friend.

Fierce comes down, ready to leave. Angel gets his things and loads them in the wagon. Hem walks over to Fierce. "I want you to ride my horse. His name is Pinto," Hem tells Fierce, walking him over to the horse. "This human is Fierce. I want you to carry him while you are gone," he tells Pinto. "Go ahead, jump on him," Hem tells Fierce, who jumps up on the horse.

Now everyone is on a horse, and the women are in the wagon, ready to ride. All the people of Timberland Forest come down to see them off. As they leave out of the forest, the people thank them and wish them luck with the Dales. Mount leads them out of the woods as the wolves lead him.

Soon, they are in the clear, and Jax starts following the map to the canyons. The wolves run ahead to clear the way of any dangers as Mount looks on with a worried expression on his face. Amanda sees the look on his face. "Something wrong?" she asks.

Mount rides up next to the wagon. "I just hope the wolves don't forget who we are without Hem being with us."

"Could that happen?" Marc asks, coming up behind Mount.

"I don't know," Mount says.

"The horses seem fine," Marc says.

"Let's check on them just to make sure," Mount tells Marc, and they both start yelling for the wolves. Soon, the wolves come running; the brothers jump off their horses as the wolves approach. All the wolves jump on Marc and Mount as they start playing around, wanting petting and fighting for more attention from the humans. Jax, Bree, and Fierce all go and join in petting the wolves. The men roll around, playing with the wolves as the sisters watch them, laughing.

In the distance, the noise catches the attention of a very large pack of wild coyotes, the brother of wolves. The coyotes are just as vicious as the wolves were before Hem used his powers on them. The coyotes follow the noise to where the humans and wolves are playing; they slowly sneak up on them, and with no warning, they attack. With Maverick in the lead, the wolves fight the coyotes.

They form a group protecting the humans from the coyotes. Maverick and Rowdy lead the other wolves as they tear through the smaller coyotes. Mount and the others climb into the wagon, getting their weapons; but before they get to them, the wolves have already defeated most of the coyotes as the others run away. "I don't think you have to worry about the wolves leaving us," Amanda says to Mount with an impressed look on her face as she watches the wolves.

The wolves come back from chasing off the coyotes. Mount goes over to Maverick and starts petting him. "You all are very good boys," he tells him, and Maverick starts licking his hand as he understands what Mount said. Rowdy and Charm come back; they each have a rabbit in their mouths and lay them down to Mount. "Thank you," he tells them and puts the animals in the wagon for dinner latter. The men get back on their horses. "Go clear the way," Mount says to Maverick, knowing now he has the wolves' trust.

The day is going by with no more problems; they travel a great distance, thanks to the horses. Jax is looking at the map. "If I'm reading this right, we should get to the canyons by dark!" he yells out to everyone.

"Shouldn't we stop and eat? The horses need to rest!" Angel yells to Jax.

They stop. Marc and Bree clean the animal meat as Fierce and Jax make a fire and set up a camp. The sisters unpack some vegetables and cut them up for the dinner.

Everyone eats, and the men are lying back next to the fire. Mount looks around. The sisters are packing up the wagon. The wolves are full, lying in the shade. The horses are eating the grass in the meadow; and the guys, along with himself, are not ready to move anytime soon. The sun is starting to go down, and in the far distance, they can see the tips of the canyons. Mount sits up. "The sun will be going down soon. I say we just set camp here for the night," he tells the others.

Marc is more than happy not to leave. Jax sets up. "It's been a long day. Plus we can be there by the middle of the day, maybe sooner, as long as we see no trouble," he says with a laugh.

They all get up, and every one of the men has a part in setting up camp as they let the girls rest. Bree and Fierce gather wood for the fire and build it up to last the night. The wolves gather around to stay warm as everyone goes to their beds made from blankets. As they lie down to sleep, they are being watched from a distance.

The spot they picked to camp at is the watering hole of a vicious group of savage cannibals who have been watching and waiting for them to go to sleep. Scared of the animals they have with them, they slowly get closer, trying to surprise them.

Soon, sounds of lovemaking can be heard as and the couples are together. Bree and Fierce laugh with each other because neither one can sleep with the noises, so the two get up and walk to the pond of water. The wolves curiously follow the two men.

The vicious group of men see their chance when the wolves get up and leave; they start moving into the camp. The leader stops them as they lustfully watch the three couples having sex. Then he decides he should be the one with the women, so he motions his group of men to attack. They scream as they run in; the couples are startled by the noise. Marc and Mount jump up, grabbing their pants and their swords, as

Mount yells for Maverick. The wolves, as well as Bree and Fierce, all come running.

The wolves, Bree, and Fierce get back to the camp just as the crazed men come running up. When they get close, the men stop when they see the wolves showing teeth and the two men who seemed three times their size. Mount looks at Jax. "Surely, these people aren't your people," he says.

"No! They can't be. Before my dad died, he talked of how our people were thinkers, inventors. These people don't look smart enough to take a bath. They probably want to eat us," Jax says, laughing.

The sisters have gotten dressed and go to the wagon for weapons out of the weapon bag. The biggest of the group of men steps forward. "Why are you people on our land? That water hole is ours!" he screams out.

Mount lowers his sword. "We are sorry. We are just passing through, heading toward the canyons. We didn't know this was your land. We will pack up and leave," he tells the man.

"We will let you leave, but payment for being here is your women. They stay here with us," the leader demands.

"You can fuck yourself!" Marc says, pulling out his sword. But Mount stops him.

"We don't want trouble with you people, but those are our life mates, and they will leave with us," Mount sternly says. Behind him, Jax is pulling out his daggers as Bree slips on the brass knuckles.

The leader of the group starts getting mad. "You can give us your women. Or you can die, and we take them. Either way, they are our bitches now!" he screams in a crazed voice.

Mount tells the others to line up next to him. "You want our ladies? You'll have to get through us," he tells the man as he holds up his sword.

The man's gotten so mad; then he yells, "ATTACK!" The twenty men behind him start running at Mount and the others.

"Wolves, do your thing!" Marc yells at them, and they charge the men, clawing and chewing through them. Mount and Marc tag team, slicing through the crazed cannibals. Jax goes to the wagon and, with the sisters, help fight all those coming. Bree and Fierce easily take out ten men.

Mount looks around just as Marc takes two more out; right behind him, Bree and Fierce make it a contest to see who could take out more. At the wagon, he sees he has nothing to worry about with Gamble's girls. They kill more men than Jax.

Mount then goes over to the one that was threatening them; he is now hiding behind a large rock, watching his men die. When the leader sees Mount coming toward him, he stands away from the rock in a fighting stance. "Without your weapon, I would kick your ass," he says.

The man is half Mount's size; he holds up his fist, wanting to fight. Mount smiles and looks at Marc. "He wants to fistfight me," he says to Marc.

Marc looks at the man. "He's going to kick your ass," he says to his brother.

Marc then looks at Bree. "Hey, Bree, you may get to save Mount's life!" he screams to Bree, laughing.

"Come on, let's go!" the man yells to Mount, motioning him to walk toward him. All the leader's men are either dead or ran off; everyone gathers around the man screaming to fight Mount.

Amanda yells to Mount, "Kick his ass for me, honey! He wanted to touch me," she says, making a sickened face.

Mount calls the wolves over to him. "Why would I fight you? My friends here will rip you to pieces if I tell them to. We all could beat you down and leave you here to suffer a long painful death," he tells the man who is now starting to show fear in his eyes.

"Fight me, and if I win, your friends let me go and your animals don't attack me," the man says to Mount.

Mount smiles. "Fine," he tells the man, then turns to his friends. "If this man knocks me out or I say I give, then let him leave." He makes them promise to let him go and to not let the wolves attack him.

"We promise," they say, almost laughing.

Mount turns around to the man attacking and trying to hit him; he catches the man's fist and twists his arm till his bones are heard breaking. The man goes to the ground, holding his arm and screaming in pain. "That's enough!" Mount screams at him, then hits him.

One punch across his chin puts the man down to the ground, not moving. "Dang, I think you killed him," Marc says to Mount.

"That was one hell of a punch," Jax tells them, laughing.

Mount looks around at the bodies lying on the ground. "We should wash up and leave. The ones that ran off could bring more back," he tells them all. They all wash up and start on their way just as the sun is starting to peak up. They get moving as Jax starts looking over the map for the village.

"Once we get to the canyons, we follow them to the end, and the Dale Village should be right around the area," he tells them as they get closer to the canyons. The sun is now up, and it is daylight just as they get inside the canyons.

"Careful, no telling what is lurking in here," Mount tells them as they ride into the canyons. The wolves run ahead to clear any animals that could be dangerous. Soon, half the day goes by; and besides a few smaller animals here and there, they see no danger.

But they also haven't seen any signs of any humans around. "We are close to the end of the canyons. You would think we would have seen someone by now," Jax tells Mount. They ride more down the path, and soon, they start coming out of the canyons to an empty area in all directions seen. Jax stops them. "Your father said we would find the village here, but I remember as a kid, my father said our people went into hiding. I remember he said to go to the middle of the canyon and look up for the way," he says.

"Well, there's nothing here. We might as well go back to the middle and see if we can find anything," Mount tells Jax. They go back through the canyons.

"This has to be about the middle of the canyons," Jax says as he stops them. Everyone starts looking up, trying to find anything.

"Does that rock near the top look funny to you all?" Fierce asks everyone. They all look up at the rock.

"You're right. It seems to be hiding a cave," Mount says.

"We need to get up there and see what it is," Marc tells them.

"Who's going to climb up there?" Jax asks, looking up at the large rock at the top of the canyon.

"I'll climb up there," Bree tells them.

"I live in the forest. I climb trees all day. I'll do it," Fierce says.

"Where I grew up, we live around trees. I've been climbing since I could walk," Bree tells him.

"I'll race you up there," Fierce tells Bree, then starts climbing up the canyon. Bree quickly starts climbing, easily catching up. Everyone starts watching the two men race up the canyon.

"I bet Bree makes it first," Jax says.

The men quickly make their way up the canyon wall, both staying right with each other as they get near the rock. Then when they get to the top, Fierce tries to get to the cliff first, but he doesn't get a good grip and falls. But Bree grabs Fierce arm's and catches him before he falls, then swings him back to the canyon wall.

"You saved me, thank you," Fierce says to Bree, then lets Bree climb on up to the cliff. Bree pulls Fierce up. They look at the rock.

"Look out below!" Bree yells to them at the bottom.

"Help me see if we can move this rock," Bree says to Fierce, and between the both of them, they slowly get the rock to move. They push it off the cliff for access to the opening to a large cave. Then from the bottom, the men disappear for a short time.

"Bree, you two okay?" Marc screams.

Bree then comes back to the ledge. "We are good! I found this rope inside the cave," he yells to them, then throws down the long rope.

Jax looks at Mount. "Do they live inside the canyon?" he asks Mount.

Mount has Jax tie the horses to the wagon, then tells the wolves, "Stay with the horses. We have to go where you can't." The wolves start whining, but Mount is sure they understand.

He climbs the rope first; then Jax ties each sister to the rope, and Mount pulls them up to the top. Jax and Marc climb to the top, and now everyone is safely at the top of the canyon. "It's a giant cave," Angel says as they all walk into the opening.

"It's getting dark," Amy says as she grabs a hold of Marc.

"Look on the wall. It looks like torches," Amanda says, pointing over at the wall. They go over to the torches. Bree and Fierce pull them down, and Mount finds sparking rocks lying on the ground. He hits the rocks together, and the spark catches the torch on fire. They light the other two torches.

Jax leads them down a long dark tunnel. "Go slow and be careful. I've explored caves before. There could be drop-offs anywhere, and watch for bats above you," Jax warns them.

They all slowly make their way down the tunnel; then suddenly, Marc gives out a yell as his torch goes flying. He steps in a booby trap and is hanging from the ceiling. Once they see what has happened, everyone laughs for a second. "Get me down!" Marc yells out.

"Calm down," Mount tells his brother, then starts shining his torch around. "Be careful. There may be others," he tells the rest. Jax starts looking around and sees how the ropes were set up; he cuts the other ropes, then cuts Marc down.

Marc stands up and gets his torch from Amy, who picked it up for him; then he lights it back up from Jax's torch. "That was luck. That won't happen again. Let's get going," he says, a little upset he got caught in the trap.

"Wait, Marc, don't go ahead without us!" Jax yells at him, but just as he does, Marc trips over another rope. When he does, two large logs come flying down from each side of the cave. Luckily, Marc falls to the ground and is able to duck under, and the logs just miss him.

From the distance, everyone thinks Marc just got crushed by the logs; as the girls scream, the men all go running. Mount gets there first, screaming his brother's name. "I'm okay!" Marc yells out; then Mount bends down to see Marc on the ground, with the logs hanging right above his head. "That was close," he tells his brother as he reaches for Mount to pull him out. Bree comes up behind and helps Mount pull out Marc; he stands up, and Amy comes running to him, hugging him, then hitting him.

"From now on, you'd better listen to Jax and your brother!" she screams at Marc, then hits him again.

He smiles as a feeling he's never felt goes over him over Amy being so worried about him. "I promise," he tells her, then kisses her.

"Let's go, but this time, slowly. And watch your step. There's no telling what will be next," Jax tells them all. They start going farther into the tunnel.

"Your people seem to not want to be found," Bree tells Jax. Jax then stops everyone; he holds up his torch to show them more traps.

Jax walks up to a rope and pulls it; as soon as he does, spears fly out of the wall and stick into the other side. "Whew! Good thing I wasn't the one to set that one off!" Marc says.

Jax looks back, smiling. "Please! Who set these traps so simple to spot?" he tells Marc. They slowly keep moving down the tunnel; then soon, the path ends as they come to a drop-off.

"What now, Jax?" Fierce asks as Mount picks up a rock and drops it; the rock hits ground quickly, so he drops his torch. It falls to the ground; light can be seen.

As they all look over the drop-off, looking at the light, Mount looks at Jax. "Think we can climb down?" he asks him.

"With the rope I brought, we can," Bree says as he shows he has the rope from the entrance.

"Good thinking," Jax says as he takes the rope from Bree and ties it around his waist. "Lower me down," he tells them, then climbs down off the cliff. Mount and Marc take the rope and lower Jax to the bottom. "I'm on the ground!" Jax yells up to them, then unties himself for them to lower the girls.

They lower each girl down to Jax; then Mount ties the rope to a large boulder, and the men all climb down the rope. Once everyone is down, Jax tells them, "Stay here and don't move. Mount and I will go see if it's safe."

Mount lights his torch back up, and he and Jax go through the dark cave, looking for more traps and a way out. As they walk through the large room, both men look at each other. "You hear that?" Mount asks Jax.

"Yeah, I can hear it. What is it? is the question," he says.

"Sounds like water," Mount says.

"If we can find the water, it should be a way out," Jax tells them.

"It has to go somewhere," Mount says. "Bree! Bring everyone over. We think we might have found something," he yells to Bree.

Everyone gathers over where Jax and Mount are waiting. "Shhh! Hear that noise?" Mount asks them. Everyone silently listens.

"Sounds like moving water!" Angel yells out.

"I hear it too," says Amanda.

"Now all we have to do is find where it is coming from," Marc bluntly says to them.

"I can find it," Bree tells them. "Jax, help me watch for traps while I listen for the noise." Jax stays out in front as Bree leads him in the direction of the water. They know they are getting close from the sound getting louder. Then soon, they walk into a dead end. Bree puts his ear up against the cave wall. "I can hear the water. It has to be right behind this wall," he tells them, and everyone else puts their ear on the wall to listen.

"I hear it!" Amy yells out.

"There must be a way to get to the water. Everyone, I want you to look around," Mount tells them all. They all start looking around.

Then Amanda yells out, "Over here! I found a small tunnel!"

Everyone goes over to where Amanda is standing. "That's not a tunnel. It's barely a hole in the wall," Marc says.

Bree bends down and crawls through the tunnel. "I'm through, and just as we thought, it's a large stream running down through the cave!" Bree yells to them.

Next, Mount sucks in his gut; and lying on the ground, he can squeeze through the small tunnel. Then Marc does as Mount, but he gets stuck. "Mount, help! I'm stuck!" he screams.

"Everyone, push while I pull!" Mount screams to the other side. He grabs Marc by his head as Bree and Fierce push on his legs; as he screams, they finally get him to push through.

"Were you trying to pull my head off?" Marc screams at Mount.

"Don't be a baby. We got you through!" Mount says as he laughs.

As Marc stands there catching his breath, everyone else crawls through the small tunnel. Jax pats Marc on the back. "Good thing your brother is here to keep saving your butt," Jax says, laughing.

"That was a small hole to a real man!" Marc tells Jax.

Mount relights the torches; when they light up, not too far away is a large stream running right through the cave. "It's beautiful," Amanda says as they walk closer to it.

The water is moving fast with huge rapids. "There is nowhere to walk," Amy says.

Jax starts looking around and notices a few logs hollowed out lying over next to the wall. "I think these were put here to ride the water," he says as he points to the logs. "Help me put one in the water," he tells the men.

Mount and Marc pick up one as Bree, Fierce, and Jax pick up another; they set them in a calm part of the water. Jax has the girls get inside and sit down, and the log stays afloat. As Mount holds on to one and Marc holds on to the other, everyone climbs into a log.

Mount and Marc then push the logs toward the rapids; then they jump into the log they were holding. Side by side, they start floating down the river; there are wooden sticks in each log to help guide the logs past the rapids. As they go farther down the stream, the water seems to move faster, and the rapids are rougher; it gets to where they are having a hard time controlling where they are going. Soon, the logs are crashing through the rapids, out of control.

The logs are crashing into rocks; everyone holds on for their lives, trying not to fall out. Then they go into a dark part of the cave; all they can do is listen for one another's screams as they try to stay together. Then out of nowhere, the water calms, and the logs go back to a slow movement; everyone starts yelling out, relieved that they are okay. Then as they keep moving, they start to hear water gushing. "We aren't through this yet!" Mount screams to everyone as it gets louder.

The log rafts begin picking up speed again as the roar of the water starts getting louder; then from a distance, they can see light. They get faster and faster, moving through the water as the light gets closer. Then as they finally can see the opening, they realize they are about to go down a large waterfall. "Try to stop!" Mount screams to Marc.

"I can't! We are going too fast!" Marc yells back.

"We have no choice but to go over the fall!" Jax screams. "Everyone, you must hold on tight!" he yells.

The rafts move toward the waterfall; when the rafts go over, they all go flying out of them. Everyone screams as they fall and land in the river below; as each one hits the water, the current sweeps them into a giant net. They all start squirming around, trying to get free from the net; then the net is pulled from the water and traps them all in it. Once they catch their breath, they look around to see they are surrounded by a large group of short, stocky men—all just like Jax.

Mount pulls himself up. "Hello! We mean you people no harm. We are here to warn you of a great danger coming your way. A large army with an evil witch as a leader is destroying everything."

The people start looking at one another, not sure to talk with the strangers.

"Please, we need your help. That's the only reason we are here," Mount pleads to the men.

Finally, the one man everyone is standing behind asks, "You are not headhunters?" He looks at Mount.

Jax then pulls himself up. "No! My dad is from this village. His name was Cur!" he yells to them.

Then one of the bigger men from the group steps up. "Did you say your father is Cur?" he asks Jax.

"Yes, sir, my father was named Cur. He said we are Dales and are from here," Jax tells him.

The men all gather in a circle and start discussing what they should do. After a few minutes, the one that was talking with Jax comes over and drops the net, and everyone falls to the ground. The Dales back away as Mount and Marc stand up, and they see how much bigger the two are than they are.

"Get the weapons!" the elder one of the Dales yells, and about the time everyone is up off the ground, the men of the tribe roll in large logs with points on them set to tightened ropes and point the weapons right at Mount and his friends.

Mount and Marc pull the sisters behind them and start backing away, but Jax goes up to them and stands right at the point of the log.

"My father once told me the Dales were the most graceful people on the earth, that they would give you the shirt off their backs!" he yells at them.

The man that set them free from the net goes over to Jax; he starts looking him in his face. He touches his cheek and shakes his chin, then starts to smile. "You have your father's chin, but those eyes are from your mother," he tells Jax.

"You knew my mother?" Jax asks.

Then the leader walks over. "We all knew your mother very well. When she got sick is when your father took you and your mother away to find a cure," he tells Jax. He then looks at the men. "Take them away!" he yells, talking about the weapons.

He then turns to Jax and walks with him closer to where Mount and the others stand. "We are very sorry for that. We have to be careful. My name is Hemp. I'm leader of the Dales." He points to the elder man. "This is my father, Thorn. He was leader before I was and is very wise," Hemp tells them.

Thorn walks over to Mount and Marc and looks up at them. "Are you boys Gargantuans?" he asks them.

"Yes, sir, our parents are. But we've never have been there," Mount explains to him.

"And you boys say a witch is coming with a large army to destroy us?" Thorn asks him.

"We have seen it with our own eyes," Mount says. "They took the city and homes of these sisters' people, and they will keep coming in this direction, destroying everything in their path till they are stopped," he tells Thorn.

Thorn turns to Hemp. "Get our guests put up in huts so they can rest. Have the women cook a feast for a celebration of Cur's son's return," he tells him. "Go rest now. We will talk at the feast," Thorn says.

"Thank you," they all tell him as each shakes his hand.

Then Hemp has a couple of the younger men help his father to his hut. "All of you follow me," Hemp says, then takes them through the village to the back side, where there are five empty huts. "We went ahead and built huts all the way back. I never thought these would ever be used," he tells them, laughing. "I must go now and make sure everything is being done. Father likes everything perfect. I will send for you when it's time to eat."

The girls go to the huts. "They're so cute!" they all scream as they go inside one.

Mount, Marc, Jax, Bree, and Fierce go to the stream that ran right next to the huts. "This place is beautiful," Bree says.

"Did you all notice all the crazy stuff they have built?" Fierce asks.

"And what is this material they are using to build their huts?" Marc asks, looking at them.

"How will we fit inside one of those?" Mount asks him.

"Come look at the beds they have in them!" Amanda yells to Mount.

Both Mount and Marc must duck to get inside one of the huts, and the bed is so small that when Mount lies down, his legs hang off the bed. They both somehow manage to get relaxed, and with the sound of the stream next to them, they all are asleep in no time.

Mount soon gets woke up by a noise; he rises up and looks around, then sits and listens but hears nothing, so he lies back down to rest while he could. Right when he gets relaxed, he hears the noise again; he quickly jumps up and hits his head on the roof. He yells out when he hits head and then hears a laugh, so he runs out of the hut, looking around. He walks around to the back of the hut and sees one of the male Dales running away. Mount laughs, knowing the people are just curious about them, so he goes back around front and ducks back inside the hut.

Amanda is awake and sitting up. "Something wrong?" she asks him.

"No, nothing. It was one of the Dales, probably just curious of the new people. He ran off when I went outside," Mount says, laughing.

"Did the big scary man scare him?" Amanda says, laughing. Mount, standing at her feet, flexes his muscles. "So what should we do now that I'm awake?" Amanda asks Mount, pulling up the cover and showing her legs.

He smiles and lies down next to her. "You are so beautiful," Mount tells her as he kisses her. He then looks into her eyes. "I love you," he tells her.

Amanda gives out a little scream as she grabs and hugs him. "I love you more than anything," she says back to him.

Mount lays Amanda back and kisses her, and they start making love; soon, the moans of the two get loud, waking the others. Both other couples are soon making love as well, getting turned on by listening to Mount and Amanda making love. Soon Bree and Fierce are out of their huts, woken by the noise of all three couples having sex. "Maybe we should go explore the village," Bree says to Fierce.

"Might as well. We won't get no sleep here," Fierce says, laughing, and they go off toward the center of the village.

Mount and Amanda are in their own world as they make love; soon, Mount gives out a loud yell, then pulls off Amanda and lies into the bed, relaxed. "That was wonderful," Amanda tells Mount as she leans over to kiss him.

Right when she does, Mount hears a noise outside; he stands up and puts his pants on, then places his finger to his lips, telling Amanda to be quiet. He then runs out of the hut. "Got you!" he says as he grabs one of the Dales by his shirt.

"Don't hurt me!" he screams, cowering down.

Mount could see he is just a boy, maybe a teen. "I didn't mean to bother you. I've just never seen any other people outside this canyon," the boy says.

"I'm not going to hurt you," Mount assures the boy as he helps him up.

"You sure are big. I bet no one messes with you," the boy tells Mount, looking up at him.

Mount laughs at the boy. "What's your name?" he asks him.

"My name is Snot. My father is the leader of our people," he tells Mount, and Mount shakes his hand.

"I'm Mount," he says.

"Where did you all come from? Is it far away from here?" Snot asks.

"We are from a small village like yours. It is a long way from here," Mount tells him.

"I sure would like to go there. I've never been outside this hidden valley," Snot tells Mount.

"You've never left your village?" Marc asks Snot, coming up behind him.

Snot looks around at Marc. "Dang! You are big too!" he says to Marc.

Mount and Marc laugh as Hemp comes up to them. "Snot! Are you bothering these men?" he yells out.

"No, sir," Snot quickly says.

"He has been no bother," Mount tells Hemp.

"Well, go to the kitchen. See what you can do to help get dinner ready," he tells Snot.

"I'll see you later!" Snot yells to Mount and Marc, waving goodbye.

"Father has rested and will be at the dinner. He wants you to join him at our table to discuss the reason you all are here," he tells them both.

Mount and Marc go get the twins and wake up Jax and Angel. They quickly get ready; then they follow Hemp to the center of the village, where tables are set up everywhere.

Most of the village are seated at the tables; and Thorn is at the lead table with Core, Ganja, and Mary Jane sitting with him. As they get to the table and start sitting down, Mount explains he can't find two of his men; then Hemp points to both over at a large hut, helping with the food preparation. Mount gets Bree's attention, and he and Fierce go join them at the table. "I wondered where you two were," Mount says to them.

"It was hard to sleep with all the noise," Fierce says, laughing with Bree.

Thorn then gets everyone's attention. "So tell us, Jax, why has the son of Cur searched us out?" he asks him.

Jax stands up. "My father found us a good place to live with plenty of fine people that live there, but now we are in danger." He points, then puts his arm around Angel. "This is my love, my life mate. The city where she and her sisters are from was attacked by a large army that is led by a powerful sorceress. They took their city from them and made their people slaves," he tells Thorn.

Mount then stands up. "Our good friend Hem was with us but stayed at Fierce's home. The Timberland people have abilities, and Hem saw in a vision how these barbarians won't stop. They use up and destroy the homes, then move on to the next one. Our village will be next, so we want to stop them. But we cannot do it ourselves. We need your help, along with the Timberlands'. And we hope the Gargantuans will help us as well so none of us ever have to worry about our homes being attacked," he tells them.

The four Dales look around at one another; then Thor looks at Mount. "Do you know why we are inside this hidden valley?" he asks Mount. Mount isn't sure what to say as he looks at Thor. "We once had another village—a great village—outside the canyons till a large group of men came to our home and killed our people. When we ran off, they took our village. We cannot help you. We stay here in this hidden valley because we are peaceful people. We don't know how to fight," Thor says.

"Besides, no one can find us here," Hemp says.

"We found you," Marc says.

"It was kind of easy too," Jax tells his people.

"You were looking for us. Plus your father told you how to find us. He is the one who found this hidden valley," Core tells Jax.

Jax stands up. "Listen to me when I tell you this woman is evil. She has the powers to know just where you are. Plus this plant you seem to have a lot of use for around here, she will want it for herself. It won't be long before they come and destroy everything around you," he says sternly.

Hemp looks at Snot, who is standing behind him. "Go get my pipe," he tells him, and Snot runs off. He comes back with a long hollow stick; it has a hole on the side. He hands it to his father; then Thorn pulls out what looks like the smelly green plant they have growing in a large area at the side of the village. Thorn stuffs the hole on the side with the green plant; then Hemp holds a torch to the plant as Thorn sucks on one end of the pipe. He then coughs and blows out a large cloud of smoke.

Hemp takes a puff, blows out the smoke, and hands it to Mount. Mount looks at Jax and Marc. "Puff on it," Marc tells him. Mount puts the pipe in his mouth and puffs; he starts choking as everyone laughs. Mount hands it to Amanda, and it gets passed around as everyone takes a puff.

Thorn starts a story. "We have been hidden in this valley inside the canyons for many of seasons now. Everything we need is inside the canyon walls. The stream gives us fish. Vegetables were growing when we got here. Plus this magical herb, we have learned to use for a lot of different things," he tells them.

Thorn takes the pipe again, hits it, and hands it to Mount. "We didn't always live here hidden in the canyons. At one time, we lived outside the canyons in the flatlands till an evil group of crazed cannibals came in at night, beating our men to the ground and raping the women. Our clan used to be so much larger. The ones that could escape ran into the canyons. Cur is the one that found the way to this paradise. We have hidden here since that day," Thorn tells them, then stands up.

"Them bastards probably still live in our homes and have some of our women as their slaves to this day. If you men can take back our village and run those bastards out of there, we will help you in any way we can," Thorn tells Mount.

Mount has hit the pipe a few times; now he is starting to feel very relaxed, but then again, he cannot stop thinking about things. "Let me talk with my men," he tells Thorn.

"How many men are you talking about?" Amanda asks with concern.

"Double the people here," Hemp answers her.

"With my sword, I could do it myself!" Marc blurts out.

"I could use a little action. What about you, Bree?" Fierce yells out.

"I'll do what Mount wants," he tells Fierce.

"What do you think, Jax?" Marc asks him.

"They had something to do with my mom being ill, I know it. I say we go kill them all!" Jax tells him.

"Let's get a good night's sleep. In the morning, we will go find their village and see just how many live there," Mount tells them all, and everyone agrees.

Mount turns to Thorn and the other Dales. "We will go to your village and see for ourselves who is living there in the morning. If we can, we will help you get your home back," he tells him. Thorn thanks Mount and the others for their help.

As they are finishing, the food is served. After they eat, Thorn is ready to lie down. "Please make yourselves at home. I must go rest now," he tells them, and two of the women help him to his hut. Hemp then has them all join him at a giant fire.

As they stand at the fire, again passing Hemp's pipe around, a man with the same color of hair as Jax's and just about the same size as Jax walks up. "So who's the son of Cur?" he asks them.

"That would be me, sir," Jax answers.

Then the man goes to him, lifting him off the ground with a hug. "I'm Core," he says as he lowers Jax to the ground.

"My dad's brother!" Jax yells out. "My dad used to tell me stories of the two of you as kids all the time," Jax tells Core.

"What happened to my brother?" he asks Jax.

"My dad was never the same after my mom died. I was too little to remember her, but what I can remember of my dad is he loved me. But he was still reckless, didn't have concern for his life," he tells Core.

"When we were small," he says, pointing at Mount and Marc, "our village was attacked. Our dads killed and ran off the attackers, but my father was hurt bad. He died from his wounds being too bad," Jax says, hanging his head, then looks back at Core.

"Mount and Marc's parents took me in and raised me like their own. These boys here are just like my brothers, and if we don't get others to help, our people could die," he tells Core.

"I'm glad you had such wonderful people to raise and take care of you. I'm sure your mother watches over you as well," Core tells Jax.

"You knew my mother?" Jax asks him.

"Your mother was a wonderful woman. Your father loved her more than life itself," Core says, smiling; then he looks sad.

"After we were run out of our village and had to live off the land, your mother fell ill. That's when your father found the cave that leads to the valley. We stayed in the cave for some time before we found the way here one day, but nothing he did helped your mother. So he left here with you and your mom, looking for a way to cure her," Core lets Jax know.

"So my mom fell ill from being run off from her home?" Jax asks. He looks at Mount, Marc, Bree, and Fierce. "Those fuckers must die," he tells them.

"Now you're talking!" Marc tells Jax.

"Calm down, you two," Mount tells them. "We need to see what we are up against and make a plan," he tells them.

"I don't care how many there are. I'll kill each one with my hands," Jax says angrily.

Core puts his arm around Jax. "Maybe I can help you from having to use just your hands. Why don't you men follow me to my workshop?" he tells them all and starts walking away. He leads them through the huts till he gets to one at the far end.

He walks up to a hut that has crazy inventions of his all over it; they follow him inside, and it is the same. Core lights a torch, and a glow from the light fills the room. Everyone looks around, amazed at all the different inventions Core has all over the room. Bree goes over to a table with different weapons lying on it. "I've invented a lot of different things with materials of the earth. But a few weeks back, I was digging in the canyons, and I found this strange black powder." He picks up a basket and opens the lid.

They all look inside the basket. "It looks like dirt. What's the big deal?" Marc says to him.

"Follow me," Core tells them, and as they walk outside, they meet the girls, who have come to find them.

"What are you boys doing?" Amanda asks.

"Core is about to show us something," Mount says as they all watch Core take the powder and pour it into a wooden box; he sets the box on the ground and walks over to everyone.

Core looks at Fierce. "You a good shot with that?" he asks Fierce, talking about his arrows.

"He's the best," Marc answers for Fierce, patting him on the back.

Fierce brings out his bow and pulls an arrow out; he puts the arrow on the string of the bow and aims at the box.

"Wait!" Core yells! He then takes a torch and lights the arrow on fire. "Okay, shoot the box."

Fierce points the arrow at the box and lets the arrow fly; when it hits the box, a huge explosion happens, and the box flies into pieces as it catches fire. "That was the best thing I have ever seen!" Marc yells out.

"We can use that," Jax says.

"Are you blowing stuff up again?" Hemp yells at Core as he walks up to them. "You have kept our guests long enough. Let them come back to the party and enjoy their evening," he tells Core.

They all follow Hemp back to the fire in the middle of the village; as they settle back, some of the Dales gather around with strange instruments that make music; as the men play a tune, the women sing songs to entertain their guests. Hemp passes the pipe around, and everyone relaxes as they enjoy the entertainment.

Soon, all three of the sisters are up with the female Dales; they sing and dance with them, enjoying the feeling of the magic weed. Then Amanda goes to Mount, pulling him up to dance with her; he does his best to say no, but she is not taking no for an answer. Right after, Marc joins Amy, and Jax joins Angel; the three couples move to the sounds from the instruments that Snot calls music as he plays what he calls a guitar. The Dales' weed make the experience so much better.

Then a couple of the Dale females pull Bree and Fierce away from the pipe and over with the others to dance. Soon, Fierce has the pipe passing around as they all spend the whole night smoking the Dales' magic weed and dancing to their music.

Jax looks around. "I know we only came here to get help with the fight against the barbarians, but I'm so glad we came, and I got to see the wonderful people I come from. We have to help them get their village back," Jax tells Angel.

She kisses him. "I love you," she says.

The next morning comes fast. Mount wakes up to the light shining in his face. He rolls over and puts his arm around Amanda as she lies there asleep. *Hemp was right. After smoking, that was the best sex we ever had*, he thinks to himself as he looks at his beautiful mate. He rubs his hand down her sexy body, and she lets out a soft moan. Amanda rolls over and kisses Mount, and that's all it takes for Mount to want to make love again. When they finish, Mount sits up. "I'm going to wash off at the stream," he says.

Amanda kisses Mount. "Let me know when I can come wash off," she tells him.

Mount goes out of the hut. He can hear talking; and when he gets to the river, he finds Marc, Bree, Jax, and Fierce all sitting around the water. "How are you fine men doing this morning?" he asks with a smile.

"We were wondering if you were going to sleep all day!" Marc yells at him, then splashes him with water. Mount tries to duck away from the water, then sits down in the water, washing off.

Mount then wastes no time. "So how are we getting out of here to go find their village?" he asks Jax.

"I hope my uncle can tells us that," he answers.

"If anything, he can blast us out of here," Marc jokes.

"I can try to climb the falls," Bree tells Mount.

"No, let's go talk with Core before we do anything." Everyone agrees, and each goes tells the girls they are going over to Core's hut to talk with him and that they could have the river.

Going to Core's, Fierce laughs. "You boys married? The way you go check, it looks like it," he says.

"I just wanted a goodbye kiss," Marc says. Fierce and Bree laugh.

"He's whooped," Fierce says to Bree.

They get to Core's hut. Jax knocks on the door, and it quickly opens. "I figured I'd see you boys this morning," Core says as he opens the door and comes out.

"Good morning," they all say.

“We are going to go look over your former home, but we were hoping you had an easier way out than where we came in,” Mount tells Core.

Core opens his door. “Come inside,” he tells them, and they all follow him into his hut.

Core pulls down a pipe hanging on the wall; he reaches into a jar, pulls out some weed, puts it in the pipe, then lights it with a torch lighting up the room. He hits the pipe, then passes it to Mount; and as Mount hits it and passes it, Core tells them, “For now, keep this between us.” He looks at each one, looking for a nod of yes. “In the very back of the canyon, behind the weed plants, I have secretly been digging a tunnel. I know I’m close to the other side. If we blast it, I think we’ll get through,” Core says.

Core takes them out of his house and leads them to his workshop. They go to the back to where three large barrels sit up against the wall. “All three are full of black powder. It should be enough to blow out the last of the canyon wall,” Core tells them, pointing at the barrels. He seals up the barrels, and between the six men, they can roll the barrels to the back of the tunnel. They set the barrels up at the wall. “Back away. This could cause the whole tunnel to fall in,” Core tells them all.

They back far enough out to where Fierce can still get a clear shot at the barrels. He sets his arrow on fire, then shoots it straight at the center barrel. All three barrels blow up; the explosion shakes the entire village as the tunnel fills with dust.

“Did we do it?” Marc yells out as they all are trying to fan away the dust. They get to the wall; it is nothing but rubble now.

“Clear out the rocks,” Mount tells them, and they all start moving away the loose rock.

All of them are pulling rock away, not sure if it worked; then right when they all are getting tired, Mount screams to them all, “I see light!” Then they all start clearing out the way toward the light.

By now, Hemp and the sisters, who are behind him, come walking into the tunnel. “What have you done?” Hemp screams. Just then, Mount and Marc move the last large bolder, and the other side of the canyon could clearly be seen. "Father has to know about this!" Hemp yells at Core, then runs out of the tunnel.

"We did it," Core says as he smiles, ignoring Hemp.

"Yeah!" Marc yells out as he slaps hands with everyone.

The girls see the hole in the canyon. "We were wondering what you all were doing," Amanda says, then looks over to Core. "I can't believe your people agreed to this," she says to him.

"They didn't," he tells her.

Amanda hits Mount. "I thought you wanted these people to like us. They will hate us now," she tells him.

They all walk out of the tunnel to the whole village, yelling hateful remarks to them. The whole village is mad that they gave a way into their village. Core tries to explain, but no one will listen to him. Mount finally walks right toward them. "Quiet down!" he screams. "Me and my friends decided we can't help you by fighting your battles. And truthfully, if you can't fight, you are no use for our cause or yourself next time cannibals attack!" Mount screams to them, and it quiets the Dale people down.

"I have come to know you fine people, and one of your own is like a brother to me. So we will help you, but we'll help you by training you to fight your own battle to win your home back, and you will feel better about yourselves and about keeping your home," Mount tells them. Chatter in the air can be heard as the Dales talk among one another. "I promise that with our training, you will get your home back, and we will be right beside you when you do," Mount tells them.

"Give us five sunrises, and we'll make you new men. You will go to your former village with a new courage and throw those crazed people out of your home!" Mount assures them. As the Dales start cheering and clapping, Mount yells out, "With your outstanding weapons and skills, all you need is to have a good battle plan." His friends look on, impressed at his leadership skills.

Then for the next five days, Mount, Marc, and Jax show the Dales how to use their weapons to their advantage.

Bree trains them all in hand-to-hand combat, showing them quick and easy moves to take down their opponents, while Fierce shows them his skills with a bow and arrow. The sisters show the women some basic moves to protect themselves if ever attacked. "Kick them where it counts," Amanda tells them.

"Hit them in the nose. Their eyes water, and they can't see," Amy follows.

"Use anything for a weapon," Angel says to them as she gets a handful of dirt and pretends to throw it in a man's face.

Day 5 is ending as Mount watches the Dales doing their last training session. Marc comes up to him. "I think they are ready," he tells his brother.

"I think you're right," Mount says, then calls for them all to gather around him. "You all have done great! We are very proud of you all. I think I can say for all of us when I say we will gladly fight beside you tomorrow!" Mount tells the Dales. The Dales cheer for him. "I said in five days, you would be new people. So now I ask again, will you fight to get your home back?"

They all yell, "yes!" They keep cheering for Mount and the others.

Hemp walks over to Mount and then quiets the people down. "We all are new people, thanks to all of you. We are so grateful Jax found his way back home and brought all you fine people with him. We all will be ready to go with you, and we will take our home back," Hemp tells them, and the Dale people start to cheer again. Mount shakes Hemp's hand as the people keep cheering and celebrating. Hemp turns to the people. "Let's have a feast!" he yells.

As the people go off to get a meal ready, Hemp turns to Mount. "Everyone is with you except for Ganja. I was hoping all of you would come with me to talk with him and make him understand this is best."

They follow Hemp around to the side of the village where all their magic weed plants are growing in a large field. Ganja and Mary Jane's house is in front of the field. When they get to the house, Ganja sees them coming; and he comes outside of his hut and walks up to meet them.

"Hello, Ganja!" Hemp yells out as they come up to him.

"If you're here to see if I'm going to the old village to fight, the answer is no!" Ganja quickly snarls at Hemp.

"I never planned on asking you! We all figured you wouldn't," Hemp snaps back.

"Why would I want to go fight for a home I don't want to live at anymore? We have been happy here in this hidden valley for a long time, and I have worked hard to triple the marijuana plants that have become so useful to us!" Ganja snaps back. "We were fine before Cur's son and his friends came here, causing all this trouble. Do you really expect our people to go stand up to those crazed cannibals? They will eat us alive, just like when they ran us out!" he argues.

Mount gets upset. "You don't give your people enough credit. They have worked hard training from sunup to sunset. I guarantee on my life they will take their homes back," he tells Ganja.

"You can stay or go. We have given everyone the choice," Hemp tells Ganja.

"I won't leave my plants. This is our home," Ganja tells Hemp. He puts his arm around Mary Jane, then leads her back into their hut.

"We can't hide forever, Ganja! Sooner or later, we would have been found by others. It's time for our people to stand up for themselves and quit hiding inside these canyons!" Hemp yells to him.

Jax goes up to Hemp. "He'll come around once we come back from running them out of the other village," he tells him.

Hemp puts his arm around Jax. "I hope so. He is a good man, but his life has become all about these plants." Then he laughs. "Not that anyone is complaining. Let's head back to the center of the village. I'm sure it will be time to eat soon," he tells Jax.

They follow Hemp back to the center to find the celebration has already started; when they sit down, a pipe is handed to Mount. Then the fire of a torch is set on the pipe, but Mount doesn't hit it; he stands up, dropping the pipe. "That's enough!" he yells out.

The music stops, and everyone goes quiet. Mount stands up, looking at all the people. "It was a great five days of training, and tomorrow, it will be time to put it to the test. These cannibals aren't going to just hand you back your former home. Some of you could die. That's why I want everyone to have a clear head tomorrow. So as the leader of this army, I suggest everyone eat, then call it a night. It will be a long march out of the canyon. I want everyone to be well rested," Mount commands to them all.

They all agree to listen to Mount; they put the weed out and stop the music. Everyone eats quietly; then they all go to their huts for a good night's sleep. When they get back to their huts, Mount stops the men. "I want you to take Bree and find the horses and wolves," he tells Marc. "Bring them back here so they will be with us in the morning," he follows up.

Marc and Bree go to the tunnel and out into the canyons; they start following the direction they came in when they first entered the canyons. Marc starts to yell for the wolves; then Bree joins in as they walk down the path of the canyons. Soon, they start yelling for the horses as well, but they don't see or hear anything. Once more, Marc yells, "Rowdy!" Just when he starts to think he has lost his best friend, from a distance, they hear a long howl. Marc and Bree go running toward the noise. Then as they turn a corner, they see the wolves running down the path, and Rowdy comes and jumps on Marc, knocking him to the ground.

Bree laughs as Marc and Rowdy roll on the ground, both excited to see each other. Bree pets the other wolves, telling Maverick, "Mount isn't here. We will take you to where he is at after we find the horses. Can you all help us find them?" Maverick gives out a bark; then he and the other wolves go running up the trail.

"I think they want us to follow them," Marc tells Bree; then the two go running after the wolves, doing their best to keep up. They go out of the canyon to a wheat field.

The men stand at the field, looking around; then they see the horses in the distance, eating the wheat in the fields. Bree calls for Bronco, and all the horses come running toward him and Marc. Marc sees Colt, goes to him, and jumps on his back, happy to see him. Bree gets on Bronco, and with the wolves leading, they make their way back into the canyons; and as the sun starts peaking up, they get back to the tunnel leading into the village. When they enter the tunnel, Maverick smells Mount's scent.

Before Marc or Bree can stop the wolf, he takes off running to find Mount. Maverick enters the village just as the Dale people are just waking up and doing morning chores. When they see the giant animal in the village, they scream in fear and go running for safety. As the wolf goes through the village, he bothers no one as he hunts for Mount; then finally, he sees Mount and goes running to him. He jumps and tackles him to the ground; all the people scream, thinking the animal is killing him.

As they watch the animal attack their new friend, they soon see Mount is laughing and hugging the large beast. Everyone starts laughing as they see he is in no danger, and then Marc and Bree come in with the other wolves and the horses. The people start to back away, not sure what to do anymore. Mount stands to his feet, putting his arm around his wolf friend, as Amanda comes running up and pets Maverick. "There's nothing to be afraid of. These animals are our friends," Mount says to them.

"They will not hurt you. They actually like to be petted," Amanda adds.

As the Dales slowly come over, they all start petting the wolves and the horses. "They will help us with our mission of taking your homes back," Mount tells them. The people are just more impressed with their new friends as no one has ever been that close to any large animals. Soon, everyone goes back to their work as Jax and Core take the horses to fix up the bigger weapons so the horses can pull them.

Soon, everyone is ready as Jax comes up to Mount, showing him the modifications he made so the horses can pull the large weapons. Mount is very impressed with Jax and Core's work. "We are ready," he tells Jax as he looks around at all the progress they've made with the Dales. That's when the sisters come up to the men, demanding they go too. Mount shakes his head side to side. "No! It's too dangerous! These people have no mercy. They will kill a woman with no hesitation," he tells the sisters.

"That's why we are going. We don't know if anything will happen to you," Amanda tells him. The men look at one another, not sure what to say.

"We don't even know where this village is. You all will not leave us here. That's final," Angel adds.

Jax smiles at Angel. "You girls know the horses will be pulling equipment. Everyone walks. Sure you girls can keep up?" he asks her.

Angel smacks him. "You men had better worry about keeping up with us!" she tells Jax, looking at all the men.

"We'll do our best," Marc tells her, grabbing Amy.

"Let's line up!" Mount yells to everyone; and as Jax and Core line up the horses, everyone lines up at the tunnel, ready to march out into the canyons for the first time in years. With Hemp in the lead, they start the march toward their old village; the wolves stay with the girls, knowing to watch and protect them. As they make their way to the village, Hemp informs them of what he remembers about the vicious cannibals and how they have no control.

"They choose to eat human flesh over having to hunt for food," Hemp tells them.

"Don't worry, we have a plan to keep everyone safe," Mount assures Hemp. Mount goes to Bree. "Unhook Bronco and take Fierce with you and go find the village so you can see what we are up against," he tells Bree.

Jax unhooks Bronco from the straps, and Bree jumps on him, then helps Fierce up. Hemp tells Bree the direction to go to find the village; as they watch Bronco run out of the distance, Mount looks at Hemp. "Bree is the best spy there is. He will see what those people are up to and see if they have any kind of watch," he says.

Hemp still has a scared look on his face. "You think we are ready for this?" he asks Mount.

"Your men trained hard and learned a lot in five days. They are ready," Mount assures Hemp.

"We will kick some cannibal ass!" Marc tells Hemp, patting him on the back. Marc then looks back at the men. "We going to kick some cannibal ass?" he screams out.

He gets a loud "YEAH!" in response as the Dale men jump up and down in excitement. "I think they are ready," Mount says, laughing with Marc.

Up ahead, Bree and Fierce are quickly making distance on Bronco; they get to the end of the canyons and head in the direction Hemp told them to go. Soon, Bree finds the trail that should lead them to the village. They follow the trail down for a good length, and then in the distance, they hear screams from a human. Bree has Bronco slow down as they listen for it again, and again, they hear more screams; they jump off Bronco, hide him behind a large bolder, and climb up a large hill.

When they get to the top, they have a clear view of the village; it is run-down and destroyed. The people they see are running around with no clothes on, some barely covered. A lot of them are fighting with each other, trying to kill one another—probably for their next meal. Clearly, they are not looking to be attacked and look in no shape to defend themselves. Fierce looks at Bree. "We could take them by ourselves," he tells him with a laugh. "I think our new friends can handle this," he adds.

Bree stands up. "We can go back," he tells Fierce, and they go back down the hill.

But while they were gone, some of the men heard Bronco and were about to club the horse to death for food. "Leave him alone!" Bree screams at them, but when he does, they all turn and attack him. With a few kicks and quick punches, Bree easily knocks all five men out. Fierce stands, almost stunned from watching Bree take them down. Bree grabs him. "Let's get out of here before they wake up," he says.

With Bronco running as fast as he can, the men make their way back to the group. Just as they get to where they see the path through the canyons, out comes the group marching. "You all are making good time," Bree says as he rides up on Bronco.

"We haven't stopped," Mount tells Bree. "What's your report?" he asks Bree.

"We found the village. It looks destroyed. The people are running wild. I took down a few men, but when they wake, they won't know what hit them," Bree says.

"There is a large pond of water not far from here to drink from," Bree tells Mount. He and Fierce lead them to the water, and Mount has Marc give the order to stop and rest as the sisters make a meal from the supplies they brought. As the women serve the food, they discuss the attack plan as they eat. They quickly clean up the camp and start their march.

As they got closer, some of the Dales are getting nervous. Marc, Jax, Bree, and Fierce talk with them, trying to keep them in fighting mode.

The sun is now up in the middle of the sky; it is getting hot. Then Hemp tells Mount, "We are here."

Mount stops everyone and gathers them to make a battle plan. "This is it. We are here to do a job. Now listen to me, and no one will die," he tells them. He has the men with arrows up front with men with swords behind them, and in the rear, the catapults and giant crossbows are placed. With Mount leading the way, they march toward the village as the sisters stay behind with the large weapons and the wolves.

Soon, the Dales see their old village; it is destroyed. They all start looking at one another, wondering why they are doing this. At the village, the cannibals have noticed the large group of people coming toward their home; the crazed people are fearless as they waste no time attacking. Mount watches the men running toward them; once they are close enough, he yells, "Fire the catapults!" The Dales release the boulders, and they fly in the air and then land, crushing some of the men; then they roll, crushing others.

Mount then has the arrow shooters light their arrows with fire and shoot them in the air toward the remaining men. Screams are heard as the arrows hit the men. Mount then calls the wolves to attack, which sends the remaining men running back to the village. He then sends Marc, Bree, and Fierce to help the wolves take out the rest. Mount has Jax unhook Stallion; he jumps on the horse and helps Hemp up with him. As they ride toward the village, Mount swings his sword, taking down the ones that attack.

They enter the village on Stallion; the remaining men lie down on the ground with the women and children. The leader grabs a child and runs into one of the huts. Mount jumps off Stallion and enters the hut. The spineless leader holds the child in front of him. "Move any closer, and I will kill her!" he yells at Mount; then before Mount says anything, an arrow goes into the head of the leader, and he falls to the ground. Mount looks around to see Fierce with his bow.

Mount walks out of the hut with the child, who runs to her mother. Mount takes the headwear the leader was wearing; at one time, the leader of the Dales wore it. He hands it to Hemp, who places it on his head. "Victory is ours!" he screams to his people, and they all cheer for him.

Mount looks at Jax as they both are happy about what the Dales have accomplished. Snot runs to Marc and hugs him. "I want to be just like you!" he tells him.

The sisters come running in and start helping the women and children that were hurt. Mount goes to Marc. "Take Snot on Colt and go tell the other village the good news so no one is worrying," he tells him.

As they ride off, Hemp yells to Snot, "I want the biggest celebration we ever had!"

"Yes, sir!" Snot answers him, and they go riding off back to the canyons.

Hemp then looks at the village. "It will take a lot of work to fix this place back up," he tells Mount.

"Don't worry with that right now. Let's get back to the canyon and celebrate your victory," Mount tells him.

It's a long journey back; the sun is going down, and it is close to dark as they get back inside the canyons. When they get to the tunnel, they find the whole village waiting on them and cheering them on. They walk into the village. Music is playing, and everyone is smoking as they are dancing to the music. All of them join in, but after the long day, the village is soon quiet, and everyone is asleep. For the first time, the Dale men sleep with pride, thanks to Mount's leadership.

Morning comes. Mount rises after a good night's sleep; he wakes everyone up to pack to leave. He then goes to find Hemp and tell him they must leave to go find the Gargantuans at the Gargantuan Shores to get their help. "We will come back when we have their help," Mount tells Hemp.

"We will be ready to help you in any way we can," Hemp tells him as they shake hands.

Marc comes to say goodbye and to tell Mount everything is ready. Jax comes riding up in the wagon with Core; they've adjusted the wagon to travel better and hold more. The men all get on the horses as the sisters gather in the wagon, and as they make their way out of the village into the canyons, the Dales follow them out, saying goodbye. Jax pulls out the map and starts leading them in the direction, and as they ride off, Amanda and Amy look back and watch the Dales disappear.

"Let's hope it won't be so hard to win over our people," Marc tells Mount.

In the last few days, the barbarians have traveled a great distance. Cobra is up, and he goes kicking the other men to get up so they could start moving. Viper rises up. "What's the hurry? We've have been walking forever, and we are no closer to finding the wizard or that traitor prisoner Bree."

As the men are arguing, Tyke comes running up. "I've found more prints. We are close, I know it," he tells the other men.

As the slave women feed them, Tyke tells them of the prints he found; he assures them they are close. Cage jumps up. "Let's go find them so we can go home," he tells them. They have the women pack up camp, and Tyke takes them to the fresh prints. They start following the prints, and they go on and on; soon, the sun is all the way up in the sky.

"Can we rest?" Cage asks Cobra. Cobra stops, and when he does, the women drop the stuff and sit down.

Viper becomes upset and goes to the women. "Who said you could stop?" he screams as he grabs one by the hair. "Might as well take a break," he tells the other men, then throws the woman on the ground and starts having sex with her.

"Is that all you think about?" Cage asks him.

Viper finishes and stands up. "What does it matter? We are lost! We probably can't find our way home—if we do find them!" he screams. Then they all start fighting among one another, throwing punches.

As the men are beating one another up, Cage finally yells out, "Stop!" Once they do stop, he says, "Listen." They all silently stand there, listening.

Then they hear animal sounds in the distance. "That's the noise the animals they rode made," Tyke says. Cobra tells Cage to stay with the women and set up camp as they go check out where the noise is coming from. They leave going through the woods and coming out into a giant field. The noises get louder, and they start running through the field, chasing the noise.

They get to a large hill and slowly make it to the top; when they look off into the distance, they see the horses running in the fields. Then a little farther away is a village larger than most, with a huge wall of protection around it. They all start cheering as they see the village. "How do we know this is it?" Viper asks Cobra.

"It has to be. Who else has animals living right with them?" Cobra tells him.

"Just in case, let's get a closer look, but don't startle the animals. We don't want to be seen. They may kill us," Tyke tells them. They sneak down for a closer look; and as they do, they see Kurt come out, playing with the horses.

"I don't see the wizard or his men, but this has to be where they live," Cobra says as they watch Kurt.

"Let's go home, boys," Tyke tells them, and they sneak away, never being seen.

"We will be heroes," Viper says.

"Let's just hope we live," Cobra tells him.

CHAPTER 9

Gargantuan Shores

THEY HAVE TRAVELED all day, not stopping; the sun is starting to go down; it will be dark soon. Mount is about to suggest stopping for the night when Marc looks up into the far distance. "What is that?" he asks everyone, pointing up at a strange object.

"I see it," Amy says.

"Me too," Amanda tells them.

Mount calls for the wolves and has them stay close in case of trouble as they ride closer to what starts looking like something man-made. "Who could have built such a thing?" Jax asks them as they get closer.

Once they get so far, they start to see other buildings around the tower; they now know they must be at Gargantuan Shores. "We must be here. Only men the size of you two could have built this amazing community," Jax tells the brothers.

"You're right, Jax. I want you all to make camp here while Marc and I go there to see if it's safe," Mount tells him.

"You two are not going alone, especially if you think these people are dangerous!" Amanda snaps at him.

"These are our people. It should be fine. I'm just wanting to make sure they are good with people that aren't their kind," Mount explains to her.

"And what if you two get captured or worse? Are we supposed to just sit here and not worry?" Amy says, looking at Marc.

"Dad never really said why he left here, but he did say these are good people. He had no choice but to leave," Marc says.

Bree walks over. "I can't save your life if I'm not with you," he tells Mount.

Mount puts his hand on Bree's shoulder. "I need you to stay here and watch the women, and if there is trouble, get them out of here," Mount softly tells Bree where no one else hears.

"I will do anything you ask, my friend. You be careful, my friend," Bree tells Mount.

"Thank you, my friend," Mount says to Bree, patting him on the back. "We will be right back," he adds, turning to Amanda.

She goes to him and kisses him. "Just be careful and come right back, or I will come find you," Amanda tells him.

The brothers get on their horses and start riding toward the strange city. As they get closer, they start hearing a strange noise they've never heard before. Then in the distance, they see the land ends; and for as far as they can see, it is nothing but water. The noise they are hearing is the water coming in as waves are crashing onto the land. Except for the twins, it is the most beautiful thing they've ever seen, but it doesn't last long as a group of large-looking men come out of the city.

"We must be at the right place," Marc says.

"Maybe we should get off the horses and walk toward them so they don't think we want to fight," Mount tells his brother, and they both jump off their horse and slowly walk toward the men.

When they get within hearing distance, Marc gets excited. "Hello, my people!" he yells out to them.

They all look at one another. "Get on your knees or die, strangers!" the biggest of them yells out to the brothers.

"We don't want any trouble. We have come here only to talk with your leader," Mount says.

The same large man pulls out a large club. "That would be me, and I never talk," he says, then swings the club at Mount.

Mount ducks away from the club and steps back. "We only want your help. We don't want to fight," he says again.

"Then you came to the wrong place," the leader tells Mount, then swings the club at him again. Mount catches the club and puts the man on the ground, taking the club from him. This infuriates the man. As he gets up, he attacks Mount; and again, Mount flips him to the ground.

Mount grabs Marc and starts backing away as more men come out of the city. The leader stands up and joins his men, and they all have clubs and start moving toward the brothers. Mount looks at the horses. "Go back to camp!" he tells them and smacks both on the behind to get them to run. Both horses run off.

"Our swords!" Marc yells out, noticing they are tied to the horses.

"It's fine, Marc. We are here to get their trust, not to kill them," Mount says.

But as they turn, they are attacked. Both Mount and Marc fight off the most they can, but there is just too many for the two of them to handle. They keep fighting till they are beat to the ground; the leader comes over to Mount lying on the ground and kicks him as hard as he can. "You boys are awfully brave coming to the Gargantuan Shores alone," he says, laughing with the other men. He pulls Mount up. "Time to die," he says, grabbing him by the throat.

"Put that man down now, Kodiak," a large elder man says to him.

"Dad! He disrespected me!" he yells to the man as he drops Mount.

"Leave them be till they say who they are and why they are here!" his dad demands.

Mount and Marc slowly get back to their feet. Marc spits blood. "You sure know how to welcome people," he tells the elder man.

"I'm sorry for my son's actions. He is kind of a hothead. My name is Doze. I'm leader of the people here," he tells the boys. "You boys look familiar for some reason. May I ask who you are and where you come from?" Doze asks.

"Yes, sir. My name is Mount, and this is my brother, Marc. We are from a village far from here that our father formed and has built up for years. We recently found out there is a giant army twice the size of your people coming into any civilization, killing or making the people their slaves and destroying the place. Then they move on to the next, and our home is the next to be attacked. We come to ask for your help destroying them before they end up at your great city in time," Mount tells Doze.

"So you have seen this army yourselves?" Doze asks them.

"Yes, sir." Mount says.

"Barely made it out alive," Marc tells him.

Doze looks at them like he is thinking. "You said your father formed your village? Who is your father?" he asks the brothers.

"His name is Dorn. He is from here, he told us," Marc says.

"Did you say Dorn?" Doze asks in an upset voice.

"Yes, sir," Marc answers back.

"And you boys are his sons?" Doze asks.

"Yes, sir," they both say.

"The sons of a no-good piece-of-shit traitor!" Doze yells out. "Kodiak, finish what you started. Beat them down, take them to the prisoner cells, and lock them in," he tells his son.

"You heard him, men. Get them!" Kodiak yells to the men, and they beat Mount and Marc back down to the ground. Then they drag them through the city to a small cell, where they lock them in.

Mount stands up and helps Marc to his feet. "What the heck did Dad do?" Marc asks Mount.

"I don't know, but we have to find out, or we will never get them to help us," Mount tells Marc.

Back where the others set up camp, Stallion and Colt come running up. Amanda goes running over to the horses. "Where are Mount and Marc?" she asks, looking at the horses.

Bree comes running over. "I knew not to let them go alone. I must go find them," he tells Amanda.

Jax stops Bree. "You can't go alone. We need a plan. I say we wait till dark and sneak in with the wolves. They will find them," Jax tells Bree.

"So they wait till it's late in the night?" Amanda goes to Maverick. "Can you find Mount?" she asks.

Maverick looks up in the air, sniffing with his nose; he then looks back at Amanda, barks at her, and goes toward the direction of the city. "Think that means yes," Amanda tells the others.

"Let's follow him," Jax tells her, then tells Bree and Fierce, "Grab what weapons you can. They may be Mount and Marc's people, but we can't take any chances." They both agree and grab all they can, giving the women a weapon and putting them on a horse. The wolf pack runs toward the city, sniffing in the air as they try to track down the brothers.

It's pitch dark. They don't want to be seen, so all they have is the light from the moon and the lights from the city. Soon, they could hear the crash of the waves, and the moon lights it up as they get close enough to see what is making the noise. It is the most beautiful thing the sisters have ever seen. As they stop looking at what seems the end of the land, Angel looks at her sister. "What do you plan to do? Just ride up and ask, 'Where are our friends?'" she asks Amanda.

Amanda looks at her sister, not sure what to say; then Jax speaks up. "I say we do just that. So far, everyone we have met has had one thing in common—everyone is scared to death of the wolves. We walk up with the wolves and demand they let Mount and Marc go," he tells them. "What do you think, Bree?" Jax asks him.

"It is our only advantage, but if they look to fight, I want you women to ride off quickly," he tells the sisters. Amanda isn't happy about it, but she agrees along with her sisters.

They slowly start riding to the entrance of the city with the wolves walking with them. As they get closer, they start to notice there is no one guarding the front. "What now?" Fierce asks, looking around.

Amanda looks down at Maverick and Rowdy. "Go find Mount and Marc," she tells them, and they both take off running through the city as they sniff out their humans. As they all try to keep up on the horses, they can hear screams from Gargantuan people, now realizing they have large beasts running through the city.

Maverick and the other wolves soon stop and start howling at a door of a building. Inside are Mount and Marc. "Are those the wolves?" Marc asks Mount. They both start trying to look out the small opening in the door; then they hear everybody outside, yelling their names.

"We are in here!" Mount yells out to them.

Amanda jumps off Stallion and goes to the door. "So you boys seem to have everything under control!" she yells to them.

"Funny!" they both yell at the same time. "Can you just get us out of here?"

Bree comes up to the door with a rope that's tied to Bronco; he ties it to the door, and Bronco easily pulls the door off the hinges to the ground. Amanda and Amy get upset when they see how beat-up Mount and Marc are. "We'd better hurry," Bree tells them.

They get on the horses to ride away, but when they turn a corner to get out of the city, Doze is standing there with all the men of the city. Kodiak looks at his father, then looks at them. "Get off your strange animals and on your knees, or we will kill each one of you!" he demands of them.

The men get down but have the women stay on the horses as the wolves stand in front, showing teeth. Mount again tries to reason with Doze. "We don't want trouble. We only came here to ask—"

But before he finishes his sentence, Doze stops him. "Yes, we know you want our help. Your father needs his people's help," he says to Mount. "Well, Mount, son of Dorn, we are not the type of people that like to talk with our mouths. So if you want me to talk with you, then you must beat our champion in a no-weapons fight," Doze tells him.

Mount looks at Bree, then up at Amanda, then to Marc and back at Doze. "If that's what it will take, then I will fight your champion," he tells Doze.

"Who is your champion?" Marc asks.

"That would be me," Kodiak tells him, cracking his knuckles.

"Good," Mount says, wanting payback.

The men walk up to each other, getting nose to nose. "Stop!" Doze yells. "Not tonight! It's late. We will do this tomorrow," he tells them.

"That is fine with me," Mount says.

"I can wait till morning before taking him down," Kodiak tells his father.

They all get back on their horses, and with the wolves leading them out, they leave the city and go back to the camp for the night. Bree and Fierce make a new fire, and Mount and Marc thank them all for coming for them; then they pet the wolves, thanking them.

Marc comes over to where Mount is, and they sit down with the wolves, each petting them all. They laugh as the wolves fight for more attention. They start watching their friends and the sisters moving around the camp, getting things ready for the morning before lying down. "We sure are lucky to have such good friends. I wish Hem was here. Maybe things would be different," Mount tells Marc.

"I miss Hem too. But we did great winning the Dales over, and tomorrow, we will convince our people too," Marc says.

"I didn't want it to come to having to fight, but it seems it's all our people know," Mount tells Marc.

"You should let me fight him," Marc says to Mount.

"No, this is my fight. I was challenged. Plus I owe Kodiak one," Mount lets his brother know with a stern tone.

Marc knows that when Mount gets like that not to push it, so he changes the subject. "The twins sure are beautiful tonight," he says to Mount.

"They sure are. I still can't believe we have them in our lives now. I love Amanda," Mount confesses.

"I love Amy," Marc says quickly.

"Let's take them to where the land ends and the water begins. It just seems so beautiful there. It's a good place to tell them," Mount suggests.

"That sounds like a good plan. Let's do it," Marc tells Mount.

Mount goes to Bree and Jax to let them know what he and Marc are planning. Bree doesn't care for what they have planned but knows he can't stop love. "Be careful and don't go off far," he tells them. The brothers get their horses, then go to the sisters and ask if they will take a ride with them.

The sisters gladly accept, both thinking of the first time they took a ride with the boys back at their home. They start riding toward the water and get to the sands. Both the couples get off the horses and go down to where the waves are coming into the shore and let the water run over their feet. Marc leans into Mount. "This place is perfect. I'm going to walk with Amy to be alone. Good luck," he tells his brother.

"You too, bro," Mount tells him.

Then Marc has Amy follow him as they walk down the shore.

Mount takes Amanda up to the sands, gets a blanket off Stallion, and lays it on the ground for them to lie on. They go to the ground, kissing. He lays Amanda back. "You are the most beautiful woman on the earth. Since you've been in my life, I have been the happiest man on the earth. All I want is to make it safe so our family will be happy," Mount tells her, and she hugs him, not letting go of him. As he holds her in his arms, he closes his eyes. "I love you, Amanda. I want you as my life mate, not as my servant," he says.

Amanda gives out a small scream. "I love you too," she tells him as she pulls back, and they kiss. Mount lays Amanda down, and they make love all night. Not too far in the distance, Marc and Amy tell each other the same and are making love as well. Both couples fall asleep on the beach from exhaustion.

Morning comes quick as the couples wake up on the beach; they get the horses and go back to the camp where the wolves are waiting to eat. The sisters feed the wolves and fix breakfast.

Mount gets Bree to show him some quick takedown moves he could use at the fight as Marc, Jax, and Fierce watch. "You sure you don't want me to fight Kodiak? I'll kill him," Marc tells Mount.

"I know you could, brother. But I was challenged. I have to fight," Mount tells him.

"Just in case things go wrong, we should be ready," Jax tells them. Everyone agrees, and Jax and Fierce go pack what weapons they can carry.

"Doze said he would talk if you beat his son, but he never said he would actually help us," Marc says.

"We have to take what we can get. We need their help if we plan to defeat the barbarians," Mount tells him.

Jax approaches Mount. "We are ready to go. I hooked Bronco and Colt to the wagon, so Bree and I can stay near the girls," Jax lets him know.

"Good thinking," Mount tells Jax. "We don't want any trouble, but if they get mad when I defeat Kodiak, they may attack. We have to get the girls out of there," he adds. The girls get in the wagon with Bree and Jax as Mount, Marc, and Fierce get on their horses.

As they go toward the city, they go by the end of the land, where the water begins. "I'll never forget this place," Amy tells Amanda, giggling. Angel joins in, knowing what they most likely mean.

Mount and Marc look over at them both with a smile on their face, but that don't last when they hear "Stop right there!" It is twenty of the Gargantuan men, all with large clubs made from wood.

"How can we help you this morning, fine gentleman?" Marc yells to them.

The man who told them to stop looks at the large wolves. He then looks back up at Mount and Marc. "You all will follow us to the arena where Doze and Kodiak are waiting!" he yells to them.

"Show the way, my good man!" Marc yells to him, trying not to laugh.

Mount looks at him. "Behave," he tells him, then calls Maverick's name. "Follow the men," he says to the wolf. Keeping a small distance, they follow the men into the city. There are people standing in the path, yelling at them; kids are throwing things at them.

Mount goes to the wagon up to Bree. "Watch these girls with your life," he tells him.

"You just watch yourself in there. I will protect the women," he promises Mount.

"Thank you, my friend," Mount tells Bree as the sound of a large crowd can be heard; as they both turn to look, they are in front of a large arena.

"You must walk from here," the man tells them, standing at a large door. They jump off the horses and tie them all to the wagon and have the wolves stay in the back.

Mount grabs Amanda by the hand, and Marc and Jax do the same with Amy and Angel; and with Bree and Fierce leading the way, they follow the men into the arena. They follow them down a large hallway lit up with torches. The men then open two big doors, and it leads out to the center of the arena surrounded by stadium seating around the giant field; it is full of all the Gargantuan people. When Bree leads them out into the field, the people start to boo.

The Gargantuan man tells everyone but Mount to follow him to a row of empty seats up front. Marc stands at Mount's side. "I'm not leaving you," he tells his brother.

The crowd starts to cheer as Doze comes in with Kodiak and three guards; they walk up to Mount and Marc. "Why is he here? This is a one-on-one fight," Doze tells Mount.

"I never leave my brother's side!" Marc yells at Doze.

Doze starts to say something, but Kodiak stops him. "Let him fight. Me and Trix will kick the shit out of them both," he says.

Doze starts shaking his head up and down. "Now that sounds good. I will allow it," he tells Kodiak. He then yells out to the crowd, "My people, we now have a double fight for you today! Our champion, Kodiak, with Trix will fight the outlanders claiming to be the sons of Dorn." The other two guards then help Doze to his seat.

An elder man comes out to them. "To win, both men of the other team must be knocked out or must yell out 'give.' So let's fight!" As soon as he says that, Kodiak and Trix both start swinging.

Neither man lands a punch as Mount and Marc both dodge the punches; then together, the brothers go back and forth, landing quick punches as Kodiak and Trix both go to the ground. In the crowd, the only cheers are from the sisters, Jax, Bree, and Fierce. Kodiak gets up, furious; he pulls Trix up, and as they back away, Kodiak holds up his arm and motions for five of his men to come into the arena. He orders them to attack Mount and Marc. All five men rush toward the brothers and start hitting and kicking them.

The cheers of the crowd are few as the people don't know what to think of Kodiak cheating. Jax and Fierce must hold Bree back. "No, Bree. They will kill you if you try to help," Jax tells him. Then down in the arena, Mount becomes angry; he breaks away from the men and starts fighting back. When Marc sees Mount, it pumps him up, and he starts fighting back. Then together, the two brothers beat the five men down; as they start getting the upper hand, the crowd starts to cheer for the brothers.

Kodiak gets really upset; he goes over to the stands, where two of the men sitting up front hand him two large clubs. He gives Trix one and tries to sneak up on the brothers; that's when the sounds of the crowd turn to boos, which gets Mount's attention. He sees Kodiak and Trix coming at them with clubs; he knocks out the man he is fighting with and gets Marc off the man he is punching. They both guard up together as the two come at them with clubs.

The clubs do no good as both the brothers dodge the swings, then take the clubs from the two and throw them away. Then together, they attack Kodiak and Trix. Again, they switch from man to man, beating them down as the crowd goes wild, cheering for the brothers. Then together, they knock Trix out, and he falls to the ground; they then turn to Kodiak, and he falls to the ground, on his knees. "Don't hurt me!" he cries out to them both.

Mount grabs Kodiak and pulls him up by his throat. "Say it!" he yells.

Kodiak refuses to say "give." Mount is tired of the spoiled brat they call their champion, so he hits him in the face so hard that Kodiak falls to the ground, knocked out. Mount then grabs him and drags him on the ground to where Doze is sitting. "Call it!" he screams at Doze. Doze looks over to the elder man with an upset look, but he nods his head to the man.

Then the elder man walks out to Mount and Marc, holds their arms up, and yells out, "Winners!" The crowd goes crazy with excitement.

Amanda and Amy come running to each of the brothers, jumping in their arms and hugging them. Jax, Bree, and Fierce come down to join in the celebration. Doze stands up. "We want you to join us for dinner," he tells them all. "We will talk as we eat. For now, I will have my people show you where you can clean up." Doze then looks at the people in the stands. "These people are now our guests. Everyone will treat my nephews and their friends like part of us. If I find out they are treated badly, the person will be punished."

Doze then turns and leaves as the Gargantuan people all gather around Mount and Marc, wanting to congratulate them. Some of the women ask them all to follow them; they take them to a building with a giant tub filled with hot water. There is a separate area for the women, so the girls go to the other side. On one side, Mount and Marc tell their story of where they went the night before, and Amanda and Amy are telling the story on the other.

They all get cleaned up and meet out front, where one of the Gargantuan women is waiting for them to take them to where Doze is waiting for them. They get to the largest building in the city, which is so beautifully structured—nothing like Jax has ever seen. They go into a large room where all the Gargantuan people are waiting; everyone stands and claps for them as they enter the room, and in the middle of the room sits Doze with a woman next to him.

When they get to the table, Doze stands. "Come sit with us." He then puts his arm around the woman. "This is my wife, Jess," he tells them all.

"Hello," they all say to her.

She then stands up, looking at Mount and Marc. "You boys look so familiar. I feel like I know you," she tells them, holding out her hand to Mount.

Doze laughs. "These boys are Dorn and Doris's boys," he tells her.

Jess then puts her hand on Mount's face. "Oh my god!" she screams, then hugs Mount and turns and hugs Marc.

Mount and Marc look a bit confused, looking at each other. Doze walks over to them. "I am your father's brother. I'm your uncle," he tells the brothers, who stand there in silence.

Then Mount says, "Father never talked about his past. We never knew of the Gargantuan people till we found out about the evil sorceress and her giant army of barbarians. Why did our father leave?" he asks.

Doze laughs. "That's a long story," he says to them.

"We have time," the twins say at the same time.

Doze sits back in his chair. "Well, I guess you all have figured out the toughest of the people is the one who makes the rules. So when we were kids, our father was champion and ruler of the people. He made us train to fight all of our childhood. Your father is older than me and was always a bit bigger. Plus since he was older, he had the right to challenge the champion first. By the time we were young men, a large Gargantuan named Wick challenged our father and won. He wanted one of us to challenge," he explains.

"But not only was I angry that your father was to challenge Wick," Doze says, then grabs a hold of his wife's hand. "I also wanted your mom to be with me at the time," he tells them, holding his head down as he squeezes his wife's hand. "Doris was the most beautiful girl in the village at the time. I didn't care that she loved your father. Then the day came when Father came to us when we were training, and he told Dorn he was ready and that he wanted Dorn to come with him and challenge Wick," he explains.

"I was very angry. I had trained just as long and just as hard as my brother. I wanted to challenge Wick, and I screamed it to our father. But he turned me down, telling me, 'Dorn is the elder son. He gets to challenge Wick. If somehow he loses the challenge, then you can have your shot,' he tells me. That was not enough for me. I then challenged Dorn to fight me for the right to challenge Wick, and your father laughed at me. I got so mad that I punched him right in the face for the first time. I knocked him to the ground," he recalls, laughing.

Then the laughing stops. "When he got up, he was the maddest I have ever seen him our whole lives. He came at me and beat the shit out of me. Then your mother came running up, screaming for your father to stop. After she pulled him off me, he left mad to go challenge Wick. Doris came over, checking on me. She took me inside and cleaned me up. That's when I took the chance and told her I loved her, but she rejected me, telling me she loved your father. That's when people came knocking on the door," he tells.

"They were going house to house, announcing Dorn's victory and that he was now leader. I looked at Doris. And hearing my brother was now leader and the woman I wanted, wanted to be with him, I was so jealous at the time. I jumped out of bed, and all beaten up, I went to find your father. He was with Dad, celebrating with all the people. I walked up to them, and I challenged Dorn. Of course, he laughed, seeing me beat-up from our last fight. And our father yelled at me to go home." Doze then stops to get a drink.

"I didn't go home. Instead, I called to the elders, who said challenges have to be accepted. And again, I challenged Dorn. This time, your father told me I was in no shape to fight and to go home and if I still wanted to challenge him in the morning to come find him. But I still didn't listen. I swung at him, and he blocked it and shoved me to the ground. Again, he said, 'Last chance. Go home, or I'm going to give you the ass whooping you are asking for.' This time, I knew not to attack. But when I got up, my final words were, 'I hate you! I will kill you in the morning!' Everyone laughed as I walked away," Doze tells them as he holds down his head.

He looks back up to them. "I went home and rested that night, planning how I would ever beat Dorn and get Doris to be mine. Morning came. I got up to my dad telling me not to go through with it, but I wasn't about to stop. I slammed the door and left the house and looked for Dorn, knowing Doris must have stayed with him. As I go through the city, people came up to me, asking about the fight. The news had gotten to everybody, and most people were at the arena. So that's where I went," he says, then gets a breath.

"The elders were there, but no one had seen Dorn all morning. Of course, I thought they were at Doris's house, in bed together. So I went there, but no one had seen Doris. They thought she was with Dorn at our house. When I get back, our father was there, and it had gotten around that Dorn and Doris were gone. As the search people went through the whole city, that's when Wick came up to the elders, claiming that if Dorn was gone, he still was champion. And the elders agreed." He starts shaking his head.

"Then Father came up to me. 'You must challenge Wick. Your brother whooped him bad yesterday. He will be easy to beat right now,' he told me. I got mad, telling him he thought I couldn't do it and reminding him of the beating I took. But Father got mad and told me, 'Dorn left saying how much he loves you, and he refused to fight you. I had no idea he was leaving home, but for the family, go challenge Wick!' he screamed at me. And I did, and your dad must have given him a beating as I won easily," Doze tells them.

"I always did my best to be a good leader. A few days after winning, I fell in love with Jess. We have been together ever since, but not a day goes by that I didn't wonder what happened to my big brother. I've missed your father every day. I stayed in shape and stayed champion for years, training Kodiak since he was a child. I made him the youngest champion ever, and he gave me the power to still lead the people, which no one complained about since I've gotten this city to what it is today," he finishes.

"Speaking of, I should go check on my son. This is the first time he'd been beaten. I'd better make sure he is okay," Doze tells Mount.

"Let us go with you. Maybe it will help if he sees we are good with each other," Mount tells him; he agrees, and they all get up and leave, with Dorn saying goodbye to Jess. They follow Doze out into the streets. Mount has the wolves follow them as he sees them out front of the building.

A Gargantuan man comes running up to Doze. "You may want to follow me," he tells him.

As they follow the man, they start hearing screams and chants in the distance. When they get to the noise, they find a large group of men surrounding Kodiak; they are all screaming to the elders why they should be named champion. Mount breaks through the crowd and stands with Kodiak. "If this man is no longer champion, being a Gargantuan, I think that would make me champion. So if anyone wants to fight, I think it should be me!" Mount screams to the men. The elders agree, with Mount being Dorn's son.

Kodiak becomes upset. "I don't need your help, stranger!" he snaps, moving away from Mount.

"Don't you mean 'cousin'?" Mount says, holding out his hand.

Kodiak looks at his father, who shakes his head up and down. Kodiak hesitates, but then shakes Mount's hand. Mount then holds up Kodiak's hand and looks at the group of men. "You men want to fight, then my family and I will take on every one of you. If all you men can take down the six of us, then Kodiak, my brother, and myself will all step down and let you men decide the leader!" The men all laugh and cheer at Mount.

When the men quiet down, Mount finishes, saying, "But if we take all you men down, not only do you listen to all three of us, but you will also come with us and help us defend our home. Agreed?"

That's when Trix seems to become the leader of the men. "So the six of you want to fight over fifteen men, and you will step away when you lose?"

“Yes, we all agree,” Kodiak says to Trix. “But as my cousin said, when we win, you all will help him and his people alongside of me,” he adds, then holds out his hand.

Trix shakes his head, laughing; then he turns to the group of men. “Do we agree to help them with their fight if they beat all of us down and make us say ‘give’?” he asks the men.

“Yeah!” they all screamed, with most laughing.

“Shall we go to the arena so the people can finally see your family go down?” Trix says to Kodiak.

“Anywhere you choose,” Kodiak tells him; then all the men walk to the arena as the sisters give the guys an earful, not wanting them to do this.

Hearing the women worry makes Kodiak start to worry. “How will we defeat all these men? It’s impossible for six guys to beat fifteen guys?” Kodiak tells them.

Mount and the others except Bree laugh. “Don’t worry, we have five men in one,” he tells Kodiak, talking about Bree. Then as they look around, they see Trix has had his men gather around them, getting ready to attack. “Go to work, Bree,” Marc says to him, and Bree says nothing as he goes and quickly takes down five very large men very fast.

Kodiak looks on in disbelief, thinking that is the greatest thing he’s ever seen, but then he hears Mount yell, “Look out!” As he turns, Trix hits him hard. They get into a brutal fight as Mount and the others easily take down the rest of the men. Kodiak looks around to see it is only him fighting Trix; not about to get embarrassed in front of his new family, he starts beating Trix down. As Mount and Marc look on, Kodiak knocks Trix to the ground and keeps hitting him in the face, yelling for him to say “give.”

Then when Kodiak thinks he will have to knock him out, Trix yells loudly, “I give!” Behind him, the people of Gargantuan cheer for the six men.

Mount and Kodiak help Trix to his feet. Trix holds out his hand. “I will fight for either of you men,” he says to Mount and shakes his hand; and behind them, the men who are slowly getting up also agree to follow their orders. Mount then gets all his family, including Kodiak, and has them follow him to the center of the arena.

Mount gets the attention of the people; he explains to them the army of barbarians and how they are led by a powerful sorceress. He tells them about the Timberlands and the Dales and how they have agreed to fight; then he has Marc and Bree do demonstrations with the weapons, and it impresses all the people in the stands. Soon, chattering all through the stands can be heard; then Doze with the other elders come to the center, where Mount stands.

Doze and the elders all kneel to Mount. "You proved you are more than a champion. You are also a wise leader, and we have all decided our best warrior men will go with you and help you and your father's home," Doze tells him. Mount helps Doze back on his feet; then Doze hugs his nephew. The crowd cheers as Marc and then Kodiak join them.

Mount then gets everyone's attention again and then calls Kodiak over to him. "I announce Kodiak to be the Gargantuan leader while we are traveling," he tells the people.

"We will give you two days to get ready to travel with us," Mount tells them.

The two days go by fast as they all spent both days lying around on the beach, getting to know their new family. The Gargantuan men are all packed and ready to go. Doze decides he will come along and surprise his brother after not seeing him for twenty years. They say their goodbyes as they start the long journey back to the canyons of the Dales.

CHAPTER 10

Gathering Everyone

WITH THE GIRLS in the wagon, the men walk with the Gargantuan men so the horses can carry supplies; plus Mount is happy to get a chance to know his people better. Not far into the march, Jax goes to him. "Maybe someone should ride ahead to tell the Dales we are on our way back so they will be ready when we get there," he tells him.

"Good idea," Mount agrees with him. "Why don't you go?" Mount tells him.

Before Jax has a chance to say anything, Marc yells, "Let me go!"

Mount looks over at Jax. "Let him go. You need me more," he softly says to Mount.

Mount looks over to Amy. "Amy, will you make sure the Dales are ready when we get there?" he asks her.

Amy laughs. "I'll go with him and make sure," she tells him.

He looks at Marc. "Take Amy with you, and you can go," he tells his brother.

Marc doesn't let it bother him as he unhooks Colt; he helps Amy up. They say goodbye, and as Marc rides away, he calls for Rowdy to come with them.

Then once they are a good distance, he yells back to Mount and the others, "Have fun walking!" Then he and Amy ride away on Colt. They all just laugh, knowing how lazy Marc has become since they have had the horses.

The day goes by as the Gargantuan men march right with them, not slowing down. The girls come to the men on the wagon, passing out water to them all. They are far inland now, coming to a small section of large hills. In the distance, they hear the wolves' growls, then one loud roar.

The men go running toward the commotion; when they get there, the wolves have the largest bear they have ever seen surrounded. Then if things don't get crazier, Kodiak runs to the bear. "Tell your wolf friends to back away. This is my bear. He must have smelled me coming," he tells them as he puts his arm around the bear. They are all stunned as they watch the bear pick Kodiak up and give him a hug. "I raised this bear from a cub, but the people got mad when he grew up," Kodiak explains.

"I brought him back here where he came from, but he never forgets me," he says as the bear keeps hugging him.

"That's what I call a bear hug," Fierce says laughing.

The bear falls to his back while Kodiak rubs his belly. "He loves this," he tells them.

Mount smiles. "It is crazy you are friends with a bear. He is beautiful," he tells Kodiak while petting the bear.

"His name is Kody," Kodiak says.

"We need to get back to moving," Jax tells them.

"You guys keep moving. I'll catch up. He has other bear friends I'll take him back to. It's not far," Kodiak explains. Then he starts walking with Kody. "I'm leaving for some time, so you be good," he tells the bear and stops. "Go be with your friends," he says and starts walking away, but the bear lets out a roar and keeps following Kodiak. Kodiak turns to the bear. "Go home!" he yells in a stern voice, but the bear refuses to leave and won't stop following him. Soon, Kodiak realizes he is going to fall behind; he just knows Mount and the rest will think he has gone back home.

Back with Mount, that is exactly what everyone is saying. Just when Mount starts wondering if Kodiak is just a spoiled kid, they hear a loud roar; and when everyone looks back, they see the large bear running at them. The girls scream before they realize that Kodiak is on the bear, riding him. "That is the cutest thing we have ever seen!" the twins say together.

"Guess the bear is coming too?" Mount asks Kodiak.

"Guess so," Kodiak says, still on Kody's back.

"Don't let him eat anybody," Mount tells him.

"Don't be mean! He's a good bear, I can tell," Amanda yells at him.

Jax goes over and pets Kody. "Hem will love him," he tells Mount.

"I can't wait for Hem to talk with Kody!" Angel yells to them.

The days go by. It takes a few more traveling on foot, but by the third sun fall, they can start to see the tips of the canyons; they will be there by this time tomorrow.

They set up camp and get an early start. Just as Mount thought, they get to the canyons and the main village with the sun starting to go down. When they go in, they find there are not many Dales there. But Core is there with a small group; they have been there cleaning and fixing the village back up. Core is happy to see them back; he calls the women there to go fix a meal for the returning heroes, and Mount introduces his cousin Kodiak and the Gargantuan men to Core.

Then as they assure the people that Kody is just as harmless as the wolves, the women come to them, letting them know it is time to eat. They go eat and decide to just stay there for the night; then in the morning, they will go to the canyon village where Marc and Amy are waiting for them.

Morning comes fast as they are up at the peak of daylight. Mount hopes they haven't fallen behind; he wants to get the Dales ready so they can get to the Timberlands. He can't wait to see Hem.

They start toward the canyon village; it doesn't take long for them to get inside the canyons as the wolves lead the way while Kody tries to stay with them. Soon, they are close; and the wolves pick up Rowdy's scent as they run ahead, looking for their brother. Inside the village, Rowdy gets the scent of his family of wolves; he lets out a howl and runs to the tunnel to go out of the village. Marc sees Rowdy go into the tunnel and runs after him; when he comes out of the tunnel, he gets on Colt.

In the distance, they hear Rowdy howl again. Colt takes off running in the direction of the howl. Back with the others, Angel yells to Jax, "Is something wrong?"

Jax is with Mount talking, then looks over to Angel in the wagon. "The wolves went chasing something. It should be fine," he tells her as they hear the wolves howl again, and they all move faster to catch up with them. Rowdy stops; he starts howling back at the other wolves. Then they all come running around the side of the canyon.

When they meet, they start jumping around and rolling on the ground, happy to have Rowdy back with the pack. Marc comes riding up on Colt; he laughs as he sees the wolves so happy to see Rowdy, and he gets excited, looking for his brother to come around the corner. He rides up to the wolves, jumps off Colt, and gets piled on by all the wolves, looking to be petted. As he pets the wolves, he looks at Maverick and says, "Where's Mount, boy?" And just as he says it, he hears Mount's voice yelling for the wolves.

"They are here with me!" he yells as loudly as he can.

Then Marc sees Angel and Amanda come around the corner in the wagon, then everyone else marching behind them; and then he sees Kody and gets behind the wolves. "Look out! A bear!" he screams. Everyone starts to laugh as they see Marc scared of Kody; even the wolves have bonded with the bear and look at Marc funny. When the girls get down to him, he quickly jumps in the wagon. "That bear won't kill us?" he asks the girls.

Mount gets to the wagon. "Are the Dales ready to travel?" he asks.

Marc jumps out of the wagon. "Really? That's the first thing you say? No 'How are you, bro? Glad you're safe, bro'?" he says to Mount. "Yes, sir, the Dales are ready to travel. We can leave now if you like, sir," Marc says sarcastically.

Mount grabs his brother. "I'm glad you're safe. I wasn't worried about that, but good job," he tells him.

"Thanks, bro, but I couldn't have done it without Amy and Snot," he tells him. "Should I go get Thorn and tell him it's time for everyone to leave?" Marc asks Mount.

"No! It's been a long trip to get here, and I want to give the Dales and Gargantuan men time to get to know each other before we have them travel. We will stay here till morning. Then we will start our journey to the Timberland Forest in the morning," Mount lets his brother know. Everyone is happy to hear they get to rest once at the village. Fierce can't wait to get there and lie back in the river with Hemp's pipe.

He and even Bree tell Kodiak about the Dales' magic weed as they walk through the canyon; finally, they see the tunnel that they blew out. "It seems like we were here yesterday," Angel tells them all. They leave the horses at the start of the tunnel; the wolves follow them into the tunnel, and then following the wolves, Kody barely squeezes in. They come out of the tunnel. Amy comes running to Amanda; they hug each other a long time, never being apart that long before.

Then as they all look around, they see the Dales are standing in the distance like when they first met. Then from behind, they hear Kody give a roar, and all the Dale people scream and start running to their homes. Mount, Marc, and Jax start trying to stop them as they yell to them, "It's okay!"

Then Snot comes up; he had been getting ready to leave. He goes over to where the wolves and the bear are all sitting, paying no attention to the people. Kodiak goes to Snot. "Want to pet him?" he asks.

He takes Snot over to Kody. Snot is a little scared, but Kody brushes his head up to his hand. Snot laughs and takes both hands, rubbing the giant bear. Kody rolls on his back as other kids slowly join Snot; then the wolves go over, begging to be petted as well.

Hemp comes up, greeting his friends. "Come in. Make yourselves at home," he tells the Gargantuan men.

Hemp welcomes Mount and the others back; he assures his best men are ready to follow Mount and do what he needs. Mount thanks Hemp.

"We will leave in the morning," Mount tells him. "We must have a celebration for you all for gathering everyone together to fight for a cause," Hemp tells Mount, then calls to his people. "There will be a celebration tonight!" he yells to them, and a loud cheer is heard as the people start going to work on getting ready.

"They love to celebrate around here," Fierce tells Kodiak and his men. They take the Gargantuan men to an area where they can put up tents for the night.

Mount and the others go to their huts next to the river; the men and the women take turns bathing and getting dressed for the celebration. It is like always—the Dales entertained with singing and music while they serve good food, then start passing the pipes around. "This is new. Mary Jane grew this," Hemp tells them as he lights his pipe and passes it around.

After a few hits, Mount is ready for bed as he says his good nights, but Amanda is not going to let him go to sleep as she lies on him in bed.

It was a good night's sleep for all, but the sun starts peaking up over the canyons. As Mount opens his eyes, it is just like the last time—he finds Snot looking in at them. "I'm ready to go!" Snot tells Mount when he sees he is awake.

Mount sits up and gets dressed; he's happy to see someone is excited to go. "Go make sure all your people are up, ready, and at the tunnel," he tells Snot.

"Yes, sir!" he yells, then goes off running through the village. "Everyone, to the tunnel!" he yells out over and over.

The Dale women have been up before sunrise, getting a meal ready for all the travelers; they won't let them leave without eating. After last night, between the smoking and lovemaking, Mount is hungry this morning. They all go to Thorn's table, where Hemp, Ganja, and Mary Jane are sitting with Thorn.

As they eat, Hemp starts thanking them again for all they have done for his people. "I must stay behind, though. Father needs me here with him," he tells Mount. "Ganja needs to stay here to take care of the harvest coming up, or our plants will die. But I want you to take my son with you. Make a man out of him while he is with you," Hemp explains.

Everyone finishes eating, and the men coming with them start saying their goodbyes to their mates and families. Hemp walks with Mount and Marc. "Please watch over my son?" he asks the brothers.

Marc goes over to Snot and rubs his head. "I'll make sure he doesn't get hurt," he tells Hemp.

Then Snot pushes Marc's hand off him. "I can take care of myself!" he yells at them all.

Hemp goes to his son and hugs him. "Just promise you will be careful," he tells Snot.

"I promise," he tells his dad, hugging him back.

Bree comes up to Mount. "Jax has the wagons tied up to the horses. We should be ready to travel to the Timberlands," he tells him.

Mount goes to the entrance of the tunnel and leads everyone out of it and into the canyons. Outside are the wolves, with Kody sitting by the wagon, ready to go.

Mount helps the sisters into the wagon; then he has Snot ride in the wagon with them. Mount calls out to all the people. "We are traveling to the Timberland Forest first before we go to our home. It could take up to three days to get there. We will try to rest as much as we can. Again, we all thank you for helping to get rid of the barbarian army and their leader, Serina. Now say your goodbyes, and we will be on our way."

So with the Gargantuan men and the Dale men with them, they go on their way to get the Timberlands.

Cobra and the other barbarians have traveled almost nonstop, trying to hurry and get back home. They are now very near the mountains, and Viper starts telling the women about the great city their people took and how their lives will be like serving Serina. Without stopping, they try to get to the mountains, each one telling what they will do first when they get home. Then before the sun reaches the center of the sky, they get to the mountains.

Seeing the entrance into the center of the mountains, which tells them they are almost home, puts a spring in their step. When they get into the mountain trail, they start realizing they are almost home and start wondering if Serina will let them live after they prove where the wizard lives. If they are somehow wrong, she will have their heads.

The sun is now starting to go down; just when they were getting tired, that's when Cage yells out, "Look, you can see the city!" They look up to see the buildings.

They come out of the mountains just as it is starting to get dark. "Finally home," Tyke says. "We should go find Boar before we do anything," he tells them, and they all agree.

As they walk up to the gate of the city, there are guards at the front. "Who goes there?" one yells at them.

Cobra isn't happy about it; as he goes to the man, he screams, "Do you not remember your captain?"

"Yes, sir," the man says as he goes to one knee.

"We are sorry, sir," the others say as they go to a knee.

As Cobra stands over the men, from a distance, Ace sees his guards kneeling; he goes out to see what is going on. "Well, look who's home," he says, laughing when he sees it's Cobra, Viper, Tyke, and Cage. "Boar has been wondering if you men were still alive, and leave it to you all to find women while you're gone. Follow me. I'll take you all to Boar. He will be happy to see you men. Now Serina may be a different story," he tells the men as they go through the city.

They follow Ace to the washroom Boar is in; he's in the giant tub, having sex with three of the slave girls. When they come into the room, Boar sees Ace. "Didn't I tell you not to disturb me?" he screams.

"Sorry, sir, I thought you would want to know Cobra and Viper are back," he says, acting like he is trying not to look.

Boar pushes the girl in his lap to the side, where he can see the four men standing in front of him. "I can't believe my eyes! I told Serina you men wouldn't fail me," he tells them.

"I thought you men were dead. Come and join me," Boar tells them as he pushes the girls out of the water. "Bring more hot water in!" he screams at the women.

The men all undress and join Boar in the large tub; as they settle in, he looks at each one. "You men look like hell. I hope you found the wizard and his men," he says to them all.

Tyke looks down at the water, then looks at him. "We hope we did—"

But before he finishes talking, Viper pushes his head into the water. "We found their village. The animals they ride were in the fields next to their homes. It's far away from here, but we marked the way to find our way back," Viper quickly tells Boar.

The slave girls have been bringing in more hot water. Boar stops them. "Go get my men some fresh clothes!" he yells at them. "After you men get dressed, we will go get some food before we let Serina know you men are back," Boar tells them.

"That sounds good," Cage says.

The women bring the clothes, and the men get dressed and follow Boar to the kitchen; everyone tries to stop them, asking them where they have been, but Boar won't let them be bothered while they are eating. Cobra finds their girls and tells Boar about them; he laughs at the story while they eat. They all get some wine; and for the first time in a long time, the men are relaxed, having a good time. Then in walks Lisa. She walks up to the table and looks at Boar. "Welcome home, gentlemen," she says.

Then all the men except Boar stand up in respect of Lisa. "Serina knows you're back. You men need to follow me to her chambers," she tells them.

They all look at Boar. "You heard Lisa. Follow her," Boar tells them.

"You coming?" Cage asks Boar.

Boar stands up, then drinks down the wine in his mug till it's gone; he sets the mug on the table. "I wouldn't miss it," he tells Cage, hitting him on the back as they start following Lisa.

They get to the chamber door. "Wait here," Lisa tells the men, then enters the door.

After a few minutes, the door opens. "Come inside," she tells them. They walk in the room, and it is very dark; the only light is where they stand and then enough light on Serina to be able to see her face. She is way into her pregnancy and is hiding it from everyone but Lisa.

"On your knees!" Serina commands the men;, they all quickly fall to their knees as Boar stands behind them. "So you men found where our enemy persists?" she asks them. Then she walks down to the four men in front of Tyke. "Give me your hand," she tells him.

Tyke holds out his hand, and Serina grips it with hers; she goes into a vision of the men's trip. She sees how the men destroyed the tribe of men and took their women as their slaves. Then her vision goes to the village they found; she can see the large animals the wizard and his companions rode on. Then her vision takes her inside the village; she sees the Cobble City slaves who escaped with the wizard. Then her vision takes her into the homes; she finds the wizard's house and then his companions' houses. As her vision takes her though the entire village, she sees proof that they live there, but she doesn't see them anywhere.

Serina comes out of her vision and lets go of Tyke's hand. "You men have done well," she tells them, then walks to Viper. "Hold up your arm with no hand," she tells him, and he holds it up. She makes it glow with her powers. Viper goes the rest of the way to the floor, screaming in pain, as the others back away. Soon, he stops screaming and stands; he holds up his arm, now with a hand.

"Thank you, my queen!" Viper says to Serina.

"You four men are now commanders under Boar and Ace. You will help train and lead the men into battle," she tells them. They all gracefully thank her as they leave the room.

Boar congratulates them. "I will call for a celebration. We will have a good time tonight," he tells them.

"Let's get some wine," Cobra tells them as they go out of the castle.

Back in Serina's chambers, she is worried about what the wizard is doing. Lisa has her rest for the evening. Serina lies in bed. "Hold me," she tells Lisa. Lisa sits behind her as Serina lays her head on her lap. Lisa takes her hand and rubs Serina's stomach. "This child will be special. He will be leader of the barbarians one day," Serina tells Lisa.

Lisa leans down and kisses Serina. "He is your son. He is destined to be a great leader, just like his mother," she tells Serina.

"I must hunt down that wizard and kill him. I feel he is up to something. He and his friends want to destroy me," Serina suddenly says.

"Rest now, my love," Lisa tells her, and Serina closes her eyes, thinking of what to do about her problem.

Back in the Timberland Forest, the sun is starting to peak through the trees. Hem rises up from his bed in the leader's room; in the time he has been there, he has settled right into the role of leading the people of the Timberlands. Hem gets up, seeing Coral is already gone; she sees over the morning chores of the people. He gets dressed, then walks out of the room onto the bridge high in the trees, looking over the beautiful homes created in the trees by Titan and the other forest spirits.

Hem then gets a feeling; he shuts his eyes and sees Mount and the others have finished their quest and are close to being back at the forest. He goes running to find Coral as he does his best to say good morning to the people he passes by. He finds her in the room where everyone eats; she is with Chantel, Blair, and Tia sitting at a table, eating. He comes up to the table and kisses Coral, then says good morning to the councilors; he tells them of his vision of his friends being close. He wants to meet them.

Coral hides the fact that she isn't happy to hear they are back because Hem may want to leave now. She agrees to get the people to make extra food for the guests who will soon be there. Coral has Hem take two of the guards with him. To keep her happy, he agrees; and the men go to the basket Hem had them build, which is like what Jax built at their home. It raises and lowers them from the trees; they lower down to the ground, and Hem starts getting excited, knowing he will soon see his friends.

It seems forever to Hem as they walk through the woods, but finally, he sees the clearing up ahead. They come out of the forest into the field. Hem puts his hand above his eyes, looking off into the distance. "I don't see anything," one of the guards says to him.

"Keep looking. They will come over that hill in three, two, one."

Then both guards' mouths drop when they see the horses come over the hill; then they see a young boy guiding the wagon and then a very large group of people, with some guiding horses pulling objects.

Mount was coming over the hill, with Marc next to him. "Look, it's Hem!" Marc says to Mount. "Hey, Hem, we're back!" Marc screams to Hem.

Hem waves to his friends, happy to see them. "About time you all got back!" he yells back to Marc.

Then the wolves come running to Hem; they all tackle him to the ground, all happy to see the one who understands them. He talks with each wolf as he waits for the others to get to them. Then he is picked up off the ground. "We missed you!" Marc yells, picking him up.

As Marc is shaking Hem, the others get there and join in. "We could have used you more than once," Mount tells Hem.

"It was very hard that day to watch my friends, my brothers leave. But I knew you all could do it without me, and as I see by our new friends, you did just that," Hem tells them.

"We still missed having you with us. I'm glad to be back with you," Mount tells him.

"You two want to be alone?" Snot says as he walks up.

Marc laughs and puts his arm around Snot. "This is Snot. He's a Dale," Marc says.

Then Kodiak comes walking up to them, with "little" Kody next to him. "This is our cousin Kodiak," Mount says.

But Hem sees Kody and goes over. "Is this your bear?" he asks Kodiak. Hem pets the bear, and then Kodiak watches as Hem has a full conversation with the bear. Kody really seems to like Hem as he rolls around, rubbing on him. "So you found him as a cub?" Hem asks Kodiak.

"Yes," Kodiak answers, not sure how he knew that.

"This place is special. It has spirits that protect it, and Hem can pull their powers and use them as the spirits do," Mount tries to explain to Kodiak.

Hem walks back over. "Kody is one good bear," he tells Kodiak. Then Hem starts looking around. "Where are the sisters?" he asks.

"In the wagon, asleep. All three have not been feeling well over the last few days," Mount tells him as they walk over to check on them. They wake the girls, and they are all happy to see Hem.

"Come up to the trees. I'm sure Coral can help you girls with your sickness," he tells them.

They follow Hem and the guards through the woods to the tree with the new lift. Jax is impressed with it, seeing it's his design. The Dales and most of the Gargantuan men refuse to go up in the trees, so Mount has Kodiak see over them setting up a camp; he is sure the wolves can keep them safe of any intruding animals. Hem then leads them on the rising basket, and the men pull them all to the top. Since Hem has been with Coral, they have formed a psychic connection with each other; and Coral is there at the top waiting with Blair, Chantel, and Tia.

Fierce jumps from the basket, hugging Chantel, as Coral welcomes them all back. "I hear you girls are feeling under the weather," she says to the sisters.

"We all three have been getting sick for a week now, mostly in the mornings," Amanda tells her.

"I'll take them with me and check them out. I'm sure it's nothing," Coral tells the men, then has the girls follow her.

Fierce goes with Chantel to go tell his family he is home; and Hem takes Mount, Marc, Jax, and Bree on a tour to show the changes he's made while they've been gone.

Coral takes the sisters to the room where hurt and sick people go; it has tables in it, and Coral tells the girls each to lie on one. Then she goes to each of the girls, looking her over and asking her how she is feeling. Once she hears each girl's story, she has them all sit up on their table as she gets a chair and sits in the middle of them. She looks at each of the girls, then starts to smile. "I guess it's safe to say each of you girls has been lying with your man at nights?" she asks them.

All three look at one another, starting to smile too. Then they all nod yes to Coral. Coral then stands, excited. "You girls are not sick at all. It seems all three of you are pregnant!" she tells them.

The sisters all look at one another again, then jump up, crying and hugging one another. "I'm pregnant as well with Hem's child," Carol tells the sisters. The girls gasp and pull her into the hug.

"Hem worked fast," Amy jokes with Coral.

"How will our men take the news?" Angel asks them.

"How did Hem take the news?" Amy asks.

"He was very happy. We were declared man and wife by Titan. The spirits call it 'getting married,'" Coral tells the sisters.

All three girls get excited. "Will Titan marry us?" the twins ask together.

"If Titan appears while you are here. If not, Titan has blessed Hem. It gives him the right to do the marriage ceremony. I know he would be more than happy to do it," Coral tells the girls.

"Let's go find the guys and tell them about marriage and see what they think," Angel tells her sisters.

They go out of the room and start walking the bridges to each tree house; as they go to each tree, they don't seem to find anybody anywhere. They soon find Chantel and Fierce in the councilors' chambers, talking with each other. Fierce informs them that the others all have gone down to the ground to help with setting up a camp for the Dales and Gargantuans. The women backtrack to the middle of the village where the basket is; they all get in, and Angel and Coral lower them to the ground.

They find Mount, Marc, and Jax standing at the bottom, waiting on the sisters. Hem and Bree are standing behind them. "We would like to talk with you girls," Mount tells the sisters.

"We want to talk with you men as well. We know why we've been sick," Amanda tells the three men.

Mount looks at Marc and Jax. "Maybe we should each go off alone," he tells them.

Then each man goes off with the woman they love. Mount leads Amanda into the woods a little way till they are alone. He grabs her by the hand. "We have been talking with Hem, and he told us how he was blessed by Titan and how he and Coral are now husband and wife. I want you to be my wife," Mount tells Amanda.

She starts crying. "Yes, I'll be your wife. But I have something to tell you . . . I'm carrying your child," she tells him, and he picks her up off the ground; his yells of happiness can be heard high in the trees. The same happens with Marc and Jax as the sisters go yelling to one another.

Mount joins the others, and all three announce they will be fathers to Hem, who has already told them he is going to be one. They all congratulate one another; then Hem turns to all the people and announces he will marry the couples tonight before the celebration begins. The people cheer for the couples, and they start to fix the grounds up for a wedding as Coral and the councilors take the girls to the top of the trees to prepare them for the wedding.

Back at Cobble City, Serina has gone into a trance; she is back at the village, looking for anything that will tell her where the wizard and his companions are. Then finally, she finds Dorn talking with Ebert.

She hears them talking about their sons and if they had any luck getting the other groups of people to help them fight the barbarians. Hearing that instantly wakes Serina; she is very angry as she rises and screams for Lisa. Lisa quickly comes running in and helps Serina to her feet.

"Come with me," Serina demands as she goes to walk out of her chambers. Lisa comes behind her, covering Serina with a robe as they walk out into the castle. "I had a vision. I saw the fathers of our enemies. They talked of how their sons are on a quest to build an army to come destroy us," she tells Lisa as they walk through and out of the castle. "I cannot allow this. I must send a message to them," Serina explains as they walk out of the city, then over to a pile of large rocks.

With her powers, she holds out her hand, and the rocks rise in the air; a small lizard runs from them. Serina drops the rocks, then goes to the lizard and picks it up with her hand. As she grips the lizard, she looks it in its eyes. "The wizard seems to like using animals for his benefit. I think I'll give it a try," she tells Lisa, then puts the lizard on the ground; as she does, she says, "GROW!" As she does, the lizard starts to grow till it is as big as a mountain and taller than the trees; then it sprouts large wings.

Lisa hides behind Serina, scared, as the large beast lets out a loud screeching roar. Serina waves her hand toward the monster. "Blow fire!" she says, and it blows a giant fireball from his mouth, lighting up the sky. "Now, my pet, fly to the village of the wizard and burn it to the ground!" she commands of the beast.

The animal lets out another screeching roar. Then it spreads its giant wings and starts to flap them, and it slowly lifts off the ground, rising into the air. As it flies off, the people inside the city start screaming.

Serina gives an evil laugh. "That should teach them not to make me angry," she tells Lisa as they watch the giant beast disappear into the sky. "Back to my chambers," Serina demands, and they go walking back. "We can see what is happening inside the waters of my kettle," she explains to Lisa as they go back to her chambers. When they get to the kettle, Serina takes her hand and dips it in the water, making a circle; then an image of her new pet flying through the sky appears.

Back at the Timberland Forest, everything is ready for the wedding to start; they have cleared an area on the ground so everyone could watch Hem unite the couples. While everyone is waiting, a choir of Timberland females sing a lovely song. Hem soon walks up in front of all the people; then one at a time, each couple walks down to Hem. Once they are all gathered around him, he starts his service as he speaks of love and the love of their maker.

It is a beautiful moment as each couple declares their love for each other; then Hem tells the men they may kiss their brides, and he announces each of them as man and wife.

Then out of nowhere, Hem falls to his knees, screaming in agony. Mount quickly goes to his friend to see what is wrong with him. Hem has been learning more and more of his powers, so now he is able to let another person see his visions. He grabs Mount's hand, and they both can see the huge fire-breathing monster.

It's flying right toward their home as the people in the village are screaming and running to their homes. The beast flies down and lands right in the middle of the village; as it blows fire at all the homes, the people come running out. Then it drags its tail on the ground, knocking them down and devouring the ones that can't get up. Then Dorn comes up to the beast, swinging his sword to drive the monster back. Gamble and Ebert do their best to get the people out of harm's way.

Sometime ago, Mount suggested they make an escape route; and the men lead the people to it as Dorn, with a large shield and a sword, keeps the monster busy. The people all flee the village as Dorn does his best to hold off the monster, but the beast is just too powerful for him to defeat. Then the monster swings his tail at Dorn, and it hits him, knocking him to the ground.

Mount breaks away from Hem's grip. "NO!" he screams; it wakes Hem from the vision. Amanda goes to Mount and puts her arm around him. He grabs and holds her.

"What did you see?" Marc asks Mount.

Mount pulls away from Amanda. "It was a huge monster, and it attacked our home. Our dad could be dead," he tells Marc.

Hem is shaking his head from side to side. "This looks like something only Serina could do," he tells the others.

"We must get back home," Mount tells him.

Mount, Marc, and Hem decide to ride ahead as Hem puts Fierce in charge of the Timberlands to get them there while Mount puts Bree in charge of them all.

They get their horses; and Stallion, Colt, and Pinto go running full speed out of the forest and toward their home. They ride all night till the light starts showing. "We need to stop and let the horses rest and drink," Hem tells the brothers. So they ride till they find a stream of water and stop to drink.

Mount can't sit still. "We can't let her get away with this. Now that we have our own army and weapons, I say we go run them right out of Gamble's home," he tells Hem and Marc.

"I agree. It was meant for us to befriend our people and get them to help us. We should attack them while they don't expect it," Hem says.

"Do you really think they are ready to attack the barbarians?" Marc asks them both.

"We can get them ready," Mount tells Marc.

"Let's just get home and make sure our families are safe. Then we can think of what to do before they arrive," Hem tells the brothers. The brothers agree with Hem, and they get the horses and go back to riding.

The sun is up, so they can see without the torches, which makes riding go a little faster. Soon, they are in their homelands; it's not long before they can smell the smoke off the houses in the village still burning. They get to the village and ride inside; the men start yelling for anyone to come out, but the village is empty. Hem shuts his eyes. "They went to the hidden area," he tells them.

"Good thing you suggested we find a hidden area to hide if we were ever attacked," Marc tells Mount.

They get on the horses and find the hidden trail; as they ride up the trail, they hear someone yell, "Sir Hem!" They stop and look to see Kurt in the distance, waving at them. Kurt leads them to the hidden opening, where the people have set up tents.

Mount and Marc go running to find their father; they find their mom and sister, and they all hug. Doris takes them to the tent where Dorn is resting; both boys go in the tent and drop to their knees in front of their father.

Dorn opens his eyes to see his boys are home. "We are so sorry," both boys say, hanging their heads.

Their father holds up his hand for the boys to grab; they both grab his hand and hold it. "Did you boys succeed in getting help with the fight?" he asks them.

They both say, "Yes, sir," raising their heads.

"Then it was worth fighting off that thing," Dorn says, getting a frightened look on his face. "It was the size of three houses, taller than the trees. It could breathe fire. It attacked by dragging its tail," he tells his sons.

Marc giggles. "It was dragging its tail? And breathes fire? I have to see this dragon," he tells Mount.

Dorn, still holding on to the boys, pulls them down to him. "If this dragon comes back, you'll wish you didn't. But you boys have to kill it if it does," he demands from his boys.

"We will kill that dragon, cut off its tail, and bring it to you," Marc tells his father.

"I'm not giving that thing time to attack us again. I plan to just keep marching back to Cobble City and take it back when the others arrive," Mount says with anger.

Dorn sits up. "I can't let you do that," he tells Mount, who looks at him, not sure what to say.

"Father, that witch destroyed our home. We have to end it now," he says to Dorn.

"From what I've heard from you and Gamble, the others are not ready to face such an evil army. They will get destroyed with or without Jax's weapons. Take the time to train them to use our new weapons. Let them know what they will be facing. Make a battle plan, son," Dorn demands.

Mount stays quiet as he looks at Marc, who says nothing; then he looks at his father. "You're right, sir. I'm just so angry—I want revenge,"

Mount says in a calmer voice. "When everyone gets here, we will train each group of people to use our metal weapons and see what skills each group are best with that will help us to win," he tells his father.

Dorn lies back down, smiling. "That sounds more like talk of a leader," he tells Mount; then they leave the tent to let their father rest.

Mount and Marc go find Hem with Ebert and Gamble; they tell the boys their story as they walk to the village to look it over. The three boys start helping the others clean up the burnt mess; they spend the next few days helping. Then on the fourth morning, just as they are about to start working, they hear the howls from the wolves in the distance; they get their horses to go meet the others. They find them at the start of the wheat fields, and the wolves come running to see them.

All three stop to pet the wolves; then when Bree and Jax get to them, they welcome them back, and Mount and Marc go running to the twins. Then to Hem's surprise, Coral comes running to him; he hugs her. "I thought you were staying at the forest?" he asks her.

"I couldn't stay. I had to be with you. Blair will run things while we are gone," she tells Hem, who is happy she decided to come.

When they get to the village, everyone is heartbroken when they see the destruction.

As they look around, Marc tells them, "It was so much worse. We've been cleaning it up since we got back."

"How is your father?" Amanda asks the brothers.

"He is good for a man who fought a dragon," Marc says.

"A dragon?" Bree asks.

"It was knocking people down by dragging its tail on the ground, so that's what I've been calling it—a dragon," Marc says.

"Where did this so-called dragon go to?" Bree asks them.

"They said it just flew away," Marc tells him.

"I've tried to use my powers to find it. But I felt Serina blocking me with her powers, so I did the same to her. She shouldn't be able to see what we are doing as well," Hem tells them.

"Good. She cannot know of our plan to train these people and go take Cobble City back for Gamble," Mount tells him.

"I should be able to keep her from finding out our plans, but we should get to training in the morning," Hem says.

"Yes, but we need to build the village too. With all these people helping, it won't take long," Mount says.

Morning comes. Mount tells the people of his plans to spend half the day rebuilding their village and the other half training to fight. He names Marc and Jax to lead in weapons training. Bree and Kodiak are to train in hand-to-hand combat. Fierce is to teach the bow and arrow to the Dale and Gargantuan men. Mount helps lead with each group and, with Hem's help, thinks of the battle plan.

The days pass by, and with all the people pitching in to build, it is happening fast. Not only is the village being rebuilt, but with more know-how, it is coming together better than before. The evenings are going just as good as they train to fight; by the end of the first week, everyone has a place to sleep at nights out of the weather, and Mount has seen different war potentials in each of the four groups of people. The men of their village have been training with Mount and Marc since they were old enough to train; they are coming along nicely.

The Timberland people are excellent at hand-to-hand combat, and all are sharp shooters with the bow. The Dales are all scrappy fighters; they all picked up on all the weapons and are very sneaky. The Gargantuans, with their size, are extreme fighters; they will be able to go head to head with any of the barbarians. As Mount stands with Hem watching each group train, he is very confident about their chances; they have with another week to train. "You did good gathering everyone," Hem tells Mount.

CHAPTER 11

Taking Back Cobble City

THE SECOND WEEK of training has gone quick; it is the last day of training. Near dark, Mount is making his final rounds, watching each group doing their final practice battle. He stops them and has them all gather around him. He then calls Marc, Bree, Jax, Fierce, and Kodiak to the center of the circle with him. Mount starts off by telling them all how happy he is with everyone's efforts during training; he promises it will all be worth it to be able to sleep at nights without worrying of an attack.

Mount then points to the others. "With these men's help, we will win the war and keep you alive. That's why I called this gathering. I name each of these men captains. Along with me, you will listen to whatever one of your captains have to say," He tells all the men. "Tomorrow, we march, and we don't stop till we take back Cobble City for our new family and run off those barbarians for good!" Mount speaks to the men, who all stand and cheer for him.

Mount then calls Hem to the center. "This is the man who will protect us on our journey. Everyone, gather around as Hem says a prayer for our trip tomorrow," he tells the men. Hem has everyone lower their heads as he says a prayer to the creator; he asks to keep them all safe during their fight. Mount then tells them they are free for the evening to go eat and get rest and that they will march out in the morning; the men all cheer for Mount, Hem, and the captains.

The men all go to eat, and when they sit down, they are greeted by Coral and the sisters. Coral explains to the men how they have decided to stay behind and rest since all four of them are with child. The men all just agree with the women, knowing they already decided a few days ago that the women should stay here. The men all eat; then each of the couples go to be alone for the evening, knowing it will be a while before they see each other again. Bree takes charge of getting things ready for the morning.

With both men having a child on the way, the brothers decide to have separate homes built next to each other. Jax gets not only a bigger house for his new family, but also a new workshop that is double in size compared with his old one. Hem, not sure where he is going to call home, chooses to still live in his dad's house.

The four couples each go to their homes. Mount and Amanda try their best to make small talk for as long as they can, but she finally grabs a hold of him. "I'm going to miss you," she cries out.

"We haven't been apart since we met," Mount says as he kisses her on top of her hand.

"Don't go! This is our home now. We don't belong there anymore," Amanda demands of him.

He holds Amanda tighter. "It's not just about getting your home back. We have to stop the sorceress and her army, or we will never be able to rest at night, wondering when they will be here to take our homes from us," he tells her.

"I know," Amanda says; then they go into a deep, long kiss, and Mount takes her to bed.

The sun comes up, and Mount quietly gets up and dresses; he walks outside to see all the groups of people up and working together to get ready for the long trip. Amanda comes out of the house. "You weren't going to leave without saying goodbye," she says as she comes up behind him.

Mount pulls her around to him and hugs her. "Never," he whispers in her ear and kisses her neck.

Marc and Amy come out of their house and walk over to them. "Enough of that," Amy says, smacking Amanda on the butt.

"Everything ready to go?" Marc asks Mount.

"Everything is ready!" Jax yells to the brothers as he walks up with Angel. Then behind them are Hem and Coral.

"You men better be ready. Every one of you has a child waiting on their fathers," Coral says, with all three sisters agreeing with her.

"I'll make sure we all come back home alive," Mount tells the women.

Bree and Fierce come walking up. "The wagons are packed and hooked to the horses. We have all the men out at the wagons and lined up to march," Bree says.

Mount, Marc, and Jax say their final goodbyes to the sisters, promising they will take Cobble City back. Mount goes to the front with Hem; he has each of the captains lead their groups so Mount and Hem can lead the horses pulling the wagon. Marc is with Bree in the other wagon. They get the wagons and each group of people moving, with Dorn's people up front and each remaining group with their leader behind them. Hem has the wolves go ahead of them to warn them of any trouble.

They start a good pace, and the next few days go by with no troubles; if they keep it up, they could be at the mountains in just a few more days.

It's the end of the third day, and they find a good spot to set up camp. With everyone chipping in, camp is set up quick, and a meal is prepared. Later that night, as everyone is settling down, Hem goes to Mount. "The closer we get to Serina, the harder it is to block her powers. Last night, I could feel her trying to read my mind," he tells Mount.

At Cobble City, Serina is in her bed, resting; she again tries to find the wizard and see what he is up to. As she closes her eyes, she goes into a trance, this time finding herself inside a tent; then as she looks around, she sees it's the wizard who is lying down, asleep. Serina goes out of the tent and sees all the other tents around; she sees two men standing guard. They are talking about how many more days it will be before they attack and take back Cobble City. Serina is furious hearing they are planning to attack.

Serina wakes from her trance and calls for Lisa. Lisa comes running. "Is it time?" she asks Serina, thinking the baby is coming.

"No, not yet. But I did it. I finally was able to find the wizard, and it's just as I thought—they are on their way here with a large army planning to attack," Serina explains.

Lisa helps her to her feet. "What should we do? You are in no condition to take on the wizard," Lisa says to Serina.

"I don't plan to take him on. I'll let my new pet do it for me," Serina says with an evil laugh.

Lisa follows Serina to the balcony doors; she opens them, and they walk out on the balcony. "Awake, my precious!" she yells out.

Then in the distance toward the mountains, they hear a loud roar, and then the beast comes flying out of the mountains and into the sky. With her powers, Serina communicates with her monster as she shows it where to go. "Kill the wizard and all his men!" she commands. The monster then goes flying in the direction toward the camp.

At the camp, most of the men have called it a night, and the camp is quiet. Then from a far distance is a loud screeching noise. As the noise gets closer, the men all start coming out of their tents. Everyone is standing around Mount as they are all waiting to hear the noise again. Then it happens again. But this time, the noise seems to be closer; that's when the men from home started screaming. "It's the monster coming to kill us!" they tell all the others; then they hear the noise again.

The wolves are woken up by the noise, and they start howling. "You mean the dragon is on its way here?" Marc asks his people from home.

"Yes, the beast will kill us all. We should go hide," one of the men tells Marc.

Mount agrees with the man, and he has all the men go hide. Before they have a chance, the roar is right at them; then a large object in the sky blocks the moon as it flies by. Then out of nowhere, the dragon swoops down and blows a huge stream of fire from his mouth as the men go running.

Screams are heard everywhere as the dragon lands on the ground and blows fire in all directions as it tries to burn down all the stuff in the camp. Mount and Hem are behind the wagon. "We can't let this thing destroy our stuff! Without the wagons, we might as well turn around. We have to back the monster away!" Mount tells Hem.

Fierce comes up to them with the Timberlands. "We'll take care of this," he says; then he and his men start firing arrows at it.

All the Gargantuan men start picking up rocks and boulders, throwing them at the dragon; it becomes angry but slowly starts backing away. "How are we going to kill that thing?" Marc asks his brother.

Mount starts looking around, then yells at the men, "Back it toward the trees!" Then he runs toward the trees with Marc and Bree behind him; then all three start climbing up the tallest tree. They get to the top and wait till the dragon backs toward them. Then Mount jumps out of the tree onto the dragon's back.

Marc and Bree jump and land on the dragon. "Cut its wings so it can't fly off!" Mount yells to them. Both men pull out their swords and swing at the dragon's wings; the dragon screams out a roar and starts trying to shake the men off its back. All three men hang on with everything they have, and when the dragon tries to fly away, his wings are damaged enough that it couldn't. Mount starts climbing up the dragon's neck, getting closer to its head.

The dragon goes crazy, trying to shake off the men; then it tries its wings again and rises into the air. "Hang on!" Mount yells to Marc and Bree.

Hem comes over and fires an energy ball at the dragon, and it knocks the dragon to the ground, and all three men fall off it and land on the ground. The dragon gets up and attacks Hem, but when it goes to try to eat Hem, he forms his energy shield; the dragon can't penetrate the shield with its teeth.

As the dragon has all his attention on Hem, Mount sneaks over. He takes his sword and puts it into the dragon's chest. The dragon screams from the blow and falls to the ground with blood pouring from the wound. The dragon is hurt bad but can still swing his tail at Mount, and put him to the ground, and then go to eat him. Marc goes running toward the dragon. As Mount rolls out of the way and the dragon bites dirt, Marc swings his sword with all he has and cuts the dragon's head off at the neck, covering it and Mount in its blood.

Serina wakes from her vision, screaming, "No!" Lisa comes running in to calm her down. "They killed my pet! Get me Boar now!" she demands. Lisa calls for a slave girl to come in the room; she orders her to stay with Serina while she goes to find Boar. As Lisa leaves the room, the slave girl helps Serina up from her bed; she is at the end of her term and could give birth at any moment. She can't take the chance of hurting the child; she decides to tell Boar of her pregnancy and that he will have to fight without her.

Lisa soon comes back in the room, telling Serina Boar is waiting in the front room. Serina tells Lisa to have Boar come in. When he enters, she turns her back to him. "Kneel," she commands. "The wizard and his men have formed an army of their own and are on their way here to try and take back our home," she tells Boar.

"I will gather all our men, and we will be ready for their attack. We will kill them all," Boar promises Serina.

"I won't be able to help you. I've been hiding something," she says as she turns.

Boar looks shocked. "Are you with child?" he asks her. "I would ask how, but I saw you in the storage building with Maverick that night," he tells her.

"Is this a problem?" Serina asks.

"No, my queen, I will die for you," Boar assures her.

"Good! Now gather the army and meet them in the field. I don't want any fighting in the city," Serina tells Boar.

"They will never see the inside of this city, my queen," he promises her.

"I leave it in your hands. Now go," Serina tells Boar, and he leaves.

Back at the camp, everyone is around the dragon's body, cheering, as Marc holds up the head of the dragon. Mount silences the men. "I want to say how great it was to see everyone working together to defeat that beast. This is a sign that if we work together, nothing will stop us," he tells the men, and they all cheer for Mount and the other leaders. "Let's remember why we are all here—to be free so we can sleep peacefully at nights, knowing our families are safe!" The men continue cheering.

Hem quiets the men. "I don't want to be the one to stop this celebration, but it's late, and we need our rest for tomorrow's journey," he suggests, and everyone starts their way back to the tents to sleep before sunrise.

As everyone is settling back down, Mount calls over Hem and the other leaders. “Well, I guess we can say Serina knows we are coming. I guess the morning surprise attack won’t work now,” he says to them all.

Hem shuts his eyes. “She is so powerful. The closer we get, the easier it is to see what we are doing,” he tells Mount.

“Maybe we should forget this and go home,” Kodiak suggests.

“We can’t go home now that she knows we want to destroy her. She will hunt us down and kill us one by one,” Mount tells him.

“I say we do it as planned. Who cares if they know we are coming! Either way, they would fight us!” Marc yells out.

“I agree,” Bree says.

“We vote then,” Hem says. “Who wants to keep going and fight? Raise their hand,” he says, and all but Kodiak raise their hand; but when he sees everyone with their hands raised, he slowly raises his.

“Good,” Mount says to them all. “Maybe we should get some sleep ourselves,” he tells them.

They all go to their tents, and the wolves watch over the camp as they sleep, and the rest of the night is peaceful.

Serina awakes from her sleep; it is early morning, but still dark out. She sits up and wakes Lisa. “They will be here tomorrow. I must talk with Boar.” Lisa dresses and leaves the room as Serina sits in the bed. Not long passes before Lisa is back with Boar. “They will be here late tonight. I want every man we have outside the city. They will let no one in this city,” Serina demands to Boar.

“No one will enter this city, I promise,” he says, then leaves to find the men he has appointed as leaders.

Boar goes and finds Ace and the four captains seating in the eating area, drinking wine with Hex pouring their drinks. Boar sits for a drink and tells Hex to go around the city and have all the warriors come to the front of the city. Hex goes to do Boar’s orders as Boar tells the captains what is happening, and after they finish their drinks, they get up and go to meet the men. When Boar and the others get to the front of the city, all the barbarians are there, waiting for him.

Boar, Ace, and the four captains stand in the center as the men gather around them. "My men, Serina just gave me word that the wizard has gathered an army of his own, and they are on their way here to challenge us for this great city we now live in. Are we going to let them come here and take our home?" Boar screams out.

"Hell no!" all the men yell.

"They are not far from the mountains. We are going to wait for them outside the city, and when they enter the field, we kill every last one," Boar says.

He then commands Ace to take the captains and line them up in groups; this is new for all of them. This is the first time they are defending the city instead of taking it. They line the men up, ready to fight. "We will not let them enter our city!" Boar yells to the men as they line up, getting ready. "Take your club and crush their skulls! This is our home now! No one will make us leave!" he screams. The men are all yelling and screaming, psyching one another up.

Mount has now led them to the mountains. "There's the trail leading through the mountains straight to the city!" he yells to all the men. They get into the mountains and can hear noises in the far distance.

"They know we are coming. There was no way to stop her from knowing," Hem tells Mount.

Mount stops them as they get halfway through and tells them all to quiet down. "Hear that?" he asks them, and the men all start listening, being quiet; they could hear screams and cheers of a large group in the distance.

"There will be no surprise attack as planned. They know we are coming and are waiting for us," Mount tells them; mumbling can be heard through the group of men, with some getting scared. "Don't worry. Just stick to what we have showed you and stick together. We are ready." The mumbles turn to praise and cheers, and Mount starts leading them down the trail toward the waiting barbarians.

When they get close to exiting the mountains, Mount stops. "Timberlands, up front. Gargantuans, ready your swords and be ready to attack on my command. Dales, stay in the back with the catapults and crossbows. Be ready to fire when I give Snot the sign. Let's do this just like we trained to do, and everyone will stay alive!" he tells all the men, and they all line up as Mount instructed.

Mount has Hem pray to the creator to keep them all safe. Mount, Marc, Jax, Bree, Fierce, and Kodiak all get on horses and start out of the mountain. They all come into the field and ride out in a straight line with all the men forming behind them.

On the other side of the field, the barbarians see them lining up, and Boar and Ace walk out into the field with the large group of barbarians lining up behind them. "You have a lot of nerve coming back here, Maverick! I suggest you turn around and take that small pathetic group of men you call an army with you before you get them all killed!" Boar yells out to Mount.

The wolves come from behind the horses, growling and showing teeth. "Your animal friends don't scare us!" Ace yells out to them; then Kody comes from behind the horses, sits with the wolves, and gives an ear-busting roar.

"This was never your people's city, and I cannot stand here knowing you made the people that do own this city your slaves!" Mount yells to Boar.

All the barbarians laugh at Mount as they cheer and high-five each other for what they did. "My army is double the size of your small little group! Your animals can't kill us all before one of us snaps their necks! So you, your wizard friend, and your little brother can leave the slave Bree here and turn and leave! And we may let you get out of the mountains before we come kill you all!" Boar tells Mount.

"You want me? Come and get me!" Bree yells to Boar, which makes Boar steaming mad.

"ATTACK!" Boar screams to his men. The barbarian men start screaming and going crazy as they run at Mount's men.

Mount holds up his hand high in the air. "First captain, attack!" he yells, and with Fierce leading the Timberlands, they step to the front and fire arrows at the attacking men. Screams fill the air as the arrows hit some of the barbarians. Mount then yells, "Second captain, attack!"

Then Jax has the Dales shoot boulders from the catapults and fire the giant crossbow; then they shoot barrels of the black powder toward the barbarians for the Timberlands to shoot arrows on fire at them.

The barbarians still standing are close. "Third captain, attack!" With Kodiak in the lead, the Gargantuan men run at the barbarians to fight in hand-to-hand combat. Mount tells Hem to stay back with the Dales; then with Marc and Bree, they charge on horses toward the barbarians quickly. The wolves are leading the way; then "little" Kody comes running by. The Gargantuan men are handling the barbarians with ease, using the weapons made by the Dales.

The wolves come ripping through the barbarians as Kody rips their heads off with a swipe of his huge paw.

Boar has been standing back with Ace, watching his men; he is getting upset as he sees his men are slowly losing. "We cannot lose this war!" he screams at Ace, then runs toward the battle as Ace slowly follows.

Mount sees Boar coming in his direction; he jumps off Stallion. But before he can get to his sword, Boar is there, and they start fistfighting.

Ace comes behind Mount, trying to hit him with a club; but before he does, Marc comes up behind Ace, picks him up off the ground, and slams him back to the ground. Then the four men start a big brawl.

Not far from them, Bree is fighting through men; he now has gotten to Cobra and Viper, who have taken weapons from some of the Gargantuan men who have fallen. "We owe you, prisoner!" Viper yells at Bree as the two surround him.

"How about I get in on this?" Fierce says to the barbarians as he walks up.

Up on the balcony of the castle, Serina stands at the ledge, looking on at the battle. She starts getting very upset seeing her barbarians are slowly losing; soon, the wizard and his army will be in the city. Serina lets out a scream as she storms inside. Lisa comes running to her to see what is wrong. She helps her to her bed as Serina starts breathing real heavy; then when she looks up at Lisa, her eyes have turned bright red. As her body falls to the bed, the demon's body transforms into the room.

Lisa hides down behind the bed in fear, but the demon pays her no attention as it lets out a vicious roar before it runs out on the balcony and jumps off, landing on the ground. Then it runs out of the city toward the battle. The demon stops, watching the barbarian men being beat down by the wizard's men. "Brothers, help me!" the demon calls out, and the ground starts to shake enough to where the men stop fighting just to maintain their balance.

The ground opens, and out crawl two more demons just as big and scary as the one standing in front of them. Mount and Marc forget about Boar and Ace as they see the large demons coming toward them. "What the hell are those things?" Marc asks Mount.

"Something from hell, it looks like," Mount answers as they watch the demons come closer.

"Prepare to die, puny humans!" the lead demon says; then he hits Marc, and it knocks him in the air back three feet. Mount tries to hit the demon, but it catches his fist.

As the demon laughs, he picks Mount up by his arm. "Is that all you got?" the demon asks him. Then from behind, Bree comes in and jump kicks the demon, but it does nothing to it. Then it turns and backhands Bree, knocking him out. Fierce starts shooting arrows at the beast, but they just bounce off. Hem comes running over. "Drop my friend!" he screams at the demon, and the demon throws Mount at him. They both go to the ground and quickly stand. Hem forms an energy ball and fires it at the demon.

The demon catches the energy ball in his hand, then throws it back with more power back at him and Mount; it hits them both and knocks them back to the ground. The demon looks around to see the other two demons crushing all trying to attack them, so he turns his attention back to the wizard and his warrior friend as he walks past the two men and raises his hand to finish them both off. The demon grows out his fingertips like sharp knives, but when he goes to strike, he is hit.

The demon goes to the ground; and when he turns to see what hit him, Titan, Legend, and Energy are standing behind him. "I should have known it was you, Nefarious," Titan says to the demon. "Leave those humans alone!" he demands to the demons. The other two see Titan and quickly run and hide behind Nefarious.

"You have no say in what we do anymore, Titan! So leave and take your goody crew with you!" Nefarious tells him.

Titan starts to get upset with the demons. "You all ruined your fate. That's why you were formed into monsters and sent to hell, and that's where I'm sending you back to!" Titan tells the demons.

Then a power war between the demons and the spirits starts. Hem and Mount have woken and move out of the way of the supernatural war; they go and check on the others who were still on the ground, doing their best to stay out of the way of Titan and the spirits fighting the demons.

Once Mount and Hem have checked on the men and made sure everyone is safe, they go over to see if they could help the spirits. "One of these demons must possess the sorceress you speak of. Go find her now, and her powers won't be as strong while the demon is separated from her," Titan tells Hem and Mount just before Nefarious attacks again.

Mount goes to Marc and Bree. "Make sure everyone is okay. I'm going with Hem to find Serina," he tells them, and they go toward the city with Snot sneaking behind them.

Titan, Legend, and Energy are getting the best of the demons. "I'm sending you demons back to hell!" Titan screams at them; then the ground opens, and a force starts to pull the demons back into the hole. Nefarious, with everything he has, is able to break free from the force; he quickly leaves, going back to possess Serina before the force pulls him back to hell.

Marc and Bree have rallied all the men as they see the spirits winning against the demons, and they defeat and run off the remaining barbarians.

Mount and Hem enter the city; it is mostly quiet except for the loyal women and servant men trying to run out of the city, who become scared when they see Mount and Hem enter. "You'd better run," they hear someone say, and they turn around to see Snot behind them, holding up a sword. "Thought I'd come help protect you," he tells the two.

Mount and Hem both laugh. "Get up here with us and stay close," Mount tells Snot.

They walk toward the castle. "She's in the castle," Hem tells them, and then they go inside.

They go toward the stairs. "This way," Hem tells them, and they go up the stairs and down a long hall. As they get a little way down the hallway, they start hearing voices. They stop and sneak up on the people; it is Lisa with a group of women and men. As they listen in on them, they hear Lisa telling them all the escape plan for Serina; if it comes to it, then some leave while about five barbarian men stay to guard the room.

"She must be in there," Mount tells Hem.

Mount comes up with a plan for Snot to get the guards' attention and then run back to where he will be waiting with Hem. So Mount and Hem go wait around the corner as Snot walks up to where the guards can see him; now in his home, it is disrespectful to raise only your middle finger at someone, so he raises his middle finger and yells out, "Want your ass kicked? Come and get me!" Then he runs full speed back to where Mount and Hem are waiting. "Here they come!" he tells them.

Four of the guards come running down the hallway. "I got this," Snot tells Hem; then he yells to the men, "Come get some!" When they get to them, Mount hits the first so hard that he goes to the ground; then he takes on two of the men while the other goes after Snot. The barbarian swings a punch at Snot. Hem puts an energy shield around Snot; the man's punch does nothing to Snot, who throws a punch of his own just as Hem shoots an energy ball at the man, who then goes to the ground.

Snot's eyes get huge as he looks at his fist, then looks back at Hem. "Good job!" Hem tells him as Mount has put the other two down.

Mount sees the other man down and pats Snot on the back. "There is one more at the door. Should we go get him?" Mount asks Snot.

"Let's kick his ass!" Snot says as they start walking down the hallway.

"Go get him!" Mount tells him, and Snot turns the corner where the last guard is at the door.

"What's wrong? Are you scared to fight me?" Snot screams at the guard.

The guard is not sure what to think seeing the young kid back. "No way you defeated my men by yourself!" the guard yells to Snot.

"Come find out!" Snot yells to the man; he becomes upset being challenged by a kid, so he starts walking toward him. Once he gets so close, Mount and Hem step around the corner behind Snot. The guard sees the wizard with his best warrior. He then starts backing away, trying to get to the door; but before he gets to it, Hem hits him with an energy blast.

Snot goes over to the guard on the floor and hits him again. "Just making sure," he tells Mount, then looks at Hem. "Let's go kill that bitch of a witch," he says as he opens the door.

Mount quickly stops him. "Stop! You don't know what powers this woman has. She can kill you if she wants! Stay behind us," he tells Snot in a very stern voice. Mount grabs a hold of the doorknob.

"Ready?" he asks Hem, who gives a nod with his head. Then Mount opens the door. They walk in, only to find that the room is empty.

They slowly walk into the next room; it is dark except for the small bit of light coming from the doors that lead to the balcony. Mount looks around and sees Serina lying in a bed in the far corner of the room, where it is most dark. He gets Hem's attention and points to Serina, and then all the torches and lamps light up. Serina sits up from the bed. "I've been waiting for you, my love," she says to Mount as she rubs her stomach. He sees she is pregnant but is not sure what to say.

Hem steps up in front of Mount. "It's over, witch! We defeated your army. Now it's your turn!" Hem yells at her.

Serina, still looking at Mount, slowly starts laughing in an evil manner. "You think you can defeat me using the powers of that weak Titan? I'm a god compared to him!" she screams and wastes no time as she fires an energy blast at Hem. He is ready as he forms his shield and blocks the blast, then backs away with Mount and Snot. Serina stands, and her eyes glow from the evil.

Hem has Mount and Snot back away, then tries to attack Serina; they trade powers a few times, but then she starts getting the best of the battle.

Mount slowly sneaks up close, and when he sees the chance, he grabs Serina by her neck and chokes the air out of her. She has to think quick, so she touches Mount and gives him the memory of their night together. As he starts to see the images of him making love to Serina, he lets go of her and backs away.

Mount goes to a knee as the feelings he had for her that night start to resurface; it then hits him that the child she is carrying could be his. Then Hem gets back up and hits Serina with his powers; he has her where he wants her, but Mount stops him.

When Serina sees her chance, she motions for Lisa, who had been hiding. When she gets to Serina, they hold hands. "You win for now, but I'll be back," she tells the men; then she transports Lisa and out of the room.

Mount lets go of Hem as they disappear; he isn't sure what to say to him after letting Serina get away. That's when Marc and Bree come running in. "Are you all okay?" Bree asks them.

"We are fine, but we let Serina get away," Hem tells them.

"Well, the city is ours. The barbarians are all gone from the city. Jax, Fierce, and Kodiak have all started a sweep of the city, letting the people know they are free," Marc tells them.

Hem goes to Mount and puts his arm around him. "We won the war. That is what matters," he says.

"We will get her one day," Mount says to Hem, and they all go out of the castle. Then the people come cheering them all for driving out the barbarians.

As the groups come back from checking the city, they all start to celebrate defeating the barbarians. Mount, Marc, Hem, Jax, Bree, Fierce, and Kodiak all are celebrated by the Cobble City people.

Then Mount turns to Marc, Hem, and Jax. "I think it's time to go home before any of our children are born," he tells them.

To be continued